ALSO BY INGEBORG LAUTERSTEIN

*The Water Castle*

# *Vienna Girl*

BY

## INGEBORG LAUTERSTEIN

W · W · NORTON & COMPANY

NEW YORK · LONDON

*First Edition*

The text of this book is composed in New Century Schoolbook, with display type set in
Caslon 540. Composition and manufacturing by the Maple-Vail Book Manufacturing
Group. Book design by Marjorie J. Flock.

Library of Congress Cataloging-in Publication Data
Lauterstein, Ingeborg.
    Vienna girl.

    I. Title.
PS3562.A845V5   1986      813'.54      85-18956
ISBN 0-393-02264-1

W. W. Norton & Company, Inc., 500 Fifth Avenue, New York, N.Y. 10110
W. W. Norton & Company Ltd., 37 Great Russell Street, London WC1B 3NU

1 2 3 4 5 6 7 8 9 0

*To* JANE MAYHALL

*and to my teachers, Hugh Crawford, Otto Kokoschka,*
*Joseoh Albers, Charles Olson, Caroline Gordon,*
*Margaret Young, Alice Morris, Professor Lawrence Holcomb*

# CONTENTS

# Contents

# ACKNOWLEDGMENTS

MANY THANKS FOR HELPING ME to Linda Healey and Katie Nelson, Henry Lauterstein, Helen Rees, Ilse Goessman, Walker Hancock, Roger Kiraly, The American Army Information Service, Lincoln Digital Corporation, Ralph Gardener, the Austrian Consulate and information service, the Rockport library and Toad Hall, Barbara, Peg, Miriam, and Meg, Jeane and Edith.

# ONE

# From Boundaries in the Dark

WE HAD CANDLES in the cellar rooms, but Grandmother, in her fever, spilled wine over our matches. "NOW," she cheerfully said, "we're invisible." Her voice shook a little.

My grandmother, the countess von Dornbach Falkenburg, called war and the Russian invasion tempest, *Unwetter*, to make me feel we would soon see the sun again. After lightbulbs had flickered out time became immeasurable. Somehow it seemed colder in the dark. To keep warm we stayed in bed dressed in fur coats and hats.

This was spring 1945. I, Reyna Meinert, her only grandchild and confidante, was fifteen years old. And she promised me, next spring we would go to the Vienna woods and celebrate the first violet. She loved that age old custom. Violets were her favorite flowers and she used their perfume. I could follow that fragrance towards her bed when I tended to her. And I even taught myself to pour wine without spilling by putting a finger into the glass.

"NOW," she said. "I am more proud of you than ever." She drank to me and I to her.

"NOW," she said. "If all of Vienna were in total darkness as we are down here men couldn't shoot each other. War and the invasion would stop. The blind can't kill."

She kept saying NOW until I felt the dark teaming with

invisible Russians. NOW, after two glasses of wine I imagined groping for a button which would set off a miracle weapon, sending intruders—puff—to smithereens. NOW, I knew that any blind person could go puff to Vienna built by Kaisers, and puff to Europe the hornets' nest and all its old castles, crowns and swastikas would tumble into oblivion. I panicked and was glad my grandmother could not see my face.

Hornets of hell had been loose above the ground. The earth trembled, walls shook down to our subterranean chambers, as my grandmother shook with fever, and a cough tore her apart. Years and years, centuries seemed to pass me by. I felt like crying, what have we ever done? We're innocent. But how guilty was innocence after Hitler.

She had dozed off. I could hear her heavy breathing. Empty water pipes moaned. We had only three buckets of water left, but we would not run out of wine. We might have to wash in wine, my grandmother kept saying, like Katherine the Great of Russia. My father, the wine and beer Meinert, had filled the wine cellar at the far end of the six long vaulted underground chambers with choice wines from his own vineyards and stored smoked and canned meats, vegetables, bread, cheese, apples for us. Then he left Vienna. It had become almost impossible to travel. The Russians had been advancing towards Vienna; the British towards the mountain region and our farm. And he had made up his mind to go there and protect Mother from suspicion and possible internment.

The food he had stored for us was worth more then any treasures in those trunks and boxes hidden down here, more than the medieval Falkenburg table set with silver and crystal, where Grandmother and I had eaten until the lights went out. Now we ate in bed. I could tell time passing in the dark as our food supply dwindled. This had to be daytime. At night I would hear mice in our cooking corner. They liked to race around a large frying pan, squeaking with delight. Their fun always stopped when tanks rolled above the ground with coffee grinder sounds. And distant shots no louder than snapping my fingers would make them stop and listen. And I often listened with the mice to the madness up there.

The sound in the pipes was a gasp, then a burp. Silence again after that. An invisible whangdoodle, my childhood monster, had curled up. I pulled quilts over my head and went to sleep.

"Are you awake, Reyna?"

"No."

"I wonder whether my swallows are already coming back to nest," my Grandmother's voice sounded sad.

I opened my eyes—it was black.

"What if the Russians shoot at our birds?"

Russians spray bullets. They grab watches and women. Close your eyes and creep back down under eiderdown quilts, sheets perfumed with lavender from linen closets.

"Surely they wouldn't kill my swallows?"

Birds bob up and down, up, in the shooting galleries. Men and boys fire guns. Birds fall down. Hairy hands grab the prize, pink feather-trimmed celluloid dolls. And monsters in hobnailed boots are jigging on gravel.

Hide. Be invisible. Turn into a bird in a dream: *My Fuehrer loves birds,* Rudolf Hess whispers. He is leaning over me. His pilot's helmet made of soft, feathery stuff is sweet to touch. He offers me a sugar-glazed orange slice from his pursed lips. *My bird of paradise.*

"What is all this chirping," my grandmother's voice. "I hope it's not a bad dream."

How could I have told her she was interrupting a sunlit feast. Waltz music, velvet caresses, roast goose, Esterhazy cake topped with whipped cream, decorated with sugar-glazed orange slices. And Rudolf Hess. I felt warm, my cheeks glowed and all my secret loves surrounded me as one.

I had collected loves as a young child, during a time of hate. The changeover, *Anschluss* of Austria with Hitler Germany, madness in the air had made me gather loves quickly—quickly the way our laundry woman, Frau Boschke, gathered up sheets before the first thunderclap.

Rudolf Hess, Hitler Deputy, who had helped Hitler write *Mein Kampf,* I had seen only once, at the beginning of the war. He was sitting on a garden bench dressed as a pilot. I used to make Hess paper dolls from his photographs. It never mattered in the least that Rudolf Hess didn't even know I existed, or that he might be dead. I could not yield my hero.

My Eugene Romberg was dead. Uncle Eugene, I used to call our neighbor, Father's best friend, and the most generous man I would ever know. He had called himself son of an Arab cook; others had called him gypsy, Rumanian thief, Jew, mostly Jew . . . I had seen him die on our mountain farm in one of those high beds, decorated with painted hearts and flowers. Yet he would not pass away; his boundless admiration for me glittered on like the diamond-studded watch he had given me when I was seven years old, which I never wound up.

"Are you all right child?" Grandmother asked.

"I'm fine." (I'm not a child. I am a bird of paradise.)

"Have you noticed how quiet it has been? Could it be over . . . perhaps?" My grandmother was interrupted, contradicted by *bang—grrramm,* scatter-bursts of invisible fireworks, crackling, catherine wheels, whirring, and trickling, like shattered mirrors, glass splintering, collapse of the biggest house of mirrors in the world. I am left with fragments of dreams, shattered images.

"Into the wine barrel, quick!" she called to me.

"Not unless you come."

"You promised your father. This is close by. Hurry! And take the Kaiser."

I groped along clammy walls where she had stored some of her treasures. Got lost. The dark closing in on me, invisible Russians coming after me on cats' feet. My right hand hit the shelf, knocking over candlesticks. I felt my way towards the frame of the Kaiser Franz Joseph portrait. My fingers reading the carved letters like braille: A E I O U, the 1493 Latin-German anagram: all the universe is subordinate to Austria. Austriae Est Imperare Orbi Universo: Alles Erdreich Ist Oesterreich Unterthan . . . For seven hundred years, seven hundred and now . . . I grabbed the picture of our last Hapsburg ruler, hugged it and calmed down. I didn't have to see the kind face. It was so much like my father's. Those side whiskers, twinkling light eyes, the half smile . . . where was Father now? He had opened the back of a huge wine barrel and put velvet cushions and wool blankets inside it. Just in case . . .

My hands found Grandmother's cubicle, the cold brass headboard of her high bed. She caught me in her arms and kissed me on both cheeks. "Just leave me the Kaiser and get into the barrel. I'm too stiff and old."

Actually she was too proud and very stubborn. I put my arm around her, coaxed her. She fumbled for her comb, perfume, and a Saint Theresa picture, stuffed everything into her cloak pocket. We knocked down a chair. Tripped over cooking utensils, the spirit stove. The blind leading the blind past cobwebs, past the smell of dung and essence of pine—the throne room—a cubicle with the two commodes. And on towards the scent of apples, the wine cellar. I tapped my way along the side of the huge old barrel. We stooped, felt our way to the opening. What if someone was hiding in there? Once we got inside my legs gave way and I allowed myself to sink down onto cushions. We shared blankets, huddled. I breathed in the odor of fermented wine and the old feeling of conspiracy came back.

Years ago during wine harvest, when I had played chasing and hiding games with vintners' children, a big old barrel like this one had been "it": the end of the chase. No one could grab you. Once you were inside the old Meinert barrel you had won. I had to laugh and laugh for no reason at all—or every reason. So far we were the winners. We had out-distanced death.

"Women endure, remember Joan of Arc," my grandmother said.

I felt like saying: endure, what do you mean endure? Men burned her up. Men had locked me up in our mountain inn, when the war was lost and a time of guilt and accusations had begun. I had come away as a fugitive. "Joan of Arc was all alone and we are together," I said. "It was worse when you were so sick and kept sending me back to my own bed." We found a flask of water, and a bottle of brandy. A tin of biscuits. I felt something under my cushion: a precious bag of lozenges. Father had thought of everything. The almost invisible oak panel door in the sub-basement laundry room was hidden behind the tapestry depicting my maternal ancestor Otto Count Falkenburg, sword raised against Cara Mustafa and his invading Moslem hoards. More than three hundred years ago Vienna had been surrounded by Turks. They had brought harems, elephants, and, of course, coffee. Otto had fought victoriously, put his swords away and turned into the recluse Otto the Mad. Falkenburgs often hid away. My great grandfather, named Otto, had been unable to go a step beyond the boundaries of his estate in the end. And Falkenburgs got their name because they liked falcons that circled, hunted for them and came back.

We drank brandy and became elated inside the barrel—free, beyond fear, under the spell and protection of a heritage of invincible courage and terror and madness. And from the boundaries of the dark, dreams, ideas and obsessions blended with memories to soar and circle like birds of prey.

My grandmother said her mind had been crystal clear when she woke up and she was praying God would send us the Americans. I heard a new and happy lilt of hope in her voice. She seemed to have forgotten about American bombers . . .

"Do you realize, child, that Americans are really Austrian, all of them? The Hapsburg Empire married the American continent in 1558."

"You mean when Maximillian married his little son to that dotty child, the Spanish princess? Didn't they inherit Spain and all the colonies including America?"

"You did have a marvelous tutor in the country." She laughed and said: "TU FELIX AUSTRIA NUBE . . ."

"Let others wage war, but you, happy Austria, marry," I quoted. Austrians always liked old mottoes and old jokes. Sometimes old mottoes, of course were jokes. And I wondered about little princes and princesses being married off so young. My grandmother said it made good sense. Playmates of the same class growing up to be lovers.

"Did you hear that?" she asked and we listened to an ugly scraping sound and waited. It made my skin crawl. I found the bottle.

"Raking," I quickly said. "A huge monster raking up broken mirror glass."

"You have such wild ideas. What would I do without you!"

The brandy made me heady. I invented a scary laugh with donkey brays to drown out monster sounds and ward off evil presence. "I am mad. You're mad. It's our heroic Falkenburg blood. We've got to have monsters to be heroic."

"You, you're so funny. My little heart. But how much brandy are you drinking?"

"A lot!" I said.

The raking scraping monster noise stopped. "Mother of Heaven be thanked!" she said with a sob. We laughed and cried easily. "I was thinking of how your father bought the farm to keep you and your mother safe. And then the mountain paradise turned into a kind of hell. The avalanche burying half the village and then the insanity of it all. Your mother Hitler's secret love indeed!"

"Berchtesgaden was only a cat's jump away!" I said.

"Mountain folk like excitement. There is nothing to do but talk all winter long in that snow. And they don't trust city people."

And Grandmama only knew half the mad story. Father and I did not tell her that I had stood accused of having chained Mother's "secret love," Adolf Hitler, up in the amethyst mine near our farm among stored museum art treasures. Who but the Fuehrer would have brought Frau Meinert that fancy city invalid suddenly out of her wheelchair and got her to take a dying man into her house, smelly, unrecognizably dirty and bearded as he was, no stranger to her. And no stranger to me. Eugene Romberg not Adolf Hitler. But the villagers liked the idea of pilgrims flocking to kneel at that unmarked grave . . .

"There is bound to be a lot of gossip around my daughter. She takes after my aunt Christina, you know. I was younger than you are now when Aunt Christina took me out of convent and I was very shy. Wherever we went on our travels, Christina attracted attention. That mass of red-gold hair, those big blue eyes, and then she carried that doll. And she would talk to the doll about her admirers—quite often in their presence. I was mortified."

My mother had inherited the hateful doll and like Christina von Kortnai she had that bright hair, slightly protruding soulful violet-blue eyes, and many admirers. The doll was stolen before Hitler took over Austria or she would certainly have stuck it into her coat pocket when she went to his first big reception. Adolf Hitler had been drawn to her at once. Mother had been all for him until he kissed her hand. She took an instant dislike. Later during the summer, she had fallen off cousin Bertl's horse, and stopped walking. And Adolf Hitler had sent her flowers with a letter, ordering her to walk. I had found the letter under her hospital bed, kept it in my treasure box because I liked the ludicrous: Heil Hitler! your devoted Adolf H.; the Fuehrer hailing himself before he signed his name.

"When everybody says how much you look like me, I am not just flattered I am relieved," Grandmother said. "Your loveliness is not as provocative, it's subtler, and easier to live with than Christina's. And fortunately you have your Father's good sense. When I think of you making your way back to Vienna. Bombs falling; fighting going on. That freight train, the motorcyclist. Even if you passed as a boy in your pants, you certainly used your wits like a girl. Just to be with me." She put her arm around me and waited for a moment as though she had guessed there was more to my story. "I would never have survived without you," she went on. "Not that I am afraid to die, but I was terrified of leaving you alone in the dark with a corpse. I implored the Mother of Heaven." In convent school she had learned to turn to Mother of Heaven, *Himmelmutter,* because her own Mother had gone to heaven when she was born. "And, of course, you looked after me like a nurse. You have been so brave."

"Not really. I am scared of the walls collapsing and burying us." I could see myself squashed under the little von Dornbach palace, with it's chipped cherubs, garlands, and a plaque of the founder, bosomy Kaiserin Maria Theresa; dead before I had ever experienced what Frau Boschke's dream book called "the height of passion."

This idea always made me bite the inside of my mouth and shiver with the old squashed rose-beetle jitters which I used to get before Hitler and the war, when Fritz Janicek, the professor, unemployed teacher of history, art and languages, and an illegal Nazi, had worked as our gardener plucking iridescent beetle beauties, which he called vermin, from the heart of a rose to squash them. The enemy in a war, no matter how pretty, is vermin. Russia was supposed to liberate us from Nazi Germany, but we had fought against them. We were the enemy. There was no getting away from that. I might be exterminated. Dead after my first kiss.

I had kissed Arnold von Lutensteg, my German officer the Frog Prince, in the doorway, said Auf Wiedersehen to the rumble of aproaching Russian guns. Where was Arnold now? Was there love after life? What would Dr. Freud have said? Before Hitler took over Austria, Frau Boschke, the Laundress, had ironed the doctor's shirts. And she had suspected him of making love to all the ladies who came to see him. When she had put her ear to the door she had soon discovered he didn't have a chance. Ladies just talked and talked. All about dreams. And she had overheard the doctor say that in actuality neither great dreams nor the height of passion lasted more than a wink. Our two maids had disagreed. Anyway, ironing and listening in had perplexed Frau Boschke who liked simple answers, and so she bought the dream book at a flea market.

If life ended like a strange dream, love would remain. Nothing was ever over. After a few swigs of brandy what were three or four centuries? The present and past, the Romans, Turks, Napoleonic French, Hitler warriors, Russians—barbarians one and all raging somewhere above our heads. Noise of war turned into a tap-tap, stomp, stomp, slap-slap, slap: a monster dancing at a mountain fair, slapping great leather pants. Grandmama took the brandy away from me, curled up against me and dozed off.

I sat with my knees drawn up to give her more room, cheered myself up with a lozenge, swallowed more brandy and waited for the tempest to end like Grandmama's fever. She had taught me to consider the counting of hours and days niggardly. And she had stopped winding up her clock collection after we had lost the First World War and the Empire. There were fancy keys for winding clocks I had always admired. And she had promised me that on the day when Prince Otto, the Hapsburg heir returned to Vienna all her clocks would tick, ring, and chime in the return of the "good old days."

The bad days of our so-called liberation—the invasion—Russians adorned with dozens of watches, raping, shooting, and plundering, now made me wonder whether all the tick-tick-ticking, that persistant tune of time passing, produced insane lust. Or, whether lust could bring about a lewd passion for more and more clocks and watches? The wine warmed my body and gave me crazy ideas. I laughed to myself as I rehearsed for disaster. Grandmother chuckled softly in her sleep as though she were laughing with me; then she coughed and woke up.

"I have had a marvelous dream about convent school, the cloister garden, throwing a red ball up to a sunny blue sky. I once had a red ball like that and it was lost. In my dream I got it back. I feel so much better," she said.

In the dark we had both dreamt of sunlight. Only her dreams were innocent and mine had become outrageous since I had glimpsed my first half-naked man: a Russian soldier in the courtyard. Dressed in fur hat and tunic, sleeves decorated with rows of watches, a jingling alarm clock tied around the neck, and pants down at his boots—a buffoon of a rapist. In my dream men wore furry, feathery Russian hats and many watches, nothing else. But they were discreetly naked like dolls. The male ornament of aroused sex was missing. One by one they had entered a velvet warm dream where lust turned to love. And rapacious loves tamed by kisses, turned into male concubines. They carried gleaming platters loaded with Esterhazy cakes in and out of ornamental hedges where male statues come to life and men turn to stone holding serving trays loaded with fowl, grapes and tangerines. A never ending melody, a slow waltz played on and on in my secret garden, my harem of men.

I wondered what Frau Boschke's dream book would say about dreaming in color and to music. Frau Boschke, the laundress had been my authority. I would keep her company in the laundry room with my small scrubbing board and my big dreams. According to her old book, scary, furry monsters coming after me meant happiness. On the other hand, Frau Boschke's own repeated dreams of marriage had left her an old maid. The red ball worried me. And dreaming of men could be a bad omen. A kiss might mean I'd never kiss again.

I had kissed Arnold, a prince of the old blood, a German officer following not orders but his own beliefs, to the first thunder of approaching Russian guns. Arnold had guarded my grandmother's gate day and night. She and her monarchists had worked well for the resistance because they were considered old, feeble and eccentric, but during the final days the gestapo had gone on a rampage to round them up. Arnold knew the gestapo well.

Frog Prince, I had named him when I was a young child and took it for granted that a prince had to have an evil spell in order to transform himself. And he had appeared shiny, clean and new to me as though he had just surfaced from another world; watchful, expressionless, a forehead that bulged a little at the temples, large eyes set far apart, beautiful as a spell-bound frog. In the dark I relived my first real kiss. Running across the street and throwing my arms around his neck again and again. And with each kiss I moved Arnold farther and farther away from evil spells of war and invasion all the way to Venice, where we embraced in curtained gondolas, floating over tainted water, trembling reflections of palaces. Yet questions persisted as the wavelets lapping against the hull: how did my twenty-year-old German prince come to Vienna as one of the gestapo bloodhounds in the first place? Arnold had misled and restrained the pack, yet he had been one of them. Later he became an officer in the Wehrmacht.

I had to save Arnold from such questions, take him far away from everything and everyone, keep him all to myself. Love, my everlasting rescue mission, often turned into abduction.

"Do you realize that I have never been in total darkness before this," Grandmother said. "In convent I got used to that little candle flickering at the feet of a white statute of the Madonna. Candlelight and sanctity went together. I always had to have a night light. . . . Funny, that dream about convent. And that red ball. I suddenly remember, one of the other girls in convent actually found it and wouldn't let me have it back."

"Hanna the dwarf." I guessed.

"Hanna Roth. I don't like to hear her called dwarf. In our convent school that was never allowed. Whenever I complained to the sisters that HE had put me away into convent because my mother had died when I was born," (she never called my great grandfather Count Otto "Father" and he certainly never behaved like one) "the sisters would tell me to just look at Hanna, the only foundling among orphans and half orphans; tiny Hanna, always cheerful and busy. The sisters used to love and spoil her and they probably allowed her to keep my red ball. Whenever she wanted something she would have a vision. That's how her career as a seer began. But I must say, she knew how to hold her own without ingratiating herself even when she was a mere child and became a mascot at court. She never allowed herself to be treated as one of those pets: giant dogs, circus horses, Siamese twins, pet tutors, and poets, and Hungarians, dear, lovely Empress Elizabeth used to leave behind when she went abroad. Hanna always had pride. Always kept herself busy. Starting off with dolls' clothes. Those dolls were much more stylish than the ladies at court. At times, of course, Hanna was misguided."

"In love with Adolf Hitler," I said. Music in my strange dream had been accompanied by Hanna Roth pigeon luring, a cooo-cooo sound like someone blowing into an empty jug. "She used to send carrier pigeons to Hitler with warnings. I saw it once—"

"Hitler and his men had to have their astrologers, mediums, soothsayers, to make them feel that their misdeeds had been preordained. Evil power makes for superstition," Grandmama said.

I could never believe that my Rudolf Hess, the pilot waiting for Hanna on the bench in the deserted Romberg garden had been evil. I had stayed in hiding and rustled in the bushes. *"My Fuehrer loves birds,"* he had said in a spooky voice. I had lost my heart to Rudolf Hess the dreamer who inspired dreams and gave me hope: a Hitler who loved birds. Hitler who loved . . .

"Hanna is smart," Grandmother said. "She can forsee trends in people as in hats, and she knew Adolf Hitler would be the height of fashion. Funny how clearly one sees things when one wakes up in the dark. I really believe Hanna liked national socialism because it changed everything. From way back, during our convent school days, she had this wild notion that a change would make her change and grow tall. You see, in convent everything had been old, nothing ever changed. We all wore the same blue dresses and little capes. And, of course, Hanna never outgrew hers. She wanted new clothes. Grown up clothes, to make her grow. Now that I think of it, the two most beautiful women I knew—our Empress Elizabeth and, of course, my aunt Christina von Kortnai—had this same notion that a change would suddenly make them change." My grandmother paused. "Hanna certainly changed my life with her predictions. I consider her an instigator. She knew I wanted to become a nun and she interfered. You see, my aunt Christina came to Hanna and asked her to make clothes for the doll."

And I could indeed see a tiny, fancy and fanciful Hanna Roth, designer of hats and costumes for dolls when she was my age, take the naked doll out of a wooden box, kiss the china cheek, and call the doll "Puppe." Just doll. There never could be any other name. The sculptor Antonelli had created Puppe with the help of a famous Swiss dollmaker. The famous artist himself had molded the doll's haunting Christina von Kortnai face, hands with those tapered fingertips, high-set bosom, and also her bunioned feet. And he had sent the doll to Christina, after she had

refused to marry him and went away. Puppe was a masterpiece
of scorn. Hanna would hold the doll against her heart, and a
unique delicate mechanism would set the doll's blue glass eyes
in motion, from side to side, from Hanna to Christina. And I
could see Hanna adorn the doll in hats and dresses to match
Christina's, giving Puppe weird animation, starting the legend
of great aunt Christina and her doll, which had lasted to the
next generation, when my mother had inherited Christina's face,
her violet-blue eyes, red-gold hair, and the obsession with that
doll.

My mother had only been five years old when the doll came
to her and she had loved the wondrous obligation to comb, dress,
care for the doll, always. I had detested Puppe as long as I could
remember, and hated the way Mother addressed the old doll when
she had something to say to me. From the beginning I had wished
the doll away. Then Puppe was lost, and after that Austria was
lost; Mother fell off the horse. Peace was lost after Puppe had
vanished. The doll changed hands as houses and countries had
changed hands during the war. The lost doll to Mother was lost
luck. She had to have Puppe back and never stopped yearning
for her. Obsessions were dangerously contagious and virulent at
that time of transition. Our gardener, Fritz Janicek, the teacher,
had become obsessed with my mother. Years later, when he was
the S.S. art requisition director, I had seen the drunken Janicek
behead the doll with a pistol shot. And then he had held that
china head in his hand and he had kissed the portrait of Christina and image of Mother—a devilish work of art. Neither lucky
nor unlucky, I told myself, Puppe was a mere idol, and for that
matter, so was Hilter. Idols, as far as I could tell, never brought
good luck and obsessions brought bad luck. Yet, as sure as I knew
Mother would always want the doll, Nazis would always want
Hitler, and those scheming glass eyes of the doll would always
gleam on somewhere in the dark of my earliest detestations.

"As a matter of fact Hanna was making the sable hat you are
now wearing, Reyna, for Aunt Christina and, of course, a little
one for the doll. She had one of her visions. An inner voice had
told her she must make a third hat. For me. She predicted that
Aunt Christina would take me away with her and travel to Russia," Grandmother remembered. "Anyway, Christina simply
snatched me out of convent and away we went with the doll to

Russia, to France, Italy. And she never brought me back to the
sisters."

"If you had not been snatched away you would have become
a nun and I would not exist," I said.

"In other words, one has to be grateful to Hanna. *Ja?*" She
said Hanna had certainly forseen the Russian invasion and made
her way to Salzburg. I could smell violets. Grandmama had taken
out her perfume to make the task of combing her unwashed hair
more pleasant. Hanna smelled of violet too. She had forseen the
invasion and fled Vienna in good time. I could see her all dressed
up and wearing one of her tall hats and half veil, driving her
midnight blue car at full speed along unpaved back roads to
Salzburg, barely avoiding a broken tank, debris of war, honking
and barely missing anyone or anything that got in her way. Carrier pigeons in cages and hat boxes, would shake on her rack as
she led the way for a convoy of odious hat-salon Nazi ladies,
screened by her dust in their requisitioned limousines.

Grandmama hit the side of the barrel with her comb rhythmically. I found myself counting the pong, pong, pong, for no particular reason. Suddenly a circle of light splashed the dark: a
nimbus—halo without a Saint—on the wall behind our barrel.

"Light, light!" I cheered, laughed. Tears ran down my cheeks
as we emerged from the barrel and blinked against the three
weak lightbulbs dangling from the ceiling. We had the same
amber, owl eyes. Hers looked huge because the face was now so
small and white. She steadied herself, "Dear God in Heaven be
thanked." Then darkness returned, black, endless. Water pipes
above my head groaned.

"I'm sick of it all. Those monster noises. The cold. I lost one
of my boots. . . ." I shouted. And the light came back on as though
someone had heard my childish tirade.

At first we were afraid to speak. We stayed beside the wine
barrel as if one hasty move, one loud word might put the lights
out forever. White hair hanging down Grandmama's back, the
crumpled fur-lined cloak contrasted with the straight backed
posture of the aristocratic convent schoolgirl. We stared at each
other. Finally our eyes met, we laughed and her fatigue and age
fell away like a masque.

"You look like a young cossack," she said. "And everything is
just as it was."

The medieval Falkenburg table remained set with crystal and silver, napkins in napkin rings, but gold-rimmed china plates were sprinkled with mouse-droppings. And sprigs of forsythia she had brought in for early bloom, had sprouted pallid leaves and white roots.

I found my lost boot. Stroked the blue wool blankets in the barrel and thought of home, Mother's blue room in the Meinert-Hof near the Vienna woods. All the comfort I had known. Was there nothing left? "I want to go up to the laundry room, wash and change my clothes."

"Not yet. But we must celebrate." In Vienna, celebrations are a solemn duty. Our city had been battered and invaded, but I would always think of our feast as a victory. The bad food and great wine and our waltz. Grandmother and I got up from the table and hummed the tune from my dream. She was weak and led me with dignity. Then we gathered momentum and everything swirled around us: the smiling Kaiser portrait, dark beams, shadowy cubicles where precious things were stored. We seemed to be standing still in the center of nowhere as bygone glory and vainglory revolved around us.

My grandmother had gone back to bed and snored softly. I went to an old mirror, raised the wine glass to greet my own face with a Viennese smile that said: nice to see you again. What a pleasant surprise. You haven't changed at all. You look great. Not quite like Grandmama. She is a true beauty. I am more rustic, cheerful: pink cheeks, and a mouth curving up at the corners. I'ts the Meinert in me. And all that uncombed curly brown hair and the fur hat make my head look big and childish.

The smiling face made me sad. I felt sorry for the girl in the mirror. A beetle crawling over the glass turned into two beetles. Roachlike armies were crawling over Vienna, mindless, purposeful, sinister. The rushing sound and the thump, thump, thump, could be my own heart, my blood, or a memory of the sea. Sounds carried me as water of the Danube might carry a swimmer who knows how to drift.

Grandmama had told me to be grateful, patient. I adjusted the old hat to a rakish angle, the way Great Aunt Christina von Kortnai would have worn it. With Christina's hat came a legendary heritage of willfulness, impatience, ingratitude. Christina took lovers, left them, and moved on. Secretly had a child by the sculptor Antonelli, and put the infant girl, Traude, into convent. She had traveled with the Antonelli doll. Never once saw her own child, but snatched her niece, Reyna von Falkenburg, my grandmother, from the convent, took her abroad. Christina had done as she pleased and never came to any harm. She had not been afraid of Russians. I imagined her wearing the hat when she stopped to dance at peasant weddings, or on a country visit to the Tsarina and the Tsar, where she had rebuked an amorous Rasputin. The trappings of her reckless past seemed to create my future where there had been none.

Keys jingled in my pocket. I was my own jailer, hidden away, dirty and hungry only for one more minute, then I ran towards the stairs, up to the secret door. The key wouldn't turn. I fumbled. It stuck. Then it turned, and turned almost by itself. The door creaked open. My heart was racing. I lifted the musty tapestry. A chink of light from the boarded up window showed me the laundry room just as we had left it. I locked the door behind me to keep my grandmother safe.

The old gilded harp near the boarded up window—instrument of angels—had been my idea. I had liked to pluck it against the sound of guns. Beside the harp, on a round table, Grandmother's open sketch book displayed that last one of all her horse drawings: a Lipizzaner stallion suspended in a frenzied leap, flared nostrils, bared teeth.

Birds chirped in the courtyard. Water had remained in the big copper wash tub on the brick stove. In the cubicle the servants' tub shimmered with cloudy water from my last bath.

It was too quiet. The little pistol my grandmother had fired when Russian Mongolian troups were shooting at the stone angel in the courtyard remained in the soap dish; Grandfather von Dornbach's old saber on a chair. Nothing had been touched. I took the board off one window. It was either dawn or dusk. A silver haze hung over the old trees, the stone bench and shrine. The man-sized cheerful angel had lost its halo and was slightly chipped. Russians had forced the portal open, now it was shut. Not far from the window a cherub's plump arm and dimpled hand lay in the green, spring grass. At the stoop, where I had seen that Russian soldier jump up from a ragged woman, a primrose had come into bloom.

I stood and marveled at all that had remained above the ground until the first glow of dawn outlined Uncle Duke General von Hohentahler's town house; the top floor nothing but a jagged, charred ruin. And then I mourned for all that had been shattered over there. The top floor with my Uncle the Duke General's study—my old refuge from the French governess and the snooty Hohentahler girls—had vanished, and so had Cousin Bertl's room, the other hideaway. That narrow hard bed, a green eiderdown, my nest for reading his Karl May books. His favorite chapters had been marked with photographs of smiling girls, women, and his horse; many pictures of Mother. One of me in leather pants pushing her in the wheelchair after she had fallen off his horse. She had been expecting a child and lost it. And Cousin Bertl, who had grown up with her and knew her well, had said, "you look silly in that wheelchair. I'll take your picture if you don't stand up." Six years after he had taken this picture I had seen her get out of the wheelchair. I thought it was shock, an avalanche.

I had used that photograph as a bookmark when I read his Karl May books. And I escaped into adventure, the fantastically real landscape of the American wild west a German had dreamt up in jail. From Karl May I had learned about white men invading the territory of the red man in the New World. White villains and heroes fighting each other and fighting with Indians good and bad, who also fought each other, scalping at random. All of them smoked the peace pipes and then fought again.

My reading, as a young child, and the strategic games with Bertl's father—restaging and winning of the old lost battles with armies of tin soldiers on old Austrian maps—had been an oddly relevant education. Before Father sent Mother and me to the mountain farm, I had already learned all about war strategies and fighting men, and I was forewarned.

Bertl, one of my loves, Mother's playmate, Grandmother's favorite too—"the young knight" as Hanna the clairvoyant had always called him—could not be forewarned. Young knights look for crusades as mountain climbers look for high mountains. The tall schoolboy reading Karl May, had secretly turned into an illegal Nazi with my mother when the party was forbidden in Austria. Under Hitler, as an officer in the Waffen S.S. Bertl had fought with the German Army in the Blitzkrieg against those

who had destroyed old Austria—a thrill to even the most reluctant officer. In the end, during the invasion, S.S. dancing around
on the roof with guns and a swastika flag had looked no bigger
than the tin soldiers on General von Hohentahler's old Austrian
war maps. Tiny men had provoked destruction.

A blackbird on the shallow basin of the shrine lifted it's head
each time it drank. Then it splashed about twittering with delight
on this new day. I went to the faucet. No water. I had bathed in
the tub several times. No matter. I stripped, shivered, stood in
the water, teeth chattering, covered myself with rich lather. There
wasn't much left of grandmother's violet scented French soap.
Bertl had brought it from Paris for her, and I had heard him say
it was crazy: bursting in and creating hell on earth in other people's countries. It didn't make sense. But he had enjoyed shopping in Paris like any other officer in the German Army. Uncle
von Hohentahler, General, an Austrian Duke was quite poor. In
the Waffen S.S. Bertl had money for the first time and he spent
it on presents. A blouse for me. And when I wore that frilly Parisian blouse with my leather pants, no one ever called me little
fellow. People started to say I looked cute in a girlish blouse and
they asked Father why he dressed me like a country boy. For me
the defeat of France, the German invasion of Paris, and the silk
blouse, had led to several new dresses, a personal victory. I forgot about the hell on earth Bertl had mentioned; so did most
everyone in Vienna when we were winning.

Victories never lasted, personal victories least of all. I dried
my shivering body. My fragrant skin reminding me of the lost
luxuries, the laughing Bertl and Parisian frills. The sunlight broke
through the haze and shone onto my spindly legs and arms. I
had arrived with only a rucksack and had no change of clothes.
There was Grandmother's trunk full of trousseau linen. I rummaged around and found a funny pair of lace-trimmed pantaloons and hopped on one leg pulling them up when I heard a
dragging sound, no louder than a boat being pulled out on the
banks of the Danube.

A man laughed.

I held my breath and dipped behind a screen, as though he
could see me and was laughing at my unformed breasts, pink
nipples standing out like the center of targets. I pulled on my
sweater. Men's voices had receded, perhaps down the street.

Things couldn't be all that bad if they were laughing. I step-hopped into ski pants.

Upstairs something crashed, bashed and tumbled.

I stuck the pistol into my belt and tucked my mane into the hat and wrote: PALACE INVADED in Grandmother's sketch book, below the drawing of that wild horse.

Half of my hair slipped out and I grabbed a pair of rusty scissors off a hook and chopped it off. A daughter and as good as a son, Father used to say. I took up the old saber in a fury. Did Joan of Arc want to be a girl when she had to fight like a man? More tangled hair slipped out of the hat: I had no comb, no mother to comb my curls. She would rather have fussed over the old doll, that dead red wig, Christina's hair.

Loud rapping on the kitchen door.

I charged into the kitchen armed with my old rage, and was waylaid by clocks and more clocks. *Verdammt.* Damn. I cursed the bombed out nuns, the good women who had carried Grandmother's precious things down below the ground. And I stepped–tripped–stumbled over the long saber made for parades not invaders. The ornate rapier cut into my palm: "Go to hell. Go to the devil. Go away!" No lout in uniform would get past me, break into the cellar rooms, hurt my sleeping grandmother. The pistol slipped from my loose belt, bouncing down the steps, bang-zinging on kitchen tiles it fired against all the marauding men that ever lived and all the evil dolls.

Let an army of monsters kick the door. I'm ready. Sword in both hands now. The door burst open, flung against the wall. I heard myself screech, propelled forward, driven against barbarians.

A row of machine guns. "Halt, halt! Fraulein Reyna. Don't stab poor old Vlado." A foreign voice, and familiar. Guns were lowered. He took off his green uniform cap and turned into Vlado, my old friend the Marxist gardener. There were five other soldiers dressed like him in drab green uniforms. And—God spare me—four Russians.

Vlado grinned. There was nothing to fear. He's a Tito partisan. "We're comrades with the Russians. Easy, easy now. Put that away."

"I am official interpreter. With much education," a Russian said in German. He wore blue pants that didn't go with his uniform and had a large friendly snout-nose.

"Where is the grandmother?" Vlado asked.

I panted and heaved as though I had run all the way home to the Meinert-Hof and back. "She is fine. Fine. Sleeping."

He turned to the men. They talked. He pointed at me. "I tell them you're comrade too. Remember?" He saluted me with a communist fist. Waited. I didn't respond the way I used to. "Remember how you once put me in your front room, in your Father's green chair?"

The Russian interpreter translated it all into one word: "Partisanca," partisan girl.

Vlado grinned. Father never knew he had hired a communist to take the place of the Nazi gardener Fritz Janicek. I never gave Vlado away because he amused me. He was married to his own niece and had eight or nine "brats." All but the oldest one, Nadica, had straw-colored curls and light eyes like Vlado. His head was round like a tom cat's. He still had the twinkle of a seducer in his brown eyes, but curls at the temples had receded and were white.

"And there you were, not much bigger than the bottle, a born communist, pouring for me brandy from France as if it were water. A big crystal tumbler full, and all for Vlado, the gardener!"

To educate Poldi and Lise, the twins, our maids, he had held them on his lap, playing with breasts and skirts, while reading aloud to them from Karl Marx. His form of communism never could have converted anyone but that seven-year-old me—it made too much sense. Vlado was not the kind of red who wanted to take everything away from us and become rich. Vlado had never wanted to unseat my father, take away his brandy. He just wanted to have a turn sitting in Father's chair and have a drink. He believed in sharing anything good or bad. Rather than fight for Hilter he had dodged, and finally vanished.

"Here your father made me overseer at the vineyards and I had to leave him in the lurch and go over to Marshal Tito. I knew the master would look after Olga and the brats," he said.

"Father, where is my father? Did he get away to the mountain farm?"

"Herr Meinert couldn't get out of Vienna. Had himself locked up in a Nazi jail. No safer place during the invasion. He had the right connections. Always knows what he is doing. There is a lot of confusion. But, we'll soon get him home."

I asked about our house. Vienna.

The Meinert-Hof had lost only a few windows. And his wife, Olga, had sent him to us. Vienna was in a fine mess. "There was that General in your house. Left plenty of coal in the cellar. There's enough to eat. Comrades have seen to that. We'll take you both to your home." He put his arm around me. My hat slipped and the remaining curls tumbled down my neck. Vlado embraced me. "My Nadica, my poor Nadica. My oldest one, my own dark curly head blown to pieces by a bomb. My one and only clever one is gone."

Two of the comrades mistook his sob for passion and came to my aid. *"Nyet, nyet,* Partisanca!" One dressed in drab green like Vlado pulled me away. He smelled of garlic.

I stood before them, strands of dirty curls dangling over my grandfather's saber handle. Vlado was making slavic sounds to the men. They surrounded me. All of them talking at once. The sound was pleasant as the twitter of birds on telegraph poles.

"Not to be afraid," Vlado translated. "They say you are beautiful partisan girl. They keep you safe and get you chicken to eat."

The sun shone in now from the stair window where Grandmother and I had stood side by side watching Mongolian Russians crawl on the wall barking like dogs. Now Russians and Slovenes were telling me I was safe and I felt as though I had lost a battle. What would Joan of Arc have done if her adversaries suddenly turned into admiring slaves? I pushed the sword into the ornate sheath. Like a warrior who puts down his arms, I suddenly felt hungry for sweetness, ravenous for food and love.

# TWO

# *Carnival of Destruction*

WE HAD BEEN SPARED. Gratitude was immense and brief. I found myself running out into the sheltered courtyard and shivering in the warm spring sun. The air had a charred flavor. I unlocked the portal to a vista of waste: black bricks, charred wood debris, gray dust; so much dust, ashes, ashes.

The theater across the street and two houses on each side remained. Beyond that only twisted metal of the ovens, where the bakery used to be. I rushed across the street, leaping over a hole, a pile of bricks, as if Arnold had never left that doorway. Prince of the old blood, a prince under an evil spell, my Frog Prince; a new nobility: a German officer following not orders, but his own beliefs. The most loyal traitor I would ever know. The most honest deceiver: a man of conscience in a time of treachery. I had clung to him and his unshaven, unwashed face had the odor of newly turned soil.

I rushed past debris in search of him and me. Anytime, even now, anywhere—over a continent, across a room, or a bed—I would flee to him, reach out, throw my arms around his neck. We had kissed in the doorway and listened to Russian guns, thunder, *Unwetter,* the tempest, coming closer, closer. Easter bells had tolled for resurrection. Men, women, children had scampered towards church or shelter.

No one was about now. I stood in the midst of hopeless waste, broken walls, ruins, smashed windows. Guns were silent. Dust hung in the air. It was too still. The wind itself was dead or hiding. Then a blackbird warbled and the church bells rang out in the emptiness. Funeral bells. "You can't be dead," I said.

An empty wine bottle had remained in the entrance to the theater all through the siege. I gave the wooden post where Arnold had leaned a kiss. It was like sending him one of those messages inside bottles that I used to throw into the mountain stream during the war. Urgent childish notes ending with lots of kisses and *Komm Zurueck*—come back. A rush of wild longing had always followed a bottle under the bridge and I imagined torrents dancing my love note across all closed borders and boundaries towards the sea. I would lean over the bridge, following the bottle long after it had disappeared. Water swirling, foaming, gushing, making me dizzy with yearning.

A born bottle post writer, sending messages of love at random, I was stuck in the most outrageously amorous period of my life: six years old forever. I remained steeped in the innate erotica of the old fairy tales. Stories of the lust for unimaginable glitter and treasures and cruel magic power, castles, magic transformations had preceded Hilter's invasion of Austria, preparing me for a prince of the old blood under an evil spell: Arnold von Luetensteg, a gestapo, looking for Eli Romberg on our farm.

Love and horror were never far apart. I almost lost my life, and kept losing my heart in rapid succession only to go right back where it all began: Arnold. From the first glimpse I had known him as a friend. The young German recruited into the gestapo, had helped Father spirit my friend Eli across the Swiss border to his father Eugene Romberg. Then, when I was ten years old, it had been Arnold who had persuaded Father to send Mother and me to that mountain paradise, a dangerously safe exile. Four years later, millions of war dead later, I had seen Arnold again. My birthday wish for some excitement, Vienna for at least one visit, had been fulfilled when Arnold had been able to take Father and me to Vienna in his Wehrmacht Limousine. I had gone to sleep, Father on one side, Arnold on the other; waking up cradled by Arnold, I had kept my eyes closed.

There had been a driver behind a glass partition. They had to talk in undertones. Arnold had told Father what a rare happy

moment this was for him. He had admitted he had been horribly
lonely. He had done all he could. But it had been hard to save
Austrians from each other—impossible to save people from
themselves.

Father had declared the Nazi era an eruption; the modern
world a volcano. Arnold could not agree with this: we were all
responsible. It didn't just happen and could have been pre-
vented. He was to blame and it was all up to him.

And why did I not sit up and say that he was not to blame?
It was really the stuffy Viennese Art Academy turning down a
young Hitler while they accepted the Meinert aunts—Father's
maiden sisters—who had known the right people. Hitler could
have become a happy minor painter instead of a supreme instigator. I had nestled against Arnold's shoulder pretending to be
asleep. Like one of those nice girls from the Kaiserday novels for
young daughters that I had been reading towards the end of the
war. Stories of daughters who did not express their thoughts
and always ended up with the perfect man. A husband as safe
as a father. Mother's choice when she was my age. Was it mine,
too?

Everything lay shattered, buried in dust, dirt, ashes, guilt.
Funeral bells kept ringing. "You can't be dead!" I said again.
And almost at once, a horse and cart with two Russians came
rattling around the corner. Father had left one of his milk delivery wagons in the old carriage house, and here it was carrying
Grandmother's pink sofa. A Russian soldier with a dirty face sat
on it holding the reins. Beside him lolled an officer bedecked
with about twenty medals, and a watch on a gold chain. I soon
learned that Russian fighting men who had come away from a
land of drab, boring insistence on equality, were greedy for decorations that set them apart and made them grand.

The officer and the soldier had flat faces and the unformed
features of young children. I thought they were brothers. At first
most Russians looked to me as though they came from the same
enormous family. The cart stopped at our open portal and turned
into the courtyard. I dipped down and hid behind wooden pillars.
The officer announced himself by spraying bullets. Vlado and
the comrades shouted from the doorway and the shooting stopped.
The men hugged each other. Then they unloaded the sofa and
carried it into the little palace. I witnessed a rare moment: Rus-

sians returning something they had taken! When they did finally agree to give back Austria, they gained by giving: American, British, French armies had to get out and Austria would remain surrounded by former imperial and now communist, Czechoslovakia, Hungary, and Yugoslavia. And yet, we are as grateful now as I was then, when the pink chaise was put back into the pink Maria Theresa breakfast room.

Two hundred years ago when the Empress Maria Theresa had the little palace built for her favorite lady in waiting, my ancestor Stefanie von Dornbach, she ordered a pink room overlooking the courtyard and facing the east to create an endless rosy sunrise light of dawn which she enjoyed when she took breakfast there after early morning mass.

For two hundred years the rosy room had stayed rosy. My grandmother would say the Russians had sensed this; something compelled them to put the sofa back. When Vlado made grateful sounds and thanked the officer, the Russian stood with his toes turned in, played with his fingers and looked embarrassed, almost ashamed. Vlado patted him on the shoulder and the Russian flung his arm around him. Then they climbed onto the cart, let their legs dangle over the edge and drove off to the Meinert-Hof. Vlado wanted to tell his wife Olga he had found us. I went down to the laundry room and while I packed two suitcases, I imagined telling Arnold about the decent Russians. He would talk about world peace. What had to be done. Then I made him say he loved me forever. (Only me. No one else.) And we would kiss. In my romantic mood, I packed all of my grandmother's lace trimmed and embroidered trousseau underwear. She did not even notice.

I had to keep our hiding place a secret. Precious things had been stored with us below the ground. Above all, the last stand, and that ultimate retreat inside the wine barrel remained a starting point I could return to whenever I felt helpless or alone. I could go back to the days in the dark with my mad dreams, rebound, laugh and come away with a sense of boundless possibilities.

In order to keep our retreat a secret, even from Vlado, I had to carry everything as far as the kitchen. Grandmother had insisted on taking the Kaiser portrait. The scratchy blanket I wrapped around the picture made me think of Arnold's unshaved

face. We had said "Auf Wiedersehen" at the theater. He might
come to look for me here. "I really want to stay," I said to my
grandmother.

She didn't want to leave either, and kept talking about swallows returning, and the boarded up windows of the corridor where
they had their nests. Actually, she was thinking of her Rittmeister, Rudi, a monarchist leader, who had been stuck into a concentration camp. She was expecting him back every minute of
the day. When the countess had to cope with something she didn't
want to do, she always hurried. Vlado carrying our suitcases
couldn't keep up with her.

"She probably doesn't want to see the damage," he said to me.
"Of course it's a shame. Why should anyone want to shoot at all
the fat angels and old flower decorations. Workers must have
labored on all the fancying up without geting any decent pay.
Stupid to destroy what the Viennese workers made, but you have
to understand. Austrians did march into Russia with the Germans. And into my Yugoslavia, too. Everywhere. And it wasn't
just war. They murdered, robbed—dirty, filthy, cruel. Burned
down villages, stole little children. Now the young Russ comes
here, shoots the men who shot at him and takes the women."

"They prefer watches," I said. "They left women, and fought
for watches. Grandmother and I saw it."

"Can you blame them? They can take the watches along. They
have to leave the women. Besides, a watch is a novelty to those
fellows, and women are not."

It wasn't funny, and it made me laugh. Grandmama had not
been listening. She had stopped and her eyes wandered over the
little palace. "At least they didn't shoot the Empress."

She meant the marble relief of Maria Theresa above the
entrance. The date, 1765 when the Empress had presented the
little palace to my ancestor Stefanie von Dornbach, had been
shot away. Cherubs on the facade had been chipped. The stone
head of a horse above the stable building was untouched. I always
used to run past it because of an ugly children's story of a chopped
off horse's head that talks. Now I recognized the blank, blind,
eyes and the half open mouth of the stone head as the model for
"The Horse" my grandmother had drawn over and over again
while we were hiding. She had been haunted by her father and
his horses, had talked about him while she had filled the pages
of her sketch book with horse after horse, and her words had

circled—as he once did—unable to leave the boundaries of his estate.

I did not like the way she stared at the horse's head. To divert her I stooped and picked up two unpolished uniform buttons. "Russian, I bet." I stuck them into my pocket, as if I knew they would come in handy one day.

She walked ahead. An amazing, proud figure; tall, fragile, costumed in cloak and fur hat, from another era. She cradled the blanket with the Kaiser portrait against her chest. "Is it safe to leave?" she asked me, ready to turn back.

"It is safe," Vlado told her. "We take you to the Meinert house with your granddaughter. My wife, Olga she takes good care of you. Nice warm rooms. And food, too. Don't worry, Alexander comes to drive us. He'll see we get there. If he asks questions don't tell him much, just talk. He'll stick his nose into anything, but he's all right when he's sober. I have three of my best men posted here. They guard this place as if it were the Kremlin." He put two fingers into his mouth and whistled. Two comrades came rushing out of the little palace carrying suitcases.

"I'd rather stay. We'll stay!" Grandmama said. "I don't think I should leave." I put my arm around her. "To think, some of the bullet marks at the shrine might have come from my pistol." she whispered. Now, that we had left the cellar rooms and I was safe, she could blame herself again. "What's to become of us? What's to become of Vienna?"

"*Schon gut Gnaedigste*. All right. Wait till you see what we have in there!" Vlado shouted to his comrades and they rushed ahead of us into the carriage house.

Before the war I had enjoyed climbing up into the one remaining carriage. Only an axle and a wheel remained. In the corner stood a strange vehicle, covered by an old horse blanket. The Russian with the big, friendly nose, Alexander, pulled the blanket off and gave the hood a resounding kiss. "*Schoen*, beautiful, isn't she? The sheep!" He jumped into the driver's seat. Grandmama with the Kaiser picture followed and I jammed in beside her. Alexander patted his stubby machine gun. "Let anyone try to take the sheep. We shoot!" Vlado put the blanket over us and piled into the back with the comrades and luggage. Alexander started the engine. He told us he was Ukrainian. His people spoke perfect German. There had been a lot of traitors in Belo Russkaja, fighting on the side of the Germans, but his father was a party leader and a patriot, a fine mechanic. He patted himself on the shoulder. He, Alexander, was a fine mechanic too, and the best interpreter, and he loved Russia and Stalin.

The greatest patriots often end up as expatriots. And some men are as susceptible to our city as others are to colds. The sun was shining down on disaster, but Alexander grinned from ear to ear. Was Viennese pleasure addiction in the air, the dust? Alexander was bewitched by the "sheep." He patted the dashboard, clicked his tongue as if it were a horse; made a big show of starting the engine and making it roar, waiting for admiration when we began to roll. The affection he felt for the vehicle made me think it was Russian. I soond found out that the sheep was an American jeep, but I never got over the weird carnival feeling of that first ride through war-torn Vienna. In a jeep, I would always expect startling scenes to come along.

We no sooner turned the corner then a twisted baby carriage came running down the hill, driven by the wind it crashed into the front of the jeep and stuck. Alexander cursed and laughed. We stopped in front of the Hohentahler mansion. Vlado moved the baby carriage and pointed at the missing roof. "Too bad. Remember when I used to bring you here for lessons with the Hohentahler sisters?" He greeted the giant mermaids at the door with a closed fist.

Communist salutes, Heil Hitler, I had tried it all out in those days. It was a game I no longer played. Mermaids had once held up a charming balcony. The wrought iron railing had vanished. Stout mermaids looked like naked serving wenches holding an empty tray. The street was deserted. Church bells clanged in the distance. We swerved around piles of debris and circled a gap on a cobbled square. Dust flew into my face, my eyes. It stank of rot, smolder and gas. Of a grandiose appartment house only two walls remained; lace curtains billowed at a window. I became intrigued by stucco garlands decorating the façade: flowers without name left over from the sugar baker sweetness of Vienna, the ornate Kaisertown.

We kept looking this way and that, caught up in the hideous diversion of destruction: draped female statues strewn about, a shattered stained-glass window, telephone wires twisted around a coal bin, an overturned truck under a tumbled wall. Alexander laughed out loud.

I became stupefied by the debauch of waste. "What a mess. What a mess!" Awe crept into my voice. In Vienna houses, rooms, drawers, everything always had to be so neat and dainty. "I have never seen such a mess!" I kept saying.

Scene after scene of destruction came towards us. Grandmama and I clung to each other as if we were on a terror ride, the ghost train in our amusement park, the prater. We cried out as we swerved around an upturned street car, or a fallen lamp post, a pile of bricks, shattered glass.

The first people we saw knelt on a small patch of grass. Most of it had been dug up. It didn't dawn on me until later that they were praying at a makeshift grave. I became diverted by three bundled up figures loaded down with sacks creeping alongside buildings faster and faster as they saw us. It seemed unreal, a farce. A cracked shop window gave me back a fleeting image of the Countess Reyna and myself in tall fur hats. I thought of Hanna Roth, designer of doll's clothing and ladies hats saying: "The right hat for the right occasion—that is elegance."

Somewhere beyond the smolder and dust of Vienna Hanna Roth was smiling her never-ending smile. We reached her street, and I was not surprised to find her house untouched. Parterre windows had been boarded up. On the second floor, the Salon Roth, a geranium was blooming. "Look, Grandmama, just look!" I said.

She was leaning forward gazing at the distant Hofburg. "There it is standing, our Hofburg, the kaiser's home." She whispered to me. "Waiting to welcome our crown prince."

Stocky Russian soldiers stood around the imperial winter residence. The road was littered with charred and rusted brown metal and dotted with cow dirt. The return of the Hapsburgs into this mess seemed to me far less likely than the return of Hanna the Dwarf who had foretold the fall of the empire, the fall of Hitler, a Cassandra, a posseur, a schemer, grand and invincible, wondrous as Vienna. Before her fixed smile, her mistrust of males, Russians at the entrance to the Kaiser palace would be mere boys with guns, clumsy, helpless, forced to be here, and hopelessly out of place. I saw it all through her eyes, but not for long.

At the Hofburg, near a statute of a giant wrestling reptilian monster, we were met by a roar. Brakes squealed. We jolted to a halt. Three fur hats, three grease guns popped up. My suitcase was grabbed and hit the ground with a smack. Alexander cursed and laughed, gripping the steering wheel so hard his knuckles turned white. Vlado and the comrades got out and joined Russian guards in the noisiest quarrel I had ever heard. They waved fists, guns, snarled, barked and yelled.

"Sit tight. Don't move. Don't talk!" Vlado called to us.

This was unecessary. My grandmother had turned rigid as a threatened lady bug, and I was numb, dumb, all eyes and ears. There is no finer language for a nasty argument and gun waving than Russian. Had I spoken up, no one could have heard me. One of the guards veered around, glared at me. My throat tightened. His bloodshot eyes turned to the countess. The door was torn open. He flung himself onto us and grabbed her bundle.

I held her tight. "Don't say a word." The blanket fell. And the picture of Kaiser Franz Joseph as a young man in country clothes was thrown on top of it. My father with his kaiser whiskers aimed to resemble the late Kaiser, who had been a manly, well-meaning patriarch, happiest in the country.

Russian soldier boys emptied our suitcases and within minutes the smiling Franz Joseph was surrounded by a wild disorder of female underpants, nightgowns with tucks, ruffles, petticoats, trimmed with Brussels lace, embroidered crest and initials.

Grandmama and I, hair tucked into hats, had been weird and sexless. Now we were exposed. The guards gaped. One, serious as a monkey, held a dainty chemise up against his uniform. Another one came closer and pointed at women's watches pinned to his uniform in a row like medals. "Tell him I have no watch, Vlado!" I said. "Tell him Grandmama doesn't have one either."

He came at me. Expressionless. A tin soldier's face. His mouth fell open displaying dark metal teeth. Grease gun in one hand, the other grabbing the blanket off our knees. A hairy hand fastened around my middle. He was about to pull me down like a celluloid doll at a shooting gallery. I screamed. Alexander honked his horn, cursed and laughed. An officer appeared in front of the Hofburg. Vlado yelled something. My grandmother smacked the furry hand away. The officer shouted an order and came along in measured steps.

Salutes all around. I saluted too. He was the first Russian

without a machine gun. His uniform was neat, decorated with medals and only one wrist watch was tied to each sleeve. Around his neck he wore a toilet chain necklace with two pair of field glasses. He had not bothered to take off the wooden handle and it dangled down his chest.

Vlado grinned. They talked and shook hands. The officer trained first one and then the other pair of field glasses on the "sheep," the countess and me. Then he became fascinated with the display on the road.

"Don't worry," Vlado said to us. "The guards are a little excited. A certain Nazi, Schmiedler, is on the loose. They are hunting for him in the inner city."

The guards seemed to be looking for a Schmiedler the size of Tom Thumb among our clothes. And I did some fast sorting in my mind. Under Hilter, Father had required a Schmiedler signature. The *Geld-Mensch,* money-man, as Father always called the big Nazi beast, could be a dangerous enemy. And Father had brought along a case of choice Meinert wine. Schmiedler had not appeared to thank him, remained invisible, but the paper had come back signed. He was known as a treacherous quick-change artist and illusionist, notorious for his many faces. He also had many houses, but his favorite residence had been in our district. He had persecuted both socialists and monarchists.

"Tell the officer Grandmama worked in the resistance and she has been terribly ill. Ask him to let us take our things. We want to go home." I said to Vlado.

He talked and pointed at us. The officer seemed disinterested. He walked over the clean trousseau underwear, yelled at the guards and they scattered. Then he picked up the Kaiser portrait.

"You can't have that! Not that." Grandmama remembered Russian officers she had met on her travels and repeated this in French.

The officer did not even look at her. He spoke to Vlado.

"All he wants is this picture. Nothing else. They'll let us keep the "sheep." And we can go on."

"Tell him it's a picture of my father," I said. And suddenly I missed my father. And I thought of him getting old and sad like the emperor. What if Father wasn't locked up but dead? My mouth opened and I bawled and howled, for my father, mother, the family we had been and might never be again. The Vienna, our Vienna snatched away, bombed, overrun, shambles. "Tell him to get his boot off the clean underwear." I sobbed. Tears I had held back during the cellar days when my grandmother was ill came pouring down my face. I couldn't stop. Vlado patted me. Alexander tried to give me a piece of bread. I howled for all the children and women who had been abused, bereaved, murdered.

The officer had raised his field glasses and observed me first from one end and then the other, bringing my distorted face close and then removing it. He changed field glasses. And I kept howling like an infant. He turned to Vlado.

"He doesn't care about the picture. He doesn't like the bearded man. Russians don't like beards. You can keep it. He wants to put the gold frame around Stalin in his room. *Dobro. Gut,* all right!" Vlado said.

My grandmother slid down before I could stop her. She, herself ripped the linen off the back of the picture. I could see that she liked the idea of framing Stalin with the ancient Hapsburg anagram: All the Universe is subordinate to Austria. Vlado pried the canvas out of the frame with his pen knife. A minute later Grandmama was beside me again clutching the Kaiser picture. Vlado stuffed our things back into suitcases. The officer hung the frame over his left shoulder, and walked away.

Then our engine died. Alexander addressed it in Russian. He seemed to plead, reason. No use. The response was a grunt. The hairy knee grabber was back. His paw reached for the steering wheel. I was squeezed against the door. The quarreling in Russian started all over again. Alexander cursed, laughed and spat. The hairy one blipped his head with the gun. Vlado was trying to make himself heard. The guards felt left out and came back. The officer turned and raised his field glasses. Alexander had slumped against Grandmama, but his crafty eyes told me he was wide awake and holding on. The hairy one could not pull him out of the driver's seat. I helped by holding onto Alexander's arm.

The officer yelled an order and was ignored. I never forgot him standing there under the triumphal arch of the kaiserly portal. A tiny man, giant statues on each side of him, huge columns above and high behind him the great cupola. Any kaiser would have been dwarfed by such vast imperialist buildings, ornamentation and debris. And the officer did try again, using the voice of a town crier. His men would not listen.

First he raised one pair of field glasses. Then the other. I saw him reach under his coat. A shot rang out. I ducked. The hairy one slipped off and tumbled onto the road. His hat rolled into the gutter. The officer stuck his pistol back under the coat. The Kaiser's gilded frame gleamed in the sun.

Alexander cursed the engine in Russian and it started. He drove away leaning over the steering wheel. We all ducked. The guards scampered back to their post at the palace. One of them urinated on the statues. By the time we turned the fallen comrade had sat up to examine his hands, to make sure he hadn't lost any fingers. We were driving away fast now. Swerving around a demolished Russian tank. Vlado and his comrades were arguing. I held onto my grandmother. She held the Kaiser portrait in front of us like a shield. An old man and three women flattened themselves into a doorway. They peered out at the Kaiser picture coming along in a jeep driven by a Russian. The old man got confused and shouted: *"Gott erhalte!"* God save! and gave us a snappy salute. The Countess smiled as though her dream had come true. She was bringing a Hapsburg emperor back to Vienna.

We turned onto the Ring-strasse ensconced behind the picture of the All-Highest Franz Joseph who had commissioned all the buildings. And it was all there. Parliament, Rathaus, statues in the parks: Greek, Gothic and Renaissance hurly burly. Pagan Gods, saints, gargoyles, and dust, debris, torn up granite and bricks, bomb craters and ashes, ashes.

"A fine mess," I said.

"Cleaning all that up is work for more men than we have left," Vlado said. "There'll be no unemployment."

The chipped and charred walls, barriers at the shell of the burned-out Burgtheater, bombed University flitted by. Grandmama stared ahead. "Ah, the Votive church is standing." A symbol of Kaiserly gratitude. The mock-gothic church had been built by Franz Joseph after an attack on his life. At the Schottentohr we swerved into a courtyard. A deserted café garden. Stacked chairs, broken chairs. The top of a gigantic linden tree glittering with splintered window glass. A Russian soldier sat on a suitcase, with his back against the tree trunk milking a cow. We drove to him and Vlado dangled a watch and chain in front of his snub nose. The watch changed hands. And the cow swung its

tail from side to side like a pendulum while the tin cup passed
from mouth to mouth. The warm milk, and the sweet seclusion
of the old courtyard made us heady. One of the Slovenes produced a mouth organ from his pocket.

We drove on to his homesick tunes, all the way to the villas
and gardens where forsythia spilled over railings and glowed in
the sudden grayness. Wind had sprung up and it was beginning
to rain when we reached our avenue. And there was the Meinert-Hof. We laughed and hugged each other as we drove up at
the gate. Nothing seemed to have changed. From the street one
could see the ancestral farm, half hidden by an old willow and
rose gardens. Generations of Meinerts had added a wing on each
side at the back leaving the courtyard open to their expanding
land.

Across the street at the Romberg villa trees had been felled.
"Resi Heller, Frau Romberg used to give me singing lessons with
her son Eli, remember?"

The countess, my grandmother, did not respond. I could share
her good old kaiser days, she could never share my good old days
at the big Romberg house. My convent raised grandmother had
been shocked at my conversion to Judaism by our neighbor the
opera singer Resi Romberg and Eli her ten-year-old son. The
winter before Hilter when some people were already trying to
rake up Aryan ancestors, Resi Romberg had decided to become
Jewish, because her rich foreign husband Eugene Romberg was
supposed to be one of the chosen people. Uncle Eugene, I used to
call him. The memory of his approval and admiration warmed
me like brandy.

Singing with Resi and dancing had been a lesson in how to
amuse yourself and entertain everyone else. Just in time, before
Hitler, when I was seven years old, I had learned from the operetta singspiel of Resi's sweet Judaic myth how to be a lover and
not a hater. I hungered for those feasts of pleasantry and affection in brightly lit rooms: flowers blooming all winter long in the
warm greenhouse, birds trilling in large cages in the aviary.

Strange people were digging in the Romberg's front garden.
The mansion was no longer sugar white, but mottled as though
it had been submerged in murky water. Stucco had been nibbled
away. It had always been known as the water castle. Water—
the facetious Viennese had said—watering milk in his dairies

had made Romberg, the Splasher, so rich. And gray water seemed to have flooded over our dead friends house since I had last seen it, creating a tragic monument to the most generous of all men. I stifled a sob, and ran to our gate.

A small girl in a big, dirty apron came with keys. She stopped and eyed me and my grandmother. "Are the Russian women going to move in with us?" she asked.

"Open up!" Vlado said. "These are the *Herrschaften*. Meinert family coming home."

The girl, addressed as "General's Gredl," had stayed on with the *Frau Generalin*. The German General, who had taken over our house when he was planning the defense of Vienna, had vanished. His wife remained invisible in the new wing of our horseshoe-shaped house. And the son, I was told, had the measles and had to stay on a cot in the sewing room in case he passed it on. I was interested in the boy and felt sorry for him.

I wandered from one cozy room to the next: white walls, dark wooden beams and old hand-painted peasant furniture. The Russians had turned the library into a dormitory and mattresses covered the floor. The house seemed unbearably hot, but two of them were fast asleep and covered up to the top of their fur hats.

Vlado's wife, the buxom Olga, led me away and told me to stay upstairs. She had prepared Mother's rooms for us, because of the locks. The general had left the cellar full of coal and the pantry well stocked. Vlado promised me that Father would come home soon and asked us to keep our door locked. Olga brought our meals upstairs.

I sank into my first warm bath. Drowsy and contented for several days, I lolled around the boudoir, the only fancy room in the house. The blue silk walls had been stained under the windows as though someone had left windows open. Any clever looter would have seen the marks on the wall where pictures and the clock had been. Father had hidden everything below the ground in his catacombs, the wine cellar.

I wore a jade green velvet dress of Mother's to go with a French novel I had found to read. The story took me far away from rape and plunder. It was about a young woman at a spa in France who is married to a wealthy jewish man and can't have any children. She falls in love with a romantic lover and he seduces her by falling down on the ground and kissing her shadow. Then the cure is effective and she becomes pregnant. Her shadow becomes monstrous, and the shadow kissing lover prefers a slender young peasant girl. I wondered whether Mother had read this book when she was pregnant before the war.

Grandmother slept a lot. When she asked me whether I was reading an interesting book, I told her it was about a spa and a cure. And she talked about how everybody always took a cure, how people who were kind to themselves were also kind and easy going towards every one else in the kaiser days, and how she missed Bad-Ischl, the old kaiser cure town, where Kaiser Franz Joseph had fallen in love with his little fifteen-year-old cousin. I stood by the window to cast a shadow, imagined myself in a cure resort in France and was going through my assortment of imaginary loves without being able to find one French enough to kiss shadows, when I saw a tall woman in a gray squirrel coat walking to the gate. Gredl was with her carrying a suitcase. It looked heavy. Once or twice she had to stop and change hands. The Frau Generalin was stealing away.

The general's wife had chosen a perfect moment to leave undetected. It was two in the afternoon. On the hour, Russians who were in the house and awake, would be lined up in the morning room waiting for the cuckoo clock to perform. They clapped and cheered when the little window opened and the painted bird popped out. Slovenes joined in cheerfully. During the hubbub I went to the sewing room to see the poor boy who had been left behind.

I could hear sobbing. Gredl had hurried back and was scolding: "stop, stop that at once." The sewing room door had glass panels. I saw a cot and a pink heaving quilt. Gredl smacked it and pulled the cover off an unhappy bearded face of a young man. She wiped his tears with her apron. "Your *Mutter* was scared of the Russian with the big nose. She had to get away. I was nice to him and he let her go. I'll be nice to him again. Then he gives me some food and then we'll get out of here, Hansi. I already stuck your uniform into the furnace. Look what I've got for you!" She held up one of my father's leather breeches and a loden jacket. "All the Nazis grow beards to hide their face. We'll take yours off." She brandished a razor and shaving brush. "I don't like it anyway, it tickles."

"First you have to be nice to me," said the bearded Hansi.

She laughed. Dropped the razor and shaving brush and dove into bed.

"You're tickling. Stop it. Stop," she shrieked. Her apron came flying out and she was giggling and screeching. "Keep those bristles off me. I can't stand it."

I had not heard anyone laugh so much for a long time. She had to be about my age. Older girls had been drafted into war work. A few days later Gredl and Hansi vanished. And I hoped that somewhere they were still tickling each other and laughing.

One afternoon there came a knock on our door. "It's Olga!" Vlado's wife, shiny, smooth-faced, as though she had just dipped into water, feet flip-flopping in Father's shoes. She was sad-eyed as a seal.

"Will the lady please be so kind and come downstairs."

Why this sudden formality? It wasn't like her. She left us in too much of a hurry. "Papa is back," I said to my grandmother. "Hurry up, quick! *Schnell!*"

We found Vlado in the morning room with Alexander. Another Russian, a stranger was sitting in Father's breakfast chair.

"I thought my father had come home," I said.

The stranger was watching squirrels chasing each other leaping from one pine tree to the next. Mates or enemies, it was hard to tell. The green spring grass was dotted with crocus and primroses and blue *Leberbluemchen* flowers. He turned from the view of the Meinert gardens to me, and pointed at the door. Sending me from the room like a dog in disgrace did not keep me from my old listening post, halfway up the stairs.

"You like the Kaiser?" This unfamiliar voice had to be the stranger. He spoke good German.

"I do," my grandmother said cheerfully.

"The Kaiser followers in this town, they all trust in you and do as you say, *ja?*"

"They trust me," she said.

"You tell the truth. You don't lie." He said.

"I am a Christian," she told him.

"The crown, all the Kaiser jewels are missing. We must find this and keep it safe."

"German authorities took the Hapsburg crown jewels and regalia and they must know—"

"—Who knows? You tell me who knows and your son the Meinert he goes free."

Silence after that. Then a chair moved. Starlings were whistling in the garden.

"I want you to release my son-in-law, but I have no idea," she said. "And I am so very glad you are planning to safeguard the treasure for us. There is the crown of the Holy Roman Empire."

She came back upstairs slowly. I settled down with a book on Mother's blue sofa. We were lucky Vlado had been able to get back to Vienna so fast. Russians had not taken much. They had killed all of Olga's chickens and a piglet.

Grandmama sat down beside me with a sigh. "Looking for crown jewels," she told me. "There was a disgraceful treasure hunt and thieving going on after the First World War, too."

I had heard all about "Poor Emperor Karl" who never had a chance to reign and would have been the salvation of Europe. Such an outstandingly brilliant and decent Kaiser, ousted and in danger.

"All he and Empress Zita had left in the world were her own family jewels. They handed most of that over to a certain lawyer. They were far too trusting. That scoundrel made off with it all leaving them practically penniless. The brother of the empress had actually tracked down the thief to München, and the lawyer promised to meet him the next day and give back the jewels. Of course, he vanished. To think that our Kaiser Karl and his family actually starved in exile. He did not want to spend money on a doctor when he took ill. He died a pauper." Her eyes shimmered with tears. "Our Prince Otto takes after his father. He is brilliant. One day, who knows. . . . Anyway, I pray to God the crown jewels are in a safe place."

"Where?" I asked in a low voice. "Do you have any idea?"

She smiled through tears and snapped one of my curls.

I said Fritz Janicek would know. He took all kinds of paintings and everything from museums and kept it all in that mine below the farm. "Do you think the crowns are hidden in that cave?"

She put her arm around me. "Never talk about any of this. Never mention that Fritz Janicek. He was a dangerous Nazi. And he was your gardener once. Any link between that man and your father could do a lot of harm."

The link was really with my mother. She had come across Fritz Janicek in the soup kitchen for the unemployed where she had worked as a volunteer during the depression. She couldn't have been more than twenty-three years old. Wearing a big white apron and white cap, and the doll dressed like a cook in apron and cap would be there too. Whenever she had been pleased with herself as the young Frau von Meinert, and felt just too adorable with her doll, she would have a need for careless kindliness. She probably felt vaguely sorry for Fritz Janicek, teacher of art, languages and history, an educated man who had lost his teaching job. He had told her he loved beauty, he loved roses and she had hired him on the spot. Father would have made inquiries and found out that Fritz had been dismissed from his teaching job because he was too fond of Hitler and too fond of boys.

"No one can hear us," I went on. "And I do think Fritz would know where the crowns are. He had a lot of power, although he was so weird. I saw him shoot the head off Mother's doll. Then he held the head and talked to it. Kissed the hair. I wonder what he did with the doll's head. Perhaps it is with the crowns."

She tried to put her hand over my mouth.

"He used to write poems for Mother. And when he and his friends took over the Romberg villa some of them dressed up in Resi Romberg's old clothes and danced. The house had been empty. I heard gypsy music. Eugene Romberg's favorite. I was only ten years old. The Rombergs always kept all the lights on day and night, and when I heard the music and saw the lights, I thought they had somehow come back. So, I went over there and I saw those men."

I would not be the only one who had a sudden need to talk, tell what had really happened and leave out the worst part. Gypsy violins in my head sang a lullaby of death. I tried to tell myself it had served those drunks right. They had chased me—a girl dressed as a boy—pawed me. Fritz had told them to stick me in the empty parrot cage. I had been caged, humiliated, yet had he not kept me safe from those hands? He had danced away with his fat partner, fled the house. Gypsy fiddlers had lured the revellers out of the aviary. By the time I broke out of the cage fiddlers were playing a cradle song. A lullaby at dawn. Men in Resi's costumes had been lying around the big hall, as though they were sleeping. Some of those men had strung up our Falkenburg gypsies. And what a sweet song of peace the gypsy man had played for them all that night. And if they could not hear the song and would sleep forever, they had drunk themselves to death on Meinert Nussberger wine without any bitter taste. Theirs had been a gentle death. That's why it haunted me and I had to talk and talk around it and never come to the point.

"Those men didn't take care of the birds. The parrot died. And there was a Falkenburg gypsy man and he liked the birds—"

"Shhh. Shhh. Walls have ears. Your father did tell me some of this. I didn't want to bring it up. I thought it might be too terrible for you to remember those men."

Had Fritz not caged me and kept me safe? And how about the gypsy opening cages and windows, letting birds who could not survive outdoors fly away? A cruelty could be kind, and kindness cruel.

"You are now old enough to understand that men who go through a war are often mentally afflicted. Hitler himself certainly was," Grandmother said.

"Fritz Janicek was a teacher, you know. And when he worked for us as a gardener he used to tell me about the first war, dates and everything. And all the corpses of beautiful young boys piled up as high as walls. And he painted nothing but self portraits in the gardener's cottage. One was purple, and it stayed on the wall after Father fired him. I looked into the cottage. It's still there. I'll show it to you. And the last time I saw Fritz Janicek he was still in S.S. uniform but he had painted his face and was wearing lipstick."

"Shhhh," Grandma said. "Your voice is too loud. You are talking too much. You were almost too quiet in the cellar. And I needed to hear your voice in the dark. Now you're making me dizzy." She kissed my cheek and said we were lucky to be so comfortable and safe here, but to all effects we were interned.

"Caged in," I said.

She ignored this and said we just had to be very careful in order to have my father released. "Just remember to forget it all."

# THREE

# *Remember to Forget*

REMEMBER TO FORGET . . . Remember to forget. A great slogan for us that winter. They should have put it in sky writing. Dropped leaflets down: *remember to forget.* It should have been written in big black letters over swastikas left on plank walls and ruins. The best advice for the next hundred years at least. And I was not in the mood to listen to anyone. I wanted to talk.

My grandmother had gone to sleep. I unlocked the door and sat on the stairs. Glasses clinked. Comrades were drinking Yugoslav Slivovic, a fragrant plum brandy that burned your throat. After a few drinks they made the cuckoo clock perform. The painted bird kept announcing one hour after the other, racing through a day. Suddenly there was a click and that was the end. I heard angry words. Apparently the Russian officer who had questioned Grandmother had fiddled with the clock and a spring had snapped. He came storming out of the morning room and slammed the door.

I confronted him at once. "I want my father to come home," I said. "He was against Hitler. He saved Eugene Romberg who was supposed to be a Jew. And also my friend Eli. My father is very smart. And he might be able to find the crown. I know he could if you let him come home. Besides, who is going to get milk distribution going in Vienna? We must remember to forget . . ."

The officer looked over the rim of metal framed spectacles, which made the lower half of his beady eyes large and soulful. "You talk like a machine gun." He took out a bunch of keys and unlocked the door.

"Those are my father's keys. Did he give them to you?"

He walked out. The door was closing in my face. "I have one like you at home. Talks like a machine gun, afraid of nothing."

I heard his voice again the night of the party. Alexander had invited me, but Vlado had told Grandmama I should stay upstairs with her. And this time the door was locked, she had hidden the keys and was asleep in Mother's curtained bed. I listened to the music. None of the comrades ever played the piano; it had to be the officer. Vlado caterwauled a Slovene song. After that a Russian chorus boomed full of wild sadness.

The dancing started. I imagined comrades squatting and kicking their short pony legs with the big shouts and singing. What a party! I tried a Russian dance and tumbled. Kept trying and went down. My legs were too long. Then I looked for the keys in the drawers, Grandmama's purse, her cloak pocket, and behind the Kaiser portrait. I messed up coats, skirts in Mother's dressing room. Put on a black silk robe trimmed with black ostrich feathers.

My grandmother had left a candle burning. I took it to the mirror and pinned up my hair, smeared on some old dry lipstick and turned into the great spy Mata Hari hiding in a locked room. The music stopped. Comrades had been out to forage for food. They would be eating hunks of bread, sausage, even eggs. I was famished. But soon the sounds of a feast and laughter changed to shouts, threats, spitting, snarling words. And the angry voices came closer. Boots clomped on my stairs. Somebody went rolling, down, down.

To Grandmama these were dream monster noises. She turned over, blinked at a nightmarish me holding a candle in front of a dark mirror. Bedlam ended and she went back to sleep.

I wheeled my cot against the door, spread the robe around me in a Mata Hari pose. The piano now accompanied a single male voice, the officer, a father thinking of home. Russians were sons and fathers not just dangerous monsters. I went to sleep.

Tapping on the door woke me up. It was light and raining hard and water came gushing out of bullet holes in the rain pipe.

Grandmother was tying her robe. She took me by the hand and hers was as cold as it had been in the cellar. The knocking became more urgent. Tap, tap, pause and tap. It sounded like a code. "Who is it?" she asked.

Jingling. A key pushed into the lock. Grandmother tried to nudge me towards the dressing room and I refused to move. She smelled like a crushed violet.

"I know that tapping," I said. "Who is there?"

"A dirty old farmer."

"Father!"

The door opened to a tired looking thin man in country clothes. I flung myself into his arms. "Your whiskers!"

"Russians hate beards. I had to shave, but whiskers will grow back!"

I suddenly burst into tears.

Grandmother scolded him for scaring me like that.

"I wasn't scared," I said.

He had knocked as though playing the old love game of stranger at the door could bring Mother back into that locked room. She had always opened up throwing herself into his arms. "I'll get you and the doll dirty," he used to say. "Get us dirty. I don't care," she'd say. Then there would be wild kissing and wild rolling on the bed while the doll sat in her gilded rocker the ingenious mechanical eyes moving from side to side.

It seemed to me now that their fun stopped after the doll was lost. And after all the years, I saw my rational father caught up in fantasies, playing the old game, wanting Mother back—and he certainly remembered to forget how he had stored Mother away in the mountains with me during the war.

I laughed a lot and cried when Father told the story of his release. The Russians had let the Nazi's prisoners go, but kept Father locked up because they didn't like his side whiskers. They had moved him in a windowless truck. Locked him into a base-ment. He didn't know exactly where he was. One day he had been able to wave to a woman through window bars and he asked her to bring him a razor. He was thirsty, but saved his drinking water to shave off his beard. This helped. By the time Vlado found him, they were ready to let him go.

Vlado and Olga stayed on and comrades moved out. I asked my father for my own set of keys and we went to the gallery, on top of the old part of the house. Creaky doors made Father wince and he carried an oil squirter with him to lubricate door hinges all over the house. "There," he said, "that's more like it." He would say that often when he was able to put little things right in the midst of hopeless chaos.

Nothing had been touched in the gallery and this pleased him. All the portraits of pot-bellied Meinert forefathers and the stag heads, their trophies, faced the windows overlooking Meinert gardens, orchard, woods, an empire expanding from the Meinert-Hof, to the distant vineyards. I used to say Guten Tag, with a *Knicks,* a mannerly Austrian small girl curtsey, to each stout ancestoral man and each stag head. And then I'd throw a kiss to my favorite, my smiling Great Uncle Ernstl the black sheep with the eighteen-carat gold teeth, gold watch chain and Meinert signet ring of his own design; the shield and the grapes.

Father had the glass key case boarded over during the war. It was released by a spring that needed oiling. Each set of keys hung on its hook.

I reached for my heirloom gilded Uncle Ernstl keys and chain. Father stayed my hand. "A little dangerous." He said and handed me an ordinary set.

"I had the gold keys when I was six years old. You wanted me to be independent. Why should I lose them now? Or do you think I'm going to be like Uncle Ernstl if I have his keys?"

Father laughed and said this was not the time to carry anything that glittered. He was right, of course. I stuffed those ordinary keys into my pocket. "There is a smell of sweaty feet," I said.

Alexander in full Russian uniform and gun popped into the room. He was carrying a boot in each hand. The Russians had all moved out. I was afraid now that they'd all come back. Alexander grinned, and said he'd come to visit. Father drew me behind his back. Alexander was far more interested in Great Uncle Ernstl the lover, spendthrift, bachelor, the only Meinert who ever died poor, and the only Meinert who ever displayed wealth. "The beautiful teeth," he said at once. "Alexander brought you a little meat. There is so much gold in Vienna. I would like those teeth."

"So you like Vienna," Father quickly said. "How kind of you to bring meat. Let me invite you to drink some good Vienna wine, our golden wine, and I'll tell you about the golden teeth."

They went downstairs. I took my time locking up and my keys jingled me a tune of escape. A hunk of pork was staining the morning room table. I took it down to the kitchen and created an uproar. Frau Boschke the laundress had arrived half an hour ago, but no one knew that Alexander the Russian interpreter was in the house.

"The Russians probably kept a set of keys," I said.

Frau Boschke called to all the saints in heaven and rolled her eyes. Vlado's wife Olga made her stop and said Alexander had often climbed over the fence and got into the house through the broken sewing room window. Anyway, he meant well bringing us meat. She cut off a piece for the laundress. Frau Boschke calmed down. Five years had gone by, but she greeted me as though she had seen me on last week's laundry day. Her big belly had vanished, otherwise she looked unchanged. I had always loved the wild nest of mud-colored hair which matched her eyes.

"Your blouse needs the treatment in the tub, it looks gray. And the dirndl needs ironing. If anyone can get a hold of some soap it will be your father," she said.

Actually it was Grandmama who helped out with soap. Three of the bombed out nuns came back to stay at the little palace and brought with them a supply of soap. They rustled along the passageway in their black and white habits. And black and white swallows shrilled darting in and out over their heads as they tended to their nests. The Countess Reyna went back and forth between the little palace and the Meinert-Hof. Street cars were not running and you never knew who you were going to come across. Father walked with her and made me stay at home. I helped Vlado dig up the kitchen garden.

Vlado talked to me, as he might have talked to his clever Nadica, about the partisans in Yugoslavia, where women and children had lived in the woods and had fought like men. Only once did he tell me about the terrible reprisals in his grandmother's village, where a German officer had been shot. The Germans had rounded up every man they could find, locked them into the church and burned them. The worst of it all, the murdered German officer had been friendly towards Slovenes. The Germans themselves had killed him and then punished the villagers for that murder to scare everyone into submission. But the few young fellows and old men that escaped took all the women and children, horses, cows, pigs into the woods and joined the Marshal Tito partisans. Eighty-year-old men and five year olds all fought the Germans.

Churchill had secretly dropped a high ranking British officer into Yugoslavia by parachute. An astonishing hero who had fought with the partisans and helped them get assistance from Great Britain. As for Russian help, Tito had said no thanks and kept them out of his country while he and the Partisans chased the Hitler army out. "I had dodged the German army and the gestapo might have rounded up my family, if it hadn't been for Herr Meinert. There's no one quite like your father, and you're quite something. That's for sure."

In the evening after potatoes and chives (a great meal in those days) Grandmama and Father liked to sit around the dining room table and feast on talking about the little marvel I had always been. How I had crawled when other infants could barely sit up, walked in no time and could read when I was five.

I didn't like being discussed.

"And what an imp," he said. "Remember when you came down early one morning after a party and I caught you drinking stale champagne and smoking a cigar?"

"I don't remember," I said.

Grandmama stared at an embroidered flower on the table cloth. Hadn't she said: remember to forget? I was not a liar, but I wanted to get away from what I had been. Nor was I the only one in Vienna who would invent stories, give promises, on a quest for *Lebensraum* in the prison Vienna and Austria had become.

What was the point of talking of what we had been. It was over. Everything was a shambles. What a mess everyone had made. I jumped up from the table in a kind of Hitler rage and went to the library. I could hear Grandmother persuading Father to send me to Mother's old school, the Sacre Coeur Convent in the fall. I did not want to wear a school uniform and pray all the time, and I considered nuns old-fashioned teachers because they were totally uninformed when it came to *Sexuelle Aktivitaeten,* a subject I was studying in the encyclopedia. I became engrossed and took it to my room. Later, when Father asked me whether I had seen volume 10, I said *"Aber wo!* Of course not!" In order to discover the hidden truth, I was forced to lie.

It would take me all winter to finally decide that most facts

are brutish, especially when it came to sexuality. Ultimately I
could not help sinking back into the blundering ignorance and
wisdom of being in love.

On Sunday afternoon Father and I went for a walk and he
said how happy he was that Mother finally got out of her wheelchair and was walking. Before long she would be back in
Vienna . . .

I could imagine her on his lap, and in his arms; in her room
with him behind locked doors. I had considered it fun. Now that
I knew what went on and what the Russians had done, I had to
force myself to be understanding. "I know you must miss the
sexual activity," I said in my grandmother's voice.

He stopped. Glared at me; threw back his head and roared,
slapping his leather breeches. I had not heard him laugh like
that since his release. He refused to talk about his prolonged
internment, but he was terribly thin and there were shadows
under his eyes.

"Sexual activity is—is—not the problem. . . ." He stuttered.

Our roles had reversed. He was at a loss for words. I was not.
"The Russians certainly had no problem." I went on. "Will we
have to hide again when the Americans, the British and the
French come? Will they grab women, girls and watches too?"

"Never." he said.

"Perhaps they rape everyone they can catch because they are
mad from loneliness. Like the rape of the Sabine women."

I stopped to fill my basket with the pale green tips of pine.
We had no tea or coffee and it made a nice brew.

He grabbed my shoulder and turned me around: "Did
anything happen? I mean, did any of the Russians . . . in our
house . . ." The idea that any man might have hurt me made him
hurt my shoulders.

Long ago when Grandmama had taken me for walks in the
Schwarzenberg gardens I had noticed statues of hefty nude Sabine
women waving their arms in the air instead of smacking the
rapists away. "Let them try!" I said.

He let go, relaxed; the corners of his cheerful Meinert mouth,
curved up. There was still something unfamiliar about this gaunt
face. He got tired just walking into town to his office and back.
Street cars had been used as barricades, rails torn up. The Rus-

sians had emptied out his plant and offices. Cart horses, each one a pet with a name, had all been taken, probably slaughtered. The carts had vanished.

He breathed in the fragrance of the woods. His shoulders fell back, and the eyes regained the old sparkle, cheeks flushed. He enjoyed picking pine tips with me; popped one into his mouth and chewed it. "You know, I'd give anything in the world if your mother suddenly came walking along this path. I love her horsey walk, and I missed it all those years. When she walks you can see how she enjoys every step, every move. Just looking at her always made me forget any of my worries . . ."

He was definitely more sentimental. We picked wild violets. He himself put them into an empty jar for the Madonna at a wayside shrine. Nowadays nothing was ever done right unless he did it himself. He said a silent prayer. Much longer than usual. I could not help thinking of the immaculate conception. Strictly speaking the Virgin Mary was never asked. The Holy Ghost took advantage of her. Was that not rape? "I am not as religious as either Mama or Grandmama. I'm a realist," I said.

Father was now in the mood to laugh at anything I said. The second outburst bothered me. I had been quite serious. He touched a pair of strong young silver birches growing side by side. Blackbirds warbled in the thicket. The air was moist without that chilly bite of early spring.

"Birds are putting on a performance, as if nothing had happened." Willows on the edge of the meadow rippled in the breeze. "There are times when I can't believe that my friend Eugene is really dead. Remember our walks with the dogs? How he used to fall in step with me and limp." Father's side whiskers growing back, his scruffy face reminded me of the unshaven Eugene Romberg when we rescued him from the amethyst mine and he lay in bed at the mountain farm, a dying man.

"No," I said.

"Well, try to remember," Father said. "You have to remember the good days to help forget what's bad. It is going to be a murderous winter." He lowered his voice. Talked in undertones as though Eugene Romberg were beside him. Nazis had worried him then, now we had the Russians. They were keeping the other allies out so that they could finish looting. You could not really blame them. They had suffered a lot, poor devils. And they had their own system. Never carried food. Took what they needed.

But how were Austrians going to survive? People were starving to death. . . . He had to have more powdered milk from the Americans to save infants and young children.

"I think the Russians would be much easier to deal with if they had their wives in Austria. They are terribly oversexed." I said.

I succeeded. He did have another good laugh. We walked on hand in hand and he started to sing off key: "Little Hans went alone into the wide world."

"You taught me that song when we were in Venice," I said.

"That was when you were two or three years old. And you tell me you don't remember anything. I had invited everyone to come along. My two sisters came with their easels. The court doctor. Grandmama and the Rittmeister. Eugene Romberg and Resi were there, but didn't stay at the same hotel. Mother and I got the worst sunburns. You remember don't you?"

"I remember a lot of spaghetti and a lot of kissing," I said and thought of the happy voices on the hotel terrace; afternoon coffee. Playing in the sand by myself on the edge of the sea. A gray day. Shallow water reflecting my own round naked belly. Further out lovers thrashing around, pink, glowing. Dipping down and popping up glued together mouth to mouth, reflected on the mirror smooth water: a magnificent four-headed monster kiss.

"I wish I had some spaghetti," I said.

"We might be lucky and get a couple of scrambled eggs on the farm."

Four hens hidden in a closet had survived. Russians had taken all the equipment from the Meinert farm. The property belonged to Father's older sisters. By the time I was born they had already settled in England. Father and a caretaker had been left in charge. Under Hitler, Tanterln-Hof, the auntie's house, had been Eli Romberg's hiding place. Everything was always covered with dust sheets. Old clothes saved in mothballs. Perhaps hens had been stuck into the closet where I had hidden with Eli Romberg from gestapo agents.

I thought of Arnold, my Frog Prince, saving Eli and loving me. We walked faster and faster up the hill, because we were hungry. Vineyards always looked like sleeping porcupines in the spring. Meadow land was dotted with dandelions and edged with *Augen-Trost*.

The song of the thrush was interrupted by "one-two, one-two.

Eins-zwei, eins-zwei," trotting feet coming downhill towards us. Starlings flew off. Along came a handsome bearded man in shorts wearing a wreath in his hair; behind him, about eight or ten women row in row, all sizes, varied ages, dressed in flowing tunics made from old sheets. Half-wilted wild flowers drooped in their hair. Faces either flushed or pale, chanting and panting one-two, one-two, they passed us as if we were trees.

Father took my arm. "Don't laugh," he said. "He is a young doctor, just out of jail. His mother is an actress, Frau Hillmar, a charming lady. He won't even talk to her. Wasn't in the war, because of weak lungs and became a fanatical Nazi. He's been locked up. All kinds of people intervened for him. Especially women. He isn't allowed to practice medicine and has become a mystic and healer. Really quite harmless and he cheers the women up. Many of them lost their men in the war. So I let them have the use of a plot. He gets them to dig and plant and they all sing together."

Winter seemed far away. You could hear clanging and scraping thrusts of spades. Everyone who had a patch of land was planting. Nuns at the little palace had put in a vegetable bed behind the stable building. Grandmama was waiting at the Meinert-Hof when we returned. She was waving a piece of paper. "The Rittmeister is in Italy." Pink spots mottled her cheeks; she took both my hands and we laughed and laughed. Her old friend was in an American rest home for concentration camp victims on the isle of Capri.

After that she spent most of her days at the little palace and she carried the message in her pocket and reread it like a love letter. Sometimes friends who had lost their homes in the bombing, or felt unsafe, came to spend a few days with her. She was busy putting furniture back in place, dusting, cleaning. All kinds of people came to use her kitchen, or sewing machine. Whenever she was able to heat water, this or that tante would come to take a bath or wash her hair. The countess was getting thinner. There just wasn't much to eat. Yet she was full of energy, her eyes danced. At times she flushed as if she had been in the Italian sun. This winter we might starve and freeze, she didn't worry. Her Rudi had survived and he would be back in Vienna. Nothing else mattered.

Grandmother herself, in kerchief and smock went to work

and I helped to put furniture in place in the one big room, the
*Festsalon.* We were preparing for her first afternoon tea party. I
brought the pictures of King Ludwig of Bavaria's fantastic castles up from the cellar.

The king had sent the paintings of his castles to his cousin,
Empress Elizabeth of Austria. I had a natural fondness for the
two storybook monarchs, blessed and bedevilled as they had been
with the same beautiful face, and unappeasable taste for splendor. Ludwig had outdone his cousin Elizabeth in mad castle-
building and most of it to the tune of Richard Wagner. There
had been no happily ever after. Soon after he had sent the paintings to the empress in 1884 the beautiful king had mysteriously
drowned with his doctor in Starnberger lake. Thirteen years later,
at another lake, Elizabeth would be stabbed by an anarchist.
Before that, however, those pictures of Ludwig's dream castles
that made the sad empress sadder had been spirited away and
given to a darling little Karli von Dornbach who also loved
romantic castles. And Karli had grown up into a dashing castle-
loving officer, married my grandmother, got his romantic old
castle, Schloss Falkenburg and the stud farm. But he did not live
happily ever after either. He had spent his time with horses and
gypsies at Falkenburg. He came to Vienna, said "Auf Wiedersehen" to Grandmama, then went off to be killed in the First
World War. My mother had been born a half orphan.

Grandmother dusted the pictures before I hung them back
onto the hook, then she turned to the huge rubber plant someone
had given to her. It had belonged to a monarchist who had been
shot during the last days of the gestapo. I helped to place the
orphan in the sunny window of the *Festsalon* next to a wall
warmed by the kitchen chimney. My grandmother loved the plant
like a homeless dog. Every little brown spot or dying leaf worried
her. Rubber plants could last from one generation to the next.
One day it would be mine, she said.

# FOUR

# Questions and Answers

WHEN FATHER AND I ARRIVED for Grandmama's afternoon tea, a young man was standing beside the rubber plant
looking out into the street. It was dense and smoky. There were
too many people in the room. Most of them Grandmama's old
friends and co-conspirators against Hitler. They no longer recognized me. Who on earth had brought cigarettes? Smoking suited
my mood. I felt nifty in Mother's brown lace sack dress with a
big satin sash below the waist. Then Father turned me into an
idiot child, telling everyone how I had hidden the costume under
my cloak. He really had no idea what I had put on. "I bought it
for Annerl in Venice that time—so many years ago—as a kind of
joke. Remember? Those were the days. Short skirts, good Italian
wine."

The women flocked around Father, as usual, chatting about
dresses, children, how he had always dressed me like a boy. I
retreated.

The man at the window veered around boyishly. Shadows
from the plant dappled his face. He was smoking. "Would you
care for a cigarette Gnaediges Fraulein?" He flipped open a gold
cigarette case with one hand.

"Bertl," I felt myself flush, wanted to throw my arms around him. He was staring at me. I held back, accepted a cigarette and was glad I had pinned up my hair.

"What next," he flicked a lighter with his left hand. The empty right sleeve of his old tweed jacket was tucked into his pocket. "And I thought I would take you by surprises. I can't believe this. I saw you only a year ago. How dare you grow up to be so . . . well."

"We all change," I quickly said in my mother's voice. He had lost an arm during the war. Otherwise Mother's young cousin had not changed much. Same feathery unruly pale hair. He held his head high and it tilted back as though he were above it all. Only now the haughty, fun-loving schoolboy looked as though he had stayed up too late and got into trouble. He had to be about twenty-seven. A year ago we had hugged and kissed. Now he retreated behind the rubber tree like a shy loner unused to peo- ple. Grandmother's friends had been shocked when Bertl became a Waffen S.S., and shocked again when he had gone over to the American army in Italy at the end of the war.

"You better not let your father see you smoke," Bertl said.

We stayed concealed between the tree and window smoking like children and shared a fitful spot of sun. His love had always been like that, flickering, bright, a conspiracy, with Mother, his older cousin. Then, there had been enchanting Resi Romberg, Eli's mother, arrested by Fritz Janicek and his gang mostly because her husband Eugene had left Austria with his millions. Bertl and his Theresianer school friends had made a bet they'd smuggle her out of the gestapo jail-hotel, the Metropol. They'd rolled her up in a Persian carpet. After that Bertl had hidden Resi in the family estate, and loved her until she received a par- don from the Nazis to star in Hitler's favorite operetta, the Merry Widow. And even Bertl's enthusiasm for Hitler had lasted only as long as the party was forbidden in Austria. "What are you doing in Salzburg?"

"Working for the Americans, what else? But who wants to talk about work . . ." He had arrived from Salzburg only an hour ago. Wanted to check up on the Hohentahler house. See what could be done about repairs. He was getting quite depressed. His room had been blown away, every other room taken over by strangers. The ballroom a dormitory, smelling like a latrine. "A hopeless mess in Vienna. So I went across the street, expecting the worst. And what do I find? My monarchist countess aunt, dressed for a tea party expecting you and your father. What luck!"

I turned my head towards him. He had the same idea. Our mouths touched and the scent of his fair skin reminded me of Mother.

"Crazy that you should put on this dress. Your mother wore it in Venice. We all had the most wonderful time. You were playing naked in the sand and the water. Your father practically took over a small hotel. I was about the age you are now. Still in knee pants. Madly in love with your mother. Eager to please. I tried to row her around in a gondola. My knees burned. She was wearing the new dress and the sun burned the pattern of the lace roses onto her shoulders."

I puffed on my cigarette. Hated the taste. Blew smoke like a dragon as if I could screen from his memory the naked four-year-old me in a terrible sunbonnet. "Are you going to stay in Vienna?" I asked.

"I can't. I work for the Amis in Salzburg as a rather disgraceful go-between. Can you believe it? I really have to keep a job to feed the family. My father isn't well. Yours never changes. Does he now?" He turned and looked out of the window. "Really odd. Just as you walked in with him, I thought I saw him out there walking back and forth in the street." He put his arm around me. "There!"

I saw a man dressed like Father in a green loden Styrian hat strolling along the sidewalk. The likeness startled me into a retreat. (Father always hated to see us at a window looking out like nosy peasants.)

"And he even has that slight Ferdl limp," Bertl said.

"But he has a full Kaiser beard and Father's hasn't grown in."

We looked through the curtain. Each time he leaned over me to puff on the cigarette, he brushed my cheek or hair with his lips.

"Who is that man?" I asked.

"Perhaps he hired a double," he said.

"Why?" I asked.

"To stop someone he doesn't want at this party."

I felt a quiver of restiveness from his arm. It reminded me of his stallion, Napoleon. Before Hitler Bertl had to support his Lipizzaner by breaking in rich society ladies with dancing lessons. After Napoleon had shied, throwing my mother, Bertl sold the horse.

"I'm going out there to see who it is," he said.

We used a side door and stole out through the serving pantry. With Bertl you never walked, you ran. In the hallway swallows darted over our heads flying in and out of nests.

"I'm so grateful that nothing happened to this place," he said. "I love every stone of it. The first thing I remember is your mother pushing me around here in her big doll carriage. She trained me never to touch her old Puppe. I must have been three and she was eight when Annerl mothered me. By the time I grew to be eight we were playing bride and groom and married each other several times out there by the angel and the old shrine. Childrens' games; those good times are never far away. It seemed just like a game when she married your father, she even hid old Puppe under her veils. She made your father promise never to touch the doll. Crazy, what? I was left out until you came along and loved me. With you I always feel my old self again. It's a lot like being with Annerl." In the courtyard, the wind played with his receding, pale hair. He could never keep it combed. And it was as soft as chicken feathers. I touched it. He threw down his cigarette, pulled mine out of my mouth and kissed my lips, hands and fingers. Then, with a little shove he dismissed me like a tail-wagging dog. A moment later he held the portal for me as if I were his one and only love. The street was empty.

"Too late," Berl said. "Story of my heroic life. Always in a hurry and always too late, what?"

We sat on the sunny steps in front of the stable building. He clamped his package of American cigarettes under his stump, manipulating matches with bravado. I almost cried.

"Taking one life or hundreds, thousands, mowing down all kinds of people can become a habit. It is disgustingly easy. I was almost killed in Poland by drunk fellow officers, you know that. To tell you the truth I saw them laughing, taking pot-shots at this pregnant pig. They weren't all that bad. Oafs, that's all. And I thought to myself, another year or two, of "Today Germany tomorrow the World," and there I'd go shooting at anything that

jumps and squeaks, Russians, British, Jews, Slovaks. Had to
stop it, what? I wasn't only defending the pig. It was self-defense,
really, if you know what I mean."

Bertl remained my magician, conjuring up the truth: one
moment you see it then you don't. Pulling moments of our lives,
out of a hat, so to speak, to dazzle and baffle me. He whispered
in my ear that he had not been afraid to die. But fighting wasn't
really heroic in a modern war. You just mowed men down. It
made him sick, embarrassed and ashamed. Not a good state of
mind for an officer. He kissed my ear. Called me the best listener
in the world.

I did not like the stone head of the horse hanging above us.
When he went on and said "what a waste," he could have been
talking about my second cigarette, his lost arm, or the charred
top of the Hohentahler mansion outlined against the pale, spring
sky.

"There was a German officer, about my own age, perhaps a
year or two older, who felt as I did. I was in the hospital after
they had to cut my arm off, and I was lucky he was the one to
interrogate me. Typical *Pifke,* a true Hun, I said to myself. I
could have been in serious trouble. I had my arm shot to pieces,
but I had fired the first shots at fellow officers—over their heads—
but all the same defending a pig. I never knew what he would
do. He didn't give himself away, but his report saved me. A decent
fellow. I hope he survived. Arnold von Lutensteg. Old German
family. One hero, that's all I came away with."

I did not want to claim the same hero.

"Were you going to say something?" he asked. "You are so
quiet."

"I usually talk too much," I said.

"I haven't given you much of a chance," he offered me another
cigarette.

"I don't want to waste it. Here in Vienna you can trade cigarettes for gold."

"Nothing you enjoy is ever wasted. Romberg once said
that . . . I want you to know I really tried to get him released.
For you, your father, and most of all for his wife, Resi. She divorced him after Hitler took over, then she missed him every
minute. Crazy, what?"

That space on the steps between us became a desert. Tears
came. I turned my head away.

"Personally I never really liked him. He suddenly appeared in Vienna and he was fat, rich, ostentatious. I was a schoolboy. And I wanted cars, money, to show off for my favorite girls. We were an old family but poor as church mice."

"You were a Nazi and he was considered a Jew," I said.

"That was not the reason. He was nauseatingly importunate with my Annerl, your mother."

"Who wasn't," I said. "She was fashionable."

He put his arms around me. *"Kind, Kinderl,* child," kissing me as though I had been badly hurt. "Don't be cynical, please, don't scoff. It will turn you into a bore. And that would be the biggest waste of all, what? Keep wearing crazy costumes like this one. Loving me is hopeless, but go on being in love as much as you possibly can."

We cuddled and I put out my cigarette stub and took a puff from his. He told me he had always been jealous. And Eugene Romberg always did things he would like to have done. "He stole your heart, gave you all those expensive presents. Even that great little dog. I saw it all. Then he'd come running to your mother and beg her forgiveness for molesting her with a little trinket worth a fortune. She'd turn him down when I was there. I think she knew how I felt. But she often told me how unique Eugene Romberg was, how great. And she never knew that he would take the emeralds she had refused and give them to his wife, Resi. Later on when he was in Switzerland with that little Swedish masseuse, Resi would show me all that glitter and ask me whether he might ever come back to her. She couldn't believe he really cared for that girl. And she was quite sorry she didn't go to Switzerland with him. The beauty about Reserl is that she is always sure that everybody loves her forever."

"Do you love her?" I asked.

"As much as possible."

"Will you marry her?" I said in a strained, piping mouse voice.

"I couldn't."

"She is at least ten years older than you are. Grandmama never thought she was suitable."

"There is another, more important reason. And then, of course, in a sense, she will always be married to Eugene Romberg. And who will want to listen to Eugene this and Eugene that. I tried to save him for her. It was the least I could do, what?"

"Tell me about it," I said.

"There isn't much to tell. I was too late. Too late . . . I took the train to Salzburg. Janicek, that scoundrel was on the same train. I stirred up a hornet's nest. Found out that Romberg had been involved in some kind of money swindle with a certain Schmiedler."

I spoke up at once. And said Eugene Romberg could not have been involved in a swindle.

"He could, for your mother's sake," he said.

"What do you mean?"

There was a pause now. Shadow of cigarette smoke snaked towards the shadow of the horse's head. He said we should go back to the party, but hugged me, stayed, as though he could not tear himself away from me. We shared his cigarette again, although I didn't really like the taste.

"Did your mother ever mention her visit to Salzburg, Hitler's guesthouse, Schloss Kiesheim?"

"No, she never went to visit anyone. Resi always wanted her to come to the Salzburg festival and she refused, she didn't like to be stared at in her wheelchair."

"They sent a curtained limousine," he said. "And she went to Hitler's guesthouse just before they nabbed Romberg. You were in Vienna at the time, staying with your father." A little frown appeared on his high smooth forehead. I laughed in his face: crazy rumors. Mother and Hitler. Just because we were so close to Berchtesgaden. A lot of gossip. Typcial.

"And she really never mentioned Schloss Kiesheim?" he persisted. "How about Franz Schmiedler. Or Janicek? Used to be your gardener and became a big Nazi art collector who decorated the guest house with a lot of museum paintings and the finest old furniture stolen from all over Europe. I understand he had stored a lot of stuff like that in the amethyst mine near your mountain farm."

I talked fast and kept talking about the farm. The years in the mountains, the snow, my friend, Stopperl, who could ski so fast. Anything, hoping he did not know that Eugene Romberg had been chained to a truck inside the snowbound mine among all the museum art, part of Fritz Janicek's collection. I did not want him to know that Eugene Romberg had died of pneumonia after that on our farm.

Bertl was so much part of Mother his fair skin had her scent.

His need for his Annerl had always included me. And we had allowed her to become a deadly idol. Obsession with Mother, in the end had lead to Eugene Romberg's death. I blamed myself and didn't want him to share the blame.

"Janicek could have taken your mother to Salzburg."

"She would never have gone with him." I could say that with conviction. Then I talked on and on, remembering to forget that she'd refused to believe me that Janicek had shot the doll's head off and that she would go anywhere with anyone who promised her the old von Kortnai doll, Puppe.

"There is the American Art Looting Investigation office in Alt-Aussee. They are looking for the Austrian crown jewels. The Nazis took the treasure and kept it in Nüremberg. A city councillor of Nüremberg, Fries—not a bad sort—is saying it was all picked up by an unknown S.S. and taken to a secret place."

"S.S. Janicek?"

"They did question Janicek. He denies everything but says Schmiedler talked to your mother when she was in Salzburg last spring and she might know something."

"Fritz is a liar. He could have stuck the crown jewels into the amethyst mine. It's in the British zone. Perhaps the British have it by now and don't want anyone to know. The Russians are looking too. They questioned Grandmama about the crowns. What if they sent a few spies into the British zone to snatch the treasure? And what if Schmiedler himself made off with the crowns? No one can find him. Long ago, our laundress, Frau Boschke, used to work at his house. Before Hitler took over, Schmiedler already got his little girl to quiz Frau Boschke about diamonds at Jewish households where she worked. As soon as Germany took over, he aryanized the jewelry and took all the good stones out of the setting. What if he got the crowns from Fritz Janicek, took them apart, kept the best diamonds and Janicek got the rest?"

"There are rumors the imperial insignia has all been sunk to the bottom of a lake. Did you ever hear anything like that?"

"Not a word. Who would talk to me."

"Your mother."

"Why don't you go and see Mama and ask her whether Fritz Janicek promised her Puppe, lured her to a Salzburg rendezvous with Schmiedler, got her the crown of the Holy Roman Empire to make up for stealing the doll . . . And if she went to the Schloss and didn't get Puppe, she might have had a red-head temper fit, throwing crowns into a lake."

I did make him laugh, but then he looked worried again and said the British had my mother in safe keeping; he didn't know exactly why or where. He had been told she was well looked after, but they wouldn't let anyone near her at this point.

"You can always question Hanna Roth. She is in Salzburg, isn't she? And she always helped all the ladies find lost things."

"She probably hid stuff and then helped them find it. Old Hanna is tricky. Same as ever. I'm not exactly her favorite. I can't help teasing her, you know." He studied my face. Waited for me to speak.

To Hanna men were all unruly boys, who made the world unsafe. I felt sorry I had mentioned her and had no more to say. When he fondled me with consoling little kisses and said coming to Vienna had all been worthwhile, just to see me, I had a sinking feeling: he had come to Vienna to question me.

He made a sad clown face. Lips turned down, eyes rolling. "It will take centuries to figure out what mischief we all got into, what?"

I loved him most of all when he looked ugly, and tried to laugh because I knew he was sad.

"Enough of all that, what? Let's go and drink some of your father's wine."

We went back to the party. Wine had made everyone forgiving. The mood had changed. "Where did you go, children, where have you been?"

I mentioned the Doppelganger.

"An ugly old peasant like me. There must be thousands of them around," Father laughed.

Berthold was grabbed away from me. He didn't stay long; had to get back to Salzburg. I went to the window when he was leaving. He turned in the courtyard and threw me a kiss. Love was a seance. I had waited and waited. He had appeared and then vanished. I waited again; relived our meeting. And I was left with double images like that of my father out there in the street and at the same time at the party. There was Bertl I had always known, and then the new, explicit and illusive conjurer.

My thoughts followed him to Salzburg, and as fruit trees

bloomed, cherries ripened, so did my thoughts and ideas about crown jewel thiefs, and Hanna Roth. Lying in the orchard with my blue notebook, I feasted on cherries as I expressed my thoughts and ideas in writing. Not that I ever wrote to inform or give evidence for or against anyone. To begin with, during the invasion, my blue notebook had been a legacy in case Grandmother and I were killed. I continued to secretly write for all my absent loves. It was the only way for me. That marvelous "if he could only see this" feeling always made me go on and on the way kaisertime girls used to crochet for hope chests.

My earliest memory of this magic town of Salzburg is a Mozart Kugel—sweet of all sweets—melting in my mouth, and the fragrance of wood cyclamen. An early morning walk after one of those inevitable showers, strolling with Mother through the fruit and flower market in front of the Mozart house. Following behind her inbetween baskets filled with intoxicating cyclamen; wild strawberries displayed on green leaves, glistening with raindrops. Mother's hair hanging down her back to dry in the sun. Rapunzel hair. What if it were long enough to dangle all the way down from the castle mount of the Hohe-Salzburg all the way to the market place and Mozart's house? In Salzburg the witch and prince could have used the convenient Hohe-Salzburg elevator. I liked the idea of a Salzburg Rapunzel without the hair climbing and hair pulling, the hurt.

Sweet as the taste in my mouth was Mother's sing-song story of long, long ago oceans. A time of fish and sea creatures, time before men when the fortress mount would have surfaced as an island and the Untersberg spouted flames and lava. So we were walking at the bottom of the sea. Adrift in fancy, ever after, legends surface: the giant Reubezahl on the Untersberg counting beets, and catching the hungry little trespasser who stole one. Mother at Schloss Kiesheim looking for the doll. Hanna Roth and the crown jewels. It was all the same.

I could, of course picture Hanna Roth in this town of enchantment, spells and transformations where old stories had become new for me. And I could almost hear the river Salzach rushing and Hanna's taffeta petticoat rustling, her platform shoes stomping as she crossed the wooden bridge under her man-sized umbrella.

Infamous Salzburg *Schnurrel* rain, drizzling rain, day after day, gentle rain. A man dressed in green loden leaning on the bridge would face the enchanting cluster of the old town and the dome glistening wet. A hood hid his face as he waited. Hanna came along and he let her pass. Then he spoke to her, turned, bowed, scraped like one of those black marketeer peddlars.

I pasted the newspaper pictures into my notebook. One showed the man on the bridge holding the umbrella over Hanna Roth like a gallant, and a second one, Hanna Roth in hat, gloves, petticoat, skirt, floating, falling, holding onto her umbrella. It had appeared in the *Stars and Stripes*. I had to admire the way Americans made everything public. "HITLER'S ORACLE ATTACKED."

The sun had broken through clouds beaming down on the fortress, the old town, the bridge. And two American officers on the bank of the river clicking their cameras had witnessed Hanna trying to take her umbrella back and struggling for it as though the man were an umbrella thief. Suddenly the man had scooped her up.

And this had to be the one and only time little Hanna was captive in the arms of a man. She had developed a big voice at Salon Roth to make herself heard among chattering ladies. When she shouted for help to the American officers they had heard her above the rushing sounds of the river: "He wants the crowns, the crowns!" She had clutched her umbrella with both hands. The hooded man had swung her back and forth, playfully, higher and higher and let go. Up she went and over, out over the railing, holding onto the huge umbrella with both gloved hands. In the pictures you saw Hanna flying through the beam of sun; her tall hat must have been pinned to her hair, pouch purse slung over the arm, as though she had forseen it all and was prepared. Light as a child in the breeze, she would have landed with a mere bump at the edge of the river. Seemingly one of the two American officers had fished her out at once. The other one had gone after the hooded man, and found only the cloak hanging from a tree. It was riddled by shot gun pellets or moth holes—perhaps both.

Hanna Roth had been taken to the American hospital, treated for shock. Her fall had led to a quick ascent. Hitler's oracle attacked by a crown jewel hunter would be guarded, pampered, under American protection. And questioned.

The big treasure and Nazi beast hunt provided endless sport for the allies, because of the vast maze of Austrian and German documented evidence of what had happened, or was supposed to have happened, or never happened at all. The unwrapping of bits and pieces was rather like Eli Romberg's huge surprise birthday box. Designed to keep Eli from getting too excited or too bored all at once, the huge box had contained innumerable small numbered packages to be opened on specific dates, which contained either another box, or a note or a piece of a game, or part of a toy. By the time all the boxes had been properly opened some of the pieces were already lost and you hunted for the pieces.

In August, Austria was about to be divided like a cake among the allies. The Russians—greedy and hungry—would keep the best part. But they would not get the crown of the Holy Roman empire.

Bertl came and went far too quickly on a Sunday at the beginning of August. He and Father talked about Mother coming home. There was no mail in Austria at this point, but a loving letter from her had been brought to Father by an English officer. Bertl said the British would release Mother to Salzburg right now, but not to Vienna, because of the Russians. We sat in the shade near the fountain which sprinkled musk roses Fritz Janicek had planted for Mother when I was a child.

Father said, "Salzburg is a Nazi nest. And we need her here in Vienna!" It did not sound like him at all. And I blamed Fritz Janicek's intoxicating musk roses. When they had opened up to full bloom that first time—just after Hitler had taken over—Mother had said the perfume was just too much and made her heady and sick. And Hitler the conquerer kissing her hand, had been just too much for Mother.

Wasps hummed around the roses and our wine glasses. No one said anything. Bertl looked unhappy. He had his heart set on moving his cousin Annerl to Salzburg. I felt sad for him and took his hand.

"Is this an official request. Do the Amis want her in Salzburg to question her about the stuff in the mine, the crowns?" Father asked.

Bertl laughed and said they didn't need Mother for that. The Amis had fed Hanna Roth her favorite little cakes and she had a vision. It would all be made public before long, anyway.

I had not a minute alone with Bertl. He did not know when he'd be back. The coffee and the sugar and cigarettes he had brought for us did not last, but through the rest of the summer and all through autumn when neighbors came to share some of our fruit and vegetables and brought us their trouble we could always share with them his version of Hanna Roth and the crowns.

The little designer of hats for the select, notorious oracle, had annoyed neighbors when she finally took over the water castle. Hanna Roth fancied herself. Even her departure from Vienna before the invasion had been a spectacle. Hanna was always Hanna. She refused to accept misfortune. And, this now made her a living legend. Soon there would be as many different versions of her pranks as those of Till Eulenspiegel, the drunken doodle bagpiper of the Middle Ages, who had avoided the big plague by ignoring it and amusing himself.

Hanna Roth always had the last laugh, and we laughed with her as we relived her stories especially the one about the crown of the Holy Roman Empire. And I always thought it was really Bertl who saved the treasure by advising the American interrogaters to ply her with those delicious little chocolate Paris towers that had always preceded her visions at Salon Roth when served with good strong coffee and whipped cream.

Bertl told us how Hanna had insisted on driving her own car to Alt-Aussee interrogation center. Dressed up in a midnight blue suit that matched the car and a Napoleonic hat decorated with a diamond star, she had raced out of Salzburg as she had arrived: at the head of a convoy. Men in uniform, Americans, instead of hat salon Nazi ladies, followed in her dust. She did not have to slow down on the war-torn road because she foresaw obstacles before she turned around a bend.

At the Art Looting Investigation unit of the office of strategic services in charge of art recovery, she spoke English and made herself at home with the small team, addressing them all as "soldier" regardless of rank. Men, especially when they wore uniforms, made her uneasy. But she was as exquisitely polite and distant as any great lady would be to waiters, chauffeurs or letter carriers. They sat around the table drinking coffee with her and she plopped whipped cream into their cups with charming condescension, and kept all the six little Paris tower cakes to herself.

And while she ate they read to her documentary evidence that the regalia of the Holy Roman Empire, had been transferred from Vienna to the Nazi party city of Nüremberg, after the annexation of Austria in 1938. Then they read a statement from Nüremberg City Councillor Fries about the removal of the imperial insignia, the crown, the orb, scepter, and the two imperial swords, at the end of the war by an unidentified S.S. officer, who had orders from Himmler, and had driven away with the treasure to an unknown destination.

They had refilled her cup. And asked her to concentrate on the name of a lake or pond. There was an S.S. unit report of rumors that the imperial insignia had been sunk into a lake somewhere in Austria, perhaps even in Vienna by Schmiedler. This had made Hanna laugh.

She took her time, adorned her coffee with another scoop of whipped cream, and kept them waiting, while she ate the third cake. Then she sat back, closed her eyes, opened them with a blank stare and said: "*Unsinn,* nonsense. All those men were liars."

The fourth Paris tower was on her plate when she asked for the document signed by Fries, and the one signed by that rogue Janicek. He had not even been named and she did not have to examine his statement, to call him the biggest liar and thief of them all, a murderer who had shot the head off the priceless Antonelli doll. She removed her gloves and clasped the papers in her strong old hands. A change came over her. She lost all color, and her black eyes stared like a dead woman's. The officers had to sit still and wait and wait.

"Nüremberg," she finally shouted, as though she had to make herself heard from far, far away. When she came around, her eyes regained their sparkle and she declared that Janicek and City Councillor of Nüremberg, Fries had made up the story: the treasure was still in Nüremberg. She had a vision of the crown, scepter, orb and two swords deep down, eight feet under the ground ... The two liars would know just where. Treat them rough like lying, ugly street boys. Lock each one up in a dark cell. They'd soon talk.

Hanna had been right. After only one night of solitary con-

finement Fries and Janicek had both admitted they'd been briefed
to make up the story about the lake. There had actually been a
mock removal, deliberate false rumors about sunken treasures,
which brought about all that fishing for crowns . . .

The American team had hastened from Alt-Aussee to
Nüremberg. In a subterranean corridor, a small room eighty feet
below the surface of the Panier Platz, the afternoon of August 7,
1945, a copper container was taken out of the brick wall. Wrapped
in spun glass lay the crown of the Holy Roman Empire, scepter,
orb and two imperial swords.

Hanna, of course, was now famous. She certainly would not
be cold, she would not be hungry, this winter, but now that she
had helped to find the missing crown, they wanted her to find
missing villains, especially Schmiedler. She was questioned about
the man who threw her over the bridge and then escaped. Had
that been Schmiedler? What did he really want? Could she
describe his face? She had become evasive. Said he had been
hooded; there hadn't been much to see. She wanted to forget that
man. He was death. He had no face. And when the Ami officers
wouldn't leave her alone she had fainted.

By the time early frost flowers curtained the chilly rooms
Vienna had become a trap. Russia controlled Hungary, had
influence in Yugoslavia, and was gaining power in Czechoslovakia. Occupied Vienna was surrounded by the Russian army. They
could close the railroads and the little American airstrip and
enclose the allies in Vienna with us, cut them off. But more than
ever—and at all times since the fall of the empire—we in Vienna
were caught between what we had been and what we had become.

# FIVE

# *Lessons*

By autumn 1945 little Austria and big Vienna had been divided among the allies, and I attended school for the first time. On our mountain farm, during the war, I had been tutored by my father's cousin, Pfarrer Kronz, a scholarly priest. I felt uneasy in a class of seventeen girls, and cramped. The desk was too small, my legs too long. Big desks had vanished. Half the girls had vanished. Some had died during the bombing and street fighting; others had fled from the Russians. At all times the dead crowded in on survivors. And missing girls intruded from the beginning—especially one . . .

After zoology class, something went wrong and the bell rang and rang, stopped and started again and kept ringing, jingling my brain like the alarm clock tied around the neck of a certain Russian soldier—that buffoon of a rapist. Each time a bell shrilled I saw him again, pants around the ankles. It was a solitary game of charades played in the mirrored halls of that wax museum for lovers and monsters: my memory, story, history.

"I can't stand that damned bell," I said. "I hate school."

Nobody heard me through the din. The class was subdued. Some of the girls had put their heads down and rested on desks. Fraulein Doctor Braun, gymnastics and zoology teacher, had made us cry and laugh leaving one exhausted, shattered. We were all under her spell. Laughter and tears were never far apart in her class. The Fraulein Doctor—a compelling beauty and part Jewish—had been rehired after seven years of Nazi teach-verbot.

Girls used to faint in her class. Long before Hitler, she had earned her reputation as a hypnotist. There were rumors that she had saved herself and her family through the power of her hypnotic light eyes. She had the gaze of a blind woman. Her long neck was adorned with a mysterious scar and her black braids dramatically streaked with white.

The gymnastics hall had burned and she liked to start the day by letting us stretch and run in the corridor. Never too much. She considered our empty stomachs—not our emotions. On this day during zoology, she had talked of the migration of birds and butterflies, the miracle of animal life and animal plight: the cruelty of the hunt. Eyes full of tears and her vulnerable mouth trembling, she had faced us with years of suppressed feelings, as she described hounds tearing a fox apart.

Without ever mentioning Nazis or the war she had confronted us with the unbearable beauty and cruelty in the world; her wounds opened for us, and like the fox by the hounds we were torn apart. The other new girl, Ursel Prenner, whose socialist father had been hunted by the gestapo burst into tears. Suddenly all of us had sobbed including Fraulein Doctor. We all wept and laughed easily these days. She quickly told funny stories about a mule she had as a child. Until the bell rang we had all laughed and laughed, she with tears trickling from her hypnotic eyes down her cheeks and neck over the scar.

And the bell kept shrilling after old Professor Ditfurt, the new history teacher, an old man, walked in and bang-bashed, the teacher's desk with his baton. He was quite deaf, noise did not bother him and he smiled like an infant, at everyone, and no one. "This is a unique moment in history. Never before have the armies of four nations occupied one city." He always said that.

You grinned, you wanted to laugh, to cry all over again. The class clown aped the way he waved his baton stirring up his thoughts about Austria's glorious past and stirring up dust. During the most unpredictable winter of my life, he was predictable; I came to be painfully fond of him.

The window was open and tepid air slowly warmed the unheated room. There was no coal, no food in Vienna, but there was sun. The weather was suddenly warm as spring. I picked up my books and moved to the one big empty desk at the sunny window. Herr Professor Ditfurt never noticed anything like that.

His theme this morning was Vienna beleaguered by the Turks in 1529 and again in 1683. I was beleaguered too.

"What do you think you're doing in Schmiedler's seat!" girls hissed. "Just you wait. When she comes back, she'll boot you out the window."

The Herr Professor was gazing out of the window while he lectured against the noisy bell and the skirmish in my corner. A haze hung over the bomb damaged Schmiedler house on the other side of the street, as if dust had not yet settled during this summer of uneasy peace. Even the Herr Professor had a dusty, faded look: whispy gray hair, grayish face and smock, as though he had risen from a grave to take the place of a Nazi teacher.

When the bell finally stopped ringing he was talking about building versus destruction. And his words danced like motes from Kara Mustafa the Turk who had been chased away from Vienna, to Napoleon Bonaparte the invader. Whenever I think of that crazy year after the war, winter, carnival, I see Professor Ditfurt waving his baton conducting history with the oblivious passion of a deaf Beethoven. He reached a crescendo singing the praise of Prince Eugene, a hero who had fought against the heathen Turks and later built his dream palace, the Belvedere. "This castle radiates the magic of a fairy tale. You enter the gardens and you are a child again . . ." I could see children in the garden of the Schmiedler house across the street. They played there in fair weather. This morning they had taken the "Entrance Forbidden Sign" down and converted the pole into a white flag. Two of the boarded-up windows, I noticed, had been opened. High-pitched voices came from the back of the house. About nine children of all sizes dressed in blue trousers and red knitted hats came running along the path. Leaves rustled under their feet. A big boy dragged a metal trunk around neglected flower beds where colored glass baubles gleamed among withered roses. The garden was dreamy, typically old Vienna and the house, modern, a box.

Mother had brought me to the Schmiedler house when I was six years old and she twenty-three. Mother's Nazi days before Hitler had been an adventure, especially when she was a courier and carried an envelope for Herr Schmiedler. She had stood wrapped in admiration. Secretly she had loved anything modern and new. The Schmiedler house to her was the latest, just like

Hitler Germany. She considered all that looking back to the Kaiser old fashioned and the crumbling little baroque palace where she grew up—ornamentation, angels, flowers—definitely passé. Nazis looked ahead—towards a new age, progress—not back. Through my young mother I had gained the impression that the unadorned box, the Nazi villa, was typically German, and this had inspired me to turn an empty chocolate box into a German house for beatles. Rounding up and boxing in turned out to be the essence of Hitler modernity. Fatalities made me cry and brought my game to an end. . . .

Goldberg, the girl in front of me turned, and saw me lift the green blotter exposing "SCHMIEDLER" and a swastika. "Put that back at once! And get out of the Schmiedler seat!" Her tough voice contrasted with a soft face framed by light ringlets. Goldberg was eighteen years old. She had lost a year of school after Germany took over Austria. So had Else Schmiedler, for very different reasons. And somehow Goldberg, the one and only half-Jew, had become Schmiedler's slave and protégé.

"I have been in the Schmiedler villa and I saw him." I bragged.

The fat one, who sat beside Goldberg asked, "What was he like?"

"He answered the door and he was bald as an egg."

A man servant in a black livery half opened the door. Mother dangling the old doll as if it were my toy. Not a smile from the bald bowlegged servant, none of the Viennese: "cute girlie, cute dolly, please do come in, a cup of coffee, a little raspberry syrupy soda." A slime green reception room with a big mirror—no tables, no chairs, no coat racks. Nothing.

Puppe turned upside down loses her hat, eyes move from side to side. Mother pulls a thick envelope out from the doll's underskirt. Snatch—and the servant has it. No *bitte schön,* pretty please, from him, or *Danke schön,* pretty thank you. His snake eyes fasten onto Mother, while his big hands nudge the air around us, shooing us out. "Herr Schmiedler sends his compliments and hand kisses to the ladies." A half-open door, bowlegs scraping. My legs scraping. A fit of the giggles. Snatch. Up in the air and out I go. The door bangs; chain rattling, lock, lock. Rattle. Lock, lock, again. Door opens. The doll's hat flies out. Bang, rattle, lock, lock. Mother and I have a fit of the giggles: Schmiedler, impossible Schmiedler. Just has to be the great man himself.

Mother giggling herself into hiccups. And don't tell Pappa. Not a word.

"The bald man was a servant," Goldberg said. "He always answered the door."

"It was Schmiedler himself. He had those bowlegs. But he always turned himself into that servant when he knew Mother was coming."

"*Bloedsinn,* nonsense! A lot of people have bowlegs from rickets. Schmiedler would never have come to the door. He had to be careful. The Amis at my father's office showed me photographs. No two of them alike. They'll never be able to find him." Goldberg's father, a Jew, had returned from America as a denazification officer. Goldberg lived with her father. The mother, a Nazi, had vanished. "I was invited to the Schmiedler house quite often, but I couldn't tell the Amis what Schmiedler was like. I was not introduced to anyone—for obvious reasons. And there were always so many famous men. Schmiedler is such a great impersonator, he could have been anyone of them. He was one of the best Hitler doubles. Else says he could even fool her."

I started scrubbing the hook-cross and the SCHMIEDLER with an old, dry eraser.

"It won't come off," Goldberg said. "Else Schmiedler carved it and she made me go over it with india ink. And she made me sit in front of her and hide her from the teachers when she put her head on the desk and took her nap. She always stayed up late and danced. Her Father brought her gowns from Paris. She looked marvelous."

Goldberg looked marvelous in her American skirts and blouses, but she stuck to the old seat of a slave. Schmiedler had left her mark on everyone. We had always been traditionalist in Austria: ingrained Schmiedler laws, Hitler laws, like King-Kaiserly laws, self-perpetuated.

Father had complained all summer long about trying to cope with the bureaucracy of both "King-Kaiserly", (K.K.) and Nazi procedures. Here in my class Goldberg loyally enforced old Schmiedler rules: family names only. No first names. Herr Schmiedler had never allowed anyone to call him Franz Joseph. (The Kaiser had been Franz Joseph. Schmiedler had been named after him, and he hated sloppy aristocratic school brat familiarity). Schmiedler was Schmiedler, Hitler, Hitler. Goldberg, Goldberg, Meinert, Meinert, no matter what.

I kept scrubbing away on the hook-cross. Futile gestures were important. Professor Ditfurt, for instance, always pointed at this or that girl with his baton. He did not remember our names. And he always asked questions although he was too deaf to hear much of the answer. One of the girls said Prince Eugene, who had repelled the Turks in the sixteenth century, was a German hero. Under the Nazis heros had to be German.

"He was French," I said. "They had laughed at him in France because he was so small, almost a dwarf. He came to serve our Kaiser and he became a great hero." My tutor, a scholarly priest, had taught me facts. I liked to show off. The girl who had been answering the question, turned around and stuck out her tongue.

"Aren't you a bit of a Falkenburg?" Goldberg inquired. "There was Otto von Falkenburg, the mad. He fought against the Turks, didn't he?" Under Hitler madness had been forbidden and punished by death.

"I'm a Meinert," I said meekly. In school I had learned to be ashamed of everything I had ever been proud of. My aristocratic grandmother, for instance, a staunch monarchist, who made me disgustingly different from the other girls. And I was the youngest, tallest and best student. They had all lived in Vienna during the war, the bombing. And if I did come back just in time for the Russian invasion, so what! I seemed to be the one and only one out of seventeen girls in my class who had not been raped by at least five Russians . . .

During recess I stayed by myself at the open window while the others formed a circle around Goldberg. And they tittered and chattered and whispered: *furchtbar,* terrifically, unbelievable. A secret hotel full of perfumed French officers; as for the British soldiers doing it standing up . . . *furchtbar,* terrifically unbelievable. Russians: lurking rapists roasting spies on spits. And the Amis. *Ja die* Amis: terrifically unbelievable, love Pretzel style in jeeps. Wonderful milky chocolates, cigarettes.

Four in the jeep, soldiers of each nation policed the city. First district of Vienna, medieval city without ramparts, the international zone was the place where a brazen schoolgirl could see and meet French, British, Americans. If they were lucky they'd get cigarettes, even chocolate and chewing gum, and if they were unlucky they could vanish forever, especially during the month when the Russians were in charge.

We were in the American zone. The best. Goldberg was pass-

ing out slices of American cheese to her followers. Sometimes
Father was able to bring some home. And once in a while he
brought black market eggs and meat, never enough. Everyone
was hungry. I leaned out of the window and nibbled on my bread.
Children in the Schmiedler garden had lined up behind a tall
boy. He blew a whistle. They marched, came about like soldiers.
Dahlias in the garden glowed saffron red. Lights strung on wires
between trees above a rotunda were covered with faded Japa-
nese lanterns. Victories had once been celebrated in that garden.
The fall of Paris.

The Schmiedler daughter, eleven years old, had danced with
all the big men of the Hitler regime. Dressed in French gowns
and sparkling with requisitioned Jewish jewels, she had passed
from one Nazi Bonze to the next, slipping envelopes into pockets.
Messages from her father. A great game. Schmiedler himself
remaining invisible. An illusionist, waltzing under the colored
paper lanterns turning pink, blue, red. Deceiver, seducer. How
about killer?

Goldberg tapped my shoulder with her fingernail. Her followers stood around us watching. "You better clear out of the desk.
Schmiedler is coming back soon."

"I thought she was in Salzburg."

"She would have driven there fast as lightning. Her father
taught her to drive when she was eight years old, holding her on
his lap. Then, after the Anschluss, she had a special permit, drove
like a racing driver. But her car was stolen. An art expert loaded
it to take valuables from the villa to Salzburg and never came
back. I saw her the other day. She'll be back and you better clear
out."

"I will not!"

"Well, I've warned you. Did you know that her father is free
and hiding?"

"Probably hiding somewhere with Hitler," said the fat one.

"Hitler is dead," I said.

"A lie," Goldberg said. "The Russians are just saying that to
avoid a Nazi uprising."

"Do you have this from your father and his Amis or from Else
Schmiedler?"

"None of your business," Goldberg said and smoothed over
her new, American wool skirt.

The girls were staring out of the window. There was a moment

of silence in memory of officers in glossy boots jingling medals
up to the Schmiedler door. Or civilians in cashmere coats carrying gifts from abroad. Fairy tale riches, treasures from occupied
Europe. Lace and silk and fragrance and glacéed fruit; pictures,
china, and furs, diamonds. A big Russian sable coat for the little
Schmiedler daughter. "Open Sesame" from the Fuehrer and an
Ali Baba's cave had opened up from the Schmiedler house to the
end of the world. And even in fairy tales, some died in the quest
for wealth, and many were sacrificed. Tears in Goldberg's eyes
were for the lost razzle dazzle of Schmiedler power.

I took out my comb. The shattered window pane had been
replaced and I used it as a mirror. Whenever I felt nervous in
school I kept combing my hair.

"You are pretty, Meinert," Goldberg said. "But she is far prettier." Voice of a wicked magic mirror. "Schmiedler is almost as
tall as you are, but not as gawky. Her hair is blond, not dark and
frizzy. She always has a coiffure like a film star."

Creating envy had been an art Hitler had mastered and passed
on to Schmiedler. Else had obviously become an expert, always
changing favorites in class, making them suspicious of each other
and loyal to her. I took an apple out of my school bag and started
to munch while girls whispered and giggled. Goldberg stood in a
spot of sun. Shadow from the window grill branded her cheek
with a broken swastika. Her smile came as a shock. She seldom
smiled. "Did the Russians rape you, Meinert?" she asked.

"Did they rape you?" said the chorus. "Rape you?"

"She won't talk." The fat girl in our class bit shamelessly into
a garlic sausage. "Too stuck up." There was a rumor that her
invalid father had been forced into the black market by the fat
one's monstrous appetite. "You can have a bite if you tell us
everything," she said.

They waited and watched. I turned my back on them. I saw
a red hat flit past a broken window on the second floor of the
Schmiedler house. The children had a way of getting in and out.

"No matter what happened to her, it's nothing compared to
what the Russians did to me," Goldberg said.

A chorus shouted, "How about me, me, me. . . ."

"How about me in the coal bin with Mother and Schnaufi the
dog!" A trumpet voice from a button-nosed small girl. "They took
our socialist housing project for rich men's flats. Shelled us. White

flags, red flags. Made no difference. One woman—one of *those* . . . hung out a black pair of lace panties." She paused, grinned.

I could hear scraping and banging in the house across the street. "They shot off locks, broke in, drank wine, beer, perfume, gasoline. Some spewed; some dropped dead. The rest came after watches, clocks and us. Some barked. Schnaufi, our dog barked back from the coal bin. That's how they found us. They even did it to Schnaufi, a male mongrel, black as the devil."

"I know Frau Boschke, she lived in your building. She told me there was only one Russian. He raped her. Then he went to the butcher woman and he stayed with her. Nothing about dogs." I said.

"It's true. They did it to horses and cows too," said a dainty sprite with sweet authority and bit into a slice of bread. "Even pigs. Afterwards they killed them and ate them up."

*"Pfui, pfui!"* they shrieked and laughed.

"Corpses as long as they weren't cold and stiff," said a girl who wore American army shoes and claimed she was inhabited by a tape worm.

Up to now Goldberg's story of how she had been raped inside a Russian tank had been the class favorite. She now treated us to a new version and added a Russian with iron teeth. And this bit of realism almost had me convinced she was telling the truth. I was impressed. How could she be so cheerful. Girls and women had filled hospitals. Some were pregnant, others had syphilis. Women had killed themselves after Russian rape.

"I don't believe it," I said.

This was ignored. Who was I to doubt anyone when I had not come up with one single rape story. I was pushed aside. We had a most welcome interruption.

"The cheep! The cheep!" Years of Heil Hitler and Sieg Heil had taught them to shout in unison: "Chewing gum. Give chocolate and chewing gum!" a chorus of beggars that sent shivers down my spine.

The American jeep pulled up below our window. Girls pushing, fighting to get an arm through the grill. The tepid air had a tainted odor. Franz Joseph Schmiedler had stored ammunition in the rear wing of our school inside the gym hall. And there had been orders to defend the school at all costs. Aged storm troopers had commanded fifteen-year-old boys against the Russians. The building was blown up. The girls had lost brothers, cousins, sweethearts for the Fuehrer, or for Schmiedler.

There were rumors that parts of bodies, odd legs, arms, etc., had remained under the debris. The two Ami boys did not seem to notice the bad smell, they grinned and waited for the excitement to reach a peak. Then they put chewing gum into outstretched hands. Pitched some into the school room to watch us fight.

At the next window, older girls pushed, kicked for a vantage point to arrange meetings with the soldiers after school. Such clean uniforms, such smiling soldier boys and such sweets.

On my way to school I could have had one whole chocolate bar. The street cars rails had been torn up. Father cycled to school with me each morning and then he went on to his office. He always kept me in front of him. A jeep had come along and the Ami boys whistled. I had slowed down and smiled. They threw a chocolate bar towards me and drove on. "We have to remember who we are," Father said, and he would not allow me to pick it up. I did not even give him a kiss when he left me at the school gate.

He liked to see me in those old dirndls. I wished my old country clothes had all vanished. I was not a bit grateful to the British soldier who had been so kind as to bring my clothes in a suitcase from the mountain farm to Father's office. My winter dirndl was too short and had been patched. When I helped myself to one of my mother's old tight skirts, Father made me take it off. I had to go to school looking like an overgrown child. He said we had not changed our ways for the Nazis and would not change for the allies. You had to know who you are. I was a misfit in school and it was all his fault. Had I walked into the classroom with chocolate, even my missing rape story would have been forgiven.

Some of the lucky girls were already pushing gum into their mouth, saying, "No, Goldberg. You get plenty from your father."

"Either I get a stick this minute or no one gets to use my American lipstick before English."

They took turns smearing their lips dark red. Hitler had hated lipstick and it was still *verboten* in our school. Miss Pnevski our English teacher made her own laws. She was supposed to be Polish and formerly a slave laborer, or the former mistress of a

Gauleiter or a former spy either for the Nazis or the allies. Anyway, she had told us she had an Ami friend. Her mysteries, chewing, smoking and dark red, almost purple lipstick made English everyone's favorite subject.

The school bell rang three times. Stopped and rang again. Goldberg covered her ears. "I hate that crazy bell. That's the ring for Hitler speaking on the radio. All of you used to line up and go to the gymnasium and I had to stay in the class all by myself. It bothered me a lot."

"*Blodsinn,* nonsense!" yelled Bergner, the class athlete. "Nothing ever bothers you!"

Goldberg suddenly turned to me and handed me her stick of gum. "Here. Now tell us what really happened when you were hiding in the cellar with your grandmother, the Countess. And hurry, before Pnevski comes toddling in."

I accepted the gum as men and women must have accepted a cigarette when they were questioned by the gestapo—to gain time and gather my wits. The sweet mint flavor, laced with malt, was an inspiration. "I found a box in the cellar filled with jars of Maltaline, a tonic made with codliver oil and malt, terribly sweet." Our friend the court doctor had invented the tonic and he had tried to cure the restless empress, and he might have helped the crown prince settle down too with maltaline. The entire imperial family might have thrived with the supplement of vitamins. Three teaspoons of maltaline each day; the Empire might have survived. An overdose—I had discovered—was deadly. "I was so hungry, I wolfed down one whole jar. I threw up."

"Poor Meinert!" she spewed. "How about broiled cats, or cutlet of rat, or sparrow stew?" A discussion of cannabalism took up time. I went to my new desk, settled down to chewing and consoled myself with sniffing the wrapper and admiring the American print. We all saved the paper. And I kept the gum in my mouth until the evening—long after I wanted to spit it out. And why didn't I just spit out what I had seen in the courtyard during the invasion? I could always say I had been grabbed, thrown down in the courtyard. It could easily have happened. If the Mongolian officer on the white horse had not been shot . . .

I was lucky now too. Miss Pnevski toddled in and saved me with her: "Got morrning girrls ant sid town!"

A scramble to seats and "Got morrning Miss Pnevski," we

said in Hitler maiden unison. German was verboten. The language in Miss Pnevski's class was English. She called us lucky schoolgirls. The war had taken away her schoolgirl years. She made up for the girlie years with a baby pink bow in a nest of dough colored curls on top of her head; painted her puffy face pink, and taught English from a book of nursery rhymes.

A recital of "Humpty Dumpty" from Goldberg, the best English student, was followed by "Jack and Jill," which was repeated line by line by the class. All very boring. I had to sit and sit. In the garden across the street, the children were running around playing. A big boy blew a whistle once and they ran to the end of the garden, twice and they came back to him, three times and they vanished into the Schmiedler house and peeked out of windows, four times and they came back and lined up behind him.

Miss Pnevski asked Bergner, the class athlete to stand up and give a "Humpty Dumpty" recitation. And right away the "flat as an ironing board" tittering began. And all around me girls whispering about big bosoms. Scarce as anything among us. Gigantic breasts were all the rage. In America, Goldberg had informed us, they could be store bought. As good as real. Any size. Russian soldier women were fat and stuffed with cardboard under their tunics. Pressed up against them in a crowded street car you could hear it crackle. Female Russian officers wore monstrous balloon boobs that could be popped! We all knew that Miss Pnevski had captured an Ami officer because her boobs were mountainous. You could tell they were real, because the nipples showed when she was cold. On this day she was encased in tight, purple wool. A new pin—a small American flag—had been stuck at the very peak of her left breast as though it had been planted there by a mountain climber the size of an ant.

Whispers of: "Boobs getting bigger." "Can you wonder? With an Ami lover!" "All that chocolate."

"It is lust," said the bookworm. An authority.

Miss Pnevski said: "Shut up," to us. "Or at least speak English."

A few girls who had already gone out with Ami boys got along very well with, "shut up," or "O.K," "yes," or "no." The English lesson also prepared us for mishaps. The nursery rhymes Miss Pnevski chose all dramatized misfortunes. And as soon as she started to read "Little Simon," I knew he would never get his pie from the pie-man.

I became bored. Flipping through the cellar diary in my old, blue notebook, I considered my own plight. It was hard to be original when it came to inventing a rape story. Mongolians invading Grandmama's courtyard barking like dogs. The beautiful officer riding a white horse and then shooting at the stone angel and all the mongolians raising their guns. Grandmama firing her pistol and the officer falling and being dragged away, would leave the class unimpressed. The Meinert-Hof as a communist stronghold was nothing. This depressed me. And whether you had actually been pounced on or not, all the old feather bed dreams of wedding nights, love, roses, waltzes, secret kisses had been violated.

I closed my book and watched the children in the Schmiedler garden running back and forth from the back of the house. The big boy came around the corner at the white flag verboten sign and blew his whistle. They lined up two by two behind him. Usually they waited for the school bell and marched away like little soldiers. This was our last lesson. I could hardly wait.

Miss Pnevski lit a cigarette. "Come here, Mimi!" she said to Goldberg. Then she put an arm around her. "From now on it will be Mimi, Traude, Hilde, Gertie, Reyna. More friendly. We take it easy like de American girls. O.K.!"

"O.K. O.K. O.K." said the chorus.

Children started to run out of the garden pulling their box in a panic, as if an invisible Schmiedler were giving them the chase. The box was already rattling past our school when the bell rang. I rushed to get my cloak. Girls cornered me in the corridor. Goldberg was saying the time had really come for me to tell them about my mother and Hitler. "Did you ever go to Berchtesgaden with her?"

It was useless to deny Mother's romance. Someone's cousin or aunt had brought stories from Schladming mountain region to Vienna, about a big curtained limousine going up the mountain road and stopping near our farm. I kept insisting that limousines and trucks had stopped at the mine, where Nazi treasures had been locked away, but no one wanted to believe this. I was grilled about Hitler and Mother every day. My silence only confirmed the rumors. The bookworm got excited, grabbed my arm and pinched. "Did he devour her with his urgent passion? Rape her?"

I felt blood rush to my cheeks. They tugged on my old mountain cloak. Elbows dug into me. "She raped him!" I yelled and gave them a push. I was almost at the door. They were after me shrieking with laughter. Then it thundered. "Down, down, take cover. The *Russ!* Cover your heads."

Small girls, tall girls, loud and silent ones all curled up. Another blast shook our building. Ursel Brenner, the other new girl slid closer to me. Her teeth were biting into her lower lip. "Hitler is back. Hitler is back. The big bomb. The secret weapon." I knelt down and put my arm around her. We all turned to stone.

Silence and shhhhhh, shhh, a rushing sound. An avalanche. I was on my feet. An invisible force drove me staggering towards the window. The sunny street trembled in a haze like a reflection. I grabbed the Schmiedler desk, held on. With a gushing, rushing sound of a waterfall, a crackling roar of invisible flames and a thud, thud, thud, the Schmiedler house sank. Only three walls remained of the new, the modern, unadorned Schmiedler house and time was already washing over it.

.

# SIX

# *Rites of Love*

THE RUIN OF the Schmiedler villa stood open like a broken dollhouse. Most of the front and north wall had crumbled. Of the basement kitchen white tiles and only a large sink remained; on the floor above, a corner of green wallpaper decorated with a design of peacock feathers. And on the second floor a peach colored flimsy rag of curtain showed where a girl's room had been. From the outside the building had three rows of windows. Now you saw a huge loft barely high enough for a short man. Walls covered with broken mirror glass and the marks of an elevator shaft.

Broken mirror, seven years bad luck. Multiply this saying seven hundred times into smashed glitter and you have the ruin sprinkled with tinsel, Schmiedler's secret dressing room.

Imagine the man transforming himself. He was said to have been the best Hitler double. The inevitable multiplicity of deceit will always dazzle me. A mirror is never empty. Each fragment of looking glass quivered with light reflection upon reflection. I should have known there is never just one illusion created or perceived; A carnival of deception lay ahead of me. My story of Vienna after the war is a mosaic of broken mirror glass; The aftermath of Hitler an endless flimflammery.

Had it been a children's prank? The building itself looked like the kind of house a child could make out of a box and then destroy. Somewhere on a pile of broken brick I saw a red knitted hat. I don't think anyone else did. In the turmoil after the explosion, mothers' shrieking, teachers running around, girls shoving, pushing each other down.

Father had insisted that Olga meet me each day, but I couldn't see her. Then I heard: "Reyna, Reyna, where are you?" the sweet Hungarian voice I knew so well. "Where is my child!" Agnes, my Agnes, our Agnes, back in Vienna. I struggled through a thicket of elbows, kicking feet, butting heads; then I was caught and hugged and safe. "My beauty, my child. My daughter." Tears, kisses that made my cheeks smart; fragrance of hey, country kitchen, loden, melted snow.

All around girls whispered and stared. Minutes after the explosion and panic they nudged each other. Could this woman be Hitler's secret love? A peasant-type with a pink, wrinkled face wearing a Hungarian kerchief; this *die furchtbar Schoene?* terribly beautiful, the notorious Frau von Meinert? They had lived through the bombing and had seen other buildings fall. This was by far the greater shock. Nor did I have to play-act to sustain their deception.

The moment her warm, rough hand touched me I felt the pleasure of being mothered again. Agnes had cared for me all my life. It was natural for me to act like a daughter. But she became embarrassed, wiped her tears, and like a servant, wanted to carry my school bag and push my bike.

I refused. Agnes had been in the country during the bombing, and was terrified of explosions. We hurried away. American jeeps arrived within minutes as though they had all been ready and waiting for the Schmiedler house to blow up. Girls hung around. Army photographers took pictures.

I asked whether Mother was at home. Agnes stopped to catch her breath. Tears came into her eyes. "Thank God she isn't. Nurse and I came ahead. We just arrived an hour ago. With that kind of thing going on, I really don't know whether your mama should come back to Vienna." Agnes had been my age when she left the village of Falkenburg and came to Vienna as Mother's baby nurse. She had hardly ever left her, or me, for that matter. "Her nerves couldn't take explosions. Not after what she went through. She was almost blown up inside the mine by that scoundrel Fritz Janicek."

Agnes telling me stories, always left out the worst part that I liked best. I had learned at an early age to fill in and imagine what really happened—an education in itself. One could say she had taught me to think by leaving me uninformed.

Now she told me how Mother had hoped Father might be able to bring Grandmama and me back to the country. Many refugees from Vienna had arrived in the mountains. Mother had gone out to pick the first spring flowers and watched the road. I got the picture of Mother in the snow-speckled meadow above the amethyst mine wearing her purple wool shawl, braids coiled over each ear shining like copper in the sun. She would shade her eyes when she saw a man coming up the hill. My dog Krampus, a chocolate-colored Pekinese was with her. Agnes had become suspicious when she saw Krampus run to meet the man, sniff and flee.

Why did Mother not turn back when she saw the man was no other than honorary S.S. and national socialist art-looting specialist, Fritz Janicek? Agnes said Fritz had forced Mama to go into the amethyst mine with him. I knew better. Fritz Janicek would be bowing and scraping, saying, "Oh, Juno." He would ask his goddess to come and look at art treasures he had collected in her honor in such a way that she would think he had Puppe, her old doll in the cave. Then she would follow him eagerly.

Agnes had found the flowers and shawl at the locked gate. She had called to Fritz Janicek. His inimitable chanting and raving had echoed bouncing off rock where the light of many candles shivered casting a golden glow. He had shouted something about a sacred offering in a priest's voice and Agnes got the impression that he had finally become Godfearing.

"I bet he was kneeling in there, wasn't he? And carrying on about supreme sacrifice. Without art and beauty he wouldn't want to live and all that," I said. "And Mama would stand there stiff and tall making her spooky pop-eyes. And I bet she was asking him to give her back the doll."

Agnes grabbed my arm, "How do you know? Did she get a letter to you, or telephone?"

"No," I said. "I know because I have second sight like Hanna Roth," I said with a hypnotic stare.

She smacked my bottom and laughed. "It was your mother who saved the museum art in the cave. You see, he had this box. She thought her doll was packed away in it. When he opened it and showed her the dynamite, she lost her temper. She spotted a bucket of water and she simply poured it over the stuff. A minute later he came rushing out. Pushed me away, locked the gate again ran down the hill where he had hidden his car and drove off to get more explosives. Fortunately the British caught him. They came up to the mine and burst the lock. Fritz Janicek had told them he had collected the museum art in the mine for your mother. Hitler's orders! Can you imagine? They were hoping to find the Hapsburg crowns. And he made them think she had them. So they took her into custody. She is treated like a queen. But they don't want anyone to know where she is. I was blind-folded when they took me to see her."

"They think Hitler is her secret lover," I said.

"Don't you go around repeating that stupid talk. They treat her well because she is a heroine. She did save the museum art from being blown up. There is a nice English army doctor in charge and he arranged that Frau Schwester and I should go to Vienna and get things ready. You Mama should be coming home soon. We'll all be together again!"

I asked about my little dog Krampus. She shook her head sadly. He had run after the British car when they took Mother down into the valley. Agnes had asked for him everywhere. . . .

"He's been eaten," I said.

"They wouldn't be so stupid," Agnes said. "He was scrawny and anyone could see he was a rare dog. They could always trade him in for a hen." We reached our avenue in silence. A work gang of convicted Nazis was repaving our bomb-scarred avenue. She stopped and frowned. "I hope they make them work until their hands fall off." She was blaming the men for my sad face, the lost dog, everything.

"Father says the men working here are mostly paper Nazis. Some of the big ones like Schmiedler got away."

"They made our Falkenburg Gypsies dig their own graves before they strung them up," she said.

It wasn't like her to talk to me that way. "How do you know that these are the same men?"

"Godless, filthy murderers. That old guy in the brown jacket, He was one of those who pissed on the Jewish ladies on our avenue right in front of you and Eli Romberg."

Bomb blast had torn up the road, now it was repaved and yet the image of the Jewish ladies kneeling and forced to scrub white "DOLLFUSS" letters on the road remained. I could see my anger in Agnes. Her face was red and distorted. I left my bike inside the gate and took her hand and pulled her away.

She went on and on about those criminals, the riff-raff and all the foreigners and foreign soldiers. Never had Agnes ever given way to her feelings in front of me. She burst into tears. I could feel a monster in me stir, ready to spit, throw rocks, sling excrement at anyone who had made Agnes so unhappy and might keep my mother from coming back to Vienna.

Agnes and Frau Schwester started to dust, polish and wash as though Mother's return depended on a thorough house cleaning. When I came home from school I wiped my shoes carefully. Sniffed the fragrance of the wood floors rubbed with bees-wax. It came from beehives on the Meinert auntie's farm and I had helped flake it into turpentine.

They had left Mother's room to the very last and now they were up there. I dropped my schoolbag and turned on the radio. The sender Red White Red, controlled by the American forces played reassuring Viennese waltz music. The floor brushes had been left in the living room. I slipped the strap onto my feet and waltzed around polishing the floor. The twins, our two maids, had always danced like this.

First I went around and around the edge of the carpet, then I closed my eyes and opened my arms like the Indian chief in the *Scenes from American History,* a book Mimi Goldberg had brought to school. If the Indians could bring rain with their dance, I could bring back Mother, Bertl, Arnold, Eli, and even the young Ami officer, that smiling chocolate thrower.

Agnes interrupted and called me to help carry clothes downstairs. The great ritual of airing out had begun. It started with opening windows wide and throwing bedding onto the sill. On the line between two trees, mother's blouses were already dancing in the wind.

After Eli was safe in Switzerland, Frau Schwester, his devoted nurse, had come to take charge of my injured Mother. At first Agnes had resented the German nurse in the starched white uniforms of a hospital nun, just as she resented the German invasion. All that laundering and starching and fussing over Mother, pushing the wheelchair as if it were a baby carriage. Agnes had wanted to care for Mother herself. In the solitude of the mountain farm Agnes and the German nurse had come to share all the work. During those six years they had even come to look alike. Frau Schwester had taken to wearing Hungarian

petticoats to keep warm; Agnes started tying her kerchiefs like
a nurse's cap. Yet they always addressed each other as Frau
Agnes and Frau Schwester.

Why run up and down? When I could throw clothes out the
window. I told them. And I did so in sequence. They caught each
garment lovingly. First of all the old Falkenburg wedding veil
went sailing down. Agnes caught it. "Such a young bride, only
sixteen. She had her dolly hidden under it." An old maternity
robe brought on a ballad of motherhood from Frau Schwester,
the baby nurse; "a mere child herself, she insisted on breast
feeding." She brushed the garment with special care, making
her clacking sound. "God willing she might be blessed again." I
could well imagine her in charge of an odious infant, back to
schedules, bustling about with disinfectant the way I had seen
her at the water castle when she took care of the schoolboy Eli
as if he were a newborn. "Made for motherhood." I hoped she
meant the dress.

Sunlight flitted over the blue silk walls of the boudoir where
I had shared Mother's lap with the dreadful doll. I threw down
two English riding habits as a reminder of Mother's wild pre-
Nazi days when she went riding with cousin Bertl. Among carnival costumes I found a Pierrot suit, with a Salon Roth label. I
tried on the mask and fitted hat. The satin gave me an electric
shock when I threw the suit out the window, and the sleeves flew
apart in wierd remonstrance.

There'd never be heavy silk-satin like that again. And the
hand sewing and shirring! All that work. Agnes and Frau
Schwester admired the old costume which had once belonged to
Great Aunt Christina. Mother had worn it to her first costume
ball: no matter what disguise she chose she could never hide her
beauty. I sent down the gray chiffon Mother had worn to the
Fuehrer reception. "I still remember her picture in the paper,"
Frau Schwester said. "Hitler kissing her hand."

"Every man fell in love with her," Agnes said. "She was so
innocent, she never noticed."

The picture of Mother with Adolf Hitler was in my treasure
box. And the card Bertl had sent her of Hitler as a medieval
knight. Also the yellow silk rose. Tiny silver swastica stuck in
the center. And there were letters from a General Mother had
left around for me to pick up. Agnes had brought the box from
the country. I always wore the key on my chain with a coy guard-

ian angel. The General's letter said she had beguiled him. He would fight and die for her alone. He had died. When everyone was saying he had been driven to suicide because Hitler suspected him of disloyalty, I knew better. Mother had beguiled him. Then she had stopped answering his letters. Was that innocent?

Father liked to tell the anecdote of how he introduced Mother to Eugene Romberg at the opera. They shared a box and Eugene Romberg had brought chocolates from Gerstner's for his friend's little fiancée. Although she was almost sixteen years old, she had pretended she was feeding the doll and made Puppe dance to the music. Eugene Romberg had worshipped her, Father said, because she was so young and innocent. I had to marvel how Mother at my age behaving like an idiot child had won Eugene Romberg's everlasting love. "Did Mama go to Salzburg last spring when I was in Vienna with my father?" I asked.

"And where is her nutria cape?" Agnes asked.

"I was asking whether Mother went to Salzburg?"

"What on earth for," Frau Schwester quickly said. "You better take off that dusty clown hat and masque. Throw it down!"

I watched the black masque and hat dance on the line. Wind would shake out the dust, but not the musky odor of potent perfume. Frau Schwester was working away on stains that had sunk in like my memory of transformations, and could not be removed.

And after all the garments had been thrown out of the window I noticed the old straw hat with fruit and flowers left out on the shelf. With the hat had come Hanna's warnings: stay away from horses. Mother had worn that hat on horseback, fell off, lost her unborn child, the use of her legs. Towards the end of the war, I had heard Hanna say to Father: "Don't let the girl wear that hat." She had meant not me, but Nadica, Vlado's only clever one, the music student. Father's darling protégé had helped herself to anything Mother left behind, clothes, perfume, and especially that crazy hat. Now she was dead.

Bombs had begun to fall on Vienna, but Hitler kept promising secret miracle weapons. Nadica's miracle weapon had to be the oldest female miracle weapon in the world: "I'm going to have your child, Ferdl." She had told him it was patriotic. There were plushy resorts for unwed mothers: extra food, a lovely vacation, trained baby nurses and adoption by good national socialist family.

Father would have none of that. His child, given away to Nazis, strangers! And he had of course, made arrangements at once. He had moved the girl and her mother and the younger children to the Meinert-Hof. Nadica, Vlado's only clever one was not quite clever enough. Father had moved out. And he had gone to stay with Resi in the sunny apartment he had furnished for her near the Opera. And he had asked Nadica to leave Mother's old clothes alone. He would do his best to get some maternity dresses for her, and wool for knitting little things.

The mother of his child would no longer be a mere stand in. Nadica should have known this. She should have known that he would have cared for her always. He would have adored a child. And had it been a son—the son he had wished for, the son my mother lost by falling off that horse—anything would have been possible.

He had waited, stayed away, half expecting and dreading a phone call or letter from Nadica. And then her letter came, written on Mother's stationery. It had all been a mistake. She had been wrong. There would be no child.

Nadica should have known how kind he was. He would have made her sit on his knee and he would have assured her she didn't ever have to tell him such fibs. He might even have asked her whether she would like to have his child one day, after the war.

But Nadica had written the letter expecting him to move back to the Meinert-Hof—and he telephoned and told her mother he was coming out in the afternoon for a little visit. Nadica had felt like a fool. He had left her and he would stay away. There is no fool like an angry one trying to pass anger on: he had announced his four o'clock little visit and she had made a rendezvous with a soldier on leave, a vintner's son. Then she had dressed up in Mother's nutria cape and that crazy, straw hat. At ten minutes to four the sirens had wailed. She knew Father would want her to take shelter, but she was out in the middle of the avenue kissing the young soldier.

Vienna had been bombed during the day. Never at night. American bombers could see the church steeples, patches of winter gray parks, and yellow palaces and villas when they unloaded their bombs. A single plane had circled above our avenue in reconnaissance. The flyer could have seen no more than a spot of color. It must have been like dropping bombs on a blossom.

Nadica, Vlado's eldest one, his clever one, was no more. Who was to blame? Father? The hat?

I took the hat and put it on. An amazing creation. Crown of fertility, Hanna Roth had called it. I straightened the brim, the way Mother had worn it when it was new. Who had picked up the hat after Mother had been thrown off the horse? Who on earth would gather up a battered straw hat after the bomb had destroyed the girl and that soldier? Had the hat blown away in the wind before the bomb fell? I had questioned Nadica's young sister, a towhead of few words. She had pointed at the sky. I had gained the impression that the straw hat with the trimmings, flowers and fruit, had returned to the shelf like one of Hanna Roth's homing pigeons . . .

Agnes and the nurse worked away with sponge, needle and thread, and a brush. I leaned out the side window where they couldn't see me and let the wind fan my cheeks. And all the airing, brushing, washing, polishing and my own dance—doing things thoroughly, as we say in Vienna—seemed like a ritual to cleanse the soul, a rite of pure female exorcism.

One by one Mother's dresses were hung up on the line. Bare branches of willows swayed in the wind; dry leaves flew up and settled on the black patch of new paving on the road between the two houses. At the water castle a washing line had been tied around the neck of one of the three marble graces. It ran to a hook on the garage. Old shirts and underpants, curtains from Eli's room flapped. Cabbages and brussel sprouts remained in flower beds. A birch tree I had once seen encased in ice, had been felled and the logs lay piled up. Wooden slats had been stripped off the garden bench where Rudolf Hess had once sat talking to himself.

A jeep came along our avenue and slowed down. Two Amis sat in front, one with a note pad on his lap in the back. They stopped at several houses and looked around. When they reached the front of the water castle, one jumped down from the front seat, ran up the steps, held an overgrown bush aside to look at the house number and returned to the jeep in one single impulse. I felt quite certain he had been the one who had thrown chocolate to me the other day. He seemed to be making a study of the fantastic mansion. Then they turned around and stopped in front of our gate.

For a moment I thought my Indian dance had been an invocation. Unfortunately our house looks like an old farm from the street. No wonder they lost interest. I leaned out as far as I could. They didn't see me and were about to drive away. So I took the crazy straw hat and threw it into the wind. Up it went over the gate. "Yippeee," yelled my graceful favorite, lept up and caught it. They sped away with the trophy.

I shivered with excitement. "I know they'll be back," I said in the prophetic voice of Hanna Roth.

I started to wait and listen after that. The sound of an engine became music to my ears. On my way to a spy mirror I usually knew whether an American jeep or car was coming along. I recognized the sound of the American commander General Clark's car passing. He had taken over a big house on the hill.

Nazi refugees had made off with any car or truck before the Russian invasion. Those cars that remained in Vienna had been hidden away or dismantled; there was no fuel. Father had buried our car and a couple of trucks in haybarns on our mountain farm. Before the first snowfall, a certain jeep, a particular car stopping at our gate, would make my heart race to the tune of an idling engine from the new, the free world—land of food, money and good intentions—that promised land where everyone drove and nobody walked.

I was already brushing my teeth, one night, ready for bed when I heard a car slow down on our avenue. Then it stopped. Trees obstructed my view. I listened to the tkkkk, tkkk, tkkk, tkk. A car door banged. The night was dark. The sliver of a moon above the dome turned the water castle into a mosque. Light from newly repaired street lanterns spilled over the wet road between the two houses. I opened my window wide, leaned out. A drop fell on my nape. The doorbell shrilled.

"Hurry up. Come down. Reyna!" Father called. "Call Agnes and Frau Schwester. Your mother's at the gate."

He sounded stunned rather than happy. I saw him rush towards the gate and then stop. We had told him she was able to walk again; no one could have prepared him. For almost seven years she had been an invalid, and there she stood on her feet calling his name. His slight limp turned into the hobble of an invalid on two wooden legs. At the gate they greeted each other softly. I heard only the tkk. tkk, tkk, of an idling engine of a waiting car.

She felt ill at ease. I could tell, when she twirled through the gate like an operetta comedienne. She often imitated Resi when she felt at a loss with Father. Her white loden cape flew up and russet colored curls bounced around her girlish face.

He roared like a stag. "Your hair, what happened to your braids!"

She gave up the act; her face fell. She was about to turn and go back to the car. Father banged the gate shut. And he locked it.

She cupped her hands "I told you so, Hugh!" she called in English. The car went tkkkk, tkkk, tkk, growled into gear and slowly drove away. Father opened his arms and she threw herself against him. He almost lost his balance. This moment of weakness was not like Emperor Meinert, who had roared like a stag. He backed off to examine her.

The house was ready but she had found us unprepared. She had returned and brought with her the crisp, smokey odor of the autumn night and English verbena—an alien fragrance—clung to her coat and hair. I pushed myself between them—an old habit. We huddled and kissed like a stage family.

My mother was holding something on her left arm under the cloak. The doll! I backed away and retreated up the steps. She called me. I couldn't move. Fritz Janicek must have given the doll back. It was restored. She was all smiles cradling it under her cloak. Then it dropped and I rejoiced until it moved.

A yelp, a bark, and a whiplike shadow raced towards me: Krampus, my skinny brown Pekinese, nipped my face, my hands, leaping about with crazy loving growls. An easy reunion.

We sat at the round Meinert table with Agnes and Frau Schwester and drank champagne. "What happened to your beautiful long hair?" Father asked.

Mother smiled and watched the bubbles in her glass.

"Father cut his beard off because the Russians don't like beards," I said. "You cut your hair off because the English don't like long hair. Right?"

Father quickly kissed her hand and said she did look wonderful. Not to worry, his beard grew back. Her hair would grow back. "I am so grateful that we are all together again. Nothing else matters."

She had come fluttering in through the gate, and she might have turned and flickered right out of the gate and out of his life. For a few moments she sat there like an understudy who has forgotten her lines. They clinked glasses; we all did. Some of her champagne spilled. She gulped what was left, held out her glass. He laughed and filled it. I held out mine and he said—no more! Anyway, it was time for bed. I had to get up and go to school in the morning. Mother was tired. His voice shook a little.

He had planned her return, talked about her lovingly and he had dreaded the reunion. I knew they had not shared a bed on the farm. He had learned to live his own life but he had taken good care of his rare, beautiful, invalid. The way he had talked about my mother, admired and praised her, reminded me of Eli Romberg with the favorite from his collection of rare butterflies. Father had kept Mother transfixed with memories and pinned down for display and safely stored away.

Later, when I came in from a walk in the garden with Krampus, I heard Mother lock her door. I did not have to listen long. A few minutes and Father's slippers flip-flapped up her stairs. He knocked on her door.

"Why on earth did you lock up, Annerl?" Had he forgotten to play the stranger at her door? "If you've mislaid your key you better find it, or I'll break in." He had become a stranger.

I couldn't hear what Mother said. He seemed to be waiting. Then there was a loud crash. Mother shouted: "Go away. You're like a Russian."

I considered going to her rescue when I heard her laugh. "My own Ferdl. My only Ferdl!"

"Hey, stop it. Wait a minute. Too much champagne. Crazy girl."

It was just as well that Agnes and Frau Schwester had their rooms at the other end of the new wing. They might have come running.

"Help, help, help!" his cry receded as though he were falling through space from a mountain peak. Cries of surprise and joy soared as though they had both landed in paradise. Sounds of shared pleasure—the song of the ages—escaped through the locked door, filled the ancestral house in defeated Vienna, and triumphed in a world divided.

# SEVEN

# Rapacious City

THE DAY I SAW the picture of Nazi prisoners in Nüremburg in the paper, I also saw the photograph of Rita Hayworth. She was called pin-up girl because American army boys liked to pin up her picture. Their loves were far away. So were mine. I did not recognize Rudolf Hess among the thin, shabby men on trial. My Rudolf Hess remained a young man in a pilot's helmet waiting for Hanna Roth on a bench in the gardens of the water castle. My Rudolf Hess wanted to stop the war. My Rudolf Hess knew no harm and had never hurt anyone; he was a soaring angel of peace. My Rudolf Hess had no wife, no child, he had no memory of a Fuehrer, he only had me. Dreams of love, when I was fifteen were orgies of transfiguration.

I took out the old box of Rudolf Hess paper dolls I had made from newspaper cuttings when I was ten years old and pasted him all around the mirror inside my wardrobe. Whenever I practiced the Rita Hayworth face, opening my mouth in a half smile, half snarl, I was surrounded by all those unsmiling deputy Fuehrers: my pin-up men.

I learned to sustain the smile. And I trained my hair to hang over one eye. We now had many visitors. Everyone had to come and look at Mother, and they called my one eyed smiling face: pretty as a picture, *Bildschoen*. A bearded old government official toasted both Mother and me in English. "I love de buteful Laties!" He was taking English lessons. His pronunciation made me wonder whether we did not have the same teacher. He was

proud of his gift for languages. "I said to the Americans, Do not
boot that chemical stoff in de waterr. De Vienna waterr sie is
pure and undouched." He was smiling to Mother and me. "Our
mountain Spring water, like our ladies—the best in the world.
Notorrriously pure."

I did not like to be reminded. I was so notoriously pure, I
hardly knew how to face the girls in my class. This was partly
Father's fault. He had made certain that all of Vienna knew no
*Russ* had touched his wife or daughter.

"Unbelievable that you, Frau von Meinert already have such
a lovely daughter. You look so young, just a girl yourself. A
Madonna. He turned on me his sweet bawdy old eyes. "Beautiful
Vienna girls, beautiful Vienna," he took a good swallow of wine.
"Vienna was not seduced by Hitler. Vienna was raped."

I was certain he had heard this somewhere. It didn't sound
like his own idea. And he changed the subject at once and talked
about the rebuilding of the Opera. He said it should be rebuilt
exactly like the old house.

"Why?" I asked. "It could be new, modern, like the Schmiedler house."

No one listened to my tactless remark. Mother seemed to have
forgotten her enthusiasm for the box house and agreed that it
was essential to rebuild and restore and make everything exactly
as it had been. And our admirer quite forgot Vienna had been
raped and could never be the same.

Frau Boschke in the basement laundry room talked of nothing but her rape. "What we have been through," she clamored.
"The disgrace. No respect for anything. Not even personal property."

Rape did not seem to have changed her. She looked exactly
the same: her large head hung forward from a curved spine. Arms
and legs were long, the body short without waist. She had mar-
velously knowing eyes the color of mud, and a bird nest of hair
to match. Her mouth was sweet, smooth, pink and chatty. She
had always preferred going from one great household to the next,
could not understand Agnes, who had stayed with one family.
She had to have a change. A well-run Viennese household before
the war performed as a musical ensemble. Frau Boschke had
been the guest soloist, a wandering minstrel.

Laundry days had always been special. Agnes used to cook

Frau Boschke's favorite blood sausage and sauerkraut. "No blood sausage," I said. "After all you have been through."

"You don't know half of it . . . "

I took my place beside her, picked up my little scrubbing board and went to work.

She lifted her red, gnarled hands from suds and let Mother's chemise sink. "Not a ring left," she said. "That hussy has them all. If I hadn't lost so much weight, my rings wouldn't have come off. Believe me, that *Russ* would have chopped my fingers off to get them. And that engraved gold watch your father gave me after ten years of faithful service. Gone!"

"How many Russians were there?" I asked.

"What do you take me for, *Kind*. Isn't one enough?"

She had always kept her rings in a chipped saucer below the basement window. Now it was empty; she treated me to a description of each ring. I was really more interested in the men who had given them to her and the Russian who had taken them away, but I did miss the rings. In the days when I was too small to reach for them myself, there had been special moments when she handed me the saucer and allowed me to wear my favorite, the forget-me-not ring. It had been given to her before I was born, when she was a young girl, by a fifteen-year-old son of a household. And I had loved the forget-me-not made of blue beads, and considered it more beautiful than Mother's solitaire, or even Grandmama's Falkenburg emerald and I took great pleasure in shining it for her.

If the Russian didn't polish the forget-me-not ring at least once a week it would turn greenish-black. Childish tears came into my eyes. I really hated that Russian. "Was he a Mongol, did he bark. Was he brutal?"

"He gave me a hunk of bread. Then he went to sleep in my bed like a baby and didn't wake up until the next day. Then, down he went to the fat butcher's wife. One of *those* women. He didn't have to force himself on her. So he gave her the rings. There she is in the butcher's shop in my own building selling any kind of black market meat wearing my rings."

Frau Boschke scrubbed the delicate, well-worn chemise with such vigor, I was afraid she might tear it to shreds. I took it from her.

"Can't you get her to give them back. Can't you ask her for the forget-me-not ring?" I asked.

She grabbed one of Father's shirts. "I asked her to give me back my precious things and she says: present from an Allied officer . . . "

"Tell the police." I said.

"I wouldn't dare. The *Russ* comes and goes. That's how she gets her meat supply. The butcher is a prisoner of war in Russia. She's contented without him. I can tell you that."

Bright autumn days ended. Wind driven rain splashed my face, blinding me when I rode to school behind Father on my bicycle. Someone brought a letter from Pfarrer Kronz, the priest who had been my tutor during the war. Our mountain farm, he said, was already deep in snow. He had been able to send us some cheese made from goat's milk. I could imagine my friend Stopperl on skis, racing down into the valley. She would stop at the amethyst mine, and listen for voices of the dead. What stories she would have to tell about the British who were stationed in the mountain town.

In class I watched dust from the bomb site run down the window pane forming rivulets of dirt. Girls kept whispering all around me about the Russian zone, foreign soldiers, displaced persons. Rumors of lewd violence rippled from lesson to lesson, as muddy streamlets fed the Danube with murky water in this foul weather, this foul year. Girls giggled.

I existed as flotsam in their midst. And barely kept my head above the water, so to speak. I decided I was above it all. When I was bored in class I hid behind my Rita Hayworth hairstyle and wrote in my blue notebook. My tutor had shown me that profound study goes from the deeply personal to the universal. I decided to rise above the personal. Let them despise me as an avid student who could not even produce a decent rape story. I wrote: "VIENNA RAPED BY HITLER?"

I quoted the old government official, who had no doubt quoted someone else, but I am still proud of the question mark, and all the others wriggling over pages like tiny vipers. Questions had not been allowed under Hitler. I had grown up during a crazy and dangerous time of definitions. Questions had been answered with slogans before they had ever been asked. I no sooner wrote down any kind of definition, then I questioned it. Snap phrases had remained in my ear too, like the catchy Nazi marching tunes, yet the voice of my tutor rose above it all.

I drifted through my school days in the midst of excitement and confusion—excluded, notoriously pure. I was not much better at home. My parents played their new game. Rain kept drumming against the windows at night. Mother had come home with some rare English tobacco for Father's pipe. He smoked after dinner, leaning back in his chair. Mother stretched and yawned, making eyes at him. She was tired, she would say. I usually spread out my homework in front of the tile stove in the livingroom corner. My parents were as easy to figure out as my algebra problems. I knew Father would go to sit in his green chair, pat his knee, inviting Mother.

"You go and sit on Papa's lap," she said to me. "I'm going up to take a bath. We have hot water left over tonight. What a luxury!" She roughed up his hair in passing, when he tried to grab her, she slipped away. "Stop it now. I know Reyna can use a little help from you with her algebra."

I gathered up my books and withdrew to my room. Father stayed downstairs smoking and reading the paper. He had all kinds of worries. His supposed aryanization of the Romberg industries had become a public issue. In school Mimi had asked me whether my father had Eugene Romberg done away with. It sounded almost as though she were questioning me for the American denazification unit, since her father, now an American officer, was in charge. She didn't want to believe that my father had bought the Romberg Industries and even took his friend Eugene across the Swiss border with his money before Hitler took over. Father had nothing to do with Eugene Romberg's going back and forth between Switzerland and Austria during the war until he was finally arrested. Mimi had told the class that my father had arranged the arrest. I had to throw a book at her. Now she had not spoken to me for a week. I did not want Father to know what happened. When I told him I hated school, he simply said I had to learn to fit in. He only half listened to me now that Mother was back.

The downstairs was heated by the slow burning tile stove. The bedrooms were unheated; we had to save coal. I had a good reason for keeping my door wide open. Mother had left hers open too. After she had her bath she finally closed her door and I could hear the key turn in the lock. She started to push her furniture around. That was part of her new game. She barricaded her door. She shut Father out, put obstacles in his way. I had become one of those obstacles too. She would nudge me towards him when he wanted her. Grandmama had probably noticed something and she had invited me to stay with her. Mama had said she would miss me too much.

In the days before Hitler, Father had always knocked on her door, humbling himself, he had called himself a dirty old peasant, and he had waited to be admitted. Then she would throw herself into his arms. I had always joined in this old routine to delay the moment when she would send me out of the room and lock herself in with him.

Now she locked him out to entice him. And she encouraged him to kick the door until the old lock yielded. I would hear her shout: *"Nein, nein.* No, go away! Then he would push furniture around, knocking down her barricade to reenact the night of her return to Vienna. By now Frau Schwester and Agnes knew what was going on and discreetly stayed away.

I pictured Mother lunging at my father. It gave me a queazy feeling to imagine what was going on in that room and yet I had to giggle. Mother assaulting my strong father. In school I had said Mother raped Hitler, and the class had liked that.

"DO WOMEN RAPE MEN?" I wrote in my notebook. Girls in class were quite capable of assault, especially the big ones. And I had to laugh to myself when I imagined Frau Boschke going after her *Russ* with a scrubbing board. I pictured women in uniform with short machine guns hunting for men. Then I had an inspiration and wrote: "RAPACIOUS CITY."

It was still raining when I was in bed with my blue notebook. Krampus curled up beside my head on the pillow, his eyes closed and his chocolate brown nose twitching. Some of the hair on his Pekinese muzzle had turned white. I read "RAPACIOUS CITY" out loud and then I had to giggle and couldn't stop. Krampus started to roll and kick his legs like a puppy. I took up my fountain pen and he nibbled my hand. "Hitler raped Vienna," I said in an aged, official voice. The dog growled. I sat up in my flannel night gown and imagined Vienna as it must have been before the First World War when my two maiden aunts had shared my room and took painting lessons at the Academy which had rejected Hitler. And he must have wandered around Vienna poor as a beggar, the fragrance of the sugar bakeries tantalizing him. If he stopped to look at the display he would see wealthy women buying cake he could not afford. The currency in Austria had

been the *krone,* a gold coin. How it must have glittered on count-
ers. Cheerful women brushing past him in furs and silk, stout,
sweet smelling, wickedly enticing Viennese.

Resi had come to see us at the mountain farm after she had
been commanded to sing for Adolf Hitler and his guests at Berchtesgaden. And she told my mother that Hitler's cook was Viennese and sustained him with cakes, whipped cream. He had never
been able to get enough of that sweet richness. He had loved to
gossip with the cook, or Resi, to hear the Viennese voices. Vienna
had put obstacles in Hitler's way like Mother with Father.

"DID HITLER RAPE VIENNA, OR DID VIENNA RAPE
HITLER?"

I was getting very sleepy, but I kept writing about Hitler in
Vienna. How he must have both loved and hated the city which
overwhelmed him. And how he had wished to destroy and rebuild
the city according to his own plan. Hitler had sent orders from
his underground headquarters to hold Vienna at all costs. Tanks
from Berlin came to Vienna leaving the Reich's capital open to
the Russians. I read all I had written to Krampus and he twitched
his ears. And I considered my observations brilliant, universal.
One day I would show those vixen in school. It wasn't easy. During recess they whispered of this or that "Ami" boy.

One morning, I simply went right over to the circle around
Mimi Goldberg. "Do Amis rape you?"

"Of course, of course, if they get a chance," said the bookworm.

"I bet you rape them and you snatch their chocolate and their
chewing gum and cigarettes!" I said.

Their laughter sounded like an admission.

One night Father came home with new shoes for Mother and
me. He grinned and put them on the table. Beautiful, sturdy,
brown new leather; perfect, wide enough, big enough. Now I
wouldn't have to go to school in my old heavy boots anymore. I
sniffed the new leather. Amazing, wonderful, how on earth did
he find them, pay for them? I hugged him, kissed him, kissed the
shoes. The new brown leather shone like newly peeled chest-
nuts. The moment I put them on I felt I could walk to the end of
the world. Leather tassels on laces dancing at each step.

Why not walk into town in our new shoes? break them in,
enjoy the sun. I could miss a day of school. Mother agreed almost
too readily. When I think back, I have a notion the new shoes

broke me in during the year I wore them. I would pick them up and polish them lovingly. They were like no other shoes. When I wore them I was in love—quite often with my own ideas. Especially that first day.

Monumental clouds rose and tumbled under the onslaught of the wind. My American hairstyle was blown into childish ringlets. Mother wore an old wide-brimmed gray hat from Salon Roth. It was too big without her crown of braids and she had to hold onto it when we turned corners in the wind. This was our first walk. I had grown to be her height during the war while she sat in a wheelchair. She looked young and supple in her old, gray suit. I had borrowed her prewar winter coat with the fox fur. Black and tight enough to make me look like her sister or friend. We fell in step taking long, easy strides and swinging our arms.

The wind brought tears to our eyes and made our faces glow. Nazis who had to clean up bomb sights, clanged down shovels and axes as we passed. We made a provocatively cheerful picture to the more reluctant penitents. You could always spot such men by their old Hitler mustaches. Those who had not been rounded up grew beards to hide their faces.

One of those men at the scaffolding of the gothic votive church, doffed a big, black slouch hat. "That looks like Fritz Janicek!" she said.

"Why should he want to come back to Vienna and get himself arrested?"

"Because he haunts me," she said. "I'll never get rid of him."

"Are you sure it's him?"

"Don't tell Pappa," she said.

I recited a poem Fritz had written for Mother.

> To you, oh Juno.
> Scorched by scorn of your unearthly eyes
> I make my sacrificial offering.
> And lay my tribute in the vale of darkness
> at your marble feet.
> To you, oh Juno.

Mother grabbed my arm. "You really remember everything. Don't you."

The sacrificial offering had not been the stolen doll, it had been Eugene Romberg, chained to a truck in the amethyst mine.

And in the end it could have been Mother. The supreme sacrifice when Fritz had decided to blow himself up with the museum paintings and his goddess, and die with art and beauty. "They'd never let him out of jail. Can't be him."

We walked on in silence. Wind stirred up dust at the bombed university. Mother had to take grit out of my eye. She had come home with English "vanishing cream." For the first time she was trying to hide her amusing orange freckles. She did not succeed. I could smell the cream and the verbena perfume.

"How about the English doctor. Is he in love with you too?" I startled her. There seemed to be an unspoken rule not to ask her any questions.

"That is quite different. Janicek never loved me. He molests. Threatens. The doctor is a great gentleman. He cares for me. That's why he helped me to come home. And he has not tried to get in touch with me."

I thought I heard a note of disappointment.

"Did you ever get the doctor to break into your room?"

She stopped. Her mood changed. Eyes brimmed over and she shrieked with laughter, doubled over, she gurgled, giggled. I had to laugh with her. I had broken the ring of silence that surrounded her. We were wild with relief and forgot everything. Men came away from the burned out Burgtheater carrying a half nude statue of a woman towards a cart. This made me laugh all over again.

One of them gave me a nasty look. "What's there to laugh about?"

I made a game of looking at all the naked statues. Nudes were definitely the most favored decoration. Bombs and bullets had chipped a plump buttock here, a big stone breast, or blasted away sculptured drapery. I saw enough mutilated erotica to excite invading foreign soldiers from Napoleon to doomsday. When I stepped into a cobbled courtyard to look at a nymph on a fountain, a young man in a belted trench coat came though the doorway and we exchanged a smile. Mother remarked how few young men were left in Vienna. Those who had survived the war were either in Russian prisoner of war camps, or Nazis in jail.

"You are so interested in statues and houses," Mother said. "You must have inherited an artistic streak from the English Meinert aunt."

On a corner plaque a knightly saint was killing a dragon. A tall woman in a short, fuzzy coat came wriggling towards the young man, grabbed him around the waist. I noted how the two dragon heads had her lusty female smile, dimples, and her fiesty expression. Sparrows were pecking around on dust heaps in the medieval, narrow streets of the inner city. Our new shoes tapped along worn cobblestones. A window was open at an old palais, two thin, long arms threw bedding out to air on the sill. Inside someone was playing a violin. Sounds were trapped in the narrow streets of old Vienna, so was silence, an expectancy lingered here from century to century.

We leaned in the doorway and listened. A jeep came along, flags dancing on the hood. Military police, soldiers of the four allies. All but the British in steel helmets. They slowed down; heard the violin and stopped. The thin arms fluffed a plump pillow. It snowed a few feathers. And the sun slanted down like a stage light touching a stucco naiad here, and a rose bud there. The soldiers were young and solemn.

Hitler had been their age when he had stomped through these streets. On an autumn day like this, he might have heard music drifting towards him and felt the stab, the blatant sweetness of a Schubert melody. Vienna will haunt young strangers, taunt them. No one could escape our heritage, the invincible ardor of generations who had worked to make life prettier.

Even the Russian guards marching back and forth at the Hofburg, the Hapsburg winter palace, now had a pallid subdued look. Mother never asked how Grandmama and I survived deep down under the ground, or how we made our way to the Meinert-Hof. She had become accustomed during her years as a pampered invalid to carefully avoid food and talk that might not agree with her.

"When we were passing here after the invasion, the Russians were looking for Schmiedler. They had caught him, but he escaped."

"They won't catch him," she said.

"Did you ever actually see him?" I asked.

"I don't really know," she said. "He is like a clown. In fact he was a clown, or a something like that at one time. Hitler had a weakness for actors. Schmiedler was useful as a double."

"Did you visit the Hitler Guesthouse in Salzburg when I was in Vienna last year?"

"Who gave you that idea?" She seemed to be prepared as if she had been asked this question before.

"Bertl asked me," I said.

We came to a bomb crater covered by a plank and she gracefully balanced over it holding her arms out to the side like a child walking around the rim of a sandbox. "Your father thinks he came and asked questions for the Americans. That isn't so. Bertl always had to know everything I did or didn't do, even when he was three years old. He hasn't changed."

"I think he has," Once I started talking about him I couldn't stop. I went on and on hardly noticing where we were going. Suddenly we stood in front of the Roth house. Mother had led me to the hat salon.

"Vienna isn't Vienna without her," Mother said. "Everybody just had to hear what she had to say."

"But you never listened to her warnings."

"I wonder whether anyone ever did." There was a moment of silence for the days of the hats, coffee, the cakes, and predictions.

"Perhaps she's come back to Vienna. There is a geranium at the window."

"She wouldn't dare," Mother said and went to the door. The lock had been torn out. We went in. I had never been interested in the mural decoration on the right side of the entrance. Now I was drawn to the Leda and the Swan. You had to stand close to the faded fresco to see what was going on. Then it became clear that Leda held the beautiful bird captive between her strong plump thighs. The Greek God had made a mistake when he turned himself into a swan. The bird was depicted flapping its wings trying to escape. Leda, hips tilted, head thrown back, clasped the Swan's neck with powerful plump arms, taking advantage of the bird. Zeus, in this picture was raped.

Proud of my interpretations, dazzled by my own perceptions, I followed Mother to the first floor. "She used to have the stairs scrubbed every day," she said. "She'd be horrified." The old brass signs "School of Dance and Etiquette," then below it "Salon Roth," looked as though it had not been polished for years.

"Why did she leave up that old Kaiser-day dancing school sign, when she took over and turned it into the hat salon?" I asked.

"*Ach, ja,* etiquette and hats. She just liked the idea. Gloved ladies dancing at arms length."

But Hanna had also preserved the mural decoration of Leda taking advantage of the swan.

Mother rang. A key turned in the lock as if someone had been waiting for us behind the door. A chain rattled and a latch was pulled back. A short, strong man blocked the entrance. His face looked young for the mop of gray hair. "Friends of the houseowners?" he could not take his eyes off Mother. "They come here every day of the week." His accent was Hungarian. "Ladies, more ladies. They all wear hats. The janitor tells me they want to have her back to tell fortunes. Fortunes . . . isn't it funny. There are no fortunes these days, there isn't any future . . . " He concluded without the Hungarian sing-song.

I tried to get past him to look around the entrance where chauffeurs and husbands and lovers had been made to wait for ladies. He stepped right in front of me and said there was nothing to see. Allied investigators had already come and gone more than once. Drawers had been emptied, every closet searched. Even the oven in the kitchen. The house owner had been thick with Hitler. They had confiscated papers and photos. "A big one of you, Madam. That one they really liked because of the naked shoulders and the big doll that has your face."

His voice sounded quizzical, slightly muffled, and impudently familiar like a puppet's. Mother did not say anything and her violet blue eyes moved from side to side, like the mechanical eyes of the lost doll. The man talked fast, answering questions before they were asked. He told us he had been a groom for a Hungarian general and also his driver. During the war, he had once brought the General's wife and young daughter to Vienna to buy clothes. He remembered the house and hat Salon because it turned out that the owner's friend was related to the general. The Russians had taken the general and the Hungarian army prisoner, even their families and those priceless horses. He was lucky he got away, it was hard being a displaced person. He knew how to make saddles and he could sew. He had found the place empty and took good care of everything. If she was still among the living she'd thank him for saving a couple of old sewing machines. Gave him a chance to barter by turning old uniforms into civilian clothes. "See my suit? I made that from a Luftwaffe uniform and you'd never know it. I can make the prettiest little skirts out of old Nazi pants."

Mother simply turned around and started walking down the stairs. "It was a high honor," he called after us. Mother stopped. He bowed and scraped. We left in a hurry. Mother didn't believe his story. He had probably bribed and threatened his way into the house. Just like the squatters at the water castle. Now they all claimed they were connected with the Rombergs.

"How about General von Kortnai?"

"He is a Hungarian nationalist. Your grandmother considers him a traitor. Never had any time for him."

"How about the daughter?"

"She could have been his granddaughter, and she was pretty and quite spoiled. The chances are they'll be all right in the end. Hungarians can charm anyone. As for that man in Hanna's apartment, God knows who he really is," she said. "But he does have the legs of a rider."

We were near the Spanish riding school and she told me about the Lipizzaner at St. Martin. The English doctor, Sir Hugh, had taken her there. And thanks to the Americans the stud farm had been saved too. General Patton loved the white horses and he had given orders to get the brood-mares out of Czechoslovakia before the Russians arrived. And she had even met the general at St. Martin. "Sir Hugh wanted me to ride and stop feeling guilty for losing my child. And there I was cantering around and I didn't know that General Patton had arrived. I had borrowed man's breeches and a hat. He came across to me and asked how such a young fellow like me was left riding instead of fighting in the war. I pulled off the riding hat and he saw I was a woman. He laughed and said I sat in the saddle like a man. Called me a veritable Amazon."

"I don't think Amazons rode," I said.

"Who cares. He meant to pay me a compliment."

That very evening I went to the library room to look up Amazons in the encyclopedia. My parents and Frau Schwester and Agnes were discussing my new interest in art. The Meinert aunts had studied painting at the Academy. Father called them eccentric old maids, said I was way ahead of them. It was too soon to decide what I would like to do. Learning to get along with girls from varied backgrounds was more important than anything else. I was fortunately brilliant and interested in many things. "What are you reading?" he asked.

"History," I said, because he would not understand my interest in legendary women who had fought men.

On the following Saturday I saw two women overwhelm three men in the front garden of the water castle. The foreigners and bombed out ones over there often yelled at each other at the washing line, and fought over clothes. Now the two women chased the three men around the overgrown ornamental hedges. Females over there were in the majority and seemed to be in charge. I noticed this only a day or two later when I came home from school and saw three American army vehicles parked in the street in front of the big house. A group of about six women were facing the American soldiers at the gate.

Neighbors had come out into the avenue to see what was going on. The Grabeners, a couple who had always lived on our avenue, looked worried. They had sold their own little house during the war, and bought a large house from a Nazi who had taken it away from two old Jewish ladies. The owners had been arrested and vanished. The Grabeners asked Agnes and me whether we had heard, the Americans were going to take over all the Jewish houses that had been aryanized. The wife always wore white gloves. She and her daughter had been spectators when Jewish ladies were humiliated on our avenue. "I thought you might know something through your father," the husband said. "He plays chess with officers of the Allied High Command." His wife took his arm. "Is it true that American officials are moving into the Romberg house?"

I must have looked pleased.

"It's not funny, Fraulein," his jowls shook with indignation. He had lost a lot of weight. "They might take over the entire avenue for security reasons. And that means your house too. After all, your Herr Father aryanized the Romberg Industries. As for your Mama . . ." His wife pulled him away.

The water castle was requisitioned. Displaced persons had to move out. I watched from my window through a pair of opera glasses. It drizzled. Some of them wore two coats so that they didn't have to carry them. It was all the same now whether they were Austrian or displaced persons. They tried to help each other with packages, suitcases, carts and baby carriages.

When I had been seven years old, before the war, I had seen the Romberg servants leave the house heavily laden with loot.

The cook in Resi's fur, the French maid in cashmere. They must have told themselves that the Rombergs would prefer that they aryanize the big radio, the silver, Eli's African sparrows. Father had watched in a rage. There had been no way of stopping that procession. Now American military police at the gate carefully checked each bundle, each suitcase. I saw them lift an infant out of a carriage and uncover a painting under the mattress.

By looking through opera glasses I could admire the cheerful indifference of the young soldiers. They laughed, smoked, handed out a few cigarettes while they sorted and tagged items they held back. Men and women at the end of the line began unloading their spoils as they moved along and left behind a trail of lamps, vases, pillows, rolled up rugs. To my amusement, a pink chamber pot had been left sitting right next to the statue of beautiful, naked Icarus. Then I remembered the collection of historic chamber pots at the Hohentahlers and I suddenly felt sad.

The Hohentahler house had been ransacked. My life had been ransacked too. I was bored with my homework and in a bad mood when Father came home and told us he had been asked to go across the street to help identify paintings and furnishings and help make a list of missing art objects.

"How about people," I spoke up. "They should sort out Resi, Eli, the Hohentahlers first. Who cares about art except someone like Fritz Janicek."

Father pointed out to me that there were quite a few people who preferred not to be sorted out. By now the Americans had investigated him and considered him reliable and helpful. They had even consulted with him when it came to hiring a reliable man to take charge of the repairs and cleaning of the great house. Father had offered them Vlado. The wine harvest was over. Vlado had worked as an overseer and now he was restless. In Tito's army he had been an officer. Marshall Tito had kept the Russians out of Yugoslavia and there was more food across the border. Vlado was thinking of taking his family to Slovenia.

Father was doing every one a favor. The Amis got an amazingly honest man, a true anti-fascist. Americans admired Marshal Tito and his men for having won their own victory. They paid well. Vlado made himself agreeable with stories of his partisan days. He volunteered to hire his own staff of carpenters and cleaning women and promised there wouldn't be one Nazi among them. I guessed at once that most of them would be good communists. The Americans had no idea.

I came home from school one day and heard the cheerful sound of hammering and sawing. The south wind had sprung up, the sun shone. Mother was resting in her room. The Föhn wind always made her head ache.

"Who is going to move in?" I asked.

"No one knows," she said. "Guess what, Vlado has hired our maids Poldi and Lise, remember the twins?"

"Why can't they come back and work for us?"

"It would be hard to feed two extra people this winter. Agnes and Nurse will get along with Frau Boschke doing the laundry. I know you always like to help with floors. I don't mind cooking or dusting either."

The twins had promised to come and see me. I became restless hoping they would interrupt my homework and leaned out of the window. There were no jeeps, not even a guard, but soon American uniforms would be walking in and out over there. Mimi had seen Else Schmiedler arm in arm with an American officer. I could imagine her triumphant return to school and my desk. Everyone flocking around her. What if the Americans moved in and became our friends, my friends? I should really go over there and remind Vlado to repair the weather vane. Russian soldiers had used it as a target and by now the cupid dangled like bait from a fishing line. Squatters had actually saved our avenue from the marauding troops during the invasion. Some of them spoke Russian. No one remembered that. They had been tolerated without the sympathy we had once felt for the homeless cats left behind by Jewish families—Jewish cats—as everyone had called them. Neighbors had fed the cats. No one had helped the stray people. We had no more to give.

I had looked on when they all piled into trucks. I didn't care where they went. Nor did I want to think of their hardship now. I had to turn away from suffering like most everyone in Vienna. It made you feel guilty even if you hadn't really done anything. Hundreds and thousands had been murdered. The gigantic reproach we had to face turned us into monsters. Just like the legendary monster of medieval Vienna, who had turned to stone before a mirror, so did we, confronted with the atrocity of those mass graves, acres of skeletal bodies twisting like roots of felled trees on and on to infinity.

I just wanted to get away. The south wind made me dizzy with impatience and longing for the splendor I had known over there in the big house when I had been one of the chosen people for one endless winter of love and play with my first friends, Eli, Resi and Eugene Romberg. How could I give up those days when red dahlias had blazed in flower beds in the autumn, and champagne bottles were planted in the snow during carnival.

Then I imagined spring and summer and a water castle full of happy Americans. American music, American uniforms, pockets stuffed with chocolate and chewing gum. I imagined dancing over there. The mere thought of jitterbugging on the lawn sent me running downstairs. The twins wanted to see me. I crossed the street. The gate was unlocked. I breathed in the fragrance of rotting leaves. The sun felt warmer in between ornamental hedges. Birds forgot winter and trilled in disharmony. I felt transformed the moment I walked into this garden, excited and exciting, wide awake. The south wind tugged on my old skirt. Fallen leaves swirlled around their bush in little orange flames. I whistled "In the Mood," like Mimi. When she taught the jitterbug I stood by and watched. The others twirled around and kicked their legs.

Now I swung out from tree to tree and I danced away the memory of a Eugene Romberg in his Arab costume, or a Rudolf Hess on a garden bench, or men dressed up in Resi's costumes, prancing, then going to sleep forever; and the birds, flying out of the aviary, high up over the gate, free and unable to survive outside their cage.

I leapt and swirled from shade to sun as though I could dance away the memory of the dead, and bring back the living who might never return. "In the Mood" made me dance away from the old wicked world, to the new, where no one felt sad or guilty and everyone was rich. A land of milk and honey Resi had invented for Eli and me: America.

A woman was laughing somewhere behind the house. Another one shrieked and laughed like a witch. I followed the sound of voices, whirling and bounding about over the winter grass towards the shed and the rubbish heap.

I had come this way once or twice when I had played with Eli

Romberg. He would hold his nose and blink his long lashes, and say, "It stinks." I would say, "It stinks," too, because he was older, my first friend and he was Eli Romberg, the son of Eugene. Secretly the Meinert in me always enjoyed the smell of compost as I enjoyed the sound of wild banter that came from the open shed.

A man bellowed. "Just you wait, you two. You're in for it this time." Vlado.

"You and your Yugoslav procuto and bread. All that slivovic, to get the better of us." A coarse country voice. "We'll see about that! You red you, you *Russ,* we'll show you!" Poldi the leader of the twins. That marvelous monster trumpet voice I had learned to imitate in the days when I had spied on the education of the twins in the gardener's cottage. Vlado holding them on his lap and reading to them from Karl Marx. Trying to seduce them both.

Now I could hear the sound of panting and wrestling. My view was slightly obstructed by a broken gilded chair and the chinese screen Hanna Roth had brought with her when she and Eugene Romberg's mother, her convent school friend Frau Traude had finally moved into the big house towards the end of the war. Hanna could not rest until she had her way and moved Salon Roth into the water castle.

The dragons on the screen had been ripped. A toilet seat dangled from a bush and a man's brown shoe hung up by the laces had been shot through the toes. I stayed behind a chest of drawers. The shed had lost a wall and was open like a stage. Vlado and the twins wrestled and rolled rocking Eli's broken bed like a sinking vessel among dried weeds and broken gilded chairs.

The twins, no longer girls, but raw-boned tough country wenches, kept Vlado pinned down on his back. While they unbuttoned his partisan army shirt and pants. Brass nobs caught the sun and springs made music to the writhing, rocking, kissing, grabbing, pinching.

The twins used to imitate Mother and Grandmama, braiding their hair and winding it around their head. Now they had short, frizzy, yellow curls. Vlado was holding onto Lise. Poldi bit his hand. He yelled, pulled up her dirndl skirt. The twins never wore underpants and he dealt her bare bottom a resounding slap. Lise sat on Vlado and her sister followed her as usual. He couldn't move.

"Help, help," he yelled and pulled the string of Poldi's blouse, snapping at her dangling breasts. She swung a stout leg over his arm. "I can't breathe, move, move! Get off. Give a fellow a chance, you won't be sorry."

They raised themselves like riders taking a hurdle and Poldi fiddled with his pants. On a shrub one of our tiny brazen robins twittered tilting it's head. Vlado lifted his head, grinning from ear to ear. "Now look at what you've done. Not bad, eh!" I saw him grin and gloat over his own jack-in-the-box extension. Proud ownership was written all over him, but not for long. He was attacked by the twins, grabbed, stroked, pushed. They punched each other, wriggling on him for a short ride, unseating each other. Blue and red dirndl skirts engulfed his body, aprons fell over his face.

"Hungry women, wild women, ahh, hah, ah, hungry, starving for men." Vlado groaned. The robin piped it's tune to the male bravado of the thrust. The twins squealed in their hilarious contest to touch, to tease, to straddle—envelope, possess the magic wand, in delirious combat. I heard shrieks of brief shared victory: two women raping a man.

A day or two later in school, the timid new girl, Ursel, was cornered during recess, and questioned. Ursel was almost in tears. I forced my way into the circle and said: "Leave her alone. I am in the mood to tell you everything."

They hooted and laughed. Mimi forgot that I had thrown a book at her. "Go on then, talk, before the bell rings."

"A friend and I were attacked by a Mongolian Russ. We pushed him down on a broken bed." I said.

They gathered around me, forming a tight circle. There was no escape now. "How about his gun?"

"There were two of us. We took that away."

"Did you shoot him?" asked the book worm.

"We tore his clothes off. And all the watches he had stolen too. One of them diamond studded. I have it." (Eugene Romberg had sent it to me from Switzerland). "We held him down and took turns raping him before he had a chance to rape us."

"How did it happen, where? When?"

The questions inspired me. I could see it all happening while I talked, the white horse jumping over a great brass bed. The Mongolian officer. "Girls can fight. Girls can get the better of a man if they want to. He was a little fellow and didn't have a chance against two, strong, Austrian girls."

They asked about my friend. And I created a powerful Stopperl and certainly larger than life. An avenger, kneeling on a Russian belly, unbuttoning a Russian fly. My audience clapped and jeered, hooted.

"If they force themselves on us," I said. "We'll do it to them until they'll cry for help and no one will hear them because we'll be laughing so hard." Invaders lay vanquished, degraded, taken by force against their will, violated by virgins. The kind of death men dream of.

Mimi gave me a slanting glance. "How come you're so different. You raped a Russian, a real Mongol, took off his pants and had such sport?"

"I'm different," I now said with disgusting arrogance. "A Meinert von Dornbach Falkenburg. The Falkenburgs already fought the Turks. We're fearless and mad. It's in the blood." I fixed my eyes on them one by one with a brassy Otto von Falkenburg stare.

Nothing helps fiction more than a good piece of evidence. I reached into my pocket and produced the three Russian uniform buttons I had picked up in Grandmama's courtyard. Girls gasped. Mimi handed me two sticks of chewing gum. They wanted to believe me. I had created myth from the erotica of terror that possessed us all.

Barbarian men had come after us and they kept coming into the secret hiding places—invading the mirrored halls of our mind. We were all deflowered virgins, whether in fact or fantasy. Children of war wallowing in terror to overcome it—girls stood appalled and appeased until the bell rang.

# EIGHT

# *Letter to a King*

TRY TO TELL THE TRUTH, talk about yourself and it sounds like a fabrication. Say what everyone wants to hear— anything at all—loud enough, pepper it with slogans and you have a following like Hitler's.

I enjoyed my triumph in school, but not for long. What next? My instincts told me not to stay around for an encore. I became uneasy and fled to my grandmother who always spoke the truth, deceived herself, and pleasantly involved me in her self deceptions. I found her writing a letter to the King of England. I was glad to help her.

*High Honored Serene Majesty:*

*I take the great liberty to appeal directly to your Royal Highness, king of the British Commonwealth, greatest ruling monarch on earth. In the name of Austrian loyalists whose families have served the crown throughout the centuries of Hapsburg magnificence, I turn to you in the most fervent hope that you may save Austria for the sake of all civilized mankind and help bring Prince Otto von Hapsburg back to us as our Kaiser.*

I was copying this, the first paragraph of the final version of our letter to King George into my blue notebook right next to the notes on the rapacious city, when my grandmother came and sat down beside me at the escritoire. I turned the page and started over again.

"Quite right," she quickly said. "A nice clean page shows one what it will look like." She had lacked privacy in her convent days and she respected mine. We had come to consider each other excessively during our last stand, those cellar days. I wanted her to remain old and innocent and she wanted me to stay young and innocent.

One glimpse at my rape notes must have been enough to make her get up and busy herself with the spirit burner. Gas for cooking was available only three times a day. She put the kettle on for tea. Then she stoked the pink porcelain stove and the glow from the fire lit up her face. She had regained some of her weight. A seamstress had turned an old, gray wool dress and restyled it with folds and delightful ruffles.

In this rosy sunrise room Mozart had played for the Empress Maria Theresa and her von Dornbach lady in waiting; the piano he had used was back in it's corner. A leg had come off and stacks of old double eagle pamphlets were used to prop it up. Grandmama said she finally had to have the printing press dismantled.

The moment I saw the pamphlets, I remembered the old Austrian double eagle pamphlets snowing down during Hitler's big jubilant hate-parade. A message without words when few wanted to be reminded that we had lost our country. And Frau Boschke had seen one of the double eagle pamphlets land and stick to the beard of a gigantic ugly papier-mâché Dr. Freud on one of the floats of huge monster Jews. I never found out who had risked his life dropping the pamphlets from a glider, but I thought back fondly and a little sadly to that day when I had made a game of catching pamphlets, waving to the glider as it vanished into clouds, yelling "God Save Our Kaiser." I was no longer able to cheer for one thing, then another, and I suddenly felt old, jaded, nostalgic for my younger self. Especially when a certain Tante Hermine came hobbling up the stairs and said, "You were simply adorable in the Café Wiesner days. So many awful things were going on, just seeing you gave us hope."

I had known my grandmother's tilted friends who had worked in the Austrian resistance, as aunts and uncles, never their full names, just in case the gestapo quizzed me and I gave them away. I didn't want to be careful anymore. General Clark would not allow the Russians to take over Austria. I had the impression conspiracy had become a habit with the Countess Reyna and her friends and they continued their networks of communication in the Russian zone as a kind of hobby.

Tante Hermine was half English and she had come to take a look at our letter. When she spotted an error she licked a little stub of a pencil and corrected it.

She had become old and crippled. My grandmother blamed Hitler for her progressive disease. An explosion had deafened Tante Hermine in one ear, the other one was covered by the kind of pert little dark blue hat Hanna Roth would have designed. Grandmama had to shout to make herself heard. They talked about a tomb my grandmother was buying. The shortage of graves was as serious as the housing shortage.

I said, "You're not going to die. You don't need a grave."

"I don't want to be buried in Falkenburg," grandmother said. "It's in the Russian zone. No one would ever come to see me."

My grandmother believed what she was saying. But I knew she didn't want to be buried near *him,* Count Otto von Falkenburg, whom she had never called Father. I suddenly felt cold and I went to lean against the tile stove. And I shuddered as though the aristocratic Tente Hermine had helped my grandmother buy not a tomb, but death.

I wished Tante Hermine would go home. When she picked up my blue notebook and started leafing through it, I simply took it away.

"You're just like your grandmother, not just in looks. You're clever. Original. By the way the tomb we were talking about was built for a beautiful, original young poet. He was never put to rest there. The family kept it as a kind of monument. Now they need the money."

"His body vanished after he died so suddenly. I know that tomb." I spoke up. "Looks like a greek temple. Hundreds of girls and women were in love with the poet. Some of them killed themselves they loved him so much. And they kept going to the empty tomb. Foolish, bored girls," I was quoting Fritz Janicek the professor word by word and I sounded like him.

"You seem to know more than anyone else." My grandmother's tone should have told me to stop talking.

"What is she saying?" Tante Hermine shouted.

I raised my voice. "The girls didn't steal his body. Doctors did." (I left out the Fritz Janicek "Jew-quacks"). "To study his wonderful brain, and they chopped up his body to find out what was wrong with him."

Tante Hermine did get the gist of it. "You don't worry about earthly remains," she said. "He left a rich legacy. In fact he dedicated one of his books to someone in your family. Did you know that?"

"Great Aunt Christina. Mother has the book and she reads it all the time. Was the poet in love with Christina von Kortnai?"

"She was an inspiration to artists," Tante Hermine said.

Unfortunately Christina had inspired a spurned lover, the sculptor Antonini to create Puppe. Before I had a chance to bring him into the conversation, Grandmother quickly refilled cups and told us that an American officer had come to visit her.

"So you sold him the precious copy of the 'Pragmatic Sanction'!" her deaf friend said in her deep, loud voice.

"I had to sell the paper to get through the winter without being a burden to my son-in-law. I need the comfort of a nice, warm room like this, especially when my grandchild is here and visitors come in from the cold."

I had a vague memory of a piece of vellum, decorated with a pattern of scrolls on the left side, beautifully copied by Stephanie von Dornbach in old courtly script, and hard to read. It was the copy of the document drawn up by a secret council and Kaiser Karl the Sixth, creating a new law to assure the throne for his daughter. Maria Theresa became the only female Hapsburg ruler. And all the time, even when she had to fight wars to defend her throne, she kept having babies.

"Americans can buy anything," Tante Hermine shouted.

I liked the way she slurped her tea and pushed the piece of toast into her mouth in one piece. She had the manners of a village lout. "At least they didn't buy the piano," she got up, took off the dashing old hat, hobbled over to the piano and began to improvise as she always did in the back room of the Café Wiesner. Music and thick velvet curtains had screened the conspirators from the main room. It had been safer for them to communicate in a public place. And I had wandered around, danced, or skipped out through the curtains to the front of the café. Herr Wiesner, the owner and I would go and look at his stained glass window. During the war it was boarded up on the outside, but he would pick me up and let me turn on the light. The stained-glass paradise would come to life in a mosaic of colors. A fat Eve with big breasts, knees like edam cheese, and a thin Adam in a Garden of Eden. The question Herr Wiesner asked me was as predictable as Tante Hermine's musical improvisation. "What do you think the snake is saying?"

The snake, winding around the apple tree, had a cunning girlish face, and was my favorite. "It says: Here Eve, I'll give you an apple if you put some clothes on. You're too fat to go naked." Herr Wiesner never got tired of my answer and always roared with laughter. And any gestapo informer posted in the Café would be diverted by the game of predictable question and answers. Herr Wiesner, Grandmama had told me did survive the war. I wondered about the Garden of Eden.

I sat down beside Tante Hermine and listened to her favorite melody. five or six notes that sounded like a persistant question, followed by a rollicking melodic response. My grandmother talked against the music. "It will do more good in America than hanging on my wall," she said. "We want to arouse interest in Hapsburg greatness."

Tante Hermine did not hear her. A faraway look was in her eyes. "I kept humming this tune to myself during the gestapo interrogation," she said. I suddenly understood the matter of fact sale of a tomb. A natural death, without torture, to be put to rest in your own grave, to a member of the Austrian resistance, was a blessing and a luxury.

Letter delivery had just been restored, but there was censorship. Austria had to pay for the censors as part of the restitution, and also thirty percent of the cost of the occupation forces, that winter of uneasy peace. The letter to the king, my grandmother said, had found it's way into a diplomatic puoch. The Countess and I waited for some response and I felt myself drawn to the little palace. "Has the American officer come back?" I always asked. But it was the Rittmeister who came back to Vienna.

The first time I saw the Rittmeister was on a rainy Wednesday. I didn't know he was in the house. I went upstairs, and found him asleep in Grandmother's arms. It amused me to see that the unframed Kaiser picture had been turned around on the shelf to face the wall. I stole away, returned an hour later and rang the bell.

My grandmother warned me at once, to keep quiet about the American. The Rittmeister would not like the sale of the old document. She was terribly worried that I might say something to upset him, but I talked far less when he was with her. Their happiness overwhelmed me. I drank it in and became subdued.

During the cellar days Grandmother had confided in me. I knew she had made love to a famous musician, got engaged right after that to the enchanting Karl von Dornbach; and I understood that Rittmeister was the greatest of her three loves. I also knew that my fickle, carousing von Dornbach grandfather had returned to Vienna and spent the last night with her before he went to fight in the First World War. In the morning, he had made her promise never to remarry if he didn't come back. He had been reported missing nine months later, when my mother was born. I was not yet able to understand that the promise Grandmama kept—like Mother's locked door and furniture pushed against it, like aunt Kristina's travels, and that devilish doll—was an obstacle with all the excitement of impossibility and constantly renewed passion.

Friday afternoon I rode into town on my bicycle; Father close behind me. We took back roads in the first district to avoid military vehicles. He was in a hurry, had to attend a meeting. I let myself into the little palace and found my grandmother and her Rudi sitting on the bench at the south wall enjoying the winter sun. She in a sable-lined cloak she had worn during our last stand. He in an American officer's coat. Under it I recognized an old Kaiserly uniform Grandmother had kept in her own closet after his arrest. All his old medals had been safely hidden with her jewelry.

They did not see me at once. Hands in thick winter gloves lay entwined on the travel rug they shared. I saw them silently intent like enamored travelers who share a journey but do not have the same destination. The wall behind them was patterned with bullet marks. A pigeon cooed on the roof and I was glad it had not been eaten. The Rittmeister had brought a pink, silk scarf from Italy and Grandmama wore it all the time in a rakish, silly bow that didn't really suit her.

They welcomed me with praise and kisses, moved and took me in the middle, covered me with the warm blanket. "If that famous letter had reached England," he said in the gruff voice he had acquired in the concentration camp. "You must remem-

ber that such letters must be snowing in on the king every single
day from every corner of Europe. You should have made it short,
to the point: "Dear King George, how about letting our Otto von
Hapsburg come back to Vienna and take over as president? He
is young, in good health, no crook, bears no grudges, owes no
favors." The Rittmeister kept clearing his throat. "Frankly I don't
think the prince—Doctor Hapsburg as the Americans call him—
would like to reign over connivers, opportunists, and criminals.
That's what hunger does to people who love to eat and live well.
If it weren't for the Countess, I would head right back to the
concentration camp, starve, or eat what hogs wouldn't touch. At
least I had the company of honorable Austrians. *Jawohl,* I had
friends fit for a king. We had wonderful conversations. You really
came to the point, said what you meant, just in case . . ."

My grandmother touched his arm and her hand trembled.
"You should have stayed in sunny Italy for the winter, Rudi,
with some of those fine people."

"Not without you," he said gruffly.

I sat between them safe and warm. We forgot winter was
coming. He tried to smile without opening his mouth. Concentration camp guards had knocked out some of his front teeth.
And he consistently kept his countess on his left side. On the
right side a scar ran from the ear to the corner of his right eye.
A final insult.

He and a group of elite prisoners had been taken out of Dachau
concentration camp and moved to Tyrol. There had been a British secret service man, a German general, a young Russian, a
French minister. Also a clown from circus Krone who had been
spared because he spoke many languages. Allied armies were
approaching. One of the gestapo men had shown the Rittmeister
Himmlers orders to execute the prisoners.

The Rittmeister didn't remember he had told me the story on
Wednesday, and I never got tired of it. "The prince was the one
who really saved you," I said.

"Salvaged me," the Rittmeister said. "Like rusty scrap iron."

A fellow prisoner, that German general, had had the courage
to get in touch with the local German army command and they
agreed to replace the gestapo guards with army personnel. Prince
von Lutensteg, a very humane young German officer was put in
charge. The Prince had been working in the resistance since the

beginning of the war. "Such stamina in that young Hun. Unbelievable. Just before the Americans arrived, he sat down and talked with the gestapo, trying to make them see that it was wrong to just follow orders, or to allow orders to be carried out if they involved murder. I don't know whether it was the Tyroler red wine those men had been drinking or his persuasion, or the approaching Americans. They repented. He is south German, you know, a Catholic and he marched them right off to Mass and confession.

"As soon as the Americans arrived he talked to them about forgiveness. The other Nazi prisoners, especially the German general did not like it a bit. But the Amis were decent as can be, they listened. The prince spoke beautiful English."

This reminded me of a certain English governess Arnold von Lutensteg had loved so much when he was my age. "And he talked about me. Didn't he? He told you he saw me in Vienna?"

The Rittmeister growled. "Imagine, here I barely missed being butchered. The prince comes and pats me on the shoulder and asks me whether I knew a young girl named Reyna von Meinert. He had seen that charming child in Vienna. She was staying with her grandmother. I tell you, when I heard that you two were in Vienna during the Russian invasion, my legs just gave way. He was sorry when he saw what he had done to me and wished he had kept his mouth shut."

"He didn't mean to worry you. I think he's wonderrfalll," I added in my school English.

The Rittmeister liked to hear me speak English. "Your prince is a brilliant fool," he tilted my chin and looked for a young countess in my bewildered face.

"What do you mean?" I asked.

"First the gestapo, then an investigator in the Wehrmacht, had to pose as a villain while he behaved like a saint. It's a wonder he survived. I guess he is smart and he can hide his feelings. He never gave himself away. That's how he saved us. No one could tell he was on our side when he stayed our executions."

"I can tell how he feels," I said. "I knew he didn't really want to find Eli Romberg that time when he came to the farm to look for him."

"Eli Romberg?" the Rittmeister raised his bushy, white eyebrows. "That name sounds familiar, but my memory isn't what it used to be. Another young man, I suppose. Just listen to that child. As big a flirt as you ever were, Reynerl," he said to Grandmama.

"There aren't any young men left to flirt with," I said. "The only one who came back was Bertl and he didn't stay."

The Rittmeister gave us a hug and said with the present shortage of men even he had a chance. We sat in a huddle under the warm blanket beset with memories we could not share. They basked in this moment of warm peace. I remained restless, retaining the momentum of danger the way one feels motion of the Danube when one gets off a ship.

"It's all one big masquerade," I said in memory of Eugene Romberg.

Influenza had broken out. The church was empty when thieves tore two gilded angels from the alter. Until they vanished, I hadn't been too interested in the angels below God's throne of cloud, but I remember the day I first missed them because our old friend the court doctor had been hurt and Mother had him brought to our house in an ambulance.

Sometimes I tied Krampus inside the gate and went into the empty church. Not to pray or ask for small or big favors. Using Saints as go-betweens, bartering with prayers, would have made me feel like a black marketeer. I came to church attracted by the image of God seated on a throne of cloud because the unsmiling kind, country face with the pink cheeks reminded me so much of Pfarrer Kronz, the scholarly country priest who had been my tutor.

During my five years on our mountain farm while the war went on, he had helped me to cope with my own wild ideas and also Hitler's. When the Fuehrer had screamed on the radio, about invading the British Isles my teacher had read to me from William Shakespeare. By the time Hitler decided to follow Napoleon into Russia, I was being introduced to Leo Tolstoy's *War and Peace*. The snows of Russia and snow on the mountain farm became one when I leaned against the warm tile stove half asleep. Words went on and on relentless as war and winter, great writers held forth to me like garrulous grandfathers in the priest's nasal voice.

Our old friend the court doctor spoke with an aristocratic nasal

twang. Like my tutor, the Herr Doctor knew no compromise. He
had faith, but mostly in his own remedy: maltaline. A codliver
oil malty vitamin tonic I had swallowed as a young child to please
him although it made me gag. And he had been feeding the last
few jars of this sticky sweet remedy to two young concentration
camp survivors who had moved into his apartment house. When
the jars were empty, the poor fellows—offsprings of tyranny, as
he called them—got drunk on vodka because they lacked the B
vitamins contained in maltaline. They came home at dawn, got
into a fight on the landing. The court doctor woke up, tried to
make peace, and was pushed down the stairs by Frank, his
favorite.

Telephone lines had been destroyed, Russians had shot phones
or took receivers as souveniers. We alone among the doctor's
friends and relatives had a working telephone. The hospital had
called. Mother had the doctor brought to our house, although we
had our own emergency. Agnes had the flu and Frau Schwester
tended to her day and night.

I found the Herr Doctor in the kitchen with Mother, who was
wrapped up in one of Agnes's big white aprons. The kitchen reeked
of precious, melted butter and spiced wine. She had put a pillow
into the easy chair near the stove for the court doctor and put
his feet into Father's big felt slippers. The doctor's dark blue
velvet robe had been cut to accommodate a huge cast for a broken left arm and a bandage for some cracked ribs. The bandage
on his head looked like a turban and gave him dash rather than
the pathos of misadventure. The physical abuse he had suffered
that day seemed to have injured him only half as much as the
insult of having his famous Maltaline turned down by the allied
high command, when he had applied for emergency aid.

Mother listened to him and licked the egg beater with a rosy
look of satisfaction. Her Ferdl would put in a good word for the
Herr Doctor, she said. Winter sun shone through the basement
window playing over her young face and bright hair. There was
a dab of egg white on her freckled nose. Egg shells lay piled up
on the counter. I was amazed and aghast. We had not seen eggs
for month. Father had brought us ten, worth their weight in gold.

She was about to stick one of those mountains of egg fluff,
*Salzburger Nockerln,* into the oven. I had been taught to stand
still at this sacred moment from my early years. "Don't tell Papa!"

she said as though we were still playing our old kitchen game on the maids day off. Father never knew that she loved to cook. And she believed in *Salzburger Nockerln* as the doctor believed in maltaline. I remembered it as her magic cure for sadness, anger, or migrain headaches, and above all as an antidote to the Föehn, the south wind that comes over the Alps and makes people in Vienna nervous. I had loved all that beating of egg white in copper bowls and sharing Mother's secret almost as much as the eating of that cloudy ambrosia. Our conspiracy had been beneficial to me on those kitchen days when I had Mother all to myself.

In her reckless eagerness to prepare this sweet remedy for the Herr Doctor, she had quite forgotten the rationed gas. I reminded her and she rushed upstairs to phone the gas company, told an official about the court doctor and begged for an extra eight minutes. The man knew the doctor and had been his patient. "What good things are you cooking for him?" he asked. She didn't dare tell, but she got her eight minutes.

In the meantime it was my turn to cheer the dear doctor up. Maltaline, I told him, had saved my grandmother when she was so ill during the cellar days of the Russian invasion. He beamed and praised her foresight in saving some of his tonic and taking it into hiding. Actually she had forgotten the sample box he had once given to her until she tripped over it. This was my secret. We had to comfort each other with half truths.

I wanted the doctor to be as happy as my memory of him. He was less round and pink. The pince-nez which used to drop into a wine glass or soup was missing. His wavy gray hair had turned white, and receded from the temples, leaving a becoming peak. I could imagine him as a handsome young doctor treating ladies with affection respect, maltaline and half truth—like his title court doctor.

He had actually attended the late Empress Elizabeth, but only once when she had fainted in the proscenium box. He happened to be at the opera with his doctor's bag, and was able to bring her serene majesty around with maltaline. After that his friends called him court doctor. Affectionate jokes become a habit in Vienna. The title had made him fashionable among aristocratic ladies and they thrived on maltaline.

By the time I came along the court doctor had really believed he could have cured the empress, who had starved to keep her

figure and exercized like a circus person. Had she continued with
maltaline she would have calmed down, stopped traveling around
and stayed in Vienna beside the emperor and would never have
been assassinated. Everything might have been different. The
empire might have been saved . . .

At bitter times in Vienna, sweet remedies worked wonders.
The doctor said Mother's soufflé was better than morphine. The
wine helped too. He drank to us both, smiled and felt wonderful.
No more pain. After the third glass, he talked about Frank, his
assailant whom he had come to love like a son. And I could see
the hurt in his face.

He said he had been busy with patients who had the flu and
neglected the two boys or none of this would have happened.
Frank was not yet well. The poor boy had been thin and starved
in the spring when he had come down with dysentery. The doctor had to go and scrounge from the Russians. In exchange for
his pince-nez they had handed him bread and a piece of meat.

"I thought I was going to loose that boy. Then, one night he
took my hand and called me Papa. I do believe this feeling that
he had a father pulled him through. We got to know each other
well. Last night when I heard him shout on the landing, I naturally got up and tried to stop that fight. They were going at each
other like wild street boys. Cursing, shouting, accusing each other
of saving their own skin and sending a fellow prisoner to be used
in some medical experiment. I told them to stop it at once. They
had been hurt so much already. And to stop worrying. There was
a good chance the camp doctor was only trying out a new vac-
cine."

We knew all about murderous camp doctors from the Rittmeister. Mother gave me a warning glance, which reminded me
of the lost doll, and she quickly refilled the doctor's plate.

He sipped wine and went on to tell us how poor Frank, in his
intoxicated state, misunderstood and got the idea that he, the
court doctor, had something to do with vaccines and concentration camps. "Just imagine, he accused me of doctoring him out
of self interest so that he would testify on my behalf and clear
me. I tried to remind him that I never was a Nazi and that I had
worked in the children's hospital during the war. Poor Frank
really went beserk and started yelling for his baby, asking me
what I had done to his infant son. Then he hit me over the head

with a knuckle duster he always carries, and booted me down the stairs. When I came around I was already in the emergency ward. I must try and get back home soon. I know how awful the two fellows must feel."

Neighbors had called the police. The doctor told the inspector not to press any charges. It was all an accident. The entire apartment house was in an uproar. "I must go home now. After this feast I will be just fine. And you see, the two young fellows have no one in the world, just each other, but they know they can always count on me. I must see what I can do. Perhaps I can trace that little son of Frank's . . ."

I listened to the slightly nasal voice and looked out of the window where the wind brutalized bare trees. And I could feel his hurt inside my belly. Just like dysentery, hatred and accusations were passed on among us, the survivors of the Hitler war. I could not help my fury against the victims who had victimized our dear old friend.

The doctor developed a temperature and my parents made him stay on with us. I was at school when Frank arrived at our house with a bag of apples. The doctor was all smiles when I came home. He had taken his bandage off as soon as he had heard his dear Frank's voice.

"Bad enough for him to see my plaster cast," he said. I am so glad he came. He sat down right next to me, took my hand and persuaded me to eat apples. You see, when he was released from concentration camp he was so weak and starved he couldn't eat anything. Then he saw someone with an apple. He asked for it, and after that he started to eat and gain strength. He has great faith in apples. Your Mama stewed so many apples. You must have some."

His mood was festive. We ate and drank. When Mother bent over to refill his dish the doctor contemplated her bosom politely. "Apples are a marvelous tonic," he said in a professional voice which hid his enthusiasm. "You must have eaten a lot of apples when you were growing up. *Meine Liebe,* you are blooming." He drank a little toast with the new wine. "The forbidden fruit. Pure magic. Just think of it, one bite and the first girl in the world turned into an oppulent woman," he said to me. "Mother of mankind."

I remembered Stopperl—my friend in the mountains had once

vouched that apples gave Eve breasts and made her own mother, *die Sennerin,* as big as the cows she tended and alluring to men. When the doctor admired me and said I was all legs, his meaning became clear. I filled my dish with stewed apples. Later I asked my well-formed grandmother whether she had eaten lots of apples at the convent. She told me she did. There had been an orchard nearby. In school I studied Miss Pnevski, as she liked to be called. Then, on Sunday afternoon, I studied the plaque portraying the empress Maria Theresa, definitely an apple eater too. I noticed the smug, smooth lips of all the women who ate apples, bloomed, pleased men and knew female pleasure.

Be it the Kaiserin who had lived two hundred years ago, or my mother, they all looked pleased with themselves, and this, I could not help but conclude, had something to do with the size of their bosoms. Mine remained totally unimpressive. Some girls stuffed handkerchiefs into their bras. I didn't own one. I would never need one. I was indeed all legs. We had plenty of apples from our own fruit trees and I started eating the forbidden fruit all day long.

Frau Schwester had assured me apples were binding. When I experienced side-effects of a violent nature, I was certain I had dysentery. I did not go to school, ate six apples instead of thirteen. All morning I felt restless. I wandered around the house in an old winter dirndl. The hem had been let out, and then lengthened with a border of embroidered braid. It was too short again. My knees were showing. I kept looking into mirrors hoping the bodice was getting too tight.

The gardens on our avenue were turning white. At the bomb site of the foot doctor's house stacked bricks looked like a pile of giant sugar lumps until the wind swept the snow away. No matter how much it would snow this winter, ruins could never be completely covered in our windy city. Destruction remained half hidden, like secret guilt. In the sheltered garden of the water castle all was deserted and still. Among the maze of evergreen hedges stood statues in wigs of snow and ermine white tippets, intriguing, half-naked roccoco wantons—part of our outrageous assignation with the past—half masqued, expectant like shameless Hitler lovers.

Girls in school were saying: Hitler is not dead, ask your mother—Bodies in the Fuehrerbunker were stand-ins—prisoners from concentration camps—Hitler is right here in Vienna, in the American zone. Could Hitler have secretly returned to Vienna? He had given orders to defend the city at all costs. He had chosen the Berchtesgaden retreat close to the Austrian border and Vienna. I took up my blue notebook and pen, fingered through the pages. Then I stopped. My stomach took a somersault. I could not believe it. My final draft of the letter to King George had been neatly cut out. I saw it but I searched my schoolbag in a frenzy.

The other day I had left my notebook behind in the school desk. I had been in a state after Mimi had told me that all Nazi houses on my avenue would be requisitioned by the Amis. Someone really important was going to move into the Romberg mansion. The surroundings had to be denazified. I thought of the questions Berthold had asked, those rumors about Mother and Hitler. I had fled school, left Ursel, my new friend behind, forgot my books.

The next day I found everything where I had left it. No girl in my class would have cut the letter to the King of England and left my fascinating pages on the rapacious city. I got a queasy feeling in my belly all over again and not from the apple diet. I kept pacing around the house worrying about who could have cut out the letter.

In the living room I turned on the radio. The announcer was talking about *Winter-Hilfe,* winteraid. Where to go and how to register if you had lost everything. I wished I could go somewhere to register and get back my missing page. Krampus was barking in the garden. I watched him running through the new snow all the way down to the gate. An American army car pulled up at the Bockl villa. Krampus stuck his head through the wrought iron railings, barked and barked.

Two American officers and a sergeant got out, rang the bell and were admitted. They didn't stay long. I watched them come out in the snow. From the first I recognized them as a team. And like any good team, comic, or tragic, each one had his own act: the slender chocolate-thrower and hat-catcher. Then a short, powerful one; and then the fully armed little sergeant who wore spectacles. They got back into the car and drove to the next house. I watched them move along the avenue and the car tires created a reptilean pattern in the snow. Were they afraid to walk, or did they prefer driving?

I watched the car turn. Krampus was still barking. Frau Schwester came out and called him. He did not listen. The Amis had stopped at our gate. I barely had time to practice a *"gut morrrning,"* in front of the mirror and smear on some lipstick poor Nadica had left in my room. The bell rang twice. I quickly combed my hair over my left eye.

*"Nein, nein.* No child, no. Get back into the house. You will catch your death in the snow. *Lieber Himmel!* What next . . ."

I followed the nurse anyway. Stood on top of the steps and watched her march to the gate in her gray skirt and stiff white blouse, a heavy sweater draped over her shoulders. She was greeted with Hitler salutes and "Hell Hidler!" in one big bellow.

It didn't sound right, and yet, Frau Schwester staggered back.

"Aufmachen!" A German officer's voice.

She obeyed. They stomped through the gate. Snow drifted between us and clung to their uniforms like camouflage. They advanced like storm troopers. I stayed on top of the steps, arms akimbo, Father's stance. They came to a halt, eyed me. I forgot to show my teeth, forgot Rita Hayworth and stuffed snow into my mouth.

Arms shot up. A bellow: "Hell Hidler!" They waited. The short officer challenged me with his soft, brown eyes. I gave him my very best Hanna Roth Hitler salute and yelled "hell!" Then I thought of the English word hell and laughed spitting snow.

"This is no joke," the officer with the soft, brown eyes said in Berlin German. "Surprise tactics. Testing reflex reactions."

No Nazi would ever explain himself to justify what he had done. I liked the American frankness. "You speak good German," I said. He ignored this, but the sergeant looked over the rim of spectacles and grinned like a proper Ami boy.

Up to now they had all looked clean, friendly, shiny, new as their cars and jeeps. I could not imagine them shooting anyone, or fighting a battle. The Rittmeister and Grandmama had taken me to watch the monthly parade when the allied forces changed the supreme command of Vienna. "Put the Americans into old Austrian uniforms," the old monarchist had said, "you'd have the kaiser's army." The highest compliment.

The countess and her Rudi would have been shocked and disappointed had they seen the Amis stomp through the Meinert courtyard. Not a glance at the white slope. Sun glimmered between the tall, swaying pines. No stranger had ever entered without expressing surprise at the magnificent property behind the insignificent facade of the old family chicken farm.

The Americans walked into the house without wiping their boots. Snow on persian rugs, a wet trail on floors I had polished marked their progress from room to room. Frau Schwester followed them with a large, crystal ashtray, scanning the clean, healthy looking young men for signs of foreign disease.

They were searching the downstairs rooms, opening closets and wardrobe doors, even the toilets. Then the officer with the Berlin voice looked at his watch, glanced out of the window as though he were timing the snow flakes. Suddenly he turned and faced me.

"Reyna Meinert!" It sounded like an accusation. "You were a Hitler B.D.M. right!" His face relaxed into a smile; he was enjoying himself.

"Never," I said.

"Your former gardener gave us a sworn statement."

Father had already been interrogated by the American authorities. They had asked him to raise his right hand and swear. Fritz Janicek would perform this ritual with flourish. He had been a language and art teacher and spoke good English. Men from the New World would take his word rather than listen to a girl in a short dirndl dress who shouted "Hell," to their "Hell Hidler." Girls in national dress had been photographed and filmed with the Fuehrer. American style clothing, even a mere scarf from the P.X. would have been conciliatory and agreeable.

Frau Schwester smoothed over her smooth, gray bun. Clutching the ashtray with both hands she spoke up in my defense. My early days with Eli Romberg. Bad experience with Nazis, especially Janicek. Life in the mountains. Refusal to have anything to do with Hitler youth. "Can you imagine the child was suspected of having chained Adolf Hitler up in a cave! That's mountain peasants for you." she said in her clipped, German voice.

Fritz Janicek's evidence would sound more plausible. I felt uncomfortable and this made me crave sweets. I picked up a gilded candy box Father had filled with American gum drops, remembered my manners, offered it around.

"American candy?" said the German interrogator.

The other officer smiled, took one. So did the sergeant. I popped a handful into my mouth.

"Who gave you the candy?" asked the Berlin voice.

"My father," I said.

Everybody knew Austrians had to buy food in the black market. The friendly officer said: "That's all right, *schon gut.*" In German. "We didn't come to track down candy."

"Did you come to take our house?" I asked.

"Never mind," said the German American officer and turned to Frau Schwester. "We have evidence that you were an illegal Nazi and welcomed Adolf Hitler personally. Then you moved to a house near Berchtesgaden to be close to Hitler's retreat. And your husband aryanized the Romberg Industries and lived with Frau Romberg in Vienna?"

Frau Schwester accompanied his barrage of words with her old clacking baby nurse sounds. "I'm not married," she cried out.

He cut her off. "Divorced then to please the Fuehrer."

I became hysterical and pretended I was having a coughing fit.

Frau Schwester turned red and puffed up her cheeks. "Unbelievable. In front of the child too."

"The child," he interrupted. "That's another matter."

He whipped a piece of paper out of his breast pocket and held it under my nose. "Your letter?"

I should have said, no longer, The final version of the letter to the king of England smelled of Ami tobacco and real coffee. "How on earth did you get this? Who cut it out of my notebook? It's my notebook. Did you all read it?"

I had left my blue notebook on the window table and he was staring at it. I opened the first page for him. Frogs in various uniforms and medieval costumes, crowns and top hats covered the page.

"That's real cute," said the other officer. "I think you have a lot of talent." English seemed to be the language for being friendly.

The stout officer snapped, "How about this Frau Meinert," in his Berlin voice and held my letter under Frau Schwester's nose.

She drew back. Letters to her were germ carriers. "I'm not Frau Meinert," she finally said.

At that moment Mother came running down from her room as though she had been listening for this cue. Her dress was

made of homespun, unbleached wool and clung to her figure. She
smelled of English verbena. "Good morning," she sounded
breathless, excited, her bosom heaved. Red curls danced, violet
eyes sparkled. "What a surprise," she said gaily and took them
by surprise. "I'm Frau von Meinert, Dornbach Falkenburg. I know,
I know, our titles and names are now mere ornaments, but we
like them . . ." Good, clear English, too. She carried the gilded
little doll's chair swinging it playfully on her way to the heated
living room, and drew them with her.

The family room of the old Meinert farm, a perfect square,
had somehow withstood several hundred years of Viennese decorating. White washed walls, country furniture for stout Meinerts and their plump wives had remained the same. There was
no crystal here, no silver, no gilt, no beads or tassels. Father had
bought a great sea-green Persian rug, a bargain, during the early
days of Hitler when Jewish property flooded the market. The
new slow burning stove was cunningly concealed behind ancient
green tile.

I caught a glimpse of myself beside Mother in a cloudy old
looking glass. Our height, long neck, pink cheeks made us the
same healthy and haughty breed. Our obvious well being made
us different and fascinatingly suspicious.

The friendly young officer took off his cap. I loved his neat
short curls. "What a modern room," he said.

"Not modern," the Berliner said. "Antique."

The little sergeant grinned and blew smoke rings in my
direction.

I sat in father's green chair. A daughter and as good as a son.
Mother settled down on the chaise where she had reclined listening to the great men under Hitler. "You might as well know
the truth. I was the only Nazi in this house. I had secretly, behind
my husband's back, joined the party long before Hitler took over."

The officers pulled their chairs close to her chaise. One on
each side. And the sergeant remained standing and smoking.
Frau Schwester kept vigil with her ashtray.

"You were near Berchtesgaden," said the Berliner. "Art objects
were brought to you and stored in the mine below your house by
your former gardener, Janicek."

Mother kept swinging and dangling the doll's chair while she
talked to them as if she had to protect herself against a swarm

of midges. "Janicek never gave me anything," she said. "In fact he probably stole my doll. The famous Antonelli doll, an heirloom."

I said: "Fritz Janicek shoot de toll," in my best Pnevski English. "But keeps de heat." The sergeant liked that.

Mother had not mentioned the doll since her return to Vienna and never touched any of the old doll's things anymore. Now, she went back to her old role. And she had the officers lean forward like boys at a story hour, watching like lip readers: Hitler's secret love talking of a magic doll. A court dwarf. Castles, fortune tellers. They took it all in and I doubt they could have repeated what she said in her clear, polite English.

She distracted them with her hand movements, the gilded chair; she smelled sweet. They stopped smoking and breathed her in, drank in all the wickedness of ornate lives they had hoped to expose and never saw in the defeated city overrun and dishonored, looted by the Bolshevicks. She reclined on the brown chaise, displaying her breasts, the knitted dress outlined her thighs, the light flared up in her hair, and in those eyes of a witch, and she dispelled the landscape of ruined buildings, ruined women, a country of murderers and losers, whores and beggars. She made them think of Strauss waltzes, kisses, old films: Hollywood Vienna at last.

The interrogator lost his tongue. He did not get around to accuse, catch her out. By her mere presence, her claim for restitution of an old doll, she accused. And demanded, not just to keep her home, but to get back Vienna, her town. In a foolish, uneasy gesture the Berliner held my letter to her. "Written by your daughter. Signed by your mother."

"Now you understand, don't you. It all happened when I came into the world. Nothing much was taken away from Germany after the First World War. Austria, not just the Hapsburg empire, Austria, the United Nations of Europe was torn apart by the peace treaty. Poor Austria, and poor Europe. My mother the Countess Reyna is right. The world lost Austria." With tears in her eyes she held up the little empty, gilded chair as though it were the empty Hapsburg throne.

I was awestruck. Impressed. Father, the chess master could not have done any better. Americans had come to ask for her home and she asked them for the Empire. The every day world of small and large battles, small and large schemes receded as I leaned back in the patriarchal green chair. The officers offered Mother cigarettes and she refused with as much enthusiasm as she had once refused Eugene Romberg's jewelry. She was lucky to be able to refuse. I felt grateful now that Father did not allow me to pick up chocolate from the street. I thought of him at work in the city to the very end of the war. I had looked down a little on the middle ground he had maintained and had admired my tutor, and the court doctor who did not have to compromise to protect others. For the first time I honored Father as a man who made the most of anything he had—a rare man. The chair smelled of his tobacco, French shaving lotion he had somehow obtained in the black market. Struggling, improvising, he fitted into any situation and always remained a Meinert man caring for his family, his land.

It was snowing heavily when I took the Americans to the gate. "The letter to King George was all my own idea," I lied. "I wrote it all. It was a game. The countess signed it for fun. My grandmother is a heroine, you know. And she would have had Adolf Hitler kidnapped and put away like Napoleon. The conspirators in Germany made a mess of everything and then she didn't have a chance . . ."

The friendly officer interrupted me and said: "We know about your grandmother." He admired the wrought iron work of the gate and asked me whether I played that beautiful grand piano. He loved a good piano. I told him mother played and asked him to come back to visit and play the piano.

"Nothing I'd like better," he smiled, his grave dark eyes reminded me of Hanna Roth. "My name is Mort. This is Lieutenant Kaufman . . ."

"I'm Tony," said the sergeant.

Lieutenant Kauffman had already walked through the gate. He turned. "I meant to ask your mother whether she is related to General von Kortnai."

He kept looking at his watch instead of me.

"Von Kortnai. Yes, I imagine so. My great grandmother was Anne Marie von Kortnai. I think I have heard him mentioned. Why do you ask?"

He ignored my questions. Something buzzed. I jumped. He

pulled back his sleeve. The sound came from his wrist watch.

"An alarm!" I thought of the Russian.

"The latest. *Ganz neu.* His father put it on the market," Mort volunteered this harmless information to put me at ease.

Lieutenant Kaufman did not like this. "Let's get to the point. Is it true that you lived with Russian officers in this house?"

*"Jawohl,"* I said. "I did. And there were some Yugoslav partisans, too."

Mort laughed. "Come off it Lieutenant," he said in German and made me feel he was on my side. "She doesn't know what you're getting at."

Lieutenant Kaufman surprised me. He came back and shook my hand and I could feel the power of a wrestler. "No hard feelings." He turned and looked at the water castle. "I understand the Rombergs were your friends at one time."

"Who told you? Fritz Janicek? Well they are our friends, but he hates them."

The German American officer acted as though he were fascinated by his watch. Later I understood that his sudden lack of interest was a clever trick and got me to answer questions he did not ask, as I went on and on about Fritz Janicek dressed up as a devil attacking Eugene Romberg and being knocked out with a milk bottle. And how he arrested Frau Romberg and tried to catch my friend Eli. In the end the German Ami surprised me with his wistful smile. He shook my hand and said he hoped I'd get to see young Romberg again. "It's hard to lose friends. I know. I had to get out of Berlin when I was a kid."

I shook hands with them all and said "Auf Wiedersehen." When they drove off through the snow I waved and Mort waved back. On the other side of the street the bearded doctor came in sight followed by women trotting behind him two by two. Eins, zwei, one two, one two. They had acquired American army pants. Mort waved to them. The women waved back. The doctor did not.

# NINE

# *Interlude by Candlelight*

WHERE DID ALL the candles come from? I saw the glow of flickering lights as soon as I walked up the chapel steps. Candles were scarce, so were people. Everyone had the flu, even the priest, Pfarrer Leiden. Where did all the people come from? Dark figures bundled up against the cold had formed a line inside the entrance of the little Meinert chapel. Any kind of line made you hopeful. Sometimes one cued up for an hour with bread stamps and the bakery sold out.

This was different. No one grumbled. Father must have opened the chapel for some kind of winter relief program. You always had to register. Under mufflers, furs and cloaks I recognized neighbors. The Bockls had reached the head of the line. A man sat at a folding table with a stack of forms. His face was hidden by the kind of styrian hat Father liked to wear. Herr Bockl handed him an envelope. The man dropped it into a briefcase and wrote something by the light of a candle stub. Several neighbors nodded solemnly to me as if we were all lining up for confession. The man at the table stamped a piece of paper. Herr Bockl took it eagerly. Frau Bockl stooped down to a box and came up with half a pink candle. She lit it from the table candle. They proceeded to the font, crossed themselves with holy water and marched to the altar.

I took my place at the end of the line out of habit. Frau Hillmar, an actress who played comedy parts at the theater in the
Josefstadt stood in front of me. Her black seal coat hung loose.
She had a Viennese cherub face, eyes of a frightened doe and
smelled of roses. Krampus liked to bark at her pet duck when I
walked past her little yellow house and she always came running out in terror. The duck was used to wandering around the
garden and anyone could climb over the railing, steal Miranda
and eat her.

Father said it was a shame, Vienna was full of lonely women.
Frau Hillmar had been married to a diplomat and she was a
widow. Her only son, that bearded young Nazi doctor, passed by
her house almost every day with his followers and never went to
see her.

The actress liked to chat with me when I passed by, now she
nodded to me, smiled and turned away. The line moved along
steadily to the bash, bang of the stamp hitting the ink cushion
and then a paper. I sidled up to her. "What are they handing
out?"

She buttoned the high collar of her fur as if she had to face a
storm. The man looked up from the table and grumbled something about watching the door. He saw me; doffed his hat exposing an old Hitler hairdo and mustache—definitely out of style
since we had lost the war. "Everything is no doubt in the best of
order with you, young Fraulein. You don't have to line up. Pick
up a candle from our donations and say a little prayer if you
like."

I couldn't see his face too well. The over-polite voice, the
intonation was familiar. I saw green plus fours under his loden
cloak. Everybody was so much thinner, it made them look taller.
"Herr Krummerer. Could that be you?"

"Shut your mouth!" said a voice that did not belong to Krummerer, the private detective whom father had hired to find
Mother's lost doll. Detective Krummerer had remained in Father's
pay later, under the Nazis, when he had been recruited into the
gestapo. But in occupied and chastized Vienna, there were those
who didn't want to hear their name, and had to hide their face.
I picked a candle stub decorated with a half-melted red heart.
Took my time lighting it and had a good look at the short printed
form on the table. It was already signed. The Detective filled in

Frau Hillmar's name. Then he stamped it April 1, 1938, with the official eagle and swastika. "Next!"

I was shoved aside and went to the altar in a state of confusion. The Bockls were kneeling. She looked up. "I don't think you should hang around here just now," she whispered.

"What's going on?"

"Your father knows all about it. Ask him." She put a finger to her pale lips and lowered her head.

The huge, green Christ on the cross above her had always scared me when Mother brought me here to pray. Wounds were still a flaming orange red. Before Hitler when Fritz Janicek was still working for us, he had painted all the old figures up in garish colors to show Mother that he was not a mere gardener, not a mere unemployed boy-school teacher of art, history, and languages, but a fascinating modern artist.

I tried to say a prayer, but Fritz and all the carved figures of tortured saints intruded. He had kneeled before the altar during the first air raid when I was in Vienna last spring. And I had seen him kiss a yellow rose. After my return to the farm, he had been hovering around the amethyst mine, writing poems for Mother and setting his trap. He could never stay away from her.

More neighbors came marching in with their candles. I curtsied at the altar, placed my candle among all the others and walked out.

Herr Krummerer was already folding his chair. During the war he had sat on that same chair outside the little palace. Ensconced behind a daily paper, which hid his face, he had kept an eye on the countess, my monarchist Grandmama for both the gestapo and my Father. Now I towered over him.

"Ah, how you have grown," he said with regret. "But still the same friendly little girl. I like children."

"What's going on Herr Krummerer?" I asked.

He looked around to be sure we were alone. "It is my destiny to take care of some important matters. I am known as Paul Herbster, now. Remember that!" he said in a Hitler voice.

"You're not Herr Krummerer?"

"Who cares, who knows."

"But you are still a detective?" I asked.

"A side line has become my mission. When I was your age I wanted to be on stage. And I did sing in the chorus at the opera.

One day I was asked to keep an eye on a certain diva, act as a guide, chauffeur. As a result I was recommended as a guide to embassies and one thing led to another."

"You showed people around and you kept an eye on them? Or you secretly followed them. My Mama knew you were watching her."

"For her protection. Your Herr father likes to keep his ladies safe. I was well payed and it was nice work. There were balls, big parties, days in the country. Those were the days. I hardly missed the stage."

"Working for the gestapo must have been a come down," I said.

"This was not for me. I am a professional. I chose my clients. You can throw a frog in the water but you can't make it swim."

I had tried it and the frog always swam, but I didn't say anything, and watched him fold the table with a bang.

"I worked for a young German who had been recruited into gestapo just like me. The right kind of client. A mere boy. I like children. And he is from a first class family. His mother, I found out is related to our exiled Kaiserin."

"The prince," I said. "I know him. And now, who else do you work for beside Father? Who is Herbster."

He became uneasy again. "Go home my charming Fraulein," he added in a typical Krummerer voice. "And keep your mouth shut!" This sounded like Hitler.

I cornered Father at his desk in the library that evening. He was smoking his pipe, gloating over English tobacco he had been able to get in the black market.

"I saw Krummerer, or Herbster. Whatever. Candle donations! You let him use our chapel to sell phoney certificates?"

Father got up and stared into the empty glass cabinet he had carried into the library room. "Remember the collection of red headed dolls that arrived the Christmas Puppe was lost? Your mother put them into this glass case. She never liked them. She knew perfectly well they came from Eugene Romberg. That's why she kept them all in the glass case. Well, I got rid of that doll collection and moved the empty cabinet in here before she came back. The old doll is gone and so is our dear friend. The collection would have made her sad; and it will make some children happy.

We have to clear things away. What was the point of making a
big thing of it. Get rid of cobwebs! In the house, the street we
live in, Vienna, Austria—it's all the same . . ."

He looked at me and I moved my eyes like the lost doll.

"You're growing up. So let me tell you this. A Meinert could
never be a Nazi. It isn't in us. Your mother doesn't know this,
only very few people had to know that I was forced to quietly
join the Reich Colonialists. Better than joining the party itself.
If I hadn't made this gesture, we would all have been in trouble.
I wanted to get Eli Romberg to his father in Switzerland,
remember? And I had to protect your grandmother. There were
quite a few paper Nazis like me in our neighborhood. Krummerer—Herbster—came to me last summer and told me he had
kept a pile of Nazi forms and official stamps and this way he is
able to supply Nazi certificates of unworthiness. Funny, those
dreaded bits of paper are now a salvation . . ."

Father had also obtained pork in the black market. Agnes
was still in bed and feverish. Frau Schwester and Mother were
in the kitchen preparing a rare feast. Not even the fragrance of
cooking could distract me. "Paper Nazis stood by and watched
the S.A. boys urinate on Frau Schongross and the other Jewish
ladies. Frau Bockl was there too."

"The Bockls are not my favorite neighbors," Father said. "But
believe me when the Schongross family comes back from Rho-
desia they won't find one piece of furniture missing. The house
is exactly as they left it and better. The Bockls will, of course
give it back. The fact is, that the big Nazi beasts got out or disappeared."

"Or disguise themselves like Schmiedler," I said. "Travel
around without being caught and even attack people, like poor
Hanna."

"He is a scoundrel and if he is caught, he will blame a lot of
harmless people and get them into trouble. Hanna knew the
Schmiedlers. And could probably identify him but she won't give
him away, because he might give her away. That's why denazification is such a farce. Especially our People's Court. So, both
the Amis and our authorities are making a big show rounding
up paper Nazis and punishing them. We'd be the scapegoats."
The health doctor and his followers were marching past the
Romberg villa row in row. "After the Amis came and inspected

houses here, I had to get in touch with Krummerer, or Herbster. I had to do something or they'd take over all the Nazi houses, on our avenue. Even if I were able to keep my house, I would not want to live in an area that is all American, all military." The smug voice of the chess master.

"Why not?" I said.

He lit his pipe. "The Russians have Vienna practically cut off and they are not getting along with the Americans. There is all kinds of conflict. We have had enough of that on our avenue."

"You gave Krummerer the names of all the Nazis. He gets money, doesn't he? He must be getting rich. That old Hitler hair, the mustache, and that voice. Why?"

"Let's call it residual heroics and a lot of palaver to put his clientele at ease. They are all very grateful." He kissed the top of my head. I smelled the English tobacco Mama had brought for him and also a faint fragrance of roses. Frau Hillmar had been grateful. I was not. Amis would have made a most welcome change from the boring old Nazis on our avenue.

"Amis are going to move into the Romberg house, soon," I said. "And you can't prevent that!"

A notorious Nazi official had to vacate a tower house he had taken away from a Jewish writer. The Bockls did have to vacate half their villa. One day I came home from school and an Ami hat sat on the rack, I heard the piano, an American tune.

Frau Schwester met me with tears in her eyes. "The American officer. Our house will be next."

"He wouldn't be playing the piano if he'd come to requisition our house, would he?" I said.

"So what does he want here?"

A good question which would never be answered. I stayed in the morning room to comb my hair. My feet began to tap. I danced in front of a mirror. When Mort sang, his boyish voice became deep and rich. I loved the tune. The words baffled me. Going on and on about a boy in knee pants whose mother didn't tell him that women were bad. Throbbing, sobbing tones ran into the next tune. The music took hold of me. I loved the mooing, cooing, the crowing. One moment he growled like a basso, then he cooed in a high note like a woman, sang a refrain in a basso voice again.

After a while I understood most of the simple words, the wailing and complaining had something to do with unloving, cruel babies. Babies who went away. This wild obsession with infants baffled me. After he had sung at length about a melancholy baby, he stopped. I walked into the room.

Mother gave me a kiss and Mort said, "Hi there, babe."

"I'm not a baby," I said in English.

"You're cute," he said.

Mother brushed hair from my face. "Isn't she beautiful?" she asked.

He answered with his great, dark eyes. I became embarrassed and held out my right hand like an Austrian. He took it and held it caressingly and I liked his small neat head, boyish features, a well-shaped full mouth and strong chin.

Mort took my hand again when I walked to the gate with him. I used to walk hand in hand with Eli Romberg when I was seven years old. At first Mort gave me the same happy feeling.

He swung my arm absent-mindedly, then he wouldn't let go of my hand and pressed it against his heart. I tingled from the roots of my hair to the tip of my toes and I wished Ursel or someone from my class could see me with my American lieutenant. "Talked to someone who's crazy about you," he said.

"Who?"

"You mean which one?" He laughed, took the key from my hand, let himself out and handed it back. "So long, babe," he said and walked off to his jeep.

So long meant never. Mort did not come back the next day, or the next. After ten days I told myself he had caught the flu.

Street cars were crowded with feverish, coughing people and it was already too cold and slippery for cycling. I was more than willing to walk to school and back with the other new girl, Ursel. And she braved the streets with me although she was afraid of bad weather and bad foreign men. She knew I was looking for Mort in every American car and jeep and kept her eyes on the ground as she trudged alongside me in a stylish oversized, blue coat, trimmed with silverfox around the hem. During the Russian invasion Ursel's married sister had been raped in this coat. Ursel accepted the coat and with it, her sister's terror of all foreign soldiers.

During the Nazi years Ursel's father, a prominent socialist

had to hide. Now, he had been given a big empty Nazi apartment on the hill just above the water castle. Before Hitler that apartment had belonged to a Jewish throat specialist who had made house calls at the Romberg villa when Eli had a throat infection. The Nazi had the doctor arrested and took over the apartment. Then, at the very end of the war, the Nazi fled and left everything behind. The Brenners, Ursel's family, found eight luxuriously furnished rooms. Ursel slept in a French four-poster bed.

We always parted at the corner of my avenue, at a tobacconist kiosk and newsstand. She scampered uphill in her fancy coat as though a battalion of Russians, French, British and American soldiers—and among them Schmiedler in disguise—were after her. Half her life she had lived in terror of Schmiedler, the murderous money man who hated socialists.

The company of a scared friend was not new to me. Eli had been frightened in the confinement of the water castle. My tiny friend Stopperl in the mountains would ski downhill faster and faster to get away from the souls of dead soldiers who she believed flew home to the mountains, inhabited the abandoned mine, and would come after her like rabid bats.

I don't think I would have been as foolhardy without Ursel. I had to be brazen for both of us. I confided in her and she warned me against Mort: Amis liked ordinary girls from the community housing project where Ursel and her mother and sister had lived during the war. Amis liked girls who could do as they pleased. "They take advantage of workingclass girls," she concluded. "My father does not like that."

The idea of Mort with a community house girl put me in a rage. "I think girls take advantage of them," I said. "Look at Bibi. She has an 'Ami' and he takes care of her entire family." Bibi, the class clown, was the first girl in my class to have found an Ami just by walking around with another girl. Now I was walking with Ursel to find Mort. Her fancy big coat did slow down an occasional jeep.

"If you see him and he stops," she kept saying. "I'll just run. I can't help myself."

Anything great, it seemed to me, should happen at least twice. After all, my parents played the same old love games over and over again, laughing and romping upstairs in Mother's rooms. I wanted Mort to come back and play the piano and sing his songs about babies, and then walk to the gate with me holding hands. I watched my grandmother with her Rittmeister. I was looking for constancy as I went from one phase to another in a changing world.

It snowed again, and in a drift of stinging hard flakes, American uniforms appeared in the gardens of the water castle. Soldiers raised the star spangled banner on the pole where a swastika flag had danced during the war. It was lowered every afternoon. Ursel could keep an eye on the back of the big house from her bedroom window, I watched the front.

One day I came home and heard Mother playing a sonatina. For Mort, I was sure. I charged into the living room. And there she was, fresh as a rose in an old, yellow silk Kimono performing for ladies from our neighborhood.

Father had saved our avenue. They had come to show their gratitude. Fatter, older, and hungrier than Mother, they lamented the terrible famine, danger in the streets, knitted, drank tea, devoured rare little sandwiches and ogled Mother and me. Then they wanted to know about all those years in the beautiful mountains during the war. So nice to be near Salzburg, the music festival, and near Berchtesgaden. ... A cozy scene of women loathing each other.

One architect's wife with tight curls was reknitting a pink dress she had unravelled while she was waiting for her husband to return from a Russian prisoner of war camp. "He brought me the beautiful Angora wool from France," she said. Then they all listed the dresses, jewels, perfumes, treasures their men had brought home from occupied countries.

"The war was going so well. Who could have foreseen the disaster," said Frau Bockl.

"Hanna Roth did," I said. "She told Rudolf Hess and tried to warn Hitler."

This brought on a barrage of resentments. "To think that this opportunist, this midget, turned me away when I asked her to remodel a hat. She made hats for the Schmiedlers. High society. Did you know that she went off on a trip with the Schmiedler girl during the war? Left her fat friend at home. I watched her from my window, they had a magnificent Damlier limousine and a fully armed chauffeur. Not that she needed a ride from anyone. No one touched her car. And she, of course, got out of Vienna in time. I was glad when the Russians tore down her phoney coat of arms from the gate," said an angry widow in a visor hat.

Soon after that the weather improved. Snow melted and I cycled into town on a Saturday afternoon to visit my grandmother. I disobeyed my father like an ordinary girl who could do as she pleased: I deliberately went through the heart of the international zone past the Roth house. I slowed down. A jeep stood near the entrance. An Ami was leaning against a lamppost talking to a girl in a gray fur coat. He was dangling a key. It was Mort. I rang my bicycle bell three times. He turned, smiled, took a step in my direction.

The girl wore a shawl. She turned disdainfully, twitched a sweet little nose. "Who's that?" she said in English.

She sounded impressively American. "So long," I called over my shoulder and took off as though the devil were after me.

Mort came in a car and took Mother to an afternoon concert, while I visited my grandmama. Father was grateful. She needed to get out. He did not have a moment. It was a time of total instability. The German money was finally changed back into Austrian *Schillinge*. Anything exceeding one hundred and fifty had to be put into a closed account in the bank to stop inflation. Father had made the right move again. He had spent a lot of money on buying an old truck, and also a cow for the farm.

"It will be a while before I can get that vehicle to run. In the meantime, I'm obliged to the young officer. I wouldn't want you to go into town by yourself, Annerl. This morning I met Frau Hillmar on the street car. It gets terribly crowded and a spiteful person actually cut a triangle out of her good winter coat. Poor thing. Once I have my truck I will be glad to give her a ride to rehearsal."

Soon girls at school greeted me with: "How's your mother getting along with her Ami officer. They're rich. Has he given her lots of presents?"

No good telling them that Father would not allow Mort to bring food to our house. But Mort always brought with him excitement, cheerfulness, new American songs. From the Nüremberg trials he brought back "Don't Fence Me In," a song that had blared from loudspeakers.

Mort was singing "Don't Fence Me In," when I finally walked to the gate with him again. Then I knew it was my tune. Only in my dream it had been a waltz. Many months before I knew Mort or his songs, when Grandmama and I were hiding from the Russians in the dark, I had dreamt the tune. No one would ever believe this. Everything began with a melody from my dream.

"Why didn't you stop when you saw me in town?" he asked.

"I didn't want to disturb," I said in my grandmother's voice.

"It wouldn't have mattered. I questioned a few people in that house. And brought along the girl to identify a man who has taken over the owner's apartment. You know Frau Roth, don't you?"

"I do. Everybody does."

"She knew where the Hapsburg crown was hidden," he said.

"She often told women where to look for lost things," I said. "She has visions. Do you know her? Have you met her in Salzburg? How is she? Did she mention me?"

"You're cute." This was his way of not answering my questions. He took up the song again.

Later on I came to think of the melody from my dream as a Mort overture. A bad omen. Like a Hanna Roth prediction which usually introduced disaster. And she was, in a sense, forever trying to stop something she felt she had started.

From the very beginning Mort talked to me more through songs and gestures. I became confused when he banged the gate shut between us and reached through the wrought iron pulling my head towards him. He pressed his full, moist mouth onto mine: less, and yet more than a kiss. "So long." I wondered whether he had been briefed to ask questions but not talk to Austrians.

"Auf Wiedersehen," I said.

I stayed at the gate and watched Mort turn his jeep and drive away. I felt nothing until I thought about the kiss and wanted it to happen again, exactly the same way; it never did.

Grandmother now heated two rooms at the little palace. The upstairs, pink salon where she slept on a day bed, and the *Herrnzimmer* conveniently close to the kitchen stairs. The room where gentlemen smoked was small and had a nice high window for plants to sweeten the air. She now kept the rubber plant

there and the Rittmeister had given her a chinese bowl full of
hyacinth bulbs. I was sitting in a big leather armchair with my
feet tucked under and she was watering plants. She wanted to
know about the American officers at our house. And I remembered to forget the copy of her letter to King George.

"They asked about General von Kortnai. Is he my uncle?" I
asked.

She put down her dainty, silver, watering can and said he
was a Hungarian second cousin of hers. A Hungarian nationalist
and a traitor to the crown. He had tried to make friends with
her young husband and influenced Crown Prince Rudolf. "Free
Hungary indeed! Look where they are now. If they and the Czechs
had remained loyal to the Kaiser everything might have been
quite different today."

"Sarajevo," I said in a Hanna Roth voice. "This was the beginning of the end."

"Funny that you should mention the General. A man arrived
late on Friday afternoon; he said he was a Hungarian and wanted
to know whether I had heard from General von Kortnai."

"Did he have bowlegs and a lot of gray curly hair?"

She pulled a dead leaf off a plant. "You know him?"

"He is staying at Salon Roth. Didn't Mother tell you? And her
Ami is watching him."

Grandmother looked at me through the leaves of the rubber
plant. "Mother's Ami? I really am uninformed."

I told her about Mort.

"He's the one who came here and ended up buying the copy
of the Maria Theresa document." she said.

"Vienna is a village," I tried one of Father's clichés. During
the cellar days she would have heard the false tone in my voice.
Now her mind wandered. She had been expecting her Rittmeister. The weather was changing and it snowed heavily.

# TEN

# Footprints to Infinity

I BUILT THAT SNOWMAN below my grandmother's window. A big fat snowman to make her laugh. The two Russian uniform buttons I had always in my pocket made perfect eyes. The big smiley mouth was a red leather watchstrap left on a thorny bush from the Russian invasion. And an empty American horse meat can, the ration we had eaten for lunch, turned into the kind of silly little hat that used to be sold at the wine gardens and was worn mostly by those who were round and fat. A neverending joke. Fat would melt like snow as that winter passed. All that would be left of my snowman at the end of that murderous cold would be a lump of icy snow with the two button eyes and the huge grin.

There remains a picture I drew in my blue notebook of that smiling snowman, as a monumental symbol of Viennese frivolity, *Vergnugungssucht*—pleasure-addiction—our great antidote to nostalgia and despair. Below the picture of that snowman are doodle marks wandering off the page to infinity. Footprints of lost people, hieroglyphics that remain engraved in my mind.

My grandmother leaned out of the window training opera glasses on the street, and the glow of the pink room behind her white braids and white shawl set her off, at this moment, as the

prominent ornament among snow-dappled cherubs and garlands of the Baroque façade.

"A stranger," she said, and lowered the glasses. "And I was
certain it was Rudi."

Vienna was full of strangers and we kept seeing in them those
we missed. I recognized Bertl von Hohentahler in every one-armed
man; heard my Frog Prince in every German voice on a crowded
street car. I was on the lookout, never gave up and even my
snowman faced the portal watching, waiting, a smiling vigi-
lante.

The Rittmeister was often late when he was reading his old
books of history, or gave free German lessons to Americans.
Sometimes he dropped off to sleep. I told her not to worry. I'd
take a street car and I'd be back with him in no time. She stayed
at the window to watch me go bounding out the courtyard and
sliding along the snowy street. At the Hohentahler mansion I
stopped to hurl a snowball at one of the sulky bosomy mermaids.
A small boy in a red Krampus-devil masque came out and threw
one back at me. Unfortunately his mother came and put a stop
to our fun.

Her head was draped like a moslem woman's. "Krampus is
not supposed to act like a bad boy, he comes to make bad children good. Then the kind Nicolo comes and brings presents."

At the street car stop she turned to me and told me how hard
it was. Her boy had never know a real Krampus and Nicolo celebration, he'd never seen a Nicolo-Bishop with a sack full of
chocolate and tangerines, and never tasted sweets. "All he knows
is being cold and hungry and it makes him mean."

I had been about that boy's age on this children's feast day in
1937 when Fritz Janicek in the Krampus masque had turned
gilded switches into a weapon. And after that, when Austria
became part of Hitler Germany there had been no end to the
revellery of undeserved punishment and reward; every day had
turned into an unlikely Krampus day in Vienna.

The streetcar was packed with women. There were no young
men who would give up seats to a mother and child. She had to
pick the boy up and his head in the red masque lolled against
her shoulder. More women got on at each stop as the street car
slowly screeched and rattled around the ring. A female voice said:
"I've got nothing to eat. When the gas comes on we'll just have
to drink hot water." "You're lucky. You got your water back before

we did. Remember when we had to go and fetch in buckets?" An
old couple tried to get out and there was a fierce squeeze and the
smell of unwashed women and naphtaline. We were passing
parliament. The boy lifted his head to look out at the assembly
of naked Greek statues on the snowy roof. Somebody bumped
him and he yelled "I want to get out, out . . ."

Then everyone felt hemmed in and mad. Women grumbled
in a chorus. The mother turned to me. "The old house where you
stay is almost empty now that the nuns have gone. They say the
eccentric old woman lives there all alone. Does she let you rent
a room? She must have coal. I can see smoke coming out of her
chimney. When the gas comes on we light the oven and that's all
the heat we have."

The streetcar swayed and we tumbled against one another.
"I'll go over there," the boy said from behind his masque. "I'll get
all her coal and her potatoes and take them away."

"Shut your trap," the woman said. He gave her a swift kick
in the belly. Two Russian soldiers jumped onto the platform and
pushed their way in. The crowd yielded like dough, then closed
around them.

"I'm the *Russ,*" the boy said and kicked her again.

Women told the mother to smack him good and hard. She
simply pulled his masque off. A tiny, pale face was exposed, large,
dark eyes full of tears.

Without a devil Krampus mask would Fritz Janicek have
confronted Eugene Romberg? Without that bundle of gilded
switches, would he have raised his hand? The attack on Eugene
Romberg stood out as the beginning of all the Hitler trouble. I
could not imagine a Nazi party without costumes of the S.S. and
S.A. Hitler Youth, B.D.M. girls. And I myself in pants, hair hidden under a cossack cap, had felt ordained to carry a pistol and
sword. What would Joan of Arc have been without her man's
armor, the costume of a warrior?

A week ago one of those boys in Russian uniform had suddenly raised his gun and shot at a crowded streetcar. Just now
a street car was passing, in the opposite direction. The two soldiers on the platform were hemmed in and couldn't even move
their arms. I was glad, especially when I saw the Rittmeister in
the other streetcar seated comfortably at a window, on his way
to the little palace.

I allowed myself to be squeezed out at the next stop. Then I was free and running back along the Ringstrasse in the snow, sliding over icy spots, bounding along, faster than any streetcar. I was hungry—so was everyone else, but I was lucky and never went to bed without supper.

The art museum had been damaged by explosions and repair had already begun. The monument of the one and only Hapsburg Empress Maria Theresa stood untouched by war, her lap had filled up with snow, and snow drift half covered statues of her loyal generals on horseback. She had to fight wars to defend her throne from jealous males and had sixteen, or seventeen children. I thought of how strong the empress must have been, as I ran around the statue. My cheeks glowed, I felt thirsty, scooped up new snow and ate it. At the Mariahilferstrasse I took a walnut from my pocket, cracked it on the sidewalk and devoured it as though I had to eat for that poor woman who had no supper, only hot water.

The shopping street was crowded. I had to slow down. Everyone stomped through the snow with empty bags, baskets, or rucksacks looking for food. In front of me a woman pushed a baby carriage converted into a wheelchair. The young man in the carriage had lost both legs, yet she looked resigned and far more contented than the mother on the street car. A son without legs couldn't do anything bad—could not fight another war—he was all hers.

The few men on the street were mostly old or crippled walking on one leg with crutches or canes, wearing a black bandage over an eye; and there were empty sleeves, like Bertl's. You never saw an allied soldier who had been maimed by war. They all looked healthy and unharmed.

At the crossing a policeman in a white coat raised his hand to stop a truck and shouted: "Halt! halt!" the truck didn't slow down and pedestrians turned back and scattered, some shook their fists, *"Sau-Kerl!* Swine."

A man in a light overcoat jumped off the back of the truck and fell; another one leapt on top of him. While they wrestled in the snow the truck turned right, skidded and vanished. The man in the light overcoat seemed to be winning and got on top, then he screamed and fell back. The assailant, a bowlegged man in breeches, leather jacket and cap, ran around the corner after the truck.

"After him. After him!" The police officer and a couple of men took off. "There he goes! Careful, he's got a knife! No, a sledge hammer."

*"Blödsinn.* Nonsense," the legless man from the baby carriage made himself heard. "He used a broken bottle. I saw it glisten."

The police officer could not run fast in his long, white coat, and a stout fellow hampered by a bulging rucksack gave up. "They'll never catch him."

The crowd walked around the injured man and a sturdy woman touched his coat. "Foreign," she said.

"Turn him over," I said. "His face is in the snow. He can't breathe."

They turned him over and backed away from a face smeared with blood and left a circle of dark footprints. "Terrible. *Schreck-lich.* Look at the nasty cut on his cheek, the mouth."

A young, soft, sleepy face. The Berlin American Lieutenant Kaufman. "I think I know him." No one heard me.

The invalid in the baby carriage held out a clean, ironed handkerchief embroidered with a small swastika and the sturdy woman wiped the Lieutenant's face. The policeman felt the pulse.

Newcomers scuffled to the front. "Dead? Is he dead?" they asked.

*"Nein,"* he said and searched the pockets. "No identification."

"Bunch of black marketeers, foreigners. Eating up all the food and making streets unsafe." Someone said. And a chorus of grumblers took up her tune. If anyone was hurt, abused, it was their own fault for being foreign, Jews, communists, spies. The Berlin American had lost his hat in the struggle. A woman in spectacles picked it up. Looked at the label. "English or American."

"An American lieutenant." I said.

The policeman jumped up. "In civilian clothes. Impossible. *Verboten.* Are you sure. You know him?"

"I know him," I said.

"A fine number!" said one of the women.

"Back, back. Stand back!" the officer shouted in a panic.

On the other side of the street women had gathered in front of a shop. The sign said "Leather Goods." The crowd rushed towards the store.

"Give me a hand. I need a couple of men." The inspector called after them. The man with the bulging rucksack and a small fellow in a big denuded S.S. jacket, carried the lieutenant to the store. The inspector called and ordered me to come along, but I could not take my eyes off the black footprints circling a red stain in the snow.

Women in the smashed display window were selling black market potatoes. "They're from our own allotment garden. Our own crop, Herr Inspector."

"Never mind that just now. Make way. We've got trouble. An allied officer, an Ami has been stabbed."

"Dead?" asked one of the potato woman. "We want no corpse around here. The *Russ* had been in here, stripped everything, but we pay rent for this space."

"Not dead," the policeman pushed them aside and opened the door to the back of the store. Three potato sacks blocked the way and he moved them. It was half dark and smelled of leather. A small stove gave off some heat. Broken, charred boards from burned out buildings were piled up beside it. Also a couple of broken drawers. The men put the lieutenant down on a leather sofa which had been slashed right down the middle.

You could hear women cursing and quarreling in front of the store. I kneeled down beside the Berlin American. "Please," I said in English. "Open your eyes." His expression changed. He heard me, opened his eyes, looked at me, saw the policeman and closed them again.

"Where did you meet him?" the police officer asked.

"He came to requisition our house," I said.

"I bet he didn't take the house after he met you!" said the little man and put his hat back on his head.

"Well, did they take the house?" asked the officer of the law.

I shook my head. The men laughed. "Why don't you get a doctor!" I said. "I'll stay with him."

"And you'll disappear. First let's have your name."

Blood rushed into my cheeks. I was cornered. The small man glared at me. "We don't have all day. Speak up."

"A disgrace those girls. *Blutjung.*"

The "young blood" made me remember a heroine—young, innocent, wrongly accused,—in one of those Kaiserday stories for girls. "Ilse Langscheidt." I carefully left out the "von," which is so important in any Austrian romance. The Meinert in me knew that a Viennese policeman these days might be communists, or at least strong socialists. My address, was fictitious, too. Father's name changed to Hans. The police inspector wrote slowly and carefully and I couldn't think of a good maiden name for Mother. The man with the pack wanted to leave. "You stay," the officer said.

"Don't you think the American should go to a hospital?" I spoke up and was ignored. Papers had to be in order. An American had been wounded in the streets of Vienna. Evidence had to be put down above all else. The Berlin American groaned, opened his eyes, reached into his coat cuff and took out a card. "Tell them to call this number," he said to me in English.

The policeman took the card.

"Do you work for the Amis?" The man with the pack asked me.

I felt I was, at this moment, indeed working for the Americans, and answered with a hearty, *"jawohl."*

The lieutenant looked as though he had gone to sleep. The cuts on his face were still bleeding and had soiled his lapels and the handkerchief was lying on his chest. I picked it up and wanted to dab the wound. The little man in big black coat stopped me.

"Listen," he whispered. "Death rattle." He took off a feather trimmed hat and pressed it against his chest.

The big man fumbled with his rucksack and withdrew to the wall. The policeman said a few scratches like that couldn't kill a young man. There was rattling again, a hissing. Something white popped up from the big man's pack.

"A snake!" I yelled.

"A duck," said the little man.

A long white neck. Beak tied with a rag. "A swan, a beautiful swan!" I cried.

"Where did you get that bird?" the policeman asked. The man ran out the door. "Stop. Stop him, he's under arrest!"

The women blocked the officer of the law. "You're not going to run off and leave us with a corpse," said the potato women. The policeman, a novice, got into an argument. In the end he and the little man went to the police station and I was left in charge of the lieutenant.

As soon as they had gone, I took an empty drawer and sat

down beside Lieutenant Kaufman. His one cheek was white, the
other pink and red with blood. The mouth looked as though he
had been kissed and smeared with lipstick. "I had to lie," I said
in German now that we were alone. "And I think I recognized
the man who stabbed you." I picked up his hand. It felt cold and
I rubbed it. "Why aren't you in uniform? He wouldn't have dared."

He opened his eyes. "He would have dared," he said and looked
at the cardboard partition that had replaced fallen brick. "They
grabbed me in the middle of town and threw me onto that truck.
He and some Russian agents. I could tell because they snatched
my alarm watch." He shivered. "They took my pistol. If any of
them were watching they'll come back, walk in here and kill me."

I took off my loden cloak and covered him. *"Niemals,* never!"
I said. "I won't let him!"

"What could you do?" he whispered. Blood was dripping from
his mouth onto the lining of my cloak. I was trying to wipe his
face but he kept turning his head from side to side.

"I'll kick him, punch. I'll bash him with the drawer."

"Not so loud," he said. "The women will hear you. Speak
English. Come closer."

I leaned over him. On the left shoulder his coat, like the sofa
had been slashed down to white padding. "If they come in here,
you run and if anything happens to me, you must get word to
General Patton himself. No one else. Remember. Tell him I sent
him General von Kortnai's diary through regular military channels. Understand?" He whispered in German. "Von Kortnai wrote
down important information about the Soviets. He had plenty of
experience fighting them in the Ukraine with his Hungarian third
army. Really hated Bolshevics. He believed General Patton is
the only one who'd understand how dangerous they really are."

I remembered the page torn from my notebook. "Do you always
snatch diaries?"

"The general's diary was entrusted to me and I held onto it
in good faith. I gave my promise." His head rolled from side to
side again in pain or dismay. "He surrendered to us in Czechoslovakia. They had been on the retreat through Hungary and
picked up families. Such women, such horses. Servants in Hungarian costumes, even a wet-nurse taking care of twins." Lieutenant Kaufman stared at the door and waited, listened. Women
out front bartered and quarreled.

"I once asked von Kortnai why he had fought on the side of the Germans and he said Nazi leaders were crazy and would have destroyed each other, but the Soviets would bring the dark ages to Europe. I didn't really like von Kortnai, but you had to admire him. He spoke perfect English, French, German. A great storyteller. And he was very proud of his daughter. She had a beautiful voice and she sang for the commander. Illona . . ."

The Lieutenant talked to me, as men had talked to Mother during the war, and always will talk to women who keep quiet during a time of secrets, guilt, and danger.

He reached into his other coat cuff for a photograph. Looked at it with a sigh and handed it to me. "She didn't give it to me. I found it." The picture of a girl on a black horse had been taken by someone who was more interested in the horse. The girl's face was lost in shade. She sat well, slender, upright, in light riding breeches, a dark coat and hat.

"During the ten days or so that von Kortnai and his people were in our charge, he and our commander had cocktails together every evening. Sometimes the Hungarians danced the czardas. Beautiful people. You can't tell what Illona looks like from this picture. She is not a real redhead like your mother, but there is a certain likeness. She was innocent. It showed. I can always tell. I can spot a virgin and I can spot a man who hasn't killed. This makes me an expert." He held out his hand for the picture, stuck it into a wallet pocket and winced. His hand came out marked with blood. "A jab on the left side."

He told me to take the handkerchief and look for water. There wasn't any. The back door opened into an alley. I was looking around when one of the potato women came and grabbed a sack from the corner. "This is the last one. They better get him out of here soon. We board up the shop before we leave. At least he hasn't croaked."

"Not yet," Kaufman said in English.

She dragged the sack out to the front.

"Why should the bowlegged man hate you so much?" I asked.

He stared past me at built-in mahogany drawers. Some had been ripped out, others gaped open.

"Where are all the Hungarians now?" I asked.

"For all I know they are dead, or worse, in Russian hands in Siberia. But it wasn't my fault. I just happened to get the orders.

We were told to hand the Hungarians over to the Russians.
Sometimes orders came from Washington, D.C. and afterwards,
no one could figure out who sent them. Then, again, orders could
get lost. I had the paper and didn't know what to do. Illona came
along on her horse. I stopped her and told her about it. That was
wrong, but I couldn't help myself. She ordered me to tear it up.
The idea had, of course, entered my mind, too. I told her it wasn't
that easy. I had to hand the orders over to the commander. She
got off the horse and told me that I was a European, someone
who could understand quality in people. The Russians were scum.
She came right out with it and asked didn't I want to save her. I
would have done anything. She even put her arm around me.
She was so innocent. I was crazy about her. I couldn't help myself.
She knew it. That bowlegged devil, a groom, came riding along
and yelled: "Get away from that Jew," in German. Not Hungarian. He wanted me to understand. She snatched the papers out
of my hand, got onto her horse and rode after him."

"You were insulted and you informed the commander," I concluded.

The corners of his smudged mouth went down. "I did my duty
as an officer. And for that very reason General von Kortnai trusted
me and gave me his diary. He knew I would not break the seal.
I promised to get it to General Patton. I have made inquiries and
he has not received it. I should never have sent it through regular channels."

He had a deep rumbling voice. Sounded and even looked almost
middle aged while he talked. Then he closed his eyes, lay very
still, the tension around his strong mouth and chin relaxed. Soft
features, smudged cheek and mouth made him look like a tired,
powerful, grubby boy. I thought he had stopped breathing. "Wake
up!" I said and put my hand under his head. "Please don't die."

*"Bitte stirb nicht,"* he echoed without opening his eyes. "It's
the kind of thing she would have said. So innocent. You are a
virgin. I can tell."

"Perhaps she isn't dead. Perhaps all the Hungarians are in a
D.P. camp."

He opened his eyes and I noticed they were dark blue with a
slight squint. "The general either shot himself, or the Russians
executed him. Illona. God. I don't even what to think about that.
They might have spared the horses. That's what the groom, that

devil told me when he pulled the knife and hacked into me."

"How come he was with Russian agents?" I asked.

"The best way to hide, make money and the easiest way to kill."

A potato woman was yelling. *"Aus,* finished. That's it."

He mumbled something in English about General Patton, reincarnation. I did not understand.

One of the women came rushing in. "They're here in a jeep with guns. You better get out of here girl. Clear out now. No use getting caught." She pushed me into the alley. It was still snowing hard and I had left my cloak. She told me to forget it and promised to keep it for me.

I ran all the way. Brushed snow off my sweater and dried myself with a kitchen towel. When I came upstairs, Grandmama and the Rittmeister were waiting. It was dark. I made excuses: missing a street car, enjoying the snow. Trying to buy potatoes. . . . We drank hot peppermint tea and ate some stale, dark bread. My grandmother was saying I should definitely stay overnight in this weather.

The doorbell shrilled. "Father, I bet he's coming to pick me up." I ran downstairs.

"Wait a minute," the Rittmeister called after me. "You better wait for me. You never know. And you better put on a coat . . ."

I unlocked the front door. Windows cast a pattern of gold squares onto the white courtyard and trees loaded with moist snow drooped down over my snowman. I picked up a shovel and ran ahead pushing the snow to make a path for the Rittmeister. Then I stopped. "Who is there?"

"Mort. Open up. I have your cloak."

"Wait, wait," the Rittmeister struggled into his coat. He had heard about Mort and saw him and all Americans as heroic protectors against the Bolsheviks. And he hurried after me to shake hands and invite Mort in to have hot tea with the Countess. Mort thanked him and said it was snowing so hard, he better take me home at once.

"I'm glad you brought a nice, warm cloak. The child runs around as if it were spring." The Rittmeister admired the jeep, said it was a little bit of America, helped me to get in and waved.

We drove away slowly. You could hear the scraping sound of snow shovels. Somewhere a lone car back fired. Mort said the

Kaerntnerstrasse wasn't too bad. I didn't care where we went. Nothing mattered. Finally I had a ride in a jeep with an American. I sat proud, twice as tall.

"How on earth did you get mixed up with Lieutenant Kaufman?" Mort said in English. "How long have you been seeing him?"

We were passing the bomb sight of Bitman's children's store in the Karnterstrasse where Mama used to buy my dresses. I didn't answer. He lit a cigarette without offering one to me. I was not old enough. Let him think I was running around with Lieutenant Kaufman while he escorted my mother. I hoped he was jealous.

"I didn't think your father would allow you to hang around town," he said.

At the next corner stood three girls in fur coats. I saw myself hanging around like the girls at the street corner. They looked nice standing there all dressed up in the snow. When I was only three or four years old—before Hitler—I had struck up a converstaion with some of "those girls" while Mama was window shopping. I had loved their painted faces and bright dresses. It had been a warm day. I had introduced myself with a *knicks,* a polite Viennese curtsy. One of the girls had told me her name was Lizzi; she had come to Vienna from St. Poelten because she was lonely and wanted to live in Vienna where there were lots of people and nice clothes. Mama called me away. Lizzi had shouted after me: "*Lebwohl* little angel, live well."

"I was lonely!" I said to Mort in the piping Lizzi voice which I had never forgotten.

"Lonely?" he laughed and passed his hand over my curls.

Later on I thought about his caress and liked it, but I was looking at the lonely girls and thinking of Lizzie who had said "live well." So much had been lost and destroyed. I knew it was crazy, but I wanted to see her exactly where I had met her and this time all dressed up in fine clothes.

There was one girl in a sable coat, much more beautiful than the others. Mort was looking at her too. The other girls were ambling in our direction. She stayed under the street light; snow glistened on her hair and the shoulders of an oversized fur coat. Her face was dainty and expressionless as a white tombstone angel's.

Mort drove on and said it was bad when pretty girls had to hang around town like that. I didn't say anything. He swerved around a barrier onto the Graben and I had a glimpse of poor old Stefel, St. Stephen's. Damage hidden under snow. I thought of Lieutenant Kaufman covered up with bandages and sheets. "Is the lieutenant all right. Is he in the hospital?"

"He is *wunderbar,*" he liked that German word. And I liked the English "wonderrrful." We both used overstatements when we felt uneasy.

The jeep skidded and he got it under control at once. He never fumbled. I noticed his deft hands, long fingers. He never wore gloves. I loved his uniform and he smelled of peppermint.

"What are you looking at?" He became nervous and pushed his cap forward over his face.

"How did you get my cloak? Did they see my name on the inside pocket? Did you tell them who I am? Will the police question me?"

Before he had a chance to say a word, a thin woman with a big thin mongrel came out of a dark doorway and ran in front of the jeep. He hissed a word I didn't understand. "You've got to be so careful. She might be trying to get hit. They do. So that we feel responsible, feed them. Few dogs. They eat them."

We Austrians were "they." He would take me home. Perhaps drink a glass of wine with my parents, play the piano and sing for us, but we were "they." I was forewarned. We were now in the American district. He pulled over into a side street. Stopped. "O.K. I got the cloak. No one knows a thing. But I'd like a few straight answers. Were you in that truck with the lieutenant? Who else was with him? Did they force you onto that truck?"

"You better ask him," I said. The street stretched out white and empty. Ruined houses, palaces, churches, like girls on the Kaerntnerstrasse, all of Vienna, destitute, ruined, waiting to be used by strangers who sought answers. "Didn't he tell you anything?"

"He wasn't feeling too great."

"It's up to him," I said in my grandmother's voice.

He took me by the chin and it hurt. "You do me good," he said. "You wouldn't give him away. Well, I'd not give you away, babe."

"I'm not a babe," I said.

He put his arm around me. I felt like a babe, a lonely girl with her Ami safe inside a jeep, that little bit of America. I closed my eyes. Girls in class had described the Ami procedure. They always started at the top. Kissing came first, then they undid hooks and buttons. I did not own a bosom-holder. This was a worry.

"You're a nice kid," he said.

I felt like a young goat. He was fumbling in his overcoat pocket. I froze. Ami were prepared to do almost anything in a jeep. The degrading step by step procedure—less than passion—seemed worse than violent uncontrollable passion, even rape. I closed my eyes and his lips on mine felt cold and hard.

"Open your mouth!"

I did, ready for a dragon's kiss. The taste was sweet. "Chocolate!" I shouted. Usually candy came afterwards. I felt relieved and slightly disappointed. I thanked him.

"You've had quite a day," he said. "I like you a lot."

He didn't say he loved me but he handed me the bag of chocolates.

"You're too young," he said.

Arnold had said this after we kissed. All the way home I ate candy and thought of Arnold. Mort stopped in front of the water castle. I had seen him jump out and run around the car to help Mother out. I waited. He came and took both my hands.

"Beautiful babe," he teased.

And I jumped on him. We fell. He rubbed snow on my cheeks. His cap fell off. I put snow on his head. When I get excited I eat snow. My mouth was full of that cold stuff when he kissed me. "You're too much," he said. "Too much."

I ran ahead towards the gate, rolled one of those "if you hit your target you get a wish" mountain snowballs. He caught it between his palms and yelled "Good pitch!"

I had wished Arnold would come back to Vienna, now I suddenly felt sure I would see him soon. A shadow between the curtains showed me Krampus was waiting. I could hear Mother playing the piano and Father the violin. They had not played together for years. I unlocked the gate. Mort locked it for me, then he took my hand and we walked towards the house like an aged couple.

# ELEVEN

# The Water Goblin

FATHER HAD BOUGHT the Swedish radio before the war. You could tune in on a city and a little dot lit up on a map which showed the shape of Europe in pastel colors. The radio had taught me Geography and the names of the capital cities long before I had my first lesson. During the Hitler wars the shape of Europe had changed. Listening to foreign radio stations had been punishable by arrest or even death. And Father had made the radio disappear. Now it was back in the living room, the light flickered over the map of Europe, but somehow the cities were scrambled. You tuned in on London and heard a French announcer predicting foul weather. In Paris you heard radio Oslo. Venice lit up and I heard scrunching munching sounds. I tuned in on Salzburg and the announcer spoke Russian. Quickly I turned from Salzburg to Leningrad.

"A dark hand came up from the water and pulled her down," I had found the children's hour, the voice of Hanna Roth, Tante Hanna, the new Salzburg radio aunt, deep in Russia. "You want two of my golden water lilies? You shall have them all. You will breathe like a fish, live in my castle at the bottom of the sea and you will wear diadems that sparkle on the water as a will-o'-the-wisp. You will forget who you have ever been as you lure children into the deep. Your laughter will be a whirlpool."

Scratching and whistling and crackling started up then a rushing and growling, sounds of noisy whangdoodle monsters gurgling and splashing in the sea. The doorbell rang. I turned the radio off and went to the gate. Frau Boschke had arrived to do some ironing.

I carried a small electric heater into the ironing room for her. She thanked God and the American army for the electricity in our district. She always brought her own sprinkler and her own coffee mug in a basket. The mug was decorated with a red heart and flowers and it said: coffee in this cup will pick your heart up.

And out of the cup came a bar of chocolate. "Something to keep us happy!"

It was too precious and rare, I didn't want to accept any. She said I had to. After all, she was cleaning an Ami office now and there was always more where that came from. "Certainly nice to be appreciated."

She was wearing a hat I had not seen before. Black velvet trimmed with slightly yellowed ermine tails. "Where did you get that hat?" I asked.

"Used to belong to Frau Romberg, the little nightingale. I ran into her cook and she was wearing it. I admired it and she made me accept it. Probably wants me to keep my mouth shut about all kinds of other stuff she made off with. Anyway, it looks better on me and it brought me luck. I wore it to the Ami office and that little sergeant pointed at the hat and said O.K."

I watched her peel off layers of old sweaters. Hand-me-downs she had acquired in various households, like all her clothes. A warm black angora cardigan with jade buttons Frau Hillmar the actress had worn when she was in mourning for her handsome diplomat husband. With it came the story of a popular actress hopelessly in love and neglected by the Herr Consul. There he was in Vienna for only a week and carousing at the Romberg house gobbling down poisoned goodies. Under Frau Hillmar cardigan Frau Boschke wore the camel hair Schmiedler sweater. It had only one sleeve. The other one had been eaten by the Schmiedler miniature Doberman. "I've washed it and it still smells of toadstools like Schmiedler."

I wondered whether all financiers had a rich mushroom odor. Eugene Romberg did under all the cologne and perfume.

"They could use me as a blood hound," Frau Boschke went on. "I never really got to see him, but I could sniff him out. I must confess I don't mind the smell of a man's sweat. And that goes for that scamp of a Russian who took advantage of me.

Sweaty as a horse. And that little sergeant at the Ami office smells like a newborn pony."

She opened up the ironing board with new vigor. I plugged in the iron for her and told her I heard Hanna Roth on radio Salzburg as a radio aunt. "What? Then it's true what Tony says. She's really big in Salzburg. Warnings to generals, predictions and talking on the radio. The Amis quiz me. Want to know about Hanna Roth, because I used to iron for her when she and her fat friend took over the water castle."

"What did you tell the Amis?"

"Everything. I thought they should be told about the *Russ* in my house. After what he did to me, making himself at home and all, and then going to that butcher woman and giving her my jewelry, my rings. I told them that he dressed like an Austrian and comes to her. American zone makes no difference to that one."

"Did they ask about us, about me?"

"They wanted to know about your mother, Schmiedler, Hitler. I told them they are crazy. The lady was a cripple in a wheelchair. Then they asked me did I ever see Hitler over there at the Romberg house with Frau Hanna. A different matter . . ." The hat hid Frau Boschke's wild hair. She looked stylish and ironed like a woman who has seen better days and has come down in the world.

"What did you tell them?"

"The truth, the truth. Hitler didn't have to come to her. She went to him. You know they say to me 'raise your right hant and schwear.' " Frau Boschke took the sprinkling can out of her basket and shook it over Father's shirt. Then she brought the iron down with a bang. "I saw her take off. It is the truth. She's not just a fortune-teller with carrier pigeons. She's a real witch. I watched her one evening on the balcony over there. Flap, flapping her cloak and turning herself into a black pigeon. She herself went flying off to Adolf. I saw it."

I had seen Hanna Roth on the balcony in a cloak. But I also remembered Frau Boschke celebrating Hitler's birthday with Father's French cognac. A celebration could make her see all kinds of things.

"*Ja, ja,* someone has to tell them the truth," she said and spat on the iron.

I loved the idea of her American interrogation and hoped they

wrote down all her statements. And I wrote Frau Boschke's truth
into my notebook. It was as good as any. The evidence she gave
stands out as a perfect retort to all investigations that had been
going on in Vienna from the days of the Romans, through the
migration of nations, the Babenbergers, the Hapsburg Empire,
year hundred after year hundred, gaining momentum whenever
a city was threatened. Deadly prying had, of course, been the
specialty of the Hitler years. The Russians were good at it too.
There was no end to it.

Why not look into the future and utter warnings like Hanna?
No one could become famous or notorious by looking at the present in Vienna. It was murky. Besides, a few warnings should
always precede any stupidity. Think of Hitler invading Russia,
or Mother getting on a horse with a child in her belly wearing
that crazy straw hat. And the girl wearing the same hat and
getting killed. Mort passing by in a jeep and with a yippeee!
catching and keeping it, until a certain hateful girl would take
it from his room. What would that hat have been without the
Hanna Roth warning? You could always say Hanna was an oracle. It was fate.

Frau Boschke rummaged through her big bag, found a newspaper picture, and ironed it to show me Sergeant Tony dressed
up as Santa wearing a white beard. The group was photographed at the Salzburg horse fountain where water spouted
from nostrils of giant stallions into a huge basin. Hanna looking
like a period doll, was protected from the spray by her umbrella
and children who thronged around the wonderous Tante Hanna
the new Radio-Salzburg story time aunt. You couldn't see the
face of the general, because he was stooping over Hanna Roth
and there was Tony, the Santa, at a safe distance from Hanna
and the fountain. Tony had told Frau Boschke it had been General Patton himself on an unofficial visit to Salzburg.

General Patton would have been amused by Salzburg, a town
built by horsy bishops, with statues of horses, huge paintings of
horses and fancy horse trough fountains. Water spouting from
nostrils of giant stallions. And General Patton certainly should
have been honored in Salzburg as the hero who had saved our
Spanish riding school, the Lipizzaner horses. After all, he personally had given the order for the rescue of brood mares and

young horses from the stud farm in Czechoslovakia. Patton loved horses, and more than that, he had liked to infuriate the Russians by herding the Lipizzaners across the border just before they arrived. And had he been in command, he might very well have questioned or even opposed an order to hand the Hungarians third army over to the Russians rather than let those savages take the beautiful Hungarian horses and women. I had a certain affinity with a genius who often made the right move for all the wrong reasons.

Burgomaster of Salzburg, or one of the other dignitaries must have told the Americans what a comfort Frau Roth had been to terrified children during the last days of the war; how she had made them forget hunger with her stories. And she had the distinction of having been thrown into the water by a man in disguise, a man without a face, a Schmiedler suspect. After her rescue by an American officer children had come to the hospital in droves with flowers, little pictures and letters. They had hung around waiting for her stories. What better way to be heard by children of Salzburg, and all over Austria than the radio?

And if there had been mention of rumors that this tiny woman had been a soothsayer to Adolf Hitler, the men would smile. She was only an old dwarf lady, fascinating like a Hitler dog, or servant. People would talk in front of her as if she were a child, because of her size. And it turned out she did know where the Austrian crown jewels had been hidden . . .

The newspaper described an angelic little girl who had come away from Hanna and presented the general with a bunch of Edelweiss. Children had sung the "Glockenspiel Lied" from Mozart's *Magic Flute*. In a brief address the general had said he knew that little girls hated big speeches and talked about his own children and a favorite daughter growing up. Hanna Roth had translated. Then the little girls had been invited to reach into Santa's bag.

In the picture the girls in the front row were holding substitute Puppe dolls, those red-headed dolls Eugene Romberg had once secretly sent to console Mother after Puppe had vanished. That collection of orphan dolls my father had given away in case they made her disconsolate.

How did the doll donation get from Vienna to Salzburg? How

did anything or anyone, officially or unofficially get out of Vienna but by Mozart express, the American train?

Hanna Roth knew about those dolls from way back. One look at the Puppe substitutes emerging from the sack one by one and she had staggered back towards the fountain trough, sank down on the damp fountain rim, on the verge of toppling into the water once more. "I must speak to your general," she had said. "I must warn him."

Tony had been scared to go near her. The general, officially or unofficially a fearless man, had gone to her at once.

Hanna wore a fur toque in that picture. A half veil curtained her uncanny black eyes. To the general she would smell too sweet, of violets. He would see her fixed smile; a strong chin and feel her power before she gripped his wrist and held on like a falcon. "The beautiful white horses, were bred for battle. Men used to get onto those horses to kill. They trained them to perform the magnificent *Capriole*—to leap over corpses! Now machines invented to make life better are murder weapons. I see an assassin clutching a steering wheel. Herr General Patton is in danger."

The Salzburg dignitaries had not liked this. One or two of them came forward and confronted Hanna Roth, asking how she knew the general was in danger. And all the Salzburg officials posted themselves between her and the Americans, as if to shield them and the general from ill fate with their own bodies.

No one could ever deter Hanna Roth. She had made a second pronouncement: Russians were about to cause an incident on the American train, the Mozart Express. There would be a shooting. "Run an empty train. Run an empty train for the next two days!"

"How do you know all this?" an Austrian lawyer had asked. "Who told you?"

"I knew about Sarajevo and no one listened. I knew Germany and Austria would lose if we went to war. I could not make myself heard. And I tried. Kept trying to the end." Hanna Roth's warnings to an American general, her warnings to Hitler, and certainly to me, would merely point the way.

Danger would be a challange to Patton who was himself a seer: one who looked back and remembered lives he had lived in other centuries. When he looked into the future he foresaw mostly

Russian danger and he had been against letting the Russians overrun Europe. Afterwards he would tell himself it had to happen. The Russians had to be taught a lesson. The Mozart Express would run on schedule.

One evening when the gas had come on for cooking I was on my way down to help Agnes and Frau Schwester in the kitchen. They were having a discussion. I sat on the stairs and heard Frau Schwester say she was all for elections. Agnes, influenced by my grandmother, said elections were hopeless. You didn't know who you were going to get. A Kaiser was brought up and educated for his job. Crown Prince Otto was smart. If he were in charge we would soon get gas, coal and more food.

Frau Schwester pointed out that Kaisers made mistakes too. There was no difference. Agnes cleared her throat. She always did that when she was thinking.

"A Kaiser mistake is like dropping a good china cup and feeling sorry, an accident. Hitler mistakes were like someone throwing china and smashing it. He never knew any better. He just hadn't been taught."

The mere odor of apples made me feel queasy after my futile apple diet, but I went down to the warm kitchen. Agnes said she was worried, I was always so late. Neither of them liked the idea that Father had put me into public girl school and allowed me to go back and forth by myself. Sometimes Agnes would come to fetch me home when I was loitering at the corner with Ursel. Agnes did not like this friendship. Ursel's father was a socialist leader and an atheist.

Fortunately Ursel's father was able to get a telephone. She could call me in the afternoon when he was not home. We giggled about girls in school. The power in my class was now as divided as Vienna. Girls who were already going out with "Amis" formed their own group. Mimi, former Schmiedler slave, now living with her American officer father attracted girls who wanted to be invited to her father's beautiful apartment, eat, and meet officers. Among her friends were also the better students in class. There were rumors of scholarships and holidays in Switzerland or even the U.S.A. for gifted students.

Ursel's father was a prominent socialist and she attracted daughters of civil servants, who had been Nazi party members and lost their jobs. The girls asked Ursel to speak to her father. She always promised. Only I knew that her father was strict and stern and she was afraid of him. I joined Ursel's group and brought with me the unpopular fat one, and also those girls who had suffered most during the war and from the Russian invasion, quiet girls who didn't have much to say and felt protected by my height, my grades, my wordiness. Besides I was a Meinert, my family was rich. I was a wild character who had overwhelmed a Russian. I naturally became more brazen among those timid souls.

We were having an exam. I looked up from my geometry problem. Something stirred in the Schmiedler garden. A girl was going around shaking snow off the Chinese paper lanterns. Ice on the lower part of the school room window made her look knee deep in frost flowers. Her fur coat was fluffy and white as powder snow, and snow was falling onto her fair hair. She blended— white on white—as she sauntered to the back of the snow-covered ruin and vanished.

By the time I handed in my paper the girl had reappeared and was leaning against the old flagpole with the *Verboten* sign. She stood motionless, and around her, all the winter stillness— skeletal shapes of twisted branches, the jagged top floor of the ruined house, a curved shattered lantern—gained a strange vitality.

The girl with the stone angel face. I had seen her poised like this in the hopeless deserted inner city. No matter what she had done or would do, she stands out like the winner in a vast game of statues, and all the world around her quivers, restive as street girls foraging on winter's nights.

She would fall back into the same pose again and again, motionless, unsmiling, alluringly predictable in this time of uncertainty, and not just to men.

The school-bell brought her to life. She came across the street. A minute later she was strutting along the corridor and girls flocked around her.

Mimi Goldberg said to me: "Didn't I tell you she is the prettiest girl in school!"

"Don't worry," I said. "You're just as pretty."

All Mimi's followers agreed. Ursel spoke up and voted for me. So did the fat one.

"Schmiedler. Schmiedler. Schmielder. There you are back

again!" They formed a circle around her. "*Du,* Else, are you coming back to school?" Mimi called across the corridor.

The circle opened and Schmiedler allowed her white fur coat to fall back from her shoulders. Under it she wore an old Hitler maiden uniform: black skirt and demure white blouse. "Would you want me to come back, Mimi?" A high expressionless voice. Ask her a question and you got one right back.

"*Ja, ja,* please come back!" said a chorus of followers.

"As a matter of fact, I don't even have time for school and I don't like to study," she said without feeling.

Mimi whispered to me: "What do you think of her?"

I recognized Else Schmiedler as the most exquisitely unpleasant girl I had ever seen. I was tempted to say: Schmiedler, I saw you waiting for men on the Karntnerstrasse. The careful Meinert in me held back. One day, I said to myself, one day. . . . I shrugged my shoulders, put on my cloak, ready to leave. The bookworm whispered something to Else and pointed to me.

The Schmiedler circle opened again. "You there. New girl," Schmiedler said. "Raping a Russian. That is a joke, of course. Russians are dirty and they have syphilis. You don't take their pants off, you shoot them. I shot three. No wasted bullets!"

"Did they rape you?" Ursel asked.

"Dead men can't rape." She made her exit in long, measured steps of an officer inspecting troups. Girls automatically formed a line for Schmiedler B.D.M. leader. No one bragged about having been raped after that.

# TWELVE

# *Carousel of Illusions*

I KEPT SAYING, I'm a Meinert, a realist, that winter. Yet events seemed to revolve around my dream of the carousel. I close my eyes and let the calliope music invade my mind. Memory, like a calliope, will play the tunes of my life over and over again.

My parents dancing a Czardas at the wine garden, the Meinert Heurigen, would give me an unforgettable dream of Mother dancing to the sound of calliope music, all by herself, arm raised, head held high. Suddenly huge, wooden like Kalafatti, the figure of a Turk at the oldest merry-go-round in our amusement park, the Prater; Mother is transformed going around and around to the trappings of cymbals and drums: wrists and elbows, knees, are joined like a doll's, she grows into a gigantic monstrous ancenstral Puppe. At her feet wooden Hungarian soldiers ride around and around on white painted horses. Stiff red, blue, green, black, Kaiserly tunics, tassels, froggings, shakos, chin straps, fur hats and jingling, rattling medals, sabers. I spin around with the Hungarian Third army carousel in rotating mirrors on a carousel of illusions.

Father had invited a group of friends and acquaintances to a private evening at the Meinert Heurigen, a little house in the square of the vintner's village. Mort came along. Father seated him beside the snubnosed young wife of the new government counciellor at the other end of the table.

She was pert, newly married to a gray-haired dignitary. Her blue eyes sparkled and she laughed a lot. She had been a teacher and amused herself by improving Mort's German, pronouncing words for him in a piping voice.

Our long pine table stood close to the warm tile stove. My face began to glow and I gathered dream material by staring at the decorative white round tiles with violet blue circles until they seemed to move from side to side like gigantic Puppe glass eyes.

The same widow had kept the concession to the Meinert Heurigen and I was still her favorite. My face hadn't changed at all, I still had those red cheeks, she said. I was the same sweet little heart, her *Herzerl*.

I felt like crawling under the table while the young wife lectured Mort on Viennese diminutives and tenderness. Her own name was Hilde and everyone called her Putzi, cutey.

Musicians arrived. An accordian player, a zither, and an elderly tenor. Frau Hillmar, the actress, had been invited and shared the court doctor with me. He said it was a cozy evening and he was happy Frau Hilmar could honor us although any performance would suffer without her. Mother was unpacking sausage, ham, chicken and Yugoslav goat cheese. Unbelievable luxuries. There was applause. Frau Hillmar said it was like a dream. The doctor said true. He for one dreamed of food when he went to bed hungry. He proposed a toast to Meinerts for sharing this bounty.

Father was in his element. "It all came from communist Yugoslavia and therefore it is meant to be shared."

We had received a food package from Vlado. Before Hitler, local Nazi thugs had driven Vlado, the Marxist, from the land he owned near Graz to Vienna. Now he had bought back the farm near the Yugoslav border. Marshall Tito had kept the Russians out of his country and there was food in Yugoslavia. Vlado, the partisan officer, went back and forth. Father proposed a toast to that "wonderful loyal fellow." More applause. The musicians played "A prosit to *Gemuetlichkeit*," Mort translated it into English: "a toast to coziness."

I didn't feel at all that cozy. Several couples at the table were strangers invited by Father for all kinds of reasons. Then there were all the other empty tables in the room and voices echoed. Frau Hillmar sang along with the music in a fine contralto voice, staring at Father. He was paying attention to the widow, and made her sit down next to him urging her to eat. Before she knew it the tired widow was on her feet and he was waltzing her away from the table, away from sultry-eyed women and watchful eyes. Was he dying his side whiskers? They looked much darker and the gray had disappeared.

"Come, come on children, let's dance!"

The young wife stood up with Mort. "In Austria we always call each other children." She counted one, two, three and proceeded to teach him the waltz. Her husband danced with Mother. My partner, the court doctor turned me gracefully, to the right, then to the left, puffing a little. Perhaps his rib had not healed completely. I did not ask. He was telling me he wished Frank could be here on a night like this. The poor boy did not really know Vienna. He refused invitations. It would do him good to meet nice Viennese girls, dance, be young, and forget. The doctor kept turning me around after everyone had sat down and the music played on just for us. Everyone clapped when our dance ended and drank a toast to youth. I was always the youngest. The child. I had always been admired just for being a child. In the days before Hitler, when I was four or five years old, I had sometimes been awakened by a litany of endearments. Women, in shimmering dresses like angels and men in dark suits had stood around my bed filling the air with perfume and cigarette smoke. Showing me off to guests had been a ritual. There were many childless couples and after the first World War, more boys came into the world; little girls were scarce.

In the morning I had often found presents on my bed, fancy boxes of chocolates, or a collection of those little feathered hats from the wine gardens. The day before Father had taken Eugene Romberg across the border to Switzerland, I had found a small laquered chest filled with Gerstner's candy on my bed. I would play with it, opening and closing drawers. Uncle Eugene had always loved candy so much, I saved it as though this would bring him back. All through the war the little chest had remained in my closet among old games. The chocolates had hardened and turned gray. I finally popped a piece into my mouth. Once it began to melt on my tongue, the flavors of raspberry and chocolate were revived. I savored the sweetness of my early days of waking up with presents on my bed. There was a perplexing void after the days of giving candy, flowers, endearments, diminutives, titles.

"You look so pale," the court doctor told me. "Some girls get dizzy and faint after the waltz. But don't worry. As I told your charming mother, girls your age do faint."

The doctor had come to our house to examine me after I had a couple of fainting spells. The first one in school while I was at the blackboard doing algebra. I had turned my head towards the window, trying to concentrate and I caught sight of my own hazy reflection on the window pane. My mind had gone blank. I had turned white and keeled over. About two days later it had happened again on a crowded streetcar. I had given my seat to an old lady. A nice boy from the gymnasium, the high school for boys, came and stood beside me. He told me his name was Gerhard and he was fourteen years old. He had hoped to talk to me for some time. His face was dimpled and sweet. I bent my knees and lowered my head, but I still towered over him. Through a shadowy transparent reflection of one tall and one little person, cheerless scenes of half-bombed houses and food lines at stores had flitted by the window. He said his own mother had hidden him in a wardrobe rather than allowing him to fight against the Russians. Then he recited names of dead classmates, boys who had been made to defend my girls' school. Schmiedler's orders. His voice had faded, as if he were left behind and I were moving on. Then I didn't see him anymore. He had reached his stop. I had gone past mine. At the terminal the conductor had tapped me and told me to get off. I passed out.

The court doctor had treated me with kindness and respect. He had warmed his stethoscope before listening to my heart. Said, sorry, before he had tapped my knee. Held his breath when he had to look down my throat. He had sent Mama out of the room during his lecture on the female body. He became botanical and romantic, when he had talked about the mechanics of female and male organs and their union: ferns and the beautiful little seeds in search of eternal perpetuation, the blossoming. I wondered how many little highnesses had to rely on this little lecture and grew up without facts about sexual activity.

Now the Herr Doctor told me I did have to be watched. I had grown so fast and I was slightly anemic. Maltaline would soon be available again, if only in small quantities. A perfect tonic for me. The zither began to play and he hummed. Father sang, always a little off tune. I looked at myself on the double window pane. My soft face surrounded by a puff of hair floated on the reflection of the room. A craving to exclude myself always preceded that lightheaded feeling. Maltaline would not cure that. Mort was laughing at the other end of the table. I kept staring at myself until I didn't really see my own face and became a stranger on an excursion to nowhere. I felt dizzy and remote. Suddenly a face dove up at the window and dipped down.

At the other end of the table the young wife was teaching Mort a Viennese song about going to Grinzing. "While you are in Vienna you must take voice lessons," she told him. "I think your voice is marvelous."

The "while you are in Vienna" bothered me. From that moment on I was afraid Mort would vanish like the face at the window. A Vienna without Mort seemed impossibly bleak. I emptied my glass when Father proposed a toast to all the talented beautiful ladies at the table. The melancholia of our coziness months after the carnage, sweet compliments after the rapes, gave me the hiccups. I wanted to rescue Mort from old songs, sentiments, sticky, syrupy as flypaper. I wanted to drive with him through the snow and the wind in a deserted city.

That was when Mother asked the musicians to play something Hungarian. The passionate music was accompanied by soft chatter: talk about food, the kind of meals we used to eat. Someone was telling Mort how we used to eat roast leg of veal at the wine gardens and breaded chicken. "You just don't know what Vienna was like when we had food!" Mort was watching me. I hiccuped and felt miserably ashamed of us all trying to turn our past into a storybook world. He had to listen to oranges carefully excavated and the pulp mixed with delicious whipped cream, brandy and nuts spooned back into the skin. Memories of everyone's favorite feasts—those good old days—turned into the Land of the Schlaraffs, a legend of gluttons that eat their way through mountains of pudding to get to a hellish paradise people by fat men and women who loll about and wait for roast chicken to fly into their mouth, and stretch out their hands for a cup of bubbly wine. Mother was not interested in the ode to bygone feasts either. She looked sad. The doctor noticed my hiccups, refilled my glass and told me another sip might help.

"Play me a Czardas," Mother said to the musicians. "Ferdl, I want to dance!"

Before the war, when I was five years old, I had been allowed to crank up the gramophone and turn records while my parents practiced dances in preparation for Fasching, our carnival. The Czardas had been a favorite, because Mother liked to go to costume balls in Hungarian costumes: scarlet boots, a short skirt on top of many lace trimmed petticoats I liked to count. During the last year of free Austria, Mother had become secretive and my parents stopped rehearsing for carnival.

They were still a proud pair after all those years. Father in his loden suit and pink scarf-tie; she in a clinging dark dress, right arm raised, head held high. Their feet performed the rhythmic beat. The court doctor hummed along, nodding his head: *tata, tatata, da, da, daa.*

Mort looked on with a smile. And all my pride and pleasure in watching them dance vanished. I wished I could blindfold him, lead him away so that he wouldn't see the darn on Mother's silk stockings, and Ferdl von Meinert—Emperor Meinert, wine and beer and milk Meinert—dancing in terrible worn-out old country shoes.

I thought of changing them. Imagined them in American style clothes, carefree, decent, without a blemish of guilt that sat there like Mother's darn. Mort was trying to catch my eye, he was enjoying himself. Perhaps he saw the performance of the Czardas as a comedy act of awful Austrians, Hitler lovers, murderers, swindlers, starving beggars, putting on a show. I looked at myself in the window glass and pushed my American filmstar hair behind my ears to look more like my grandmother.

Tap, tap, tap. Only I heard it. Only I saw the hand in the black gloves tap, tap, tapping the Czardas on the glass, tapping it's way up. Then a face surfaced, just eyes and nose pressed against the window. It could be anyone, I told myself, a passerby watching us. The features were flattened out, the eyes followed Mother's turns and twirls as though the spectator was about to go into a hypnotic state.

The dance ended, and the face vanished. Everyone clapped, cheered, glasses clinked. "The door," I said. "There's someone at the door."

The mistress of the wine garden got up.

"Don't open up!" I said.

No one listened.

"Who is it please?" she asked and her politeness would seem superfluous and fussy to Mort as the lace on her old winter dirndl sleeve.

Car brakes squealed in the street. A dark figure of a man scurrying around the corner taking small hurried steps of a Fritz Janicek. Someone drummed on the door. The music stopped. No one said a word. We froze like children playing statues. We had not overcome the fear of malevolence and force. Mort jumped up.

Father went to the door. "Who is that?" he asked sternly.

"Military Police. *Aufmachen!*" An American speaking German.

I ran to Mort. "You're not supposed to be here?" I whispered. "Come, quick. I'll hide you in a barrel!"

"Hey," he grinned. "What's all this about?"

He followed Father to the door and it opened to a blast of cold air. Ami M.P.s in white helmets saluted Mort. He walked out with them. Not a word or an excuse. He left his cap and coat. A minute later he was back. Everyone was standing up.

"Please sit down," he said in German. "I'm sorry to spoil the evening." He switched to English.

"What happened?" I asked.

Father gave me a warning look.

"An incident on the Mozart Express. A Russian has been shot. You will read about it in the paper tomorrow, anyway. Russians had no business on our train." Mort said in German.

No one said a word. Threats to the American Mozart train, this important link between Vienna and the American occupation zone of Salzburg could mean war. Russians had been getting on the American train when it slowed down at the demarcation line to molest American passengers and even rob them. Hanna Roth's vision had been inspired by fact. And so was mine. Frau Boschke had told me Lieutenant Kaufman had gone off to Salzburg. I emptied my glass of wine and stared into the dark window glass until lights danced like reflections of stars on deep water. Then I had a vision of Lieutenant Kaufman holding a gun that smoked like a cigar.

Mort had put on his cap and was leaving, then he looked at me and said: "Our men are O.K."

A few days later military police stood by a truck unloading office furniture and files at the water castle. And there they were again, Resi's old stage hands Stauble and Pichler, State Theater Coulisse Pushers. (Everyone in Vienna had to have an official title.) One was tall and the other small. They bumped into trees dropping a desk and bungled on towards the door. Long ago they had been fired for dropping stage props during performances. Soft-hearted Resi had hired them. I remembered them in operetta style liveries carrying fancy furniture and paintings into the house, arranging and rearranging Biblical settings. Later, after Resi's arrest, the official Coulisse Pushers had carried furniture and art treasures out of the big house for Nazi collectors. At the same time they had worked for Bertl von Hohentahler, rolled Resi into a rug and, with the help of Detective Krummerer, smuggled her out of the Gestapo Hotel. They didn't care what they carried nor did they worry about what they dropped. Now that most of Vienna was busy moving props, and bungling along to find shelter and keep from starving to death, they no longer made me laugh.

Mother and I were on our way to a little seamstress who altered and restyled Mother's old dresses for us both. Walking arm in arm we were sometimes taken for sisters. We talked in undertones as we passed the Romberg gate. American officers were supposed to move in before Christmas. There was a rumor that the wife of a high Nazi beast had been hired as housekeeper.

"Look at that!" Mother said.

Pichler and Stauble came from the house with a wreath and handed it to the guards. It was made of evergreen, the kind we use for winter funerals. But I would see one like it in the early spring decorated with wax lilies. This one was decorated with red berries and a red ribbon.

"The Nazi housekeeper moved in," I said. "And she's already dead."

Guards got onto a ladder and proceeded to hang the wreath onto the gate. My mother looked worried. "It must be an American custom to display the wreath before it is put on the grave." She stopped at the gate. The guards turned and said "Hi!" She said "Good afternoon," in her nice English. "So sorry that there is a death so close to Christmas."

"Death?" one of them said over his shoulder.

They went on with their wiring, as though they had been told not to fraternize.

"The wreath," Mother said. "I thought . . ."

The other one turned on the ladder, tilted back his helmet cap, and showed his wonderful, white teeth. "Wreath, the wreath," he smirked. "Christmas wreath. Wine-act. Get it?"

"Ah, *Weihnacht,* ja, ja, Christmas," Mother and I laughed and they laughed with us. They offered us cigarettes and said only the Wine-act-Christmas turkeys were dead.

Mother decided to follow the American custom and had a wreath hung onto our gate too. She thought Mort would like it.

He came the very next day. Mother was out and he was waiting in the courtyard ready to take me for a ride in his car. Agnes said a visit at home was all right; going out with him was not. While we argued he stood in the snowy courtyard, peeling a banana. Agnes and I watched from the window, trying to remember when we had last seen a banana. He peeled the fruit, nibbled, and finally took a bite. Mort ate slowly, I had noticed this before. Once I had given him one of my apples and he had stroked and polished it caressingly as though he had to ingratiate himself with the very food he ate. The apple had been so shiny it reflected his bite.

"He eats beautifully. Nice manners," Agnes said. "Perhaps you want to show him the deer. Nice view of the sunset from the top." Nothing could happen to me within the safe enclosure of the Meinert gardens.

The red winter sun was already sinking down towards the water castle. Father had rescued a wounded doe. I had named her Rita. At first she had run away, especially from Krampus. Now Rita had calmed down and Krampus liked following her around the garden. Mort lured the deer with a handful of hay, but when he tried to touch her shiny black nose she bolted. "Hey, come back here!" Rita flicked her tail and ran off into the thicket.

"The pink sky reminds me of Normandy. I remember the crossing. So many boats in the water. The English Channel was like a highway. It made you feel everything was under control, but we were scared. I was wounded. I didn't feel a thing. Shock. If you have too much of it, you die. I could hear myself singing as if I were someone else far away. A song from a muscial show I had been in. There were soldiers singing. The next thing I remember was a soldier yelling: 'look at that bloody sun.' It was like a bad dream."

I asked about the wound, he said it healed fast. And I told him I knew about war from a gardener who had fought on the western front in the First World War, and I took Mort to the gardener's cottage to show him the purple Fritz Janicek self portrait curling on the wall from rusty nails. A good likeness, sharp nosed, with that odd, strained sidelong stare of a man studying his own face in a mirror.

"He liked to paint," I said and remembered to forget Fritz the Professor-Gardener-S.S.-Doll-thief, art-collector, worshipper-of-Mother, creator of this or that maze that led to traps.

A piece of the mirror he had used as a palette remained on the stool. I fingered the dry dark Prussian blue Fritz Janicek had used to mix the darkest purple. I had once touched it during one of those Janicek tirades about the First World War, his mother the invalid, my mother the doll and horse lover. And Prussian blue on one little finger turned into midnight dark smudges from knee socks, to leather pants, to shirt, nose chin and curls. Prussian blue had left a mark, so had Fritz Janicek with his lectures.

"You should have seen his roses. He was a great gardener." (I left out the killing of cats who scratched up in flower beds, and birds that pecked at fruit, hand squashed rose beetles, shooting Puppe's head off and kissing that head.) "Our garden was *sooo* beautiful before the war. And the lilac!"

I found myself telling him about confirmation time in Vienna. How all kinds of parents had asked Eugene Romberg to be confirmation father, because he gave each confirmation child the most expensive ring and watch. He was so generous. I told Mort of children riding to St. Stephens, dressed up like little brides or grooms, in the Romberg's white Damlier or in a horse-drawn Fiaker decorated with lilac from our gardens. Then from church they had gone on to the traditional celebration in the amusement park, the Prater. Eugene Romberg used to treat children to all the rides they wanted, ghost-train, merry-go-round, and to shooting galleries. And then a feast at Eissvogels where he would urge his confirmation child to eat and eat.

I had to talk very fast creating a landscape of a happy Austria for Mort and myself, but I had heard Father say that many of those grown up Romberg confirmation children were trying to denazify themselves; writing to Switzerland, asking Eli for a testamonial that they could not have been real Nazis, because they were Romberg confirmation children. At the same time Romberg *Firmlings* asked for food, clothes, help. And if Eli complied Romberg *confirmlings* would multiply!

Mort did not interrupt me once. When I stopped talking, he said: "We do know about Eugene Romberg. And old purple face here certainly didn't have much time for him, did he now? The picture is a good likeness." Mort said. "I have interrogated that man."

"He's in Vienna isn't he?"

"I imagine so, although some of them sing, get payed and then skip."

"What did he tell you?"

Mort walked out. "He lies a lot. They all do. Everyone else is to blame. He did his best to save museum art. Colonel Fredricks is an art collector and took an interest in old Janicek." He made a snowball, threw it and Krampus ran after it. "I have to ask you something," Mort said. "That little midget. She knew something was going to happen on the Mozart Express before the shooting."

"Hanna Roth," I nodded with enthusiasm because I liked it when he spoke to me in English. Understanding and misunderstanding between us came naturally.

"Frau Roth talked about General Patton. Mentioned a car," Mort said. "Today some vehicle comes along on the wrong side of the street, causes a bad accident. The general is in the hospital."

I could imagine Hanna Roth's dark blue car with the crystal vase taking a curve at full speed. Big smile, driving glasses enlarging her huge, black eyes. "She's not an assassin," I quickly said. "She's a rotten driver."

"She didn't hit General Patton's car. An American truck smashed into it. But how did she know this was going to happen?"

I kicked an ice ball up the hill. Krampus came bounding after it. "Father always said men talk to women and women all talk to Frau Hanna."

"It seems so much like an accident," he said. "Not many people knew that the general was going to a pheasant hunt."

"Peasant hunt! The general deserved everything that happened to him."

Mort laughed and took a dictionary out of his pocket. "Birds," he said. "Not country folks."

We laughed. He took my hand and we ran uphill under the great pines where snow looked blue and was patterned with footprints of birds and squirrels and the deer. I told him I hated any kind of hunt. Father never hunted.

We climbed to the top of the pavillion. Gold and tangerine ripples of cloud cast a glow over the snow dusted vineyards and hills of the Vienna woods. He took off his uniform cap and put it down on a snow-covered table and his face took on a rosy sheen of the sky. "The Roth woman. Do you ever listen to her stories on the radio?"

"I did hear her once by chance. It's a children's program. I'm not a child," I said.

"Do you talk to her on the phone?"

"No," I said.

"But you have listened to her stories."

"Ahh. You think she passes coded messages on to me over the radio with her stories. Then I send them on by carrier pigeons all the way to Hitler in his hiding place. Then he gets disguised as a driver and runs into General Patton's car . . ."

"Slow down," Mort took out a note pad and pencil. "Say that again."

I tried to translate it all into English but I couldn't stop laughing.

"It isn't all that funny," he said. "The Roth woman lived over there at the end of the war?" He pointed not at the water castle but at the brilliant sky, as if Hanna had indeed been one of dark birds that now circled above the trees.

"I'm sure you know all about that. You've interrogated Frau Boschke. *Nicht wahr?* And you must know she actually did have a right to live there. Her best friend Frau Traude, Traude Romberg, was Eugene Romberg's mother."

"Her friend moved to Morocco," Mort said. "Do you know why?"

"She can't live without candy," I said. "She would starve to death here."

He walked back and forth; snow crunched like broken glass. Years ago, after the last Romberg ball, Eugene Romberg, in an Arab costume had stomped through crusty snow over there.

Champagne bottles had been planted in snow-covered flower beds. "You really think Hanna Roth had something to do with the shooting?" I asked.

"I don't think anything. I thought you might have some ideas. You knew her well, I understand." He was leaning forward. Down below, Rita the deer limped gently over pink sun-drenched snow.

"I wish you could have known Vienna before the war." I spoke slow, clear soft Austrian German like my grandmama. "Hanna Roth used to design the most fantastic spring hats, flowers, little veils." (Little hats tilted forward and Adolf Hitler. She had fore-seen it all.) "Just wait maybe in the spring the prater will be repaired and you can ride in the Riesen-rad. The merry-go-rounds, the ghost train. We even have a flea circus. See the electric wires among the trees? Well, Russians did shoot the light bulbs, but by the summer I'm sure Father will have it all repaired. It will be warm. There will be more food. Perhaps the Rombergs will come back. I mean, Resi Romberg, the singer and her son Eli and they'll live in the water castle." I talked too fast.

"Water castle?" he asked.

I explained and he listened. "Mixing milk with water? Splasher?" he repeated after me. "A joke?"

"Teasing is often a way of loving in Vienna. You couldn't help loving Eugene Romberg."

The sky slowly faded. Mort turned up his coat collar. In pro-file he had rounded cheeks, a small snub nose and the full, smooth lips of a bottle baby. His eyes bulged a little and the mustache was lighter and not quite as curly as his short hair. He looked too young for the officer's uniform. Fritz Janicek had probably been that age in the First World War when he had seen ram-parts of corpses. How about Mort? Why did anyone ever want to stick boys into uniforms and send them off to kill each other? Why not let the old fanatics and politicians go off and be heroes? What if the world agreed never to send anyone under sixty to fight in a war?

Mort turned and caught me looking at him. "Would they have called Romberg Splasher if he hadn't been a Jew or foreigner?"

"Of course," I said. "Don't they give funny names to people in America?"

He turned to me. Threw his cigarette into the snow and stepped on it hard. "They sure do! Especially kids."

"What did they call you?" I asked.

He reached for me and caught me in his arms. "Forget it," he said and pressed me against his coat. I felt his uniform buttons through my heavy sweater. He kissed my mouth three times, pushed me away then clasped me in his arms. He repeated this and I kept count. By the time we reached fifty-seven he was playing a silent tune and I was the instrument. Holding me at arm's length, his lips circled over mine, barely touching, faster and faster, tobacco and banana flavored mouth swooping down to mine. When he leaned me against the railing and pressed himself against me I glowed as if it were summer. I was afraid the old wood might give way and we might crash down into the frosted lilac bushes. To avoid such an accident I had to press myself against him. He trembled and pushed his tongue into my mouth.

I didn't like this until he began to play the tune he had played on my mouth on my body. Circling gently and pressing against me with his hips. It felt warm and sweet and ridiculous. The railing creaked. I pushed him away.

He was breathing hard. "You're just a kid." This time it was a reproach.

"Girls are never too young, only boys are." I always sound like the person I quote. He had a fine ear for tone.

He laughed. "Who said that?"

"Mother's cousin."

"Hohentahler?"

"Do you know him?"

"In Salzburg. Right? I've spoken to him. He's O.K." He lit another cigarette. "You're quite a family. Your grandmother is quite a lady. You were with her when the Russians took Vienna. Did she store a lot of stuff in her shelter?"

"A lot of very old stuff," I bragged to make him happy. "When spring comes she'll bring a lot of it upstairs. She has a clock collection. You can come and look around. I'm sure she won't mind. I know you've already been to see her and you bought that document."

He looked disinterested and sad.

"And don't worry. I'm sure General Patton will get better."

He hissed something under his breath. It sounded like a curse.

"Don't you like him?" I asked.

"You ask too many questions," he said.

"So do you," I said.

He kissed me again. When he let go, the lights of the water castle came on one by one. This had happened before. One morning at sunrise when I was ten years old. Only this time it happened slowly. Someone was looking around each room before going on to the next one.

"Colonel Fredricks must have arrived," Mort said.

"There is no car."

"It'll be at the back gate," he said. "Less conspicuous."

"Less conspicuous?" I echoed because I liked the English word and didn't know the meaning.

"It's quieter back there," he said in German. "More private too." As it turned out he was quite wrong about that.

"How many officers are moving in?" I asked.

He hugged me, relaxed for the first time that afternoon. "Lieutenant Kaufman and all kinds of other men will be working out of the office. There'll be two of us staying over there. Then, of course, there is the sergeant and the guards and the Austrian staff."

I hopped up and down, made all kinds of silly happy sounds.

"The housekeeper has a young daughter. Supposed to be cute."

I didn't like that one bit. "The woman is supposed to be the wife of a big Nazi," I said.

"Frau Schmiedler?" he moved away from me and bit into his lower lip. "She's O.K. Turns out she had a hell of a time. Mixed blood. Seems the old man kept her on as a cook. Made her do all the housework and cooking when he entertained and she had to stay out of sight for the sake of the girl."

I should have said, I don't believe it. Could have said, don't you know that everyone used to search for Aryan ancestors under Hitler? Now they're digging up Jewish grandfathers or grandmothers like mad. A Nazi with a Jewish ancestor behind him could make all kinds of excuses and even register for food from relief organizations.

"A terrible thing when you have to hide who your folks were," he said.

He actually had tears in his eyes. And tears in sympathy for Frau Schmiedler, sympathy for an Austrian, brought him closer to me. Overunderstanding was better than suspicion.

He hacked the heel of his glossy shoe into the snow. "She used to do most of the pastry cooking when Hitler secretly showed up, or Himmler, any of the big shots."

"She could have poisoned them," I said. There appeared before me a half empty pastry tray! *Happy Birthday Dear Willy, from the Schmiedlers.* A carnival of men dressed up in Resi's costumes. Fritz Janicek's Club. His friends, Gypsy musicians playing a lullaby at dawn, to a dead parrot, men in Resi clothes, sleeping, sleeping forever. Perhaps it hadn't been poisoned wine.

"She's O.K." he said again. "Might be fun for you to have the girl around. When we were inspecting houses I noticed that there aren't any kids your age around here. The tennis courts will be fixed up in the spring." Now Mort was trying to cheer me up. "Things will settle down by then. There should be more food."

While he talked soldiers came around the Romberg garage with barbed wire and started unrolling it inside the front railings.

I could already hear the ping-ping of tennis balls, and see an Else twinkling across the courts in shorts, playing games behind barbed wire. I had visions of the girl with the angel face disporting herself in the gardens, the many rooms I loved.

Lights on the top floor, even the attic lights came on. The glass cupola glowed against a now ash-gray sky. "Isn't that a cheerful sight!" he said.

"All the lights used to be on day and night when Eugene Romberg was alive," I said.

Suddenly all the lights at the big house went out at once.

"Must have blown a fuse. Turning on all those darned lights at once. Typical," Mort said.

# THIRTEEN

# Glitter on Her Hat

I CAME HOME from school and found Frau Boschke, the laundress in my room, changing my bed. Her hair had been crimped and was no longer mud-colored but black. "Well, take a good look at me. I'm now Official American Household Helper."

Everybody in Vienna liked to have a title under the Kaiser, after the Kaiser, and under Hitler. Indignities after Hitler brought on a craving for the dignity of more titles, new self esteem as insatiable as the hunger for sweets.

Frau Boschke shut the door and produced a package of American cigarettes. We both lit up. "American or not American, I told them twice a week is enough. I have to have a change. That's me. Then Sergeant Tony spoke to me. Who can refuse such a fellow. Now it's three times a week."

"I saw Else Schmiedler on Frau Romberg's balcony with an American officer," I said.

"Colonel Fredricks," she said.

"Has the girl taken over Resi Romberg's old room?"

"The colonel has," she said. "And that Schmiedler daughter has taken over the colonel. That's how her mother got that job in the first place. The colonel thinks they are bait. Schmiedler will come out of hiding. The Americans will nab him and then Frau Schmiedler and the girl will at least be able to tell them whether they got the right man. It's a joke. The chimney sweep came the other day. Else went to meet him, let out one big shriek, Vati, Pappa, Daddy! Threw her arms around the man's neck and got herself all black. The poor man had a time shaking her off."

I had to laugh at Else with our local chimney sweep who went around covered with soot from top to toe, brushes coiled over his left shoulder with a certain dash, because he had the reputation of a ladies' man. "Did the Amis think the chimney sweep was Schmiedler?"

"You should have seen the colonel and one of the guards jump on the poor fellow with pistols, scaring him so much he dropped his ladder on his own foot and cracked a bone. He showed them his identity card. They decided his papers were forged, had him locked up in the exercize room with the mechanical horse. I talked to Tony. He believed me and they called the local police. It took two hours to get straightened out."

"What happened to Else?"

"She said she couldn't help herself. She missed her father so much, and the chimney sweep was black from top to toe, how could she tell who was underneath it all. . . . That girl is poison. Always was. Our sergeant Tony says she is 'no gut.' And he studies people. He noticed me when I was cleaning Ami offices. Took a great liking to me. If you want to know the truth he is the only one who has any sense. That Lieutenant Mort he comes and he goes and he goes. . . . The colonel doesn't know whether he's coming or going—some Abwehr officer! Then there is a third one who shows up at the office every day, smokes cigars and sticks his nose into everything. A real Berliner big mouth. He goes into Herr Romberg's gymnasium and lifts weights every day. The chimney sweep had tried out the riding machine while he was locked up. So the Berliner has his ride the next day and gets his seat covered with soot. I have the mess. And my Sergeant Tony wants me to keep an eye on the Schmiedlers. And as far as the big Nazi money beast Herr Schmiedler himself goes, he can put on beards, wigs, dress up as a grandmother. I washed his clothes and he can't fool a good Viennese washerwoman. No two men ever smell the same. I can sniff him out."

"You say he smells of mushrooms," I said. "But he's not the only one."

"More like toadstools," she said and put a neatly folded nightgown under my pillow right next to my treasure box, patted it lovingly.

"How do I smell?"

"Of mischief and that English toilet water you steal from your Mama."

"Did you tell Sergeant Tony that Schmiedler smells of toadstools?"

She sat down on my bed, crossed her thin legs and grinned. "You don't tell everything right away."

"What beautiful stockings. The Sergeant gave them to you."

"And plenty of cigarettes."

"It is true that he trades with coffee, soap, cans of meat, almost anything for old Nazi uniforms, swastika pins, flags, pistols?"

"Isn't he a wonder? What would we do without him this Christmas. Nothing to buy, nothing to eat. They should all be grateful and keep their mouth shut. And they should be glad to get rid of the old stuff and clear out the attic."

She busied herself smoothing my pillows and quilt. We puffed on our cigarettes. Neither of us knew how to inhale. "What does he do with it all?" I asked.

Her eyes danced. She enjoyed carrying stories from house to house. Like any first-rate gossip she would forget who told her a story after she had passed it on. "When I used to iron for the Romberg family there was that big room I could never get into. He had the key and kept it locked. Now the Herr Colonel Fredericks has the key. Else is driving him crazy. And he forgets to lock it . . ." She hummed the "Merry Widow Waltz," emptied my dirty linen bag into her laundry basket, danced out with it and shut the door. She often left me hanging like this with all kinds of unanswered questions. There was always a "to be continued," at the end of her stories.

It was Tony, the sergeant, the boy wonder who put up a gigantic Christmas tree at the window of Resi's old music room days and days before Christmas. I saw it from the hill near Ursel's house and drank in the jolly sight of green, blue, yellow, and red electric lights twinkling like a nightclub sign announcing Christmas. Everyone was saying it was simply awful destroying the wonder of Christmas for Austrian children who all believed the Christkindl came flying through the window with the tree on Holy Eve. But Ursel and I loved the American tree.

This would be a dark Christmas for many. Candles were scarce. During mass I would stare at dancing candle flames until

I felt dazed and closer to heaven. And gazing through the back railings of the big house at those twinkling lights, the gigantic American Christmas tree, I felt closer to Lieutenant Mort's America: a paradise of catchy songs, dancing lights, dancing pairs, cars bright as easter eggs, young men kissing smiling young girls. The Americans we saw were young and unhurt by time or war. I stared at those twinkling lights and had visions of a new world without old wickedness or old age. Mort seemed to have forgotten me since he moved into the water castle. Once or twice he had waved to me in passing and smiled from a car or a jeep. He didn't even slow down.

I was walking down the hill from Ursel's house one afternoon and stopped near the empty cobbler's hut. Only one jeep was parked inside the back gate of the great house. Rolls of barbed wire alongside the railings created a frilly edge to the doily of snow patterned with shrubs and lacy shadows of twigs. Smoke was rising from the tennis pavillion occupied by the guards. It was very quiet and Christmas lights in the window winked and blinked.

I heard a thud. Else Schmiedler had jumped out from the French window of Eugene Romberg's secret room. Nothing could have prepared me for the shock. She came away as a trespasser from the room Eugene Romberg had unlocked for me the morning after the last costume ball. He had been dressed as an Arab. The furniture had been from Morocco and he had talked to me of the big shadowy house in Mogador, where as a small boy he had played games of chess against himself with bowling pegs on the chessboard tile floors. Then, one day, the Arab cook had interrupted his games and claimed Eugene as his son. "They call me Romberg the Jew, Rumanian, Gypsy, and thief. Actually I am a thief. Izaak Romberg thought I was his son, and I became his heir."

Else came away from his house like a thief, avoiding the main path. One moment I saw her white fur coat among evergreen hedges, then she blended in with the snow or vanished behind statues and huge trees. I loathed her in that black mannish hat, which she had trimmed with a fascinating glitter chain from the christmas tree. When the guards came out of the tennis pavillion she doffed it and they gave her a cigarette. The glitter chain danced in the wind while they smoked and laughed their way to the back gate. They unlocked and held it open for her and she left them behind like servants.

I took cover behind the cobbler's hut. Ursel had told me she sometimes saw a light in the window. I peeked in and saw the dark shape of a man. A glass sat on a shelf. The man reached for it, a ring sparkled. Shelter was scarce. Many people had come down in the world. It would be boring and cold in there. And who wouldn't want to watch Else Schmiedler stride down the hill.

The wind shook trees. Snow fell on her. She shook it off the hat and I saw dark roots on the parting of her pale, smooth hair. Beautiful, flaxen-haired Schmiedler, a Hitler blond! part of that sham Aryan master race. It should not have made me glad. I had been on our remote mountain farm, enjoying lessons with the tutor I loved, playing in alpine meadows with my friend Stopperl, while a ten-, eleven-, thirteen-year-old Else had to have her hair bleached to beguile the great architects of carnage.

She had been used, but I didn't see it that way. I followed the glitter of her hat down to the street car stop with such fury, I came out of hiding. She didn't turn her head. Looking over her shoulder was not her style. The man inside the hut must have seen me standing there. I didn't give him a thought.

A streetcar came along almost at once. Else threw away her cigarette, jumped on ahead of other people who had been there before her, and took the best front seat. A dignified neighbor, a music teacher in a dark overcoat, stooped like a beggar for the butt of her cigarette and stayed behind to smoke.

Smoke from the tennis pavillion slithered up towards the cupola of the water castle. Lights of the American Christmas tree still twinkled and the streetcar screeched over icy rails and vanished around the curve. There would be men gazing after her, gaping, and she wouldn't know it. And she would leave them behind like the neighbor smoking her cigarette butt. Her disdain glittered like the chain on that hat. Else was on her way. She didn't wait around for love like me. I could imagine her taking her place at the corner of Kaernerstrasse among *"those"* girls.

Among ruined buildings and ruined girls the Schmiedler daughter appeared as a misplaced ornament. Decked out in this or that fur her father had taken from unworthy owners, unworthy lands I saw her flaunt the superiority of an initiate to cruelty. What was done, was done. To Else Schmiedler everything was baloney, *Wurscht*. She didn't care and she did as she pleased. Corpses, suffering, *pfui*, bilge. Men—*Quatsch*. The future was hers.

Before the war, Mother had expected a second child. And she had the room next to mine painted not pink or blue but sea green, just in case the baby Eugene, Father expected, turned out to be a Eugenia. The room had remained empty. My grandmother now used it when she spent the night, or took a rest. When she came to stay with us the week before Christmas a little slow burning stove in the nursery was lit for her. We opened the connecting door and shared the warmth.

She was taking a rest in her room. My parents had gone into town in Father's truck. The quiet house bothered me. At the water castle lights were on, military cars drove up and down the hill. Mort had gone to Germany and would not be back for Christmas. I felt disgruntled. And whenever I felt life was passing me by I turned to the mirror.

I swept up my hair and tried out an Else Schmiedler face. The brush fell from my hand. "My Rudolf Hess is gone!" I got down on my hands and knees. There was no sign of my favorite Rudolf Hess picture, the smiling one.

The Countess Reyna came at once and sat down on my bed. In the mirror the remaining Rudolf Hess paper dolls formed a crazy crown above her white braids. "It probably fell down and was swept up and thrown away. And you still have quite a collection of pictures left." I saw on her face both the amused amazement of a girl, and the fatigue of aging. "I had no idea he meant so much to you. Most of these pictures must have been taken when he was young. Even before you were born. Now he's old enough to be your grandfather." She interrupted herself and laughed. "I know. I know. Time doesn't exist, age doesn't matter when it comes to such infatuations."

"Loves," I said.

"How many great loves do you have?"

"Several," I admitted.

"I was the same way. After Aunt Christina took me away from the convent, out into the world, I became infatuated with every handsome man; even our Kaiser, long before I was presented." She smiled at herself in the mirror. "You gain time dreaming of all those incredible loves."

Creations preceded experience. And choosing one, would have meant losing the others. She understood this. Our eyes met in the mirror and her face took on my expression. I knew what she was thinking.

"I am a realist," I said. "Rudolf Hess is really quite ugly, especially the mouth." I spoke fast, without conviction, and her lips moved with mine shaping words. "He does have beautiful eyes, so sad. He tried to stop the war. And he might be condemned to death because he signed papers condemning Jews. Could it be that he hated Jews because he was born in Alexandria? Egyptians were mad at the Jews from way back because the Jews were runaway slaves and made off with some Egyptian jewelry." I was spouting Resi Romberg's version of the history of the Jews.

She touched my arm and said, "Calm down, little heart. You don't have to make excuses for him."

I went to the mirror and pulled the Rudolf Hess paper dolls off. Deep down I couldn't and wouldn't believe that my Hess ever condemmed anyone to death.

My grandmother knew me well. "Perhaps the missing picture bothers you because you were almost ready to take all those photographs down, but don't throw him away," she said.

I got my treasure box out from under a pillow. Took the key off the chain I always wore around my neck. I didn't need it. I had left the box open. I stuck the Rudolf Hess paper dolls into the top, quickly shut it. The lock seemed to be stuck. I shoved the box out of sight under my pillow with an amazing sense of relief. That night I had a happy dream: Water lapping against the hull of a gondola, wavelets crimping the reflections of palaces, laughter bouncing off dank walls in narrow canals. A man singing "O Sole Mio" and the oar creaking, the smell of rot. *I am here, here I am.* Giving myself up to warm shallow water, wallowing yielding as a cloud yields to a breeze. I am in each grain of trickling sand. I am nothing, everything in warm ripples of drousy delight. I woke up. My lips were still saying: *I am here, here I am.*

In Frau Boschke's dream book happy dreams were a bad omen, and unhappy dreams good. After Christmas, when she was so much in love, she started carrying the old tattered dream book with her sprinkling can and American soap, because she herself was dreaming so much and was trying to figure things out. Perhaps the dream book is right. You console yourself with happy dreams when you know bad things are going on.

I woke up and said: "Grandmama I've been dreaming of Venice. It was beautiful!"

She was kneeling on her bed. The little night light shone on her faded paisley shawl. White braids dangled down her back. She was looking out at the white garden lit up by an invisible moon. "*Ja, ja,* our beautiful Venedig!" Venice lost. The empire lost. I heard it all in her voice. "You were only three years old. You had such a happy time. Your father took over a small Italian hotel and invited everyone. The Meinert sisters brought their easels and parasols. I played in the sand with you. We built so many castles, you and I. And there were other children. One who had a little wooden trowel you wanted so much. A lovely little child. Schmiedler family. The father turned out to be a scoundrel."

"Did you ever see him?" I asked.

"Yes and no. He seemingly slept all day and stayed up at night. He changed his appearance, wore wigs, outlandish clothes. He was a speculator and an illusionist. His wife was a handsome woman, Rumanian, I think." She seemingly didn't know anything about Frau Schmiedler the housekeeper. I did not want to interrupt her happy memories. She sat back on her heels. The lace on her white nightgown was now slightly frayed around the sleeves and hem. "I had never played like a child until you came along. You changed everything. Especially Christmas. In my own home, as a young war widow, I just recreated a convent Christmas for my Anne Marie. My little girl always carried her doll. On Christmas day Hanna Roth often came to make a doll's Christmas, and your mother loved that. You were so different . . ."

She praised the toddler and made me long for the child I had been. "I wish we could go back to Venice," I said.

"I know. We all feel hemmed in this winter. I was thinking of this, looking out into the enchanting garden. I have my dream, too. You married, settled at Falkenburg with a wonderful family. I could almost hear the little feet of grandchildren running along the ancient passageways, chasing away the ghosts. When the Russians leave I will somehow have the place repaired. Our

Franzl goes to check up on Falkenburg. He gets along well with
the Russians."

Franz, the monarchist peasant leader, had been a courier for
the monarchists during the war. Now he sometimes brought food
from his farm for my grandmother. "He gets along fine with the
Russians, because he looks like Stalin," I said.

"To think he's going to marry my friend Hermine." A log
crackled in the stove. I lay back and closed my eyes and listened
to the love story of Tante Hermine. Alone, on a run-down estate
at the end of the war. Her eyes giving her trouble, her left arm.
Then she became lame. She told her friends she had sprained
her ankle, she was a little arthritic. But she knew she couldn't
continue to work for the resistance unless she had some help.
Someone she could trust. The man she had loved had been killed
in the first World War. She had never married. And she simply
put an ad into the paper: "Lady, landowner, old family, handi-
capped, wishes to meet suitable partner between fifty-six and
sixty years old."

Franzl had been using the paper for kindling and saw this by
chance. His own marriage had been arranged. The girl had
brought him land, but also bad blood. She wasn't all there. Their
only child had been a half wit. Franz's wife had died during the
war. And only a few month ago his boy had vanished from the
farm. Franzl loved that boy and kept looking for him. Never gave
up. He was lonely. He had answered the ad with a short note.
He loved old families. And he could trace his peasant stock back
hundreds of years.

Hermine had received a long, wild letter from a seventy-year-
old Casanova. And another one from an opportunist. The note
Franz sent, had dignity. He did not give his name either. She
arranged to meet him at a coffeehouse. He would know her by a
black Hungarian sheep dog. This way he could see her, and if he
didn't like her, simply stay away. She walked into the coffeehouse and there was Franzl. He jumped up, petted the dog, took
it off her hands and helped her find the nice private table she
wanted. The coffeehouse was almost empty. She kept watching
the door. He had remained standing up respectfully. They had
lots to talk about. The same problems, the war, the land, the
Nazi danger. After fifteen minutes she had invited him to sit
down. They had talked and talked until dark. Finally she had

asked. "What brought you all the way here, Herr Franzl? Anything serious?" She was, of course, thinking of his lost son. Everyone knew about that sorrow.

He told her it was very serious and grinned. Then he admitted he had answered her advertisement.

Hermine, an Austrian princess, had laughed. Ordered more tea.

"They fell in love," I concluded.

"Quite suitable. When our Crown Prince comes to the throne, Franzl should get a title. He is a great patriot. A noble person. A country man. Hermine is a country woman. Fortunately her property is in the British zone. They didn't want to get married until after the war. There will be a wedding at Christmas."

I closed my eyes. A piece of coal dropped and hissed inside the stove. One by one I placed my loves at Falkenburg until I had assembled them all. The unhaunting of the castle, turned into a haunting: Rudolf Hess waiting for me on a rickety bench in the overgrown herb garden. Bertl in a boat on lake Neusiedel. Eli in the old library. Mort in the music corner of the dining hall singing "Prisoner of Love" and "Don't Fence me in." I took Arnold, my Frog Prince, by the hand and showed him the winding staircase with the portrait of a dwarf in armor.

You could tell yourself, hey, what's the matter with you, all this dreaming of love. Life isn't an amusement park. It's pretty hopeless and even dangerous. You can't go around town after dark. In the sunlight who wouldn't take a chance. Imagine the winter sun in the first district, medieval Vienna, those narrow streets and squares, the fountains, the debris and all those foreign soldiers; all four allies in charge. And all the secret agents watching each other and looking for someone. Vienna, city of dreams, always has, and always will be a city for spies and loves, young and old and that includes snoops like me and investigators of the soul like Dr. Freud.

A dapper French officer seemed to be following me. Had he noticed my new wiggly walk? Would he think I am old enough? If he said something would I run like Ursel? On the Graben a shop window reflected the person behind me. A woman! The officer has vanished. My ears were too red. That was it. I stopped and let down my hair. I breathed in the icy hair. Combed it out. No one came along and said, what lovely hair you have. No Bertl appeared by mere chance. Eli hadn't arrived unexpectedly from Switzerland. I hummed Mort's "Prisoner of Love." My kind of love prison was a crazy mirror house.

I was on my way to Mother's furrier. He was turning her old black muff into fur lined driving gloves—a Christmas present for Father. Mother had been glad to get rid of the old muff and old memories. Puppe had been stolen out of this muff years ago; she hadn't touched it since. And Father had no gloves. His hands got terribly cold driving around in an old rusty truck. especially when he had to crank it up.

Actually Mother's furrier, a Jew, had gone to America. The employee who had aryanized the firm was still the owner and answered the door himself. He said, "good morning Countess," kissed my hand and made his excuses. I had to have a little patience. He had Russian customers.

The parquet floor in the big reception room was stained. The gold and brown Persian rug had vanished. So had the silk curtains. One window was still boarded up. Partitions had been torn down from private fitting rooms. A woman was facing a mirror trying to squeeze herself into a tight black Persian lamb coat. Another one helped and got her stuck. They negotiated with the furrier in broken German. Two or three furs were lying on a chair. They picked up another black one and the idea was to make the two coats into one to allow for the monstrous balloon bosoms. Girls in school had been right. I was impressed. In the circus vulgar clowns wearing huge balloon bosoms invariably ended up in some kind of conflict. I was quite prepared for a pop as the furrier struggled to get the stout woman out of the tiny coat. He promised them anything to get them to the door and then he locked up carefully. He might not ever see the women again. This had happened before. He was left with their orders.

"Gloves are not our specialty as a rule, but we oblige. With what can I serve, gracious countess? You have the perfect figure for a fur. We create a new model from something old. This is what we specialize in now." I admired the gloves, stuck them into my pocket and paid him with American cigarettes. He led me to the back door and bowed over my hand again.

I had only walked about one block when a man stepped in front of me. He lifted an Austrian felt hat. I recognized Alexander, Valdo's comrade by the big friendly nose. We shook hands.

he inquired after my grandmother, grinned and dazzled me with a display of new, gold teeth. "You like?" he asked. "Just like the picture in your house. Gold is better than steel."

I laughed and he laughed with me. "A lot of gold. The best. Eighteen carat. A nice job. A lot of chains and rings. A lot of gold hidden away in Austria. A lot of treasures. You saw it, *ja*? In the mountains. A cave. How many caves are there?"

I hesitated and he encouraged me with a smile displaying his gold.

"Perhaps the Americans have the crowns, perhaps not. Perhaps they only say so that no one will look and find. You tell me what you know and you get a present from Alexander. What you like? A fur coat? Nice ring, something to eat?"

His gold smile held both the promise and the threat of Ali Baba's cave. He was friendly. Trying to bribe me like a child. "How about setting General von Kortnai and all his Hungarians free?"

He glared at me. Took a dirty notebook out of his briefcase and asked me to write it for him. I was telling him about the general, the daughter, the horses, everything.

Suddenly he pointed at a man who was staring at a window display of a single parasol. "We talk another time." The man came towards us so fast, a pigeon flew in front of his face. Alexander vanished around the corner.

"*Ach,* Fraulein von Meinert. I have the honor. You remember me."

Green plus-fours, the hat, Krummerer, alias Herbster. The candle donation. He had a watchful face, soft jowls, and two protruding rabbit teeth showed under his Hitler moustache. "I hope you were careful talking to a stranger. The man you talked to is a Russian."

"I know," I said. "He stayed at our house."

"An agent. I hope you have not given him any information." He took my elbow and kept looking from side to side. Following people is outdoor work and gave him a florid complexion. He said he would be so free as to escort me. "I've always loved little ones. Sorry I never could find that dolly for you."

"Mother's. Have you forgotten?"

He muttered something about having much on his mind.

"Did Father ask you to follow me?"

"None of that. I don't do that kind of work anymore. This is pure coincidence."

"Why are you suddenly Herr Herbster?"

"Safer," he said. "Krummerer had been hired by the gestapo. They wanted an experienced private detective and no one could refuse the gestapo. And now Krummerer would be in jail, accused and punished for what they did. Your Herr father and I we had an understanding from way back."

"Who is Herbster?" I asked.

"Dead," he said without feeling. "I did my best for him. He could trust me. When they put him into a concentration camp he left his documents with me for safe keeping."

"A Jew?"

He nodded. "A Dutch diamond merchant. They made him an honorary Aryan and he talked like a German Nazi and got involved with Eugene Romberg and Schmiedler in financing the Russian campaign. Some kind of swindle. They got Herr Director Romberg too in the end."

I stumbled and he gripped my arm. "What happened to Eugene Romberg after he was arrested in Salzburg?" I asked.

He didn't want to talk.

"I saw him die, you know. He was locked up in an empty amethyst mine. My mother and I found him during an avalanche and took him to our farm."

"So he told you how he got there?"

Black windows of bombed out houses confronted me like hollow eye sockets. "I know most of it," I said. But I didn't have to encourage him to go on. With secrets, conspiracies and mistrust comes the natural urge to tell all.

"I had nothing to do with his capture. They questioned him and stuck him into a concentration camp. I didn't know about the experiments until it was all over. He was picked out because he was a chess master. They wanted to test a new drug. God knows, maybe they were planning to feed it to Hitler and Himmler and everyone else later. The camp director, a chess lover had this idea. Romberg and a young Russian chess master were to play and the winner they promised would go free. And they put this power drug into their water. Romberg won. They actually did let him go. Without money or anything, to see how the power drug would help him make his way."

"How about the loser?"

"Whoever lost the first game was given another dose of the drug. If he lost again, he was given more."

"Did it kill the loser in the end."

"It did."

"That made the winner a murderer," I said.

"They had promised the winner a head start of half a day, shoes and an overcoat. They followed him. Power drug, or no power drug, Romberg went straight into a trap."

"Why didn't you tell my father. He could have done something!"

He glared at me.

I walked away from him at a trot like a fugitive, slipping on soiled icy snow. But I had to know exactly how it happened. And he had to keep talking.

"Romberg had the idea that your mother was in danger up there in the mountains. All Janicek had to do was wait."

A Fritz Janicek maze, of course. He had once created them for mice in the gardener's cottage. "Why didn't you stop Eugene Romberg. Why didn't you help him?" I tripped, fell, got up quickly before he had a chance to help me up. The votive church supported by scaffolding, in the distance, was sham-gothic, so was Eugene Romberg's fate. Had he not been desperate to get to Mother, he might have saved himself. I walked ahead, leaning into the wind.

"I didn't know what they were going to do until it was all over. And what's over is over. He had his chance. But Romberg was always Romberg. Couldn't get away from himself. No escape. No escape at the end."

I had heard too much. Life seemed like a Fritz Janicek maze. "Why did you tell me this!" I shouted into the face of the stranger Krummerer had become.

"I told you because you asked," he said in a new fatherly tone of voice. "And I like children. But it is your turn now. What did that *Russ* want?"

"Treasures," I said. "A box filled with treasures."

"Whatever he offered you, I can give you more."

"Who's paying you?"

He ignored this. "One must trade to survive. How about your own father? Don't tell him I said so. But it's all over Vienna, anyway. He traded a train for bacon, ham and a Christmas carp. You're a lucky girl. I have some lovely stones, Fraulein."

"Herbster diamonds?"

He actually reached inside his coat lining into a hidden pocket.

"I'm not interested in diamonds," I said.

He cautioned me without saying a word. I saw his gift as a mime. He held out his hand offering me anything, anything at all. And this reminded me of another hand, the plump, white hand of Eugene Romberg, who always wanted to give me everything and never asked for a favor in return.

"You can't give me back Eugene Romberg," I said. "So get General von Kortnai and his daughter and his Hungarians away from the Russians." I ran away from him, jumped onto a moving streetcar before it reached the stop just like Else Schmiedler. The crowd trying to get out, pushed and scolded me. I turned to stone. Krummerer, Herbster was left behind and his last gesture was a despondent salute, the gesture of a mime portraying a lost general.

Knowledge of evil hurts. I went to bed early. My belly ached as though I had eaten something poisonous. I wanted to be alone. Bad experience was supposed to wash over me like winter rain that ran over the cupola of the water castle. When I am troubled I often sink into sleep.

It was dark when I woke up. Only the stove door in the nursery glowed. My grandmother was asleep. The wind rattled windows. It had stopped raining. A car door banged like a pistol shot. Men laughed. I heard a whistle—one high, one low. It went with Ami boys looking at girls up and down. A jeep had stopped between trees in front of the Bockl house. Else was standing beside it. She doffed her hat to the jeep and the tinsel sparkled in the headlight.

# FOURTEEN

# *Parables of Fancy*

FATHER AND I WERE LOADING Christmas boxes onto his truck. I heard someone whistling "Prisoner of Love." Mort, I thought. Then Else Schmiedler turned the corner: oversized sable coat, the man's hat decorated with tinsel chain and a three-legged miniature Doberman, hop, hopping alongside her straining on a bejeweled lead. She strutted on the other side of the street whistling the tune over and over again, staring straight ahead. We didn't exist.

I dropped the box I was holding.

"Careful, careful," Father was saying. "There's a precious egg in each box." Our gate was open. My dog, Krampus came out and sniffed a tree.

"Get him!" She dropped the lead and a snarling, yippy black canine monster darted at Krampus and had him by the neck. Then there was rolling, yelping, growling, hopping rolling again. Krampus at the bottom, then Krampus on top. I took hold of his tail and pulled him away. "Scram!" I yelled not merely at the vicious cur. "Scram, scram, scram! Get away!"

I meant get out Schmiedlers. Leave the beautiful house, get out and away. Get away! Get. I kicked a piece of ice, sent it flying against the ever present insult of monstrosities. She picked up the lead without slowing down and went on whistling. "Don't Fence Me In." The song Mort had sung for me. My song. That glitter chain from the big American Christmas tree danced down her sable clad back. Someone else's coat. Much too big. A dead woman's coat and never even altered to fit. One of her many stolen coats. As for that black hat—a man might have had his head chopped off so that she could wear it. Schmiedlers only enjoyed what they took away from someone. She whistled Mort's song on and on all the way uphill. I could feel her boots stomping, strutting, over the dispossessed.

"Just look at that. Crazy old Krampus." Father was saying. "At your age. Look at your muzzle, getting gray just like mine."

I leaned against a tree and waves of detestation passed over me. "That damned girl told her dog to attack. She let go of the lead. I hate her! She is a street girl. Someone should warn the Amis."

My father said: "Not you, I hope." He put the last boxes onto the truck in a great hurry. I didn't want to spoil his fun and allowed him to laugh it all off. And, of course he was right when he said my dog and I had a lot in common: we both stuck our nose into anything good or bad.

He mumbled something like "very pretty." A misguided remark whether he meant Else Schmiedler or the rusty old truck he was patting. "Come on, come on be a sweet girl!" And he might have used the same tone of voice with his wartime girl Nadica, who was now dead. The truck started, grunted and died. Father coaxed the engine with kind words and a crank. I thought of Alexander talking to his "sheep," Mother with the doll, bestowing life to the inanimate, which surely had something to do with the two world wars and all the war dead.

"Now that's more like it," Father said when the engine purred. "You'll get a nice coat of red paint next spring!"

Spring did not exist within the confines of my lucious detestations. I whistled "Don't Fence Me In" claiming Mort. I can whistle that tune now, anytime, it puts me right back there in the snow, clutching my keys harder and harder. "Prisoner of Love" turns me into a prisoner of hate to this day. Young hatred like young love is monumental. And memory a mirror that turns lovers and monsters of my life into stone medusas.

The old truck rattled along. My father beamed. "Remember when you came with me to deliver Christmas baskets before the war?"

I shook my head and remembered to forget.

"A big goose in each basket in those days. Delicious fruit . . .

I might not be able to give much away this year, but I bet you
anything I'm the only employer in town giving away food packages."

"Is it true that you bought a locomotive and traded it in for
Christmas food?" I asked.

"Who told you that?"

"Everybody in school is talking about it."

He beamed. "Nothing has changed. They're still talking about
me."

"And they dress like you. I have seen that man again. He has
your side whiskers and he even limps."

He merely laughed at this. "Here are all the allies, the con-
quering heros in their fine uniforms. Austrians had to put their
fine Nazi uniforms away. So out come the old Austrian national
costumes, leatherpants, the loden jackets with the horn buttons,
the green hat with the badger brush. Very understandable and
quite practical, too."

"I wore nothing but old dirndls all during the war. And I would
like to look normal."

He laughed at me. Told me not to worry. I looked wonderful.
He couldn't bring much food, but seeing me would cheer everyone up. First there was Father's secretary on the Stuben-ring.
Her husband had died in the war and her apartment had been
destroyed by bombs. She lived in three rooms with her pampered
ninety-year-old mother-in-law. Tiny old Frau Schrompl sat in a
big arm chair and her aged monkey eyes flickered from Father
to me, back to father: "Kaiser Franz Joseph." she said. The sec-
retarial daughter-in-law told her the emperor was dead. This
was her chief, the boss, Herr Director Ferdinant von Meinert.

"Herr chief boss, boss, boss that is impolite. The all highest,
our emperor. Help me up. One must curtsey."

Then there were Resi Romberg's parents. The bakery. Still
the one bright spot among dark tenement buildings in Hernals.
I used to admire the wild urchins playing and fighting in the
street. No one was about. One of the bakery windows was boarded
up. Resi's mother laughed and cried when she saw us. Her ringlets had faded to the color of unbaked rolls, but her sweet little
face had remained pert and pink. Father told her she still looked
like Resi's twin and gave her a hug and kiss. She dimpled like
Resi when she smiled.

Her husband, Master Baker, as she always called him, had a fever and was asleep. The bakery was unheated during the afternoon. She wore two overcoats. And she was proud of the blue cashmere shawl Resi had given her years ago. "And we have nothing to give this year. Nothing. No coconut kisses. Remember how you used to love those, Reyna? You are so lovely, so lovely. And I am so lucky to see you again." She shed some tears. Tiptoed into the back room and came back with a picture of a slender youth in a blazer. "Doesn't he look like a film star? Our Eli. A gentleman from Switzerland came and brought us money from our grandson. Fancy, Eli remembering us! One of these days I hope I'll get to see him again. Not now. In the spring. By that time my Master Baker will be feeling better."

I took the picture to the light. Eli's face had not changed that much. It was thinner. His large eyes were half closed, the full lips half open. He was holding a tennis racket. No more asthma, his grandmother told us. Graduated from high school with honors. I kept looking for my Eli in the unfamiliar complacent graduate and missed the dreamy sadness.

When we were back in the truck Father said he was quite disappointed in Eli. Not one word. When he had been able to get through to Resi on the phone, she had complained too. Eli had grown away from us all. "She thinks rumors must have reached him."

"Like your poisoned wine in his father's cellar?" I asked "Someone told the Americans that you had planned to poison Eugene Romberg."

"The Romberg cellar was full of Meinert wines. We all drank it. If it had been poisoned he and I would have been the first to die. Eugene and I liked to talk or play chess with a glass of wine. Eli must remember that. Who could possibly make him believe such stupidity?"

"The denazification people."

"Eli Romberg was already eleven years old when I hid him. And he should certainly remember how Prince Lutensteg and I got him across the Swiss border to his father. And he must know I made sure Eugene got safely out of Austria with most of his money long before the Anschluss. Even you must remember that."

"Nazis thought you got Eugene and Eli Romberg to Switzerland so that you could take over the Romberg industries without any complications."

He took me by the ear and said I had the biggest ear-*Waschln* in the world. And a good memory for the wrong things. I caught his hand and kissed it, the way Mother sometimes did, and snuggled up against him. He smelled of roses. I was not surprised when he finally stopped at the back of Frau Hillmar's house and said: "No need to start a lot of gossip . . ."

"Did her husband die in the war?" I asked.

"One doesn't talk about it, but Consul Hillmar was one of the men who were poisoned at the Romberg Villa. You wandered over there. I hope you have forgotten all about that."

I had never told anyone that I had seen Puppe seated in Eugene Romberg's old dining room chair. Fritz Janicek the S.S. had bowed to the portrait doll, talked to her as he had always talked to my mother. And if he had made off with Puppe, I was glad. I'd rather she possess him than obsess Mother. Fritz and old Puppe richly deserved each other I had told myself when I had seen the old doll presiding over the mad scene of men dressed up in Resi's costumes. "What did the Consul look like?" I asked.

Father turned the engine off and then started it again, trying it out. "Handsome. Tall, dark haired. Liked to play the piano and was tone deaf. Awful."

I had not forgotten powerful hairy arms bursting Resi's floral gown. Thumping hands pounding out a waltz, and murdering the piano.

"He made his career as a diplomat under Hitler. A shady character. Could have been that someone tried to poison him and killed them all. At that time I hardly knew the Hillmars. We ran into each other at parties or the wine gardens no more than two or three times a year."

"Did he work for the *Abwehr* or the gestapo?" I asked.

"Who knows. He certainly was abroad a lot. At the German Embassy in Bulgaria. Probably stole museum pieces for Janicek, that great art collector. If nothing else Consul Hillmar left his wife provided with enough rose water to last to eternity." He climbed out of the truck, tried to change the subject and said things certainly could not get any worse in Vienna—they just had to get better.

The way Frau Hillmar came tripping out of the house reminded me a lot of Resi Romberg. Miranda, her pet duck was standing in the doorway and led the way into the sunny, small yellow house. Frau Hillie—as Father called her—was plump, soft looking with a tiny waist. Chairs, the sofa, the table, everything in her house was small and made her look big. I played with her collection of miniature ducks while she opened the Christmas box and exclaimed over everything. "Miranda, just look at that? all these good things to eat. Bacon, even bacon." She held up a green woolen shawl. "My dear Prospero how on earth did you perform such magic?"

She turned to me and told me that so much had been stolen from her. Someone broke into her house one night while she was asleep. Fortunately Miranda had been in her room. "She knows I'm talking about her. See how she flaps her wings?"

She always included the duck when she talked to Father and this unpleasantly reminded me of Mother with Puppe, the old doll. Mother had sometimes addressed him as Emperor Meinert. Frau Hillie called him Prospero. This had more meaning to me later on that year when I read Shakespeare's *Tempest*. By that time I understood how Frau Hillmar must have observed my mother and Resi with my father. Long before Frau Hillie and my father got acquainted she had studied her role.

Although everything in the little yellow villa was dainty, Miranda went around soiling the Persian rugs. The actress gave me a bread crust and allowed me to feed the bird. Miranda wagged her tail everytime she ate. Then she sounded off for more. And Frau Hillie said: "That's right. You speak up. It's a disgrace. That horrid man wanting to eat you up!" Her rendition of the horrid man from the point of view of a duck, was a perfect portrayal of Herbster alias Krummerer. Herbster had tried to blackmail her: "He gave me such a piercing look and said I would not be allowed to go on stage anymore, because my husband had been a Nazi criminal. He went as far as offering me a diamond as big as a bean for my Randa bird. A cold, glittering stone. That's what he offered me, that murderer."

I giggled. Father put his arm around me. It was not supposed to be funny. On the way home I wanted to know more about the blackmailing. Father didn't want to discuss this. Instead he told me that the real Miranda had been stolen. The bomb on our avenue had shattered some windows at Frau Hillie's house. The duck got out and vanished. Father had been lucky enough to get another white duckling. It had cost him a fortune and at first the duck was neither tame nor friendly. Frau Hillie thought it suffered from shock and the actress never found out what had happened.

He looked a little sad. "That one bomb. Remember Nadica? Valdo's girl, the music student? She had such promise as a pianist. Funny, Hillie and Reserl also came from poor families. Viennese girls have such talents." He turned right and stopped between trees in front of our gate. "Your mother too. If I had not married her when she was still a schoolgirl, there is no saying at all what she might have done. She is musical and a great bookworm. A linguist too. I should have let her finish school after we were married. It just wasn't done. So she stayed at home." He sighed. "She must have been bored . . ." He squinted out into the snow. We both remembered Mother the rebel and illegal Nazi. Hiding under those wide brimmed Hanna Roth hats that always gave her away. "I don't think I want you to marry so young."

How else would I ever have a chance to make love in Venice, in a cozy boudoir? Haystacks, the woods, jeeps would be embarrassing and uncomfortable. "If I wait too long everyone will be married. A lot of young men have died in the war," I said.

He roared at my good, practical Meinert sense. I let him lift me down from the truck as if I were still a small girl. "Who do you have in mind? I hope it isn't an American soldier! That's all."

"Why not?"

"Has Mort proposed?"

"Stop it," I said. "You wouldn't like it because he would take me to America." We were almost the same height. Arm in arm we walked towards the house. "Or, perhaps, you think Mort isn't quite tall enough."

"He's really all right," Father said. "Decent, I suppose. Fun to have around the house and play for us. I am so busy. He is a nice escort for your mother. But he just doesn't count."

I let go of his arm and felt a chill as though I had been insulted. "What do you mean?"

"He won't last," he said.

Morning brightness filtered through shirred curtains into a milky light, played over Mother's bright hair, shimmered among breakfast crockery, making blue forget-me-nots dance. Father's spectacles sparkled. He was reading the morning paper and giv-

ing us the news: General Patton had died from injuries he had
sustained in the car accident.

American guards across the street had lowered the flag and
it flapped against the pole making the sound of horses' hoofs
galloping over snowy fields of infinity, carrying a horse-crazy hero
to a beyond that was a starting line. The general believed in
reincarnation. So did I. Paradise for horse lovers would be a meet
beyond the demarcation lines of life.

The English doctor called that afternoon. Mother was out. I
answered the phone and Sir Hugh said: "How are you my dear,"
because he thought it was Mother. Then he said girls my age
always sound exactly like their mothers on the phone.

When I mentioned General Patton's death and his former lives,
he cleared his voice, and said: "Awful shame." Then he went on
about the windy day, the sun. And finally he promised to call
later and hung up with a bright "cheerioooo" that would ring in
my ear. I couldn't understand that hanging up, was his response
to me from the beginning. He had cut me off, before I had a
chance to ask whether he had meant those former lives were an
awful shame, or the general's death, or whether I should be
ashamed. I did my homework in the cold morning room near the
telephone determined to speak to the English doctor again and
clear this up.

No more than ten minutes later Mother walked in and she
was upstairs hanging up her fur coat when the phone rang again.
I decided the doctor was sorry, he had cut me off. And said, "Good
Afternooooon," every bit as seductive and British as Mother.

"So we speak English now. My new poem is, of course in German," said Fritz Janicek Mother's devoted gardener at his insi-
nutating best." " 'Enchantment at dawn.' " Inspired by memories
. . . Schloss Kiesheim, you know."

I could hear him change into the professor, artist, Nazi prophet
as he recited in a marvelous high-pitched voice trembling with
emotion, which I had always found hard to resist when he used
to lecture to me in the gardener's cottage:

> Enchantress,
> at dawn
> you rise veiled by mist
> I am drunk with your dreams

> A mere tremor of dew on silver web
> torn by your marble feet.

I stifled my giggles. Mother walked in and I quickly handed her the receiver. She heard the familiar voice, flushed, lost her temper and slammed the receiver down. "How can you laugh? He could have killed me. He is mad." She studied her polished finger nails. Her cheeks were pale and orange freckles stood out on her nose. She looked tired. "And he is responsible for the death of Eugene Romberg. *Ja, ja,* I knew although I just couldn't let on."

"Why not?"

"I had a need to mourn for Eugene privately."

"So you said you took in a stranger and everyone believed it was really Adolf Hitler."

"She turned her face to the window where icicles sparkled in the sun. The calliope music started up in my head. The Hungarian third army merry-go-round spun around and around on painted horses to the soft flap, tap, flap of the American flag.

"Janicek will go free as long as he talks to the allies. They will take him seriously, they won't laugh," she said.

"Because he speaks good English," I said.

I went to stand in line at the bakery and met Ursel and recited the poem in a Janicek voice and it made her laugh. We were not supposed to go beyond the park but we went for a walk later, all the way to the ninth district, to take a look at the American Club, the Clam Gallas. The Amis had taken over a charming little palais set back in gardens. We went to the gate and the guards told us to move on. They had their orders.

You couldn't wonder. There had been a scandal. Austrian schoolgirls had been caught dancing half naked for some Ami boys in the backroom of a coffeehouse. Ursel and I were watching American trucks, cars, and jeeps coming and going while we talked about the two thirteen-year-old girls from our school who had been dismissed. A jeep came out through the gate, and slowed down near us.

"Good afternoon, girrls!" said Miss Pnevski.

We hesitated. Ursel gaped. I fixed my eyes on Miss Pnevski's curly hair and her pink bow to keep myself from staring at the driver: a Negro.

He grinned and said "Hi there."

"Come here. Don't be shy," she held out two chocolate bars. "It's Christmas time." She told the officer we were learning to speak English very fast. And he kept watching us with flashing eyes and smiled. I had only seen two other Negroes before the American Army came to share the occupation of Vienna. There had been a retired boxer, married to a Viennese girl who had lived not far from us before the war. I was told not to stare and never got close enough to see his face. After that, when I was eight years old, I had much admired a Negro roller skater in the circus. I had been dazzled by his conspicuous zippers on the sleeves of his white lamé shirt, and his black pants. Austrian pants fastened with buttons. When we went to the back of the tent after the performance to visit the animals, the roller skater and a midget clown had stood near the bear cage to keep children from trying to pet or tease the animals. I had a chance to tell them both my name. We shook hands. The roller skater was Bob and the midget called himself Goliath. They had invited me to feed the elephant named *Buberl,* little boy. For weeks I had dreamt of joining the circus.

Ursel hung back. I introduced myself to the handsome man with the circus smile and held out my hand to shake his. Miss Pnevski put the chocolate into my palm. I said "thank you" in English and felt like a beggar.

Miss Pnevski said: "Come here, Ursel. Don't be shy," in English. Then she told her friend that Ursel had suffered a lot during the war. And I was a good English student. He said we were nice kids and flashed his teeth again.

Miss Pnevski handed me a candy bar for Ursel and said "Merrry Chrisamas." They drove away and we watched.

"I am scared of Moors," Ursel said.

"He was not going to eat you up," I said. "Or strangle you."

"Moors in Africa do eat people," Ursel said.

"Ha," I said. "They sold human meat right here in Vienna last spring, just like the Africans. I don't think it's half as bad to kill because you're starving than it is to kill millions out of hatred and spite."

Ursel burst into tears and said she never hated anyone, never ate anyone. I put my arm around her and we both devoured our chocolate.

No one knew whether or not Father actually traded a train for Christmas food. We did have a priceless Christmas carp. Our house was festive with pleasant secrets on the twenty-fourth. Father went down to his private little wood-panelled room, the catacomb where he had once hidden Eli Romberg. He brought up Mother's gilded clock and her paintings and Vlado was in Vienna, ready to help hang everything back on the blue silk wall of her boudoir. Vlado was rather disgusted, he told Father, the American OSS were using German intelligence services against the Russians. Those Nazis were quite capable of arranging a murder or two of Americans and pinning it on the Russians to make trouble between the allies. Mother came into the room and he stopped talking and hammered a new hook onto the wall.

Father hung the original Fragonard himself. "So, there you are again." The picture of the red-headed girl on a swing never resembled Mother all that much. He just liked to see her as that idle girl in a pretty flower garden swinging and dreaming.

I followed Vlado and asked him whether former Nazis working for the Amis could have disguised themselves as Russians and caused trouble on the Mozart express. He laughed and said he wished he could blame them for that.

"How about getting disguised as Americans and driving trucks and running into people? How about running into General Patton's car?"

"They know who drove that truck," Vlado said.

"Nazis could have bribed the driver, couldn't they?"

Vlado said I was very sharp and tried to just walk away from my questions. I asked rather pointedly whether the twins had gone back to the country . . . "Those girls, those girls. Crazy. Wild girls. Who knows where they are."

As soon as Vlado left, Father went down into his private cellar rooms again. I supposed the Christmas tree, and presents were hidden down there. He did not lock the door behind him. "Can I come down?" I called.

"Wait. We're coming up."

Footsteps. Then a white head appeared. It was my tutor, Pfarrer Kronz. Everyone wanted to see my surprise. I became embarrassed and stiff. He drew me into a corner. I kissed his hand like a shy country parishioner. When we were alone he gave me a bunch of Edelweiss from my friend Stopperl. She had

won the ski race held by the British and could ski faster than
any men. Of course, there weren't that many young fellows left.
Some of the houses destroyed by the avalanche had been repaired
during the summer. Not his own. He was still living on our farm.
I interrupted, finally, and asked the question no one had
answered: "Did Mother go to Salzburg that time when I was visiting Father in Vienna?"

"Did she tell you she did?"

I shook my head.

"Then you shouldn't ask me, should you now? Is it that
important?"

The court doctor interrupted our conversation. He arrived pink
from the cold and loaded down. In one hand his doctor's satchel,
just in case someone swallowed a carp bone, in the other a small
overnight case because he was sleeping at our house. Had it been
four or five years since we had all spent Christmas together? He
inhaled the fragrance of cooking and baking.

Soon it was time to go to the back of the house and wait for
the Christkindl. I placed a footstool between Pfarrer Kronz and
my grandmother and tried to imagine Christmas eves when other
generations of Meinerts had gathered in this back room. It faced
the south and the old, floral upholstered sofas and chair had
been bleached out, white-washed walls had yellowed. My tutor,
Father's second cousin, looked at home here. His white hair and
rosy face always made me think of wild rambling roses. He had
a gift for fitting in.

Father filled our glasses with sparkling wine. Frau Schwester came into the room and brought the radio. She knew how
much Pfarrer Kronz loved Christmas music. A children's choir
sang "Oh Tannenbaum." "Merry Christmas, Frohe Weihnach-
ten, little ones near and far . . ." The voice of Hanna Roth. "I
wish you were all sitting here around the Christmas tables set
for us by the American High Command. I will tell you a story of
a doll's Christmas." Whistling, crackling and a sound of rushing
water drowned her voice.

"Of course, it might just be the weather," the court doctor
said amiably. "Who would want to block a story about a doll's
Christmas."

I thought of Mort who had asked me whether Hanna Roth
sent coded messages with her stories. She had predicted the death

of an American general. Once more she was suspect and grandiose. I imagined her in one of her silk dresses a matching tall
hat trimmed with bows or fur, or feathers. She would be smiling,
her veil would be thrown back and she would eat as fast as any
child. American officers would be there too. I thought of Mort
and Lieutenant Kaufman.

Father wanted to call Mother and he kept tuning the radio.
"She would love to hear the story. Women are all little girls.
Especially when they are spoiled and beautiful. Dolls, ducks, they
all have to have mascots."

"There is a difference between animals and dolls," my teacher
said. "One of my favorite pupils never touched a doll and loves
her little dog."

"A dog has a life of its own. But you have to make believe
with dolls," I said.

"I remember a certain officer who kept a room full of life-
sized dolls in his room. Remember the Redl case?" The court
doctor said. "A spendthrift, fancy car, fancy nephew. Imagine
the Schlamperei. For seven years he had been a chief of staff
and he was in Russian pay. They called me in when it was all
over. I was there when they found that doll collection.

"What happened to officer Redl?" I asked.

Frau Schwester took Father's place at the radio. She considered herself an expert with radios from the days when she
had tuned in on the forbidden British station during the war.

"Was he murdered?" I asked.

I could tell by the disgusted look on her face that she knew
all about the officer Redl, and was desperately trying to drown
this unsanitary conversation out with Christmas music.

"One could call it murder," Father said. "Officers came and
handed him a loaded pistol. Then they waited."

"Franz Ferdinand, our heir to the throne, a devout Catholic
was simply horrified." My grandmother spoke up. "He felt the
monarchy was to blame for this self murder."

"Then Franz Ferdinand himself was shot with his poor wife,
because she didn't listen to Hanna Roth and didn't wear the lovely
yellow hat in Sarajevo," I said. "It was a special hat. Trimmed
with daffodils. She would have been the image of spring. The
pistol would have dropped from the assassin's hand." Before
anyone could respond to this Hanna Roth version of the murder

that brought about the First World War and the fall of Austrian
Empire, and the end of so much more, the sound of the old Meinert Christmas angel bell was heard.

I ran ahead of everyone as I always did, but the bizarre image
of an imperial officer celebrating Christmas in a room full of huge
dolls flitted through my mind. I saw him possessed by the dolls
as Mother had been by Puppe. Idolizers had created monsters—
even Hitler. And sooner or later they themselves became monstrous. I thought of the way Mother used to sit around stiff as a
doll allowing herself to be worshipped by all kinds of terrible
men. Now she was walking to the piano in a long, green velvet
gown swinging her arms gracefully.

She played "Holy Night," everyone sang. Unholy idols hov-
ered somewhere. Did I imagine it, or did the tree tremble? It
tilted. I darted forward and caught it. Krampus was under it
tugging at his Christmas bone.

Almost everything under the tree this year was for me, the
child. I had sat on the floor among books, bits of jewelry, blouses
made from a table cloth. A coat made from a blanket. A chorus
of praise formed: how good I had been in the mountains, what a
great student. Such a sunshine. Without me, Grandmama said,
she could not have survived the war. All their hope for me, the
admiration, the love made me an idol: through me Vienna would
be Vienna again.

I slipped away from it all. Dipped under the curtain to look
across the street. The water castle had been all lit up. I treated
myself to a moment of hearty dislike for the girl over there. I
imagined a wild party abounding with American food and American uniforms. And I would have traded all my presents at that
moment for the company of Americans, especially Mort.

The Meinert chapel overflowed with vintners and neighbors
at midnight mass. Afterwards they all lined up to exchange
Christmas greetings with my family. Grandmama was pale from
the cold, Mother pink. They walked arm in arm in dark coats.
Father and I followed with my teacher. The court doctor had met
up with Frau Hillmar. The actress carried a shopping basket. I
knew quite well she had smuggled Miranda the duck into
Christmas mass. Mother used to bring Puppe to chapel under
her coat or in her muff.

The chapel bell rang out and then all the other church bells in the distance. "Watch out, slippery, careful. Here take my arm. We better hold on." Father led the way with Mother on one arm, Grandmama on the other. Actors, youngish men and two older women, followed behind singing "Oh Tannenbaum" in harmony.

Pfarrer Kronz and I followed slowly. He was wrapped up in a heavy muffler Frau Schwester had knitted for him from unbleached mountain wool. I had my hands deep in the snug pockets, my head covered by the hood of my new coat made from an old honey-colored wool blanket.

Below us lay the valley. The actors were sliding down the road, laughing and yelling like children. Then Miranda got out of the basket and had to be caught.

"The village has donated a gravestone for Eugene Romberg's grave," the Priest said. "We have held a memorial mass."

"How about Mother and Hitler?" asked the monster child in me. "She was in Salzburg when they arrested Eugene Romberg. You must know about this. She must have talked to you." Then I poured out the story of Eugene Romberg at the concentration camp. The game of chess. Everything. "I hate the Schmiedlers living in his house," I said.

"Watch out, watch out. It's slippery at the foot of the hill!" Father called to us.

My teacher, the country priest, knew how to walk over ice, sliding step by step. So did I, but I held onto him. Our long shadows blended on the blue moonlit snow.

"Do you think the water castle is a cursed place?" I asked.

"No. There are no haunted houses or cursed houses. There are haunted people who have no faith in God. Hitler and his sort have left suspicion and a lot of envy behind. That's the real curse."

I listened to him and told myself, he was too old and too good to understand what I was talking about. The wind had swept clouds away. Bells stopped ringing. The air was miraculously still. A lopsided moon looked as though it had been through the war. And stars sprinkled the sky like splinters. Under a thin layer of soft snow was ice. And peace was a veneer, we were moving on treacherous ground.

A pool of water had frozen at the bottom of the hill. The actors got onto it laughing and sliding. Vintners joined in. Someone swept snow off with a hat. From a small beetle of a car came zither music. Then there was a man in a green loden suit caught up in the midst of the excitement on the ice.

"Look, look," I said to Father. "Anyone would think it's you."

"Not anyone who has seen me stumble around and limp," Father said. He turned to Pfarrer Kronz. "Remember. Not so many years ago, you saw nothing but Hitler moustaches. Now we're going back to the Kaiser whiskers. Soon I'll see myself all around town." Father called himself a peasant, simple, down to earth and considered the priest, unworldly, a scholar, a bit of a saint. They were second cousins, had the same strong nose, chin, amazingly beautiful hands. And they knew how to sound outspoken but kept secrets.

The father double had retreated to the dark under the trees and watched the actors sweep Mother away into the dancing sliding crowd. The dark coat showed off her figure and the wide brimmed Roth hat hid her face. A partner leaned forward, and twisted peering under the hat admiring her rosy cheeks, her eyes. And she stopped, backed away, as though he had just peered under her skirts.

I could see the allure of her tall, shy, unworldly and totally self-possessed strangeness. Mystery surrounded her as haze surrounded the moon. She created the illusion of space, possibilities; offered *Lebensraum* and didn't know it.

The actors and bystanders watched Father kiss her hand and help her over the wet edge of the ice, and the Meinert imitator faded away. What were Kaiser whiskers, Austrian loden, without that Meinert smile, twinkling eyes? No one could ever imitate my fortunate father. Without knowing why, everyone suddenly clapped and cheered. On this first Holy Eve in the midst of disaster Ferdinand von Meinert—our Ferdl, to so many—stood out as protector and survivor. Without even trying he had created a certain aura which at this moment enveloped both Mother and me. He was pleased with himself, a man without envy, a rare man. I then turned to him, clapped my hands, inviting another round of applause.

# FIFTEEN

# *Children's Crusade*

EACH TIME I heard Hanna Roth on the radio, I had the feeling she knew I was listening to her story. Like Hitler, her idol, little Hanna addressed multitudes and made you feel she spoke to you alone. You wanted to hear the old stories but you waited for her to add a new little twist. She was like a master chef, who takes old recipes and makes them unique. And when she surprised and even shocked you with a new story, the ingredients were always familiar enough to make you comfortable. She repeated words and phrases; mouthed them with relish as she carefully mixed the old and new to achieve a revelation.

Pfarrer Kronz came into the room, sat down beside me and said, "When have I heard that ranting and raving before?" the Pied Piper threatening wicked town fathers sounded so much like Hitler threatening the Jews. Then there was the Pied Piper's silvery flute. Just three or four notes. *"Komm mit! Komm mit!"* Come along, Come along, repeated by children she kept with her during the broadcast.

Something inside one began to turn somersaults, skipping, rolling down snow-covered mountains jubilantly leaving behind the world of grown-ups who had spoiled everything and could not be trusted; ready to follow the piper in the green suit from winter to spring over fragrant meadows towards *Lebensraum* a sapphire blue sea and a ruby red sun, to forget everything and play happily ever after.

Pfarrer Kronz must have known how much I was listening

for the sound of a silvery flute that winter. After the broadcast he talked to me of the Middle Ages, the children's crusade. Big and little ones taking each other by the hand and leaving the war-torn towns and villages, the sins of their fathers behind walking towards the sea, the Holy Land. He said to me that trying to get away from it all was only natural for the young especially these days. I confessed to him my mad longing for the sea, Venice, and my admiration for everything American.

"You haven't even been here a week," I said to him. "Why can't you live in Vienna. We all need you. I don't really like school, you could be my teacher again." How different my life would have been that winter had he given in and stayed . . .

I cried like a child when his bus moved away, turned to a shop window to hide my face. On the glass pane I watched the reflection of the bus diminish and disappear. The shop window was almost empty. A few pine branches, tinsel and wooden spoons remained from a Christmas display. A small wooden scoop trowel caught my eye. I ran into the store and asked for it at once.

"They come in handy in the flour bin, if there is flour in it. There isn't much to sell," the shopkeeper said. "I'm glad you found something."

I found something that had once been taken away from me; and clutched the trowel inside my pocket, consoled beyond all reason. Just touching the smooth wood brought back the sensation of wallowing in warm, shallow water, endless sand. The Lido beach near Venice. Children's voices, indulgently lazy grownups.

I had been three or four years old, digging a deep hole in the sand with a wooden trowel exactly like this one. A man had come along carrying a glass of red wine in one hand and leading a tiny doll of a girl on the other. The trowel had been pried from my hand. It had belonged to that child. She had left it lying around. I had found it. Now she had to have it back. I held on. My hand was pried open and the trowel taken away. I howled. A red sunburned father said too much sun and ordered us all into the shade. Suitcases had to be packed. We left at once and drove to the mountains. If I had only been able to hold onto the trowel I would not have howled, and I would have been allowed to play naked in the warm, salty water and dig in the sand, and eat spaghetti every day without end.

Eugene Romberg had loved to watch me inhale spaghetti at his table. He had not only admired my greed, he felt I was promoting international peace, and held me up as a glorious example to his finicky son Eli: if everyone learned to enjoy food from foreign lands it would lead to better understanding in the world. He had promised me that one day we would all travel around the world on a yacht. And he would hire the finest teachers for Eli and me. We would learn languages and study geography and history in each country we visited, and, of course eat the national food. Only months before Hitler took over Austria, Eli and I had shared Resi's conversion to Judaism, and Eugene Romberg's promise of that sea voyage had turned the whole world into our promised land.

The trowel in my pocket gave me back the promise of Eugene Romberg, Venice, the sea, and my days of contented games. As soon as I got home I went to find my old sled and made my way to the nearest hill. The sun had come out. A group of younger children had gathered at the top of the slope. I recognized the blue trousers and red, knitted hats. In the autumn this gang had been playing in the Schmiedler garden, and later in the park, at the frozen lake.

One of them waved to me. "*Du,* you, big girl bring your sled! Come help."

I might have turned back, if it had not been for the trowel in my pocket and the memory of that interrupted game. And I would have missed the creation of the big *Sauser,* the Whiz.

We worked hard stacking all kinds of sleds, boxes and an old rocking chair with old boards and pieces of knotty string and rope. The children worked together as an expert team. My sled and two old bob sleds were tied to boxes and covered with charred boards. The children had a big metal box on wheels and used it as support in the center below the rocking chair. The sun was warm, the air icy. Cheeks glowed, our breath steamed. We lifted heavy boards, arranged, and rearranged the three layers.

There were those who could not understand what I was saying, and talked with their hands using sign language. I was the tallest one and useful. The little ones came and passed their hands over my mountain sweater, and one girl with startling light eyes stared into space and said to me: "I want to touch you and see how tall you are." She was blind. Two girls always stayed close to her and helped her climb aboard the sauser. "I can't see," she told me. "Some of the others can't hear too well. And I can almost see with my ears. I knew you were tall before I touched you. Your voice came from higher up."

The leader, a big boy, perhaps eleven years old, had a small clever face, clear, gray eyes, a shock of tawny hair. He never said a word, but gave his signal with the whistle I had heard when the children had played in the Schmiedler garden. He slowly lifted the whistle and gestured the signal for children who could see, but not hear. And he, the tallest of the children took his place as the captain of the sauser in the chair on top of the metal trunk. Two pieces of old rope he held had been tied to the supporting outside sleds—a poor steering device—a fine symbol of power. I never heard him speak.

Children who sat on the edge of the boards had to steer by digging their heels in. I naturally became a member of the launching crew pushing the whiz over the crest of the hill. Then I would leap aboard and clamber up to take my place behind the captain. We were off, snow flying up and the sky rippling past foaming with clouds. "*Weg, weg,* away, away!"

The big sauser, this supernatural escape vehicle, had to be repaired after each run. And each time we had this sensation of transcending, rising, flying away and coming back. We kept improving the structure.

The blind girl said to me. "Listen to those dogs barking! They are lucky, they are American and they belong to General Clark. He came to see us and he brought us sweets because we have no families and stay at a children's home with nuns. There is a flag, isn't there? I can hear it flap. Red and white stripes. *Ja?* Stars . . ."

Up we went and down—faster and faster as the sun sank and the slope became icy. The wind dropped, the sky darkened; a slither of a moon appeared and the snow gleamed. The leader, named Jan, put the whistle into his mouth, blew short signals, and the children started to take the sauser apart.

"What a shame. I wish we didn't have to stop," I said.

"Come, come," said a small boy. "You've got to help with those big heavy boards. We'll hide some of that sutff where we can find it again."

Sometimes when I am bewildered or displeased, and want to get away from everything, I lie in bed in the dark. Then, suddenly I go through the routine of reassembling boards, boxes, sleds, rebuilding the sauser, that extrordinary escape vehicle made of nothing and everything. I relive this winter's sunset, the skinny moon, darkness, and the light of snow, assemble all I have— forget what has been lost—put it all together again into a sauser and push off once more. Something in me shouting a triumphant jubilant, "*Weg, weg,* away, away."

They did not ask me for my name. I was the tall girl and they took me along. The blind girl Eva said: "Hurry, we've got to get back. It must be getting dark. The gas has come on. I can smell smoke. People are cooking down there." She felt for the rope of my sled and helped me pull as I helped her make her way along the lane. The runners, crates and rocking chair, and the metal box hissed over the icy snow.

"What's in that metal box?" I asked.

She smiled.

"You're not supposed to blabber," said one of the others in a foreign voice.

"Where are you from?" I asked.

"Who knows."

We walked in rows between snow-covered hedges. A big crow flew up and cried out. Some saw it. Those who could not see, listened, flapping their arms like wings. And the bird seemed to follow. They threw it crumbs. "It talks," Eva said. "Sometimes that bird talks. And it always follows us."

"What does it say?" I asked.

"Cocoa-Cocoa! It's name. It's brownish isn't it?"

At the foot of the hill Jan, the leader, turned right. The sled grated over cobble stones. I had forgotten this lane. It led to a high ornate gate. We stopped and I saw the yellow villa with a pointed tower set back in spacious grounds behind huge snow laden oak trees and silver pines. The walls had dark wet patches. A small adjoining building, stable or garage, had collapsed.

Jan whistled three times. And we lined up sleds and boxes and the rocking chair behind snow-covered shrubs. He whistled twice and we fell into formation around the gate. The blind children groped for a cast iron stag among fancy fretwork. "Dear, dear, stag," they stroked it, feeling for the antlers.

"Is this where you live?" I whispered.

"No, *aber wo.*" they said.

Jan rang the bell. No one spoke.

"Tell me when the big lights come on," Eva whispered to me.

A spotlight at the door and another one at the gate came on.

"Now," I said.

"It looks like a search light, like a flak gun post, doesn't it?" she asked.

"*Ja*. Only now it shines down not up."

Jan blew his whistle once. Not a sound now. No one stirred.

The door had opened. A man in a trenchcoat and boots appeared. The children stirred, and made a sound of Foehn wind rustling frosted trees. Jan blew the whistle and they shot up their right arms in a silent Hitler salute. Stiff as statues they anticipated the drab little figure of a man crossing the beam of the floodlight and approaching slowly in the dusk.

"Hitler, Hitler give us bread! Dear Kind Fuehrer give us bread!"

Could it be true, Hitler hiding in our district? And could those charred bodies in the bunker in Berlin really be a deception? And would Hitler risk being seen here in Vienna by war children, maimed foreigners he disliked. Yet, the children, just like Hanna, the dwarf had remained loyal.

"Hitler, dear good Hitler give us bread!" the children chanted again. One of the youngest broke formation and climbed up on the gate. No one said anything. Jan gently lifted the deaf boy down.

The crow suddenly flew out of the trees and perched on the gate. And said it's "Cocoa, cocoa" The man they had beckoned marched on bandy legs and carried a basket. "Bread for the children. Bread!" he shouted in a Hitler voice. It was Krummerer. A tall man came up behind him carrying a bag.

"Hitler, Hitler!" the children shouted. "Heil!"

"Stop that at once children! Schluss!" the tall man yelled to them from the dark under the trees. A command in clipped German. They obeyed. Their arms dropped. Krummerer, Herbster came closer. The children were jumping up and down reaching through the fretwork of the gate, the fencing, not only for bread, they wanted to touch his sleeve, his hand.

How could they call him Hitler? He did not resemble any of the pictures I had ever seen?

Krummerer in the role of Hitler the benefactor accepted the worship with stiff condenscension. Then he saw me. "Good evening, young Fraulein," he doffed a styrian hat. Some of the children eyed me with awe and a little envy which excluded me from their ranks. I suddenly stood alone, tall, different. I fell back and they lined up to reach into the bag one by one.

The tall man had stayed in the dark under the trees. When the bag was empty he came forward and handed Krummerer a second one. Then he saw me, stared as though I might vanish if he blinked.

"Arnold, Arnold," I yelled like a child.

He had changed from a boy into a man. High cheekbones. A generous large mouth. His military haircut had grown out into a shock of wavy sandcolored hair.

All around me children were eating American bread. The bird was sitting on Jan's shoulder. "Danke Hitler, thank you Fuehrer!" Another salute. Arnold did not seem to hear or see anything or anyone. He did not take his eyes off me. Slowly he approached the gate.

"I heard about a girl from the Meinert-Hof killed at the very end by a bomb. Couldn't bear to go near your family."

Children went to get their sleds and crates. Jan whistled. They fell in behind him again. Sleds began to hiss and bump over cobblestones. Off they marched along the snow lit lane. The bird flying along with it's "Cocoa-cocoa, coa." It was getting dark. "Big girl," Eva called. "Where are you?"

Suddenly I grabbed my sled, left Arnold standing at the gate with Krummerer, Herbster. Helter skelter, I ran after the children.

Footsteps behind me. He was slipping on icy cobblestones. "Stop at once, Reyna!" The voice of the Herr Kommandant, monster Manqué, boy officer with the beautiful frog prince face who I had loved ever since I was seven years old.

I turned around and ran towards him, stopped—wordless as any maimed war-child. Here I was in my old ski trousers and the old sweater Frau Schwester had knitted for me from Mother's mountain-spun wool. For him I wished the frost and snow on my uncombed curls could be a veil and the ice balls on my sweater ermine. What was there to say? He took my sled, reached for me. Our entwined arms tightened, cheeks touched. We were equally tall—blessedly tall—as Hanna the dwarf would have said. And we fell into step at once.

On we went like happy sleepwalkers through deserted lanes

and empty winding streets. Now and then we stopped and kissed.
At the allotments, working men's garden plots just above the
cobbler's hut he enfolded me sharing his coat, kissed my eyelids.
I waited for words I had had him say hundreds of times. "It's a
miracle," he began and was interrupted by sounds of sawing and
hammer blows inside the hut. Floodlight suddenly turned the
snowy gardens of the water castle into a stage.

"See the tree down there near the field." I said. "That's where
Hanna Roth had parked her fancy car. She was looking for Rudolf
Hess. He had flown away. She cried and said he was flying into
a trap. She was right, wasn't she? He would land in that empty
field and meet her in the Romberg gardens."

"Whoever he was, you took to him, didn't you?" He scruti-
nized me for a moment. "Perhaps the way you took to me. Your
heroes have to be an enigma."

I tried to look into his eyes like a soulful female in love with
an enigma.

He laughed. "I always hoped I was special to you, because
you stole my heart when you were only this big." His gesture
reduced me to the size of a Thumbelina. "I hated being in Austria after the Anschluss. Coming across you that day made it
easier. I knew I could be useful. Then I got to know your father
and he taught me to use my power in the gestapo to prevent
some of the vile things that were going on. I was quite inexperienced and there were times when I had to rely on him."

He stopped talking and stared at me in disbelief. Snow flakes
swirled around us. His ears were pink from the cold. Only a few
months ago it would have been easy to simply say "I always loved
you," like a girl in a romantic story. It wasn't the same. He had
thought I was dead. The girl he had kissed before the Russian
invasion didn't exist anymore. I felt like an inopportune ghost.

Smoke rose from the cobbler's hut. Windows were boarded
up but you could see light through the cracks of a shed at the
back. Work was going on and a man was singing: *A bullet came
flying, is it for me or is it for thee.* Song of the good comrade. Song
of German war heroes. To the ten-year-old me an anthem sung
by the doomed. Heroes and villains dressed up in Resi Romberg
costumes at the water castle. And I, placed on the table for display, a girl in leatherpants, a girl as good as a boy. In empathy
with the gang of Hitler soldiers, troopers. Villains, heroes in silk

and velvet, rouged and perfumed and sweaty: men as good as women?

The hammer banged like bullets. *My eternal life is yours, my good comrade, my eternal life is yours.* Then there was shrill laughter. Else appeared down there in the white gardens of the water castle.

"So it is true. She's here," Arnold took my hand and led me downhill so fast the sled ran into the back of my legs. Else kept on shrieking and her laughter like the glitter on her hat was tinsel. Arnold wanted to see what was going on and peered into the garden quite unabashed; in Vienna this was not done.

"They'll see you," I said and hid behind a tree.

Arnold was as deaf to me as some of the war children. "I can't understand the Americans," he said in a loud voice. "Sharing a house with the Schmiedlers. Are they really that naive? I thought I was a simpleton."

I had only had a glimpse of the American colonel coming and going. Now he stood on a square of light cast by a window, stiff as a chess figure while Else imitated her three legged dog, in a game of hop-scotch. The dog ran in our direction and she followed hop-skipping and laughing. Arnold did not move.

"Can it be? Is it possible. My prince!" Else doffed that hat. "Funny, I was thinking of you the other day. I heard you're working for the Ami now. Then, who isn't . . ."

She displayed herself for him in a dark garment that fitted her like a pelt, moving restlessly, exciting and excited. Then she stopped close to the gate and the light chiselled the sweet perfection of her young stone angel face. "You swine-dog! You ox. . . ." On and on. Gutter language poured out of her lovely mouth.

Arnold pulled me behind his back and shielded me.

"If it weren't for you, they'd be fishing for crowns in every lake and pond in the Reich, the Amis, the *Russ,* the English and the French and everybody else. I had this fabulous story, *wunderbar.* That Janicek had picked up the crowns in Munich and dumped them into a lake." She was puffing on a cigarette, blowing smoke at us. "But you won't catch Vati Schmiedler, that's for sure. I told him long ago that you were an oaf, but he liked a real German prince. Such an Aryan. All that old blood. Remember how I used to sneak into your room at night?" She laughed, kept on shrieking.

He took my arm and led me away.

"I'm wearing the boots you gave me. Did you notice?" she shouted.

The colonel called her. She went to him, but the black shadow of a dog kept hopping alongside the barbed wire barking after us.

"She is right," Arnold said at once. "I am a simpleton. One thing always led to the other."

I wanted him to forget Else, forget everything, talk about love, instead he talked about himself, at my age when he had volunteered for the Hitler *Arbeitsdienst* to work as a laborer. Partly because he had been rebellious and found the atmosphere at home stifling. His conservative father had wanted him to go to university, study history and go on into the diplomatic service. From the *Arbeitsdienst* boys were drafted directly into Hitler's army. His father objected. Boys Arnold met in the work duty could not think of anything they wanted to do better than fight for Hitler. They were outstanding and decent. Hard workers. Idealists. They had built a reservoir and a road. They ate in a mess hall, drilled not with rifles, but polished spades, and talked of saving Germany and Europe from the Bolshevics. Then, one day, during a rally, a torchlight parade, marching along singing Arnold had come to stand close enough to really look at the Nazi leaders.

"A terrible shock. Usually I can look at a man, or woman, and of course, a little girl child and trust my first reaction. That's how I survived the war. At that rally I looked at men on the podium and suddenly I asked myself: what am I doing here? Hitler addressing the youth of Germany. I listened and heard nothing but slogans, rubbish. It made me feel terribly ashamed for him, and for myself. I wanted to sink into the ground at every vulgar promise and threat. I thought he sounded crazy and wished I could get away. I could not move. I turned to stone. I actually keeled over. When I came to I was in a car with a stranger in civilian clothes.

"This one and only time in my life my good instinct for people failed me. I regained consciousness feeling lost, and uncertain about everything. It was dark in the car. I couldn't see his face. He knew my name, asked for my parents. Said he had danced with my sister at a ball. Then he said that I had been a wonderful boy. Exceptional and very mature for my age. It was fate that he should come across me like this. A decisive moment. He took me straight to a doctor, who pronounced me to be in superlative health. He never introduced himself, but he knew more about me then I myself did. He told me not to act rash and just keep on. I was doing splendidly. And, of course, my loyalty for boys who were my friends drew me back.

"For half a year my benefactor appeared regularly and took me out to dinner like a father and encouraged me to talk, gave me little presents, courted me and flattered me as if I were a girl. Names, titles, had been important in an old family like mine. He fascinated me because he never told me his name. I was allowed to call him Herr Bank Director. I knew he had several houses and one in Vienna. He promised one day I could be of service to my fatherland. One day soon I would hear from him. I had the right face, the right family, this could be of utmost importance. Then he vanished.

When the time came, I did not join the army, but went to university. About a week before Hitler took over Austria the dean called me to his office and presented me with an urgent official summon and I was sent to Vienna. The same man met me at the station. That's how it all began. That moment of revulsion at the rally led to my being singled out and recruited into the gestapo."

"That man was Schmiedler," I guessed.

"Everyone is looking for him. It's not that easy. Vienna is full of all kinds of suspicious characters, nothing but changelings these days. And Franz Joseph Schmiedler could disguise himself so that his own wife didn't know him."

We reached the foot of the hill in silence. He brushed snow off my hair and kissed both my cheeks and said it was all so strange. Here he was back in Vienna, walking with me and he had seen Else Schmiedler.

"You used to stay at their house?" I asked.

"I had to," he said. "I needed information. Schmiedler had no secrets from Else. He thought he could trust her and she was in the room when he talked to some of the top Nazis in Vienna. Baldach von Schierach had Else photographed and used her for posters and propaganda films. Well, Else isn't all that clever and she was spoiled and liked to show off. She'd walk into one's room anytime day or night without knocking. You couldn't keep her out. There were no locks or latches in that house. Then she'd threaten to yell and say I dragged her in. I had to give her cigarettes and shoes to keep her happy and talking. She was wild about shoes."

"Did Eugene Romberg stay at the Schmiedler house when he came to Vienna secretly during the war?" I asked.

"He did. I could never figure him out."

"I'm sure Else denounced Eugene Romberg," I said.

"Anything is possible, but I doubt it. I never met him, but he was very kind to her. She showed me shoes he brought her from Switzerland and she had helped herself to one of his hats and liked to wear it. She took what she wanted. Her father encouraged her to snoop around in various guest rooms."

"What is he like?" I asked.

"A husky fellow with a blond goatie. Everybody tells me that was a disguise. Who knows. No description seems to match. I was a simpleton and thought of him mostly as a money man and an opportunist. Now, Else has given the Ami a sworn statement that her father was the only double who even sounded like Hitler. She says Hitler had been shot in Hamburg years ago, and after that several doubles took his place in case one of them got killed." He laughed. "Who knows. She'd say anything. But sometimes she helped save lives with her chatter."

"I don't believe that," I said.

"Well, not intentionally. You see, I had found her those fur trimmed boots. And she put them on at once and said they reminded her of the Kaiser days. She had a good laugh and said those stuck up aristocrats were all going to be rounded up and shot. There was a printing press in Palais Dornbach."

We were now walking along the avenue towards the Meinert-Hof. He stopped under a street lantern and talked about my grandmother and her group of heroic friends who had drawn attention away from the activities of the young members of the resistance.

"How about the printing press?" I asked. "Grandmama used to have the old Austrian double eagle printed you know."

"I had it taken away piece by piece. Your father helped. You wouldn't believe the chances he took during the war."

I reminded him that he had taken more chances than anyone else. Saving many people. Eli Romberg, then our Rittmeister. He said that was nothing and took the rope of my sleigh. We then

walked side by side like children. I led him as I had led blind
Eva. With his words he was groping blindly. He talked about his
responsibility as a German. Soul searching: cleaning away debris,
you found lost treasures, and you unearthed putrid matter. You
had to clean up the mess and try to make amends. Survivors of
camps had to receive compensation. And there were those war
children. Simply kidnapped from occupied countries to replenish
Germany. Himmler's idea. They ended up roaming in packs. Some
had actually been used on the front. He went on and on. Finally
he announced that one had to shoulder the responsibility for the
destruction of civilized Europe, the threat to Christianity. He
was to blame. His self-accusations impressed and depressed me;
it was like a Christian wearing a hair shirt.

I memorized his words—Meinerts have this habit, perhaps a
trait passed on from ancestral chicken farmers who could neither write nor read. And while I listened I admired the shape of
his face, the dimple on his chin and his large expressive mouth.
He would clamp his lips tight during his self-incrimination, then
he looked at me and turned back into the handsome frog prince.
And the seven year old in me nudged me to transform him with
a *Bussi*, a kiss on his cheek. It was magic. His face changed. He
beamed, and his mouth became full, moist. He took me into his
arms and I could feel his heart pounding, but he kept on talking
about himself: how he had left home, his room full of books, and
lived in barracks, then in a dormitory at the university, and in
Vienna in a guarded house, finally the army.

"I was never alone, and yet totally isolated. Except for one
good friend when I was still at the university, I had no one to
talk to. In Vienna, with the gestapo, I could not speak a private
word to anyone. I had a high position although I was so young.
Only rudeness gained me respect. The men under me were Austrian. I was German and they were afraid I had been placed
there to watch them. When they wanted to torture and kill a
prisoner I would say: a wounded man can't think and a dead
man can't talk. And I myself was tortured by all I knew and saw;
I was afraid of going mad if I had to keep my mouth shut much
longer."

He said he could not trust anyone until he met my father. He
remembered how he had followed his truck to this suspicious
farm: the owners, Meinert sisters lived in England and were

British subjects. "One look at your little face and I knew that
your friend, the Romberg boy was hiding somewhere in the house.
I saw through your father's game, playing the simple peasant,
admired his courage and most of all yours. You looked at me
with those big bright eyes, no matter what I asked, you had the
right answer. A chit of a girl dressed like a boy and already a
female who could beguile men who had come to do harm."

He had been barely twenty years old and many times he got
dangerously depressed and felt sorry for himself. The world was
coming to an end for him. He didn't see how he could possibly
survive. Thought they would find out what he was really doing.
He would have been tortured until he couldn't talk and killed
inch by inch.

We were coming close to the gate of the Meinert-Hof. "Your
father had seen how I took to you. Decided I loved children. And
he cunningly met with me in private. I came to honor this
uncompromisingly decent man, acting like a clown, anything, to
save his friend's son. After that we had to be careful and met
secretly whenever we could."

He sounded formal, over-educated, very German, as he went
on about my father during the war and about me as a tot. I wanted
him to tell me how much he loved and admired us now. "Are you
sure you won't come in and eat supper with us and see my father
again?" My voice was dull and grown up, decorous, my feelings
were not. I could not imagine the evening without him. Wanted
to keep him, and see his face change, his lips became amorous
for me.

He held me tight for a moment and then he said: "*Es tuht mir
Leid,* I am sorry. I have no right . . ." While he refused his lips
touched my hair, my neck. His eyes asked me for invitations
beyond belief. We kissed. I found the little wooden trowel and
held it in my left hand. And all the pleasure of safe, rippling
water returned. I felt naked and warm.

"I thought you had been killed. And here you are. You are a
miracle." He passed both hands over me. Gently at first, like the
thorough court doctor. "Here you are." He kissed me again and
his hands slipped under my sweater and he cupped my breasts
just barely touching. "During a war there were girls who meant
nothing, and remained strangers. I learned how to please the
hard way."

Was Mort a stranger who had taught me how to please?

"Then, suddenly, I hold a girl and she feels as if she were part of me. Something that has been torn away and then put back in place."

Under the warm shield of his hands my small breasts grew warm as rising yeast dough.

"If I should never see you again, or something should happen to me, I would feel I have had a rich life."

Morbid, sentimental, I thought, also frightening. "You're going away again?"

He let go of me. Smoothed down my sweater like a parent. "I do have to go."

The devil in me suddenly asked: "Are you going to visit Else Schmiedler?"

His mouth tightened. "How kind of you to think of this. It will, of course be my duty to find her father. But she is pitiful. And she could get into a lot of trouble—"

"—She causes trouble," I said. "I bet she had Eugene Romberg arrested. She'll get you into trouble, too. Are you going to be in danger again?"

"We're all in danger," he pulled my sled to the gate. Hurriedly helped me to unlock it.

I dragged the sled into the garden, banged the gate shut, locked up again and missed him as though he had already been deported to Siberia. "It's always up to you. And it was always up to Eugene Romberg too. He told me he wanted to help Germany lose the war and all of it for us, for Mother. Now he's dead. You say you want to make things decent again—for me. You'll go away and never come back!"

"You're crying," he said. "Don't cry. It scares me."

"You'll stay?"

"Just for a moment."

"Then I won't unlock the gate," I said.

He reached through the fretwork and took my hand. Wrought iron hearts, flowers, stylized leaves obscured the structure and the very purpose of the gate with harmonious patterns. A barrier quite typical in Vienna: delicate and unyielding as the ornate entanglements of our lives that brought us together and yet held us apart.

# SIXTEEN

# *Will-o'-the-Wisp*

I RETURNED TO EVERYDAY LIFE like a drunk after a spree. You can overimbibe on reality when you are fifteen. My fantasies and dreams had been a stage where I had created scenes, old and new. Leading men had been far away, missing. I had played all the parts. Sampling kisses had been like tasting this or that new wine which has to be stored to reach it's sweet perfection. Now Arnold had appeared and created havoc.

I somehow could not talk about Arnold without sharing him and I wanted to keep him to myself. I did say to my friend Ursel: "Just look around our class, either awful things happen to us or nothing happens at all because we are too young. It's always child this and child that. We are really grown up and no one wants to know it and we're old enough to choose a lover." I had to try ideas on Ursel before I could ever convince myself. She seldom disagreed.

Her face lit up with admiration. We were sitting surrounded by books on the high four-poster bed in her dainty aranized and then denazified room. "I'm much too scared," she said and closed the door. "Not just of the Russians and all the other foreign men. My mother has always been scared too. She runs away from my father. Sometimes he chases her at night."

"My mother is not scared in the least. She grabs Father," I said.

"I guess it's in the family. You grabbed that Russian."

"Why not," I said. "Women have always been up for grabs.

Just look at history." I took out bread and dripping sandwiches I had brought along as a snack. We left a history paper we were supposed to work on and ate.

"Men are stronger," Ursel said. "It took two of you to get the better of a Russian, right?" She wanted to believe it.

"Men like to be grabbed," I said.

"By two girls?" she asked.

"Why not!" I said.

"How about love? Would you want to share?"

I certainly did not want to share Arnold. When I was walking home after dark, the Christmas tree at the water castle was all lit up, twinkling and winking. What if he was in there with Else, standing at a window, and he saw me go by carrying my books looking like a child. The sickening suspicion that Arnold might be sharing a never ending American celebration with Else Schmiedler made me rush downhill, all the way home in a panic.

Frau Hillmar's duck was sounding off; this was unusual after dark. I was already walking towards our house when a man came along on the other side of the avenue dressed in country clothes like Father. Loden cape waving in the wind. At dinner Father declared he would like to drop everything, get out of Vienna with us all and take up mountain farming, raise poultry like his ancestors. Keep a few sheep, a cow and a pig and lead the simple life.

Mother stared into her empty cup as if she were reading tea leaves. "I have had enough snow and solitude," she said. "I want to be here in Vienna during Fasching, go to balls."

"People are starving to death. Who do you think will dance?" Father said.

"Everyone," she said.

"Vienna by night is becoming more and more impossible. You'd be attacked and robbed in the streets at night. Who'd take a chance," he said.

"Everyone," she said.

The moment we had put the angels, the glass baubles, the glitter chain and silver bells and shiny stars away, I became restless. Two endless days had passed. No Arnold. I came home from school and decided to make it happen all over again. I grabbed my sled, like one possessed, raced to the hill. Tracks of the sauser, that giant escape vehicle remained engraved in icy

snow. Dogs barked at General Clark's house as though they had
never stopped. Birds sat on telephone wires. I lay down on my
sled and took the hill at full speed, as though I could somehow
catch up with the children, retrieve something that had passed.
I hurried along the same lane. Snow drifted down onto my head.
I would ring the bell. He would come out. And then? could I really
throw my arms around his neck? I reached the gate, wiped snow
off the iron stag for luck, and rang just once. My heart throbbed.
I rang again, ran away like a teasing street urchin and hid shivering with excitement. Nothing happened. I rang again and again.
No one came.

I gave up, walked away half relieved, half disappointed and
retraced our walk, haunting deserted snowy sidestreets, flitting
around in the dusky cold. Voices came towards me, chanting "one-
two, one-two, *Eins-Zwei, Eins Zwei!*" Frau Hilli's son the bearded
doctor muffled in a hooded cloak rushed past me like a fugitive
monk. Bundled up women panting and gasping followed: "One-
two, one-two." I followed at a distance, falling in with their rhythm.
The end of the war had brought the end of parades and processions in Vienna. The allies marched. We looked on.

Not even funeral processions passed our house. No more black,
plumed horses, weeping mourners. Too many people were dying
of hunger and the cold in Vienna. There would have to be one
funeral procession after another. And horses had mostly been
eaten.

I thought of Arnold marching at a Nazi rally carrying a torch,
feeling like a fool. I felt silly too, following the doctor and his
troup, but I also liked it. Most anyone who joins a parade for no
particular reason has fun stepping it out.

On the hill above the water castle, near Ursel's apartment
house, I gave up, and fell back. The cobbler's window was dark
but someone was sawing wood in the back shed. At the back gate
of the water castle jeeps and several cars stood lined up. I could
see children in Resi's music room running around the Christmas
tree which had been lit up long before Christmas and now twinkled on as though the holidays would never end. One of the guards
saw me and opened the gate: "Hurry up, you're late!"

I went in as if I had been invited and left my sled at the
tennis pavillion. Two officers stood under a rosy green winter
willow. Lieutenant Kaufman was back in Vienna and acted like

a stranger. The other officer, Colonel Fredericks was tall and
gracefully slender. I noticed his deep set, speculative eyes, fierce
jaw line, and the small mouth made for talking in undertone.
"The wormy apple is always the sweetest," he was saying. Lieutenant Kaufman said: "Not for me. I'm fussy." Then he turned
and called: "Entrance over there, child. On the right."

What did I care about sweet wormy apples. I was back in that
fantastic garden walking towards the house I loved. Stucco scrolls
reeled before my eyes, winter bare trees gestured with black,
twisted limbs and white statues posed as if bewitched.

At the door I hesitated. My palms began to sweat inside mit-
tens. Before I had a chance to ring the bell the door was torn
open by a maid: chocolate-colored uniform, apron and cap with
frills.

"Surprised?" Frau Boschke chuckled. "Remember the girl from
France? Frau Romberg's maid? A sparrow. Her uniform. Who'd
have thought I could squeeze into it. It is a little short, but there's
someone here who thinks I have great legs."

My face in the old hall mirror looked foolishly pleased. A
moment of shock always preceded a feeling like sinking into a
tub of hot water when you entered the overheated rooms of the
great house.

She plucked the knitted hat from my head and hung it on a
hook. "So they invited you. Come in, come in. The food, the food!"

The entrace room had been transformed into an office. The
everchanging decor of all kinds of overstuffed, bright sofas and
chairs, carved tables, and a memorable glass swan had vanished. A motorcycle stood where the bust of Beethoven had been.
The skinny little sergeant Tony sat ensconced behind a gray metal
desk and a barricade of file cabinets and boxes. He was sipping
coffee. I drank in the fragrance.

Frau Boschke beamed. "Our Tony. Sweet isn't he. Our carrier
pigeon. Learning to ride a motorbike." The sergeant didn't say a
word and retained his serenity. Soulful brown eyes enlarged by
spectacles, dainty features and large pink ears gave him the alert
look of a schoolboy on his best behavior and ready for mischief.

"Didn't I tell you the *Amerikaner* took a fancy to me at that
interrogation? Everything has changed for me. The food! That
food . . . " I had never seen Frau Boschke so happy since the
day she had celebrated Hitler's birthday in the laundry room

with a bottle of Father's French cognac at the beginning of the war. She was scurrying around between me and the young Ami sergeant like a happy June bug. How could the water castle be a cursed house if it brought such joy to Frau Boschke? She was chatting away about days when she had been a girl and came here to iron for the Cannon Baron who had built the house. How she had been ironing his silk nightshirts and heard a bang bang bang. He'd blown out his brains, because he had lost all his money. We'd lost the war, Frau Boschke lost her pay until Herr Director Romberg bought the house. A big change. He had even honored the dead man's debt and given her back pay with interest. "He knew how to live and let live. May he rest in peace." She pointed at the wall. There was that framed newspaper photograph of Resi, all dimples and ringlets, posing as a Madonna with a four- or five-year-old Eli in baby clothes. A monument to her whim and Eugene Romberg's indulgence.

"Took me a good half hour to iron the frills, bows and ribbons on that baby dress and bonnet. Frau Resi's idea. Making herself look younger for reporters. The boy could talk like a grown up. She told him to pretend he was little baby Moses, keep his mouth shut . . . So much has gone. They came and they went and they went, Nazis, S. S., Janicek and his gang. Then the chocolate crazy fat Romberg mother and that little *Meisterin*. The boss dwarf. She put the curse on those men so that she could move in with hats and hats and apprentice girls, stuffed her carrier pigeons into cages where fancy little birds used to be. Then they all flew away to Salzburg. And here we are, and no one touched that picture of a pretty mother and babe. Not even the homeless ones or the *Russ*."

The three-legged little dog came bounding along the corridor yipping at me. Frau Boschke said: *"Kusch!"*

The sergeant said: "We'll fix that," and grabbed the dog, put it into an empty file drawer, and let it lap coffee from his saucer. The dog seemed to be used to this and settled down.

"Will you still be coming to our house on laundry day?" I asked.

*"Natuerlich,* naturally," she said. "I come and I go and I come. You fix this for your *Madl,* Tony?"

"For my Madl I fix anything," he said gravely in schoolboy German. *"Wird gemacht."*

"Listen to him speak German. He is really smart. It's for my

Tony that I stay put so much." She cackled and adjusted the
frilly cap on her newly crimped hair. "And the food. The food!"

Frau Boschke had washed dirty clothes of the fortunate, the
unfortunate and the doomed. She had scrubbed, boiled, ironed
and gossiped on laundry day with the same gusto no matter what
went on. And special meals had to be prepared for her. Agnes
used to say Frau Boschke had the appetite of three farm hands.
I, however, had seen the aluminum utensils she carried with
her, filled and carried home for her evening meal.

"I'll be back in a minute, Sergeant." She gave a sharp salute.
Wiped her hand on her little apron as if it were wet from the
laundry tub; took mine and rushed me through the passageways. "Wait till you see. Your eyes will pop out of your head.
Here for the day. Flown in specially with all the good things to
eat."

"What?" I asked.

She often liked to keep me guessing. We passed through empty
rooms filled with cartons marked U.S. Army. I let go of her hand
and ran ahead into the big hall. The giant chandelier swayed
gently from the hook on the glass dome and chimed in the draft.
It had been sadly defoliated. Furniture had vanished. One
embossed table remained from the days of Resi Romberg's Biblical setting. On this table, Frau Schwester, as Eli's hovering
nurse, used to place the Romberg pasteurized baby milk. I could
hear children laughing and clapping and felt like bursting into
tears. "Everything has gone," I said.

She turned on me, hands on hips. "What do you mean? We
still have the piano. Can't you hear it?"

*Danube so blue, so blue, so blue.* Sounds of the inevitable Blue
Danube Waltz. The American radio station played it to please
us, we played it and will keep playing it to remind the world of
great sweet old Austria and make them forget about the dismal
Ostmark.

Snow melted on the dome and it dripped from the old bullet
hole into a metal wastepaper basket. Resi Romberg had considered the self-murder of the ammunition manufacturer
romantic. The water dripped like a metronome to the waltz in
the memory of this or that ruined man. And Resi's heavenly
harmless tunes echoed over all the grim years of hellish trampling down grabbing and slaughter.

*Danube so blue, so blue, so blue.* Another waltz, another celebration. Frau Boschke picked up her apron with two fingertips
and waltzed towards the library. The music ended. She stuck
her head inside the door and kept me waiting. "Now," she pushed
me in; shut the door behind me. And there, standing on a podium
I found Hanna Roth exactly where I had last seen her.

A year ago last spring in 1944; it seemed as though a hundred
years had gone by. My visit with Father had been coming to an
end as the daytime bombing of Vienna began, when I had seen
Hanna the foundling on this podium as a determined Falkenburg. After an unsigned letter directing her to the portrait of a
dwarf in armor at Schloss Falkenburg, she had transformed herself. Out of the smoke and ashes of Hitler's Thousand Year Reich
Johanna von Falkenburg had risen, briefly claiming a title and
gaining control of the water castle. I had seen her on this podium
in a wig of white braids, costumed as my grandmother's half-
sister and my great-aunt, she had appeared sad and funny as a
clown.

She was back on the platform. The American army had taken
over the great house, she had lost her one and only Traude, had
given up white braids, and regained her dignity. A lone figure
looking at me over the heads of about thirty spellbound children.
Her fixed smile I always felt was for me. Although she had pro-
fessed she hated war, she wore her dark military coat with frog-
ging, brass and tassels and the fur hat of a Kaiserly hussar, only
a saber was missing. Behind her, in the adjoining music room
twinkled the gaudy multi-colored lights and tinsel decorations
of the American Christmas tree. Officers and civilians, stood
around holding long stemmed wine glasses. Mort was not among
them. They seemed subdued. Her rich Kaiserly costume made
them look drab, almost deprived.

She knew how to turn her freakish size into a spectacle, using
her disadvantage to gain advantage like a general. She always
astounded me and never showed surprise.

"Welcome," she said. And exchanged with me the usual curtsey, dismissing with this old Austrian gesture of esteem and self-
esteem, any degradation or defeat. Her curtsey simply fitted into
her story of Tiny Doll meeting a butterfly. "I won't get onto your
back. You like to fly from flower to flower. I'm on my way to find
my own happy place." Hanna used her hands like a mime for

children who could not hear or could not understand words. Jan and his gang formed a row with a nun who had dozed off leaning against the wall. I sat down at the back.

The curtains had all vanished and the colored glass decorating the top of the French windows cast rose and gold lights onto the children. They were not aware of this. Hanna saw it all and was inspired to depict with words butterflies flickering over hills and meadows and blue water, a tiny doll adrift on a rose petal boat in search of her happy place.

Hanna Roth's back was turned on the music room. She faced one of the many strategic mirrors she had placed around the walls when she had recreated Salon Roth at the water castle. In mirrors she could always see what went on all around her. She knew how to read lips. In the days towards the end of the war, she had looked into those mirrors for whispered intrigue. Ladies who had come for hats and advice, had no doubt inspired those predictions and warnings to her Fuehrer. Now she used what she saw in her story.

She had a quick eye for the portentous. And I could trace the moss backed sea monster in her story to the green livery of a man-servant. The tiny doll said: "Please don't throw me into the water, I have to find my happy place. If you've nothing better to do, take me there!" And the tiny doll climbed onto the monster's back. And who would not have climbed onto any monster's back to try and find a happy place that winter? It was any child's story, Hanna's story, my story. Some of the children cheered.

"And where do you think Tiny Doll found her happy land?" Hanna Roth asked.

A boy jumped up and shouted: "America, America!"

"No, Germany!" yelled the stout little blind boy from Jan's group. "The Reich, the Reich!" the gang echoed.

Hanna fastened her eyes on me. "You tell them. You tell them, little Highness."

My old title made some of the children turn around and stare at me. "Tall Girl," one of them said.

Little Hanna Roth watched me cower to make myself small, invisible. "She landed at home where she had started." I quickly said.

"Bravo!" Hanna said. "*Ja, ja.* She returned where she had started only now it was a happy place," Her dark eyes filled with tears. A spot of sun on the right side of her face, showed up wrinkles like cracks on an old portrait. Was she thinking of Traude Romberg, Eugene's mother, her best friend and assistant who had somehow sailed away from her and was eating candy in that shadowy big house in Mogador, Morocco?

Some of the youngest children of Jan's gang nodded to each other. The word Hitler was on their lips. That's what they had been taught, drilled to believe in. They didn't know anything else. Jan the captain of the sauser, the whiz, got up and stood at attention staring into the music room. Else Schmiedler had walked through the door with Lieutenant Kaufman and Colonel Fredricks. She laughed, twirled and the skirt of her light dress flew up and shimmered.

"Will- o'- the-wisp. Will- o'- the-wisp." Hanna Roth chanted.

Jan blew his whistle three times. The members of his gang fell in behind him. He pointed at Else and shook his head. With a faraway look he marched the gang towards the door. The nun woke up, hurried after them, took Jan by the shoulders, talked in sign language, whispered foreign words, brushing hair from his eyes, and pointed at long tables set up for all the children alongside the walls. Else filling children's cups sent a bewitching fragrance of hot chocolate around the room.

Jan pointed his finger at Else Schmiedler like a gun and shook his head. He signaled with his whistle, his gang fell in behind him and they all marched out. The nun threw up her hands and ran after them and the colonel followed.

Hanna stiffened and her eyes stared into the distance. I anticipated a trance, wild warning and prediction. "I should not have come," she said. "It is dangerous, but I am always drawn back here."

I asked what was so dangerous and what had upset her.

"Boys!" she said too quickly. "They always get restless and disturb the peace."

Males had not been allowed to enter the inner sanctum of Salon Roth. "Remember how the ladies used to come out here in droves?" I had seen her here with stout Frau Traude after they had installed Salon Roth in this room. How could she go into one of her marvelous trances without hats, ladies, whirring sewing machines, the smell of steaming felt? Now only the mirrors and a few of the gilded little chairs remained from those days of her luxuriant intrigues.

"Do you want to come back and live in this house again?" I asked.

"It is in my name, you know. Traude considered it safer in those days. But I wouldn't want to make this my home. I abandoned this house at the end of the war. Once you abandon a person or a place you must not ever return." Her black eyes fixed on me.

Traude Romberg had abandoned her. I had not turned away from Hanna Roth, but from Johanna von Falkenburg an invention of master maze-maker, Fritz Janicek. His lure had been that anonymous flowery letter leading to the old Falkenburg estate; melodrama of a winding staircase, old portrait of that dwarf in armor. The inscription: Johannes von Falkenburg 1768 leading to a family chronicle in the library open for anyone who cared to see: *Johanna von Falkenburg* written in war time ersatz ink below Count Otto my great grandfather and his sister. A hoax. I had said so, not that it made any difference. The entrapment of a Fritz Janicek maze always lead to an irresistible deadly end: Falkenburg dwarfism, possible incest. Family disgrace. Mother the decendent of dwarfs . . .

Hanna had shed her title, regained her power. I sensed this as she turned her head this way and that following Else the will-o'-the-wisp around the room

"Why do you think the boy pointed at Else?" I asked.

She did not answer my question. Her eyes fastened on a tall middle-aged American woman who was seating the children who remained. "Look at that! Only one hat in this room. And what a sad one!"

The hat was small, black, placed carelessly on gray short cropped thick hair.

"A rich American, the child rescue lady, most important and well meaning. And such an unfortunate hat! Only circus clowns wear that kind of nothing hat and they usually trim it with a huge paper flower." She kept her smile, but her voice shook. "Do you realize what has happened?" She gave way to a heavy sigh. "They might put crowns back into glas cases and guard them. How about hats? My glorious hats that made my ladies feel proud and safe? They have gone. Gone. With it all the self-respect is lost. No individualism left. Here I am back to telling stories to little ones. There is nothing else. Remember how I used to design *the* costume, and *the* hat for your glorious Mama? And the doll . . ."

"For great aunt Christina von Kortnai before that."

She chuckled. "Ja, ja. Those were the days. When the snow melts they will start rebuilding, restoring buildings. But can they restore my ladies? Here you are dressed like a country boy. Will I ever see you dressed in wheat-colored cashmere, a tiny tilted hat in your curls, gloves to match . . ." Her dark eyes were drawn back to the unfortunate hat. "I could trim her hat with a hazy blue ribbon, the color of her gentle eyes."

"I wonder why those war children ran off when they saw Else Schmiedler. I don't like her. Do you?" I said.

Hanna pulled a half veil down over her fixed smile.

"You made hats for Frau Schmiedler, didn't you, during the war. Did you ever see him? Where is he now? You must know . . ."

Hanna Roth left me standing and headed towards a table miraculously loaded with cakes, cookies, wine and cheese. I followed, so did the lady in the unfortunate hat.

"How you stand out. The picture of health," she said to me in slow loud English and loaded a plate for me with a big piece of chocolate cake. I thanked her in my best English. And she held onto my arm with the determined informality of a shy American and told me that my rosy cheeks, my curls, reminded her a lot of her daughter. She had a deep, soft voice. Her face, like the hat, looked as though it had been packed on a long journey and irreparably crushed. "You are older than the other children and you must certainly remember your parents well and you must know where you came from. We will do everything we can to find them."

I assured her that my mother was just across the street and Father at his office in town and told her my name. The American lady held onto me and said she should have known. I spoke English so nicely and I just looked different. And she was sorry that the neighborhood children had not all been invited. The poor war children, torn away from their homes, should get to know other children and families. Some didn't even remember their parents. And, of course there were those that had been hurt. Frightened and disoriented. No wonder they suddenly ran out of the room. She was making a great effort to find parents or relatives. She was sure they would soon come forward."

"Don't be too sure about relatives," Hanna Roth said in English with a decorative French accent. "These are hard times," and she ladled sugar worth a small black market fortune into her coffee cup. "Relatives might not be so eager to take in a handi-capped child."

The child-rescue-lady said she understood this and would make sure to find foster homes in Switzerland for each child until things improved.

"What?" I said with a sudden fury of a disoriented war child. "The children are a family. They help each other. You can't sep-arate them."

The kind American lady smiled with invincible goodwill. Hanna and I had disappointed her. Colonel Fredericks had just come into the room and she turned to him. Hanna joined a French group of civilians and officers. And I was left to the pleasure of eating the first chocolate cake in about five years, until Lieuten-ant Kaufman touched my shoulder.

"Well, here we are," he said in his Berlin German. "As if nothing had happened." He looked pleased with himself and seemed to have recovered from the stabbing.

"A lot has happened," I said. "The Russians and Americans could have started another war. Did you shoot a Russian on the Mozart express?"

He looked annoyed.

"How about the man who stabbed you."

"Let's put it this way. If a man tries to kill you, Russian, Hungarian, or whatever, you certainly have a right to shoot him."

"The war is over," I said in an Arnold voice. "The Allies are supposed keep order. You could always arrest anyone who threatens you. Killing is murder."

"You certainly have all the answers. Why didn't you speak up like that under the Nazis."

"I was too young and they would have killed me and my par-ents." He turned his back on me and looked out of the window and I liked his broad shoulders and narrow hips. "Is the groom dead?"

He said "crazy kid," to himself rather than me. "As a matter of fact he's disappeared."

"Perhaps he has disguised himself," I said.

He picked up a nut from a half empty plate and nibbled, as though he weren't listening. I didn't know that this had been part of his training and tried to get his attention by going on and on about Schmiedler, how some men dressed up as women. I had seen it once during the war right in this house. This very room.

"You were sent over here by your father to poison the wine and most of the men died," he said.

I became furious. "Who said that? I bet it was Fritz Janicek. He's a liar. Lieutenant Mort knows that. Is he back in Vienna too?"

"Unfortunately." He took me by the elbow and led me to the end of the table. "I do owe you a favor." He put down his empty wine glass. I ate the last of my cake fast like Hanna, hoping he would show his gratitude by giving me more. He ignored my empty plate and leaned towards me confidentially. I got a whiff of fragrant clean skin and hair. "I hope you're not getting tangled up with Lieutenant Mort," he said. "He is a trouble maker."

He walked out. I hoped no one was looking and took another piece of cake.

"You there. I don't know how you got in here." Else Schmiedler accosted me across the room. Her dress had a tight bodice, excessively full skirt and tight sleeves. I hated that pretty picture.

"I used to come here all the time," I said. "The Rombergs are our friends."

"There are no Rombergs," she said. "He is dead. And she divorced him."

"There is Eli!" I said.

"Who's that?"

"My friend. The son. He is in Switzerland."

"Your friend. Is that so?"

Before grapes formed in our vineyards she would repeat this again and laugh. Her reactions lacked variety. Never once did she pretend to be friendly towards anyone. She went around the table filling cups without a smile or a word. A hazy sun and snow cast a white light onto the children solemn as dolls. Suddenly a powerful engine roared and growled, stopped and then sputtered. Some of the children ducked under the table, others jumped up. The motorcycle I had seen in the entrance room came wobbling along the snow covered path. The rider, Sergeant Tony, equipped with an oversized white helmet, and a dispatch bag sat hunched over the balking machine. It shot forward, shaking him, crashed into frozen bushes. Frau Boschke came running, arms waving, coat unbuttoned and flying. She caught up with him and took hold of the back of the seat, and ran trying to keep him steady. He blew his horn. A guard came out of the stone pavillion and raced ahead to open the back gate. The motorcycle swerved, and got away from Frau Boschke. Children jumped up and left their cake to cheer Tony on. He brushed the gate post, shot out into the street and was gone. Frau Boschke at the gate waved and waved.

The children clapped their hands. So did I. During the hub-bub Else and the Colonel walked out and left the door open. I devoured my cake. The servant handed me a cup of hot choco-late. I was stuffing cookies like a hamster when I heard sounds of a distant Resi Romberg record playing "Vilya, what you have done to me," selections from *The Merry Widow,* Hitler's favorite operetta. I left the room, crossed the great hall where crystals used to chime with Resi's trilling, soaring and expressionless choir boy soprano "Vilya, oh Vilja." I followed the song along passage ways, past the gymnasium, the stable of the mechanical horse; the empty conservatory and the empty cages of the aviary.

"No human made love and kissed like this." Heat and a cloy-ing perfume were trapped in the windowless passageway with the song. Seven years had passed since Eugene Romberg had brought me here, led me to his secret room and unlocked it. Now I found it half open. Actually I could have walked into the room. Else Schmiedler and the colonel would not have seen me.

In his secret room Eugene had apologized to me as he usually did when he gave precious gifts. Diamonds, or rubies, gold, could be lost or stolen. The story of the interrupted game of chess, invented, imagined or real, I would keep as long as I lived. He had entrusted me with his dread of the Arab cook who had appeared among bowling pegs; claimed the right to kill his mother, kill little Eugene. The cook had vanished almost at once, and yet he remained ever present in that locked room. "All one big mas-querade," Eugene Romberg had said.

His crystal flask and glass had remained on an embossed table. The display of whips, hangings, and those unforgettable por-traits of a young, pale Traude, and her husband the bearded Izaak Romberg—a man and woman looking in opposite direc-tions—had been replaced by posters, photographs and paintings of Adolf Hitler in a variety of costumes and uniforms. Ceramic pots and urns had vanished. Two long banquet tables covered with white cloth displayed the red and gold and silver and black glitter of Nazi emblems: golden party badges, iron crosses; the silver lightning rods of the S.S. Service medals; a gold honor cross for German mothers. And when I did go into the room in the end I was not surprised to find Mother's yellow silk rose which I had lost from my treasure box. In the heart of that silk rose, would be that flea-sized silver swastika Mother had worn before Hitler took over Austria. Afterwards I told myself, I was not just a voyeur. I had to wait and take back my lost treasures.

The secret room was L-shaped, exactly like the music room. The French windows remained covered with heavy draperies. Spotlights beamed down on the display. Old leather seats had been pushed together in the dark recess to clear the floor for dancing.

Else was leading the colonel in a waltz. His uniform coat had been replaced by the black Leibstandarte, S.S. tunic. She looked naked under her transparent dress and he danced badly and kept staring into a tall mirror, which had a swastika encrusted frame. "I don't know why you won't let me lock the door." He was saying. "It should at least be closed. Anyone could come by . . ."

"And what is there to see. A little dancing. Right under everyone's nose. We like that best, ja?"

"Now tell me about Hitler," he said in a lovesick voice.

"Shot in Hamburg in 1935 and buried secretly."

"How did you find out?"

"How many times do I have to tell you? Vati shot him."

"There were three Hitlers after that."

"Nein, nein. What's the matter with you are you getting senile? Four. I told you so. My Vati could really make himself look perfect."

"Wasn't he afraid you'd talk."

"A little girl who talks and laughs a lot. Who would believe me?"

"And you really saw the four doubles?"

"How many times do I have to tell you?"

"Where?"

"In Vati's dressing room. All the walls were mirrors. And I danced with each one. So many little me's, so many Adolfs . . ."

Else turned the colonel in front of the big mirror where they floated among Hitler memorabilia. The thin colonel arched forward and pressed himself against her sturdy female thighs. Her bouncy behind kept time with catchy tunes in much the same way as Agnes kept time beating dough while listening to the radio. The rhythm was perfect, involuntary. They belonged together as the egg beater belonged in the bowl.

"You worry too much. It's only a little dance, ja! and I always keep my pretty clothes on," Else spoke German.

"Keep the pretty clothes on," he repeated like a language student. But clothes-trees loaded with all kinds of old uniforms looked as though a gathering of National socialists had stripped. And I wondered whether the uniforms had been left behind by the men who had died wearing Resi's dresses.

The gramophone was running down. Resi's boy soprano voice turned into a drawn out lulling falsetto. The colonel grabbed Else hard, clutched her, and the record kept turning and turning with the caressing swoosh, swoosh, swoosh of long, silk skirts.

"Right under everyone's nose?" Else pushed the colonel away. He chased her around the room shouting. *"Darf ich bitten,* may I have this dance please." And went to crank up the gramophone again. She kicked his hand away, picked up her petticoat, swung it above her head and ran.

I fled into a broom closet and the floor boards creaked.

"What was that?" he said.

Else stopped. "Rats or mice. There were rats or mice in this house a long time ago. My father had to do something about that."

"Where is he?" I could tell this was part of a game they had played over and over again.

"Dead," she said.

"You're teasing me again. You are a terrible tease and liar!" This was no reprimand. He liked the idea and fairly glowed in the presence of so much wickedness.

She laughed and ran off. He gave chase. I rushed into the room and took back the silk rose, pricked myself on the flea-sized swastika. Hitler eyes stared down from all the big portraits and posters: Fuehrer the brown-shirt, Fuehrer the Austrian country man, Fuehrer in a belted raincoat with a dog. Fuehrer the undertaker in a black suit and black tie. All the same face, the same stern instigator. The same staring eyes. Fixed and seeing nothing. I felt myself surrounded by the portraits of a multitude of blind voyeurs.

# SEVENTEEN

# *Beware of Carnival*

ON MY WAY OUT I found Frau Boschke sitting behind Tony's desk drinking coffee. I asked her whether Hitler had been long dead and about Hitler Doppelgangers.

Frau Boschke produced a small flask from a file drawer and poured something into her cup, added a scoop of whipped cream. "Every second man tried to look just like him. You must remember all those Hitlers. From the age of four to eighty. Even our chimney sweep." She drank and the whipped cream gave her the mustache of an aged Fuehrer. "Hitler or a hundred Hitlers, real or not real? What's the difference. One devil or a hundred when everyone is bedevilled."

"Did you open my treasure box and take my yellow rose and some other stuff?" I asked.

"I made your bed and all that stuff fell out of an old box. Hitler picture, letter. Could be misunderstood. Safer here with the colonel. I gave it to Tony for Christmas. He was as pleased as a child. You like books. So I brought you that nice book the Schmiedlers had lying around. And made you happy too!"

She was right. I loved the *Handwriting of Great Men*. Hitler, Goering, Goebbels, etc., etc. Mussolini, Napoleon, and, even Rudolf Hess. Letters slanting forward, backwards, or straight, it all had meaning. Pointy letters, rounded letters, tiny letters and big ones. To "Else from her Vati," Schmiedler wrote in rounded even large letters of a generous personality. His handwriting was no doubt disguised.

Frau Boschke had sometimes brought me a toy or books children in another household had left lying around. I used to put hateful dolls ignorant acquaintances had given me into the dirty linen basket for Frau Boschke. It had always been a fair exchange until now.

"You could have asked me first!" I said.

She drank down her coffee, wiped her mouth with the back of her hand and sighed with pleasure. "Ask a lot of questions and you get a lot of answers," Frau Boschke said. "I use my own judgment."

Hanna came into the entrance to get her cloak and umbrella, ready to leave. "Ah, there you are, *meine Liebe,*" she said to me with a new little swagger. "I have to fly back before dark."

Frau Boschke helped her with her cloak and winked. "You can always turn yourself into a nightbird, Frau Roth." She was half serious. And we both liked the idea of Hanna Roth flapping her arms and flying over the American zone, the British zone, circling the French and soaring under the stars over the Russians all the way to Salzburg.

I often think of Hanna in wintery Salzburg at that little Bishop castle in a white park, where snow-saddled unicorns guarded the gate before an ice glazed lake. Hat, veil, gloves, umbrella, predictions, warnings, story hours.

Hanna Roth in the Getreidegasse under the trade shields. Or in the cathedral before altars where doll-faced angels drenched in gold swam to the music of Mozart who had kneeled here in his day. Siren voices of boys echoing in penitent hearts year hundred after year hundred luring souls to paradise in a glorioso to secular power and unearthly wealth: the equestrian spirit of the bishops. Lords who had known how to stay in the saddle . . .

Little Hanna would refer to the attack on her person as "the Christening." Court dwarf, Hitler fortune-teller, she had been thrown into the river by a villain and emerged from the river as Hanna the Brave. A heroic little Austrian rescued by a heroic young American officer. Had she not sewn jewels into hatbands of the famous actress who had to flee from the Nazis?

After the incident the actress wrote to the military government of Salzburg on behalf of Hanna Roth. And the American

protectorate suited Hanna Roth's fancy rather like those unicorns at the gate facing the frozen lake: positioned guardians.

Since she could not foresee danger for herself, Hanna carefully circumvented bomb sites, bridges, lonely streets. Soon after
her return from Vienna, strolling in the gardens late one afternoon she would see the sinking sun reflected on the ice. She
stopped and suddenly she heard herself calling my name. There
was an echo.

Afterwards she had no recollection of walking back, taking
off her cloak or climbing the stairs. She found herself sitting on
the piano stool at the telephone. It was kept in a niche decorated
with a fresco of Saint Solanos surrounded by birds. The gilt eyes
of all the birds stood out from the faded colors, so did the halo.
She would make the sign of the cross before she telephoned to
warn me. In Salzburg the occult and the sacred are never far
apart. The operator in those days would say "Just a minute,
please." Then Hanna waited and waited. Listening to the rushing crashing sounds like oceans that had covered the Salzburg
land before the time of men. She would look out of the narrow
window over the unicorns, the lake dotted with an island, to a
distant peninsula in the white distance between snow and clouds:
Untersberg—home of legends. And the rumbling on the telephone line—thunder, roaring, crackling and hissing sounded like
the vulcanic anger of the legendary giant, Rubezahl. The Tur-
nip-counter, guarding his crop, small minded in his anger as many
a giant, catching pitiful little thieves.

Rumbling gave way to twitter, then, finally a distant ring. I
answered. And she said. "Greetings, *Gruess Dich,* little Highness. Listen to old Hanna, little Highness. *Ja?* No costume parties."

"Why?"

"Doesn't a storm oppress the air long before it comes," she
said. "I can always feel it hours before it thunders. The future
does affect present . . . you understand? No masquerades."

I rather liked thunderstorms and I loved Carnival. "What's
going to happen to me?"

Her reply—if you can call it that—was the ratched sound of
something turning, grinding. The telephone clicked. I had questioned her warning and she had hung up. Some years later, by
chance, I visited the castle by the lake and found the shrine, the

telephone. Beside it a convenient piano stool. I turned it and got a picture of Hanna Roth winding herself up and down making the grinding ratched sound of one of those carnival noise makers, after her warning, spinning me into carnival mischief like a whirligig doll.

The warm wind was blowing over the Alps, old and new graves of unknown soldiers, and across borders, graves of concentration camp victims, and the grave of Eugene Romberg in the mountain town. In Vienna snow dropped off statues like plaster casts. Cherubs, dryads, gods and godesses, saints and madonnas emerged as amputees. The Foehn always brings thaw and melancholia to Vienna and with it a mania for diversion, pleasure.

The damp was more penetrating than dry frost, and trying to keep warm kept the Meinert family closer together. The living room and kitchen were cozy, the rest of the house barely warm enough to keep pipes from freezing. I would spread out my school work and books on the carpet in front of the slow burning tile stove and my parents would stay at the dinner table over a glass of wine. They talked freely as if I weren't there or deaf, about matters I was not supposed to understand because I was too young.

Mother said: "You're saying that no woman really knows a man until she lets him make love to her, Ferdl? Women don't really know whether they are in love until they allow themselves to be taken. You might as well say that only the victim knows about murder and he is dead. I really got to know the men who sat around here at the beginning of the war and told me about themselves, because they never touched me."

I, however, remembered a conversation when Resi had told Mother that a man she did not know at all, had surprised her in the bunker in Berchtesgaden. She would have gone with him to the end of the world. And Mother had admitted that a man had surprised her at the meadow farm—only with a passionate kiss— and yet, he had stirred her the same way.

I would watch Father and Mother getting ready to go to the vintner's ball, the baker's ball, apothecary ball, artist's ball. Touch the old Hungarian costumes, or evening dress, and tell them to have fun in a parental tone of voice. They told me that next year I would be old enough. This year one had to go early and stay all night, it was too dangerous to come home before dawn.

During breakfast Mother would tease Father about Frau Hillie, and he would tease her about a masqued stranger who had
kept cutting in when Mother danced. Soon they began to yawn.
I would go to school and they would go to bed. Costumes dish-
evelled, Father carrying Mother's shoes, stumbling with fatigue,
still talking about everyone they had flirted with as if they had
to borrow passion. Then they would make love among her lace
trimmed crested pillows as an afterthought. Disgustingly casual.
I pictured them on the same bed naked and entangled as if by
chance. Nothing more shocking.

"Fasching is supposed to be for young girls," I said one evening when Father was waiting for Mama. "I don't see why I can't
come along to some of the balls. I know Grandmama would not
approve. She still lives in the Kaiser-days, but she doesn't have
to know about it. All the girls in my class go out." I only knew of
Mimi and the fat one. "Ursel is younger than I am and she is
going to a union ball in a dress made from a pink organdy bed-
spread with thousands of little frills."

Father glanced at the cuckoo clock. "Thousands of frills," he
said. "We'll have to talk to Mother about that."

Same old costumes, same old attitude towards me. Mother in
a gala dirndl with black, velvet bodice. She had lost weight and
it hung loose. I fluffed up her blouse sleeves. "Father says you
have do something about me. All the girls are going out to balls."

"In thousands of pink frills," Father helped out.

Mother tucked her hair into one of Father's green felt hats. I
held the cloak for her. "Just look at me having to hide in a man's
cloak and hat," she said. "Your father wearing an old watch in
case we have an encounter with watch collectors."

"I can stay out all night. And I can dress up as a man."

Father looked over his shoulder and said he would speak to
the principal of my school. It seemed to him there used to be a
little ball and the girls even put on a show.

"Mother was engaged to you when she was my age. I never
go anywhere. I don't want to hop around with a few pimply
schoolboys left over from the war."

"Better than a lot of decrepit old fellows like your father.
Rejects from the first war! By next year some handsome Nazis
will be let loose from the internment camps and jail and some of

the prisoners of war might come back from Siberia. Then you'll have some exciting dancing partners."

"I don't know," Mother said. "But couldn't she go to the vintner's ball with us? It's nearby. We don't have to stay all night."

They faced me. Definitely a pair now, light eyed, half smiling, dressed like brothers. "What do you think your mother would say if her only grandchild made her debut at the age of fifteen among a lot of tiddly vintners?" Father said.

Their roles had reversed. He had been the one who wanted to give me freedom before I was able to stand up and walk. He had encouraged me to crawl around the house sliding down the stairs on my rounded stomach. When I was six years old he had handed me Uncle Ernstl's golden keys and allowed me to make my way to the water castle whenever I pleased. A girl in leather pants, as good as a son. Ready for anything.

"Next year," he said. "By then the Amis will be dancing at our balls, the French and Russians. *Ach ja,* the British too. There must be something about the English. I always thought they were rather reserved and cold . . ." he needled Mother about her Sir Doctor.

"That's not funny," Mother said.

"It isn't. Just look at my sisters . . . In love with England."

"I don't particularly want to look at your sisters. They have nothing to do with the fact that our girl is restless. I'd rather she go out with us. I get the idea you'd like to see her safely married and go to balls afterwards, just like me." Hysterical laughter. Trying to have a good time when everything was awful and hopeless. They argued and I was the pawn. Siding with me, prodding me into rebellion, Mother relived her pre-Hitler days, the thrill of hidden flea-sized silver swastika's, her own luxuriant rebellion linked, of course, with the revelry of her delicious acquiescence to Father.

"All in good time. Married or unmarried, next year is soon enough," Father said. I did not agree and yet my sympathy was with him. He started fumbling around in his pockets. "There was something in my pocket. Don't tell me. Lost. I am so absent-minded these days . . . I try to hide things, in case someone picks my pocket in the street and than I can't find it. *Ach, ja,* Reyna, Look inside my hat band."

Tickets. A box for the Volksoper, the little opera house. He knew I needed to have a little fun. He had invited a few people, including a certain Ami officer . . .

"A harmless little evening," I said to hide my pleasure.

There was not an empty seat in the house. It was unheated. We wore coats. There was a youngish couple: a Count Provost and his willowy, shy wife; the court doctor and Mort. Grandmama had telephoned and said she was too tired. She had a cold and could not get over it. I missed her, and yet I was glad she didn't come. While everyone was greeting acquaintances in neighboring boxes and looking around scanning the audience through opera glasses, Mort and I settled in the recess of the box. He did not want to talk about his stay in Germany or about Hanna Roth and seemed dull.

We had not been alone for weeks. I asked him how he liked the Schmiedlers. He said they were O.K. No more. As soon as the lights were lowered and the overture began he took my hand and his fingers began to creep over mine like waltzing spiders. It gave me goosepimples.

Mother turned around and smiled to us and he deftly put his program over our hands. This made my pleasure slightly indecent and more intense. He had once said to Mother that he never noticed a piano, he just played it. I thought of that when he played with my hand, and then turned it over and kept sliding his fingers in between mine. He actually kept his eyes on the stage and later he played much of the music from memory, while I couldn't even remember the name of the operetta.

By the time the curtain went down on the first act and we separated to applaud, my face glowed and I was pleased with myself and worried, as though I had been under a quilt with a carnival lover. This was the first short intermission. Father said with pride that our lieutenant was the youngest and most accomplished American officer in Vienna. Learning to speak German like a Viennese. Charming company. A fine musician. Such rhythm. *Echt amerikanisch.*

When the lights dimmed and the curtain rose again, I put my hands into my coat pockets. And I felt excited and ashamed when I allowed Mort to invade the pocket to the tune of a march. His finger gently and persistently slid into my palm, then out, rhythmically. The curtain rose, the ballet performed. I closed my

eyes and my fingers curled around his each time. And each time
I clasped him I reached out ecstatically to Arnold. I felt a crusad-
er's bride left behind to grow old, thinking of the absent one,
borrowing passion, finding and giving the pleasure of an absent
one away.

The act ended with the chorus of girl dancers in tights and
top hats parading through the parterre audience. And when they
wiggled up the side of the stage, Mort wiggled out of my hand.
The lights came on.

The doctor turned to talk to us and said: "My dear child, you
look flushed." He touched my forehead. Told me to keep wrapped
up. I had a temperature. There was a lot of influenza around.
And Mort eyed me with infuriating sympathy. I jumped up.
Everyone went out to stretch their legs or smoke. There had been
a rumor that the buffet, the old snack bar, was open. Father said
it would be a dangerous stampede. He knew of an inn where one
could get a little something after the theater and it would be his
pleasure . . . While he talked, I looked down into the parterre at
the Russians in the audience. One officer had brought a boy in
officer's uniform with him. They both kept their caps on. The
only other American, a Negro officer, was getting up, escorting
a lady dressed in red.

"There is my English teacher, Miss Pnevsky," I said to Mort.
"With her American fiancé."

He looked down at the crowd and did not say anything.

"I met him once. She introduced me. Let's go down and talk
to them," I said.

"No." He left me and went to mingle with my parents and
their guests. I didn't have a chance to ask him whether it was
true that Negros had their own regiments, their own schools and
churches in America. Girls often discussed Magda and her
American Negro soldier during recess. Magda Stengler from the
graduating class was famous in school for her green, slanting
eyes, wild dark hair and little black moustache. Her Negro soldier was jolly and very generous and she wanted to go to America with him.

We often referred to Negroes as Moors in Austria. I preferred
this. Just as Grandmother had always chosen to call Jews
"Hebrews." Polite, less personal . . . Besides, Moor sounded
romantic and dramatic like Othello the Moor of Venice. Ugly

slogans, name calling, that went with racism, had been around too long. That pure Aryan, German, farce in our hodge-podge Vienna, seemed part of a dirty old game of winner takes all that grown-ups had played.

We all felt ashamed of our parents in some way. Mimi the "mixling" of her Nazi mother. The fat one of her black marketeer father, I of my beautiful and conspicuous mother and an eccentric father who dressed as if he were on a farm. We secretly blamed those we loved best for being hungry, poor Austrians. Everything different, unknown, foreign won our hearts.

I could see the superiority of Miss Pnevski's fiancé by the way he towered over the pushy crowd with an easy smile. He was walking with his arm around his lady's waist, quite unhurried. The uniform showed up his elegant tapered torso. People were staring at the pair and he held his head so high it tilted back. This reminded me of Bertl von Hohentahler, Mother's cousin. Aloofness seemed a natural reaction to either admiration or to scorn.

I excused myself. Mother embarrassed me by asking whether I wanted to come along. And I ran off quickly and went down the stairs. The little jewel box of a theater had only been slightly shaken up and chipped. The railings had already been repaired. Wooden posts supported a ceiling in the lobby. And under a crack stood my teacher with her love. Her face had changed and looked less puffy. The diamond on her left hand sparkled when she waved her cigarette and called to me in a breezy American tone of voice.

She was pleased to see me, perhaps relieved to be greeted instead of ogled in her red skirt and coat. Her officer said his name was George Williams. We shook hands and he whipped chewing gum out of his pocket so fast I flinched.

"Fast on the draw," he laughed heartily.

I did not understand. And he entertained me with stories of the fast guns of the West until the first bell rang announcing the end of intermission. We shook hands again. He offered me another package of chewing gum for my parents. When I refused, he said he had some chocolate in his coat. He'd give it to me on the way out. I said that would be too much. His face fell.

"I love the chewing gum," I quickly said.

He smiled again. Said I spoke good English. Had a great teacher.

I made my way through the crowd. Mort was watching, but did not come to meet me. He followed me back to the box and did not pull out my seat. Miss Pnevski was walking towards her seat leaning against her George. The lights dimmed. A conductor was applauded. Music filled the little Volks Oper. Mort had not said a word to me. He was staring at the curtain and held the program with both hands and chewed on his moustache. I remembered a walk through the vintner's village, when he was singing for me and we had run downhill, sliding and laughing. The street had been empty and he had shimmied up a lamppost. I felt as though years had passed. He seemed to have aged since his return to Vienna and moving into the water castle.

I stared at his face, remembering how I had loved him when he had clung to the lamppost singing a song about a mocking-bird. He felt my stare, turned and took my hand again. Until the end of the performance our fingers were entwined. Partners on stage were dancing to jolly nostalgic Viennese music. And I was nostalgic for a jolly Mort—remembering, borrowing love—and this made me sad. He sensed something and caressed my wrist, touched it with one finger, giving me the message of a consoling kiss. During the final scene he slid his fingers between mine clasping and releasing and than clasping faster, more and more until my fingers turned into yielding thighs. When the music stopped, all through the applause my heart pounded.

When the lights came on, the kind doctor asked how I felt and I was afraid he might touch my wrist and discover not a mere fever but the symptoms of a heart attack. I was quite relieved when Mort said goodbye. We went on to eat gulyas in the back room of an inn. I missed Mort, wondered when I would see him again and gulped my food. This reassured our medical friend. Whatever I had caught, he said kindly, I would soon get over . . .

# EIGHTEEN

# Satin Pierrot

MY FIRST CARNIVAL COSTUME, the hand-me-down satin Pierrot is half black, half white. Pantaloons and overblouse loosely draped to play and shimmer over breast and hips are gathered into ruches at the neck, wrist and ankles. A tight fitting cap half white and half black swallows my curls. Pompoms bounce and bells jingle at each step. The masque is half white and half black. Lips are too smiley and red. Too much lipstick, too much rippling silk, too much perfume: you can smell me coming.

Only Hanna Roth could have designed such a costume; only Great Aunt Christina and her doll would have worn it. And then Mother, of course, at her first masque ball. I had thrown the Pierrot suit out of the window for the Agnes–Frau Schwester doing-things-thoroughly rite. Not sun, or moonlight or Föhn-wind could ever air out mischief.

My parents were dancing somewhere. Agnes and Frau Schwester had gone to visit our local priest, Pfarrer Leiden, who had fallen on the ice and broken his hip. My note said: "Off to study English, back soon." It was not a complete lie. Mort had spoken English to me on the telephone. "I bet you're bored all alone in the house doing your homework! Want to play a trick on someone? Have a little fun? O.K. Put on a cute costume. Meet you in front. We'll only be gone an hour. I'll be waiting. Fifteen minutes. O.K. Hurry!"

How did he know I was alone? Hanna Roth had said, beware of carnival, but there was nothing wrong with a little bit of fun.

I could see the car waiting, stuffed Mother's high-heeled slippers into the deep cloak pocket. I'd be back in an hour.

I saw two uniforms under the trees. I had thought I'd be alone with Mort. There was the little sergeant examining something in the trunk. When I appeared he picked up one of those round, gray fur uniform hats. He tried it on and it slipped down to the rim of his glasses.

"Russian!" I said.

"We have everything," Tony said.

A woman came along with a black Alsatian. The dog's eyes glowed in the dark. Mort snatched the hat off Tony, threw it into the trunk, closed and locked it.

"Let's look at you," Mort said and drew me towards a street lantern. I took off the hood, unbuttoned the cloak.

Tony whistled one high and one low. "Great," Mort said. "but you won't want that masque. We're going to see someone who likes a pretty face . . ."

"Are you going to dress up as Russians?"

"Shhh," Mort said. "Let's get going."

The woman with the dog was passing by, her face half-hidden in a shawl, not just against the cold. The dog had gone crazy during an air-raid and bit the tip off her nose off. She went around veiled like a Turk. I had a queazy feeling as if all of Vienna this winter was costumed to hide pain.

"What's the matter?" Mort asked. "Are you scared. You'd rather not come along?"

I told him about the woman and her dog.

Mort said pilots who had their face ruined could have it repaired. I had read about a British surgeon who was going to turn a pilot into a woman. My parents had refused to answer any of my questions. I had asked the court doctor whether the British surgeon could make breasts and everything, and whether the pilot could have babies after he became a woman. The doctor had become evasive.

"In the U.S.A. we can fix anything." Tony said.

I never would meet another American who had more faith in his country, yet, as far as I know he never went back. Perhaps the greatest patriots are destined to be expatriots, deserters, fallen angels who loved their homeland from far away cozy coffee houses. And to me in the warm safe American car, fully masqued, wedged between two Amis and a piece of chocolate melting in my mouth, Vienna was the sweetest place in the world.

The sergeant was driving. Street lights which had been fixed in American Vienna, reflected on his metal rimmed American glasses. Mort put his arm around me. "There is one of our civilians, a practical joker. The kind of guy who'll put a rubber spider into your glass. He's big and fat. Always ready for a good laugh. He just moved into a new apartment and asked me over for a drink."

I no longer recognized streets. Mort had his arm around my shoulders. I smelled alcohol on his breath for the first time. He looked at me, smiled, and hummed that song about a mockingbird and told me that it was from "Finnigans Rainbow." Mort said he had been the leading man in this musical play at his high school and I reminded him of a girl at home who had made him do crazy things. "I feel just great!" he concluded.

"Like shimmying up a lamppost?" I asked.

"And don't you think he won't." Tony said. "The lieutenant will do anything!"

"Wait til I put on one of those Ruskie uniforms," Mort said. People and houses flitted by in unlit streets. Near a socialist housing project a group of men and women in costumes walked arm in arm with a one-legged figure who wore a stork beak and white masque. "Now, listen, pretty girl. All you have to do is ring the bell. We'll stay out of sight. When he opens the door we'll pounce on him. He'll kill himself when he sees Tom here in the big, Russian uniform."

There would never be a night quite like this. You have to be forewarned to savor such a moment. *No masquerades. No costume parties* . . . Why did Hanna Roth design costumes if she didn't like carnival? Tony kept his eyes on the road, sober, serene, attentive. "My girl thinks a lot of you," he said to me. "Boschke thinks you're smart as a whip."

Mort translated this for me, gave me a hug and said he agreed. Later, when Mort's arm wasn't holding me I thought about the expression and did not really like it so much.

Black alleys, gardens, a church with an onion shaped steeple and then we slowed down at a square of Viennese modern box houses which had been romantically adorned with old wrought iron lanterns, window grills and a gate that enclosed a cobblestoned courtyard. We had arrived. I had never passed the square before and have never seen it again.

Mort told me to duck. We stopped at the gate. The guard knew him, saluted and let us in. Cars and jeeps stood at each building. We parked under an old tree in the half dark.

Unique moments—good or bad—often have the inevitability of slapstick. Mort and Tony ducked down behind the open trunk of the car and popped up as Russians with grease guns.

Mort gave the orders: "No giggles! upstairs without a sound." I entered the building as though I had lost my will. Perhaps it was the delicious fragrance of coffee, the sound of American voices, music behind closed apartment doors. On the first floor the ghost of a swastika showed through a film of puke-colored paint.

"Take off the masque."

Tony, kneeled down and pushed my feet into Mother's gold evening slippers.

"Put the cloak on the banister. First door on the right."

The door was black and glossy. A name plate had been removed leaving marks. And the peephole stared at me like the eye of a heavy lidded monster with the thick lipped mail slot for a mouth.

"O.K. Ring!."

I rang twice. The monster eye opened.

Tony's fur hat popped around the corner, his glasses twinkled. Mort signaled. I remembered to smile. A key was turning. The door swung open. I confronted Lieutenant Kaufman in a blue, slik robe decorated with dragons, belt and tassel. We faced each other for the blink of an eye.

"Yahoo, yipp, yahoo!" a barking howling masquerade came between us. Machine guns, Russian hats, clumsy coats. The German American threw himself to the ground yelling something in Russian. The tassel on his belt slithered. He lay face down covering his head playing dead like a frightened insect.

"Hey there, hey," Tony said. "It's only us. Trick or treat. Wrong door."

"Mix up. Sorry. How about a drink?" Mort drew us inside and shut the door. "It's a joke. We went to the wrong floor. Come on. Get up Herb."

"Shock," Tony said. "We'll fix that." He put down his gun, clapped his hands and the German American shot up, shoved him aside. "Nigger," he yelled into Mort's face. "Rotten, damned nigger. Nigger. Nigger." He yelled it over and over again.

I had not learned that word and did not know the meaning.

Mort walked out, slammed the door. Tony opened it again, grabbed my hand and pulled me out. He lost his fur hat on the stairs. I picked it up. Remembered my cloak. Ran back to get it from the landing.

"Hey there. What's going on. Is that Kraut having a party and I'm not invited?" A fat civilian, cigar in mouth. Perhaps the practical joker who had missed our joke. "Hey wait. Cute costume. Don't I know you?"

I escaped down, out. It was snowing. I saw the tail light of Mort's car and Tony running after it with his grease gun. The guard pounced on him. There was a brief struggle. A few curses. Tony took off the Russian coat and hat. They were laughing. Tony came back. Lieutenant Kaufman was watching from his window.

Tony saw him up there. "They hate each other's guts," he said with satisfaction.

"Was I sent to the wrong door on purpose?"

"Who knows. That Schmiedler bitch set us all up. It was all her idea." Snow was streaking down on us now. I shivered. "How?"

"I wouldn't know. My *Madl,* crafty B. smelled a rat. Didn't want me to go out. Now my cap is in the car. Good thing the guard is an O.K. guy from Pennsylvania. He'll get us a ride back."

I asked him about "hating someone's guts," "smelling a rat" and finally about "nigger." Tony translated.

"Lieutenant Mort is white," I said.

"Kaufman says he's a cross over. Has a touch of the tar."

You could still see footprints Mort had left beside the tire marks of the car. A few minutes later they were covered by new snow. I felt deserted. Left behind to ask questions and get puzzling answers. "Tar? Cross over?"

"Black blood, but it can't be much. Who gives a damn."

Same old turmoil as Austria under Hitler Germany. Confusion. Jewish blood, Aryan blood, Prince of the old blood like Arnold. I had become enlightened when Grandmother had pricked her finger with a needle and I saw a drop of blood—red not blue. One drop of blood had taught me everything when I was eight or nine years old. Now, after all the bloodshed, how could soldiers believe that blood came in different colors? I thought of Mort and started chewing on my lip the way I always did when I was afraid for Eli Romberg.

"The Lieutenant Kaufman up there was scared shitty. Lucky he didn't mow us down like Russians. Thought they had come to get him. Now I'm without my cap. We've got to get out of here. Don't know what the hell made Mort leave us behind. Boschke-*Madl* will go wild when she sees him come back without me."

I stood in the snow, deserted, a female clown. This was carnival, you got carried away, acted a part. "I've got to go back up there," I said. "It's up to me. I was the one who rang the bell. It was my fault." I sounded like Arnold. Tony could not hold me back. I marched back, ran up the stairs and Lieutenant Kaufman was waiting at the door, pulled me in and locked up.

"I want to tell you," I said in German.

"O.K., then talk!" He said in English.

He was still in his dark, blue silk robe. A tippet of curly brown hair filled the neckline and hair covered his legs. He was holding a glass. The room was sparcely furnished and neat. Among bottles on a table, lined up like soldiers on a parade stood a few "Meinert Spaetlese."

"I truly regret," I said in Arnold's brisk *Hochdeutsch,* high German.

"Typically Viennese," Lieutenant Kaufman took off my cloak. "The clown suit is just right. Find an Austrian, accuse him of what went on here, it's always the same. No matter what he or she did it's never their fault. *Es tuht mir wirklich leid.* I am really sorry. I have had it up to here." He slid his hand across his throat.

I felt color rise to my cheeks. "You should regret what you said to Lieutenant Mort!" I said.

He emptied the glass and banged it down.

"A crazy masquerade," I said. "I know I shouldn't have come. A mix up. A practical joke meant for someone else. The man upstairs. . ."

"Using Russian uniforms for a masquerade? A joke? I had a right to shoot . . ."

"You had the right."

He half closed his eyes and looked me up and down as if he were taking aim. Russian drunk officer on American train, or satin Pierrot, sinister intent or buffoonery, in the end it's all the same: trespassers will be persecuted.

The robe suited him better then the uniform. You could see the torso of a wrestler, a strong, straight neck. His face was boyish and the eyes reproachful and tragic as an ape's. "You fooled me. I only saw the girl who had stayed with me when I had been sliced up by that maniac. *A good kid.* I forgot about the Nazi favorite, the mother. That diary with all that Rudolf Hess stuff, Hitler, rape. I didn't ask myself how the hell did she get past the guard." He was scolding me in English.

I held out my hand as if I could reach through some invisible bars. He grabbed my arm, pawed my body all over as if he were searching for a weapon, especially in the silk folds on the blouse. When he didn't find anything he said to himself: "In spite of all, the only possible virgin I have come across in Vienna—and the last one. Nothing more innocent, nothing a more wicked tease."

He gripped me. Little bells on the hat and sleeves jingled when he picked me up and carried me into the next room. I had not been carried around for many years. He unloaded me on a large unmade bed. I had a chance to romp and battle as a child. No one had ever overpowered me and pinned me down. My guilt vanished. "Let me go!" I squirmed, struggled; his robe fell open and the hair below his neck turned out to be a mere bib. He had a powerful white torso, notched by the knife scar below the left shoulder and he smelled of soap. Snug white underpants at the pit of the rounded belly bulged like a diapered infant's.

He pulled up my blouse. I was naked under it. Instead of bosoms rising like Austrian mountain peaks, I had two insignificant swells. *"Ach, ja,"* I heard him say with profound relief. "Unformed, untouched. A Nazi virgin. Desertion on rape. Wild about that Jew-hating lunatic Hess." This was the Nazi stalker briefing himself. A Nazi hunter breathing wine on me and gloating over guilty innocence. "From ten years old and up. Rapacious city—that's putting it mildly. Vienna's one big whorehouse."

*"Eins,"* Kaufman the wrestler counted and undid the first hook on my pants.

I could not move my arms, but I kept holding onto the black and white Satin Pierrot cap with both hands for supernatural protection. Ripping off my clothes, I guessed, would not be his style. At all times he took pride in procedure. Struggling with hooks made him sweat. He smelled pleasantly of dog paws.

*"Zwei,"* the second hook. The lieutenant kept wresting with

well-sewn, first quality old Austrian hooks and eyes, I sustained
the position of a corpse while he bragged about breaking in virgins the way Bertl von Hohentahler used to talk about breaking
in his horse.

He held me down and I held onto the magic hat worn by
Christina von Kortnai. Where, when? Had she been wrestled
down? How about Mother as the satin Pierrot? A hazy memory
of a man whispering to her in front of the hall mirror: "You will
come as the clown? For me, please? Without the doll or you will
be recognized." So, now I could blame everything on the Pierrot
suit, the way men blamed what they did on their uniforms. I
focused on the ceiling, turned my mind into a fly and gained a
fragmented perspective: of a satin Pierrot holding onto its hat;
weighed down by a baby-faced monster fiddling with hook on
pants that stay up like a chastity belt. Each particle of percep-
tion formed one monstrous absurdity. I couldn't stifle the giggles, gurgling, into laughter-shrieks.

He propped himself up and watched me roll around, stop,
then spatter and start all over again, all the tiny silver bells
jingling. Color drained from his face. Then he flushed. He had
not coped too well with my pants, now he tugged on his own and
got as far as another bib of fur.

"What if I'm not a virgin?" I hiccupped. "How do you know
I'm a *Jungfrau?*"

He let go of his pants as if he had been stung. "You let Mort
touch you? I asked him about that. He must have lied to me
again."

"Is that race-shame in America, just like Hitler's *Rassensc-
hande?*"

"A shame. Because he is ignorant. Doesn't know what's what
with girls. No thinking ahead. Can do a lot of harm without half
trying. Then blames it all on someone else. A girl is entitled to
pleasure. The first experience has to be safe and right." He rubbed
his fur bib, sat up beside me and let his wrestler's legs dangle
over the edge of the bed. Most feet are ugly. And I couldn't help
loving his dear little perfectly square feet decorated with matching little fur bibs. "You have to create a first night," his toes
wiggled.

Dear little perfect feet, irresistable as kittens. Could you fall
in love with feet for one night of learning what's what?

"Let me get my book." he said.

"A book?" Sergeant Tony waiting; Agnes calling Ursel, and finding out that I wasn't studying English with her. And then the police. Parents rushing home from the ball. All this for the bookish creation of my first night . . . No honeymoon room, no curtained bed overlooking lagoons, no big golden orb of a moon looking in on a Venetian night of love.

The little feet ran around stepping over fallen clothes, papers, and wine glasses frantic for that book in a bedroom that looked as though it had been searched by a bookthief. In Austria rooms had to be neat. I had never seen a messy room and the carnival of disorder thrilled me. A night could pass before the German–American expert Austria cleaner found that book and got on with his mission to break guilty innocence.

"What a mess!" I could not keep awe and admiration out of my voice. "You know, you should tidy up!" This was a mischief-making satin Pierrot speaking in a German Frau Schwester's *Hoch-Deutsch* demanding order in the midst of chaos.

"Tidy up," he repeated. *"Sauber machen."* He put on his robe, tying the sash in a double knot.

I fastened my hooks. And he started to pick up a uniform shirt, pants, socks. I made my way to the other room, the floor moved as though I had been on a sea voyage. A mirror in the neat room, showed me Kaufman going through a stack of papers. "Lost. *My God!"* I became interested in my own pink face in the mirror, mouth curving up in an involuntary smile, pompoms dancing over a few loose curls: a wicked Pierrot snatching the keys from the door would have locked the Ami investigator in. He was saved only by those *herzigen,* dear little, feet pattering around in despair. A daughter, and as good as any bosom-, or rump-loving lusty son, put the keys down and said: "enough is enough." An old Meinert motto.

He had forgotten me. His bare feet pattering around stacks of secret folders in a messy room. He seemed to have forgotten the book and was reading some of the papers. I picked up the cloak, took the masque from the pocket and put it on, saluted the guard of honor: bottles of Meinert wine labeled with our ancestral crest great uncle Ernstl's design: shield and grapes. *Enough is enough.*

"I truly regret," said a polite Meinert. I left him kneeling on the floor lost in the profusion of confused files. "It's one big mas-

querade anyway." Words of Eugene Romberg. Why did I have to
be so smug? *Enough is never enough.*

On the stairs I met the fat civilian. He grinned from ear to
ear. "Hey," he said. "It's you again. Is there a party I'm missing?"

I found my old shoes, picked them up and jingled past him.
"The party is over," I told him.


My party was over. I felt worse with each day that passed as
though nothing had happened. Mort stayed away. I came home
from school and saw an unfamilair squirrel coat hanging in the
entrance room.

"Frau Boschke's," Agnes said. "Can you imagine. The Americans are really making a lot of her. I don't know how she will
like eating just plain soup and bread for lunch."

I went down to the laundry room at once. She was ready for
me. "Next time you're off on some kind of *Spampanadl,* some
crazy escapade, you just leave my Tony out. He was so worked
up this morning he fell over on his motorbike. Now he's in the
Ami infirmary and I can't go near him. Just as well he's laid up
just now. There's been a complaint. Lieutenant Curly-head has
been transferred. So that hussy Else can have the house to herself with the colonel. In the meantime she's hiding out somewhere too, just in case. She had a falling out with the German
American and it was all her idea. I told my Tony to stay out of
it." She reached into her pocket and gave me a piece of chewing
gum. "Sorry about the little lieutenant. God be thanked, you're
all right. Or are you?"

"O.K." I chewed and savored the dank odor of boiling linen
and old stone. She picked up one of Father's shirts and saw a
wine stain, held it up to the light. She examined stains on garments as an expert. "Tyroler wine," she said. "Not much of that
around Vienna these days. I know where he has been."

"Where, at Frau Hillmar's?" I asked.

"No one can keep a secret from a good Viennese laundress."
She laughed dipped the shirt into a basin: *"Cold water, cold water,
never hot for Tyroler wine and virgin's blood."*

She had many sayings that went with the music of her scrubbing board. My favorite was: *"Fishy caviar, fishy love, has to be
soaked to get if off."*

Frau Boschke wore lipstick for the first time and a new frown.

"*Ja die Else!* Believe me. She'll get the colonel himself into hot soup yet. My Tony was the one who raked up those *Russische* uniforms. I don't want him in more trouble. You just keep your little mouth shut and play dumb."

My *Goscherl,* the Viennese diminutive for mouth, would not stay locked. Ursel, I knew, would be more shocked than anyone else.

She let out a shriek. I had to clamp my hand over her mouth. "You shouldn't have said you were at my house. I have to tell the truth. My father will take the carpet beater to me if I lie." She was far more afraid of the carpet beater, than the sin. Her father was an atheist; although her mother secretly took her to church. God the father in heaven to Ursel was just another man to be afraid of. She rolled her eyes. "Will you get smacked?"

I assured her I would not get smacked. My father had slapped me only once when he was nervous just after Hitler had taken over. Then he was very sorry.

"My sister and I got smacked a lot," Ursel said. "When one of us did something, *Vater* used to smack both of us and never asked whose fault it was. He said the one who knew about it and allowed it to happen was just as bad. We were a family and responsible for each other. I was glad when my sister was married. I was always spanked for things she had done."

Ursel's father, the socialist, and his form of justice, or injustice made me almost wish for an indignant father with a carpet beater who would punish and absolve all the Americans and Else and also me. Then everything would be done and over with.

"Are you sure it was that German American officer with the kind face who tried to take advantage of you? He sometimes speaks to me. I was running past his car as fast as I could. He was just coming out the gate. And he called after me in his German voice, not to worry, he would never run down a nice little girl like me. The next day I saw him again. He was with the officer that looks so stern. And he spoke to me and asked me for my name." You could already see how lovely Ursel's face would be one day when she gained a little weight and got rid of the dark blue circles under her large, bewildered eyes. "If the lieutenant had shot you all it would have been your fault."

"If I had been shot dead, what would it matter whose fault it was?" I said.

She raised her fine eyebrows: "It would matter to your family and me, and the girls in our class, everyone. You would have hurt everyone. My father says you have to have a social conscience . . . He says going to church and confessing, getting absolution so that you can get to heaven, is egotistical."

I went home as impressed by my own wicked behavior as Ursel had been. And I wanted to feel blameless again. I ate in a hurry. First I telephone my grandmother.

"Anything wrong?" she asked. "You sound funny. Why don't you come on Saturday and stay for a day. I have something exciting to discuss."

My mother was practicing the piano. Then she answered the phone and talked in English about Charles Dickens. The subject—oddly enough—social conscience. I couldn't settle down to geometry, put on my new coat and left carrying books as if I were going to Ursel's house. It was cold, unusually dry and clouds all moved in my direction. The sun came out as I walked faster and faster. I arrived at the gate of the yellow villa excited as the war children had been. Tracks of their sleds and small footprints had frozen. I went to pat the cast iron deer and rang the bell. The thought of those little Hitler pilgrims made me feel like a nonbeliever at a pagan shrine.

Krummerer-Herbster appeared at the door. "Coming, child. Coming. Just a minute." He hurried towards me in boots and belted coat carrying a paper bag. "Ah, *guten Tag*, Fraulein Meinert. Please excuse me. I took you for one of the children."

I interrupted and asked for the prince. And he cleared his throat, hesitated. "Does your Herr Papa know you are here?"

"He knows Arnold von Lutensteg well." I said.

"The captain is resting. He was up most of the night. In a state of stress."

I had come too late. He already knew of my escapade. I quickly mumbled something about not wishing to disturb.

"Please, please. *Bitte schon.* Do come in. You might be of help. The captain might like to interrogate you."

He made me feel almost welcome. I was able to follow him comfortably as though I had been summoned to answer questions. "Is this your house?" I asked.

Krummerer's questions were usually direct, but not his answers. The villa, he told me had belonged to a former client who now lived abroad. "The lady of the house had been given a priceless necklace by her husband. There was a rumor that it was one of those personal family pieces that had been stolen from Empress Zita when the Kaiser and him family had to flee after the first war. The lady of this house did not like the idea and she hired me, Detective Krummerer, to trace the necklace. It turned out that it had really belonged to your gracious grandmama and she had to sell it during the days of hunger following the first big war. Jewels were sold just as they are now. They are flooding the market . . ."

"Poor Kaiser Karl almost starved to death. He was a great man." I said.

"A sad story of injustice," he said without conviction and held the door for me.

The rooms had high ceilings, large windows and neglected parquet floors. Krummerer's boots made no sound, but my walking shoes announced my presence. The house was unheated and smelled of dust. We passed a desk or two, a few office chairs and a glass cabinet displaying a waterfall of papers. Then a sunny room where planks had been placed on crates to create two long benches facing a blackboard on an easel. And children's games, a teddy bear, a stuffed dog and picture books were lined up on a bookcase.

"The prince takes an interest in the war children. He is trying to find special teachers. In the meantime he uses my humble talents to assist him with simple lessons."

He took me up creaking stairs, opened a door with the bow of an operetta footman. "If you will wait here, I will announce you, *Gnädiges Fraulein.*"

I found myself alone in a huge room. Tall windows framed the view of a walled in sheltered oriental garden, where specks of snow, melted and then frozen sparkled on twisted dwarf trees and evergreen shrubs. Birds pecked crumbs at an oriental feeder. The room was unfurnished except for a table and three chairs under a pink, Venetian glass chandelier. For a second it chimed to overhead footsteps and I could hear the sound of glass touching glass of a thousand delicate toasts. Bygone music, voices resounding in the empty stillness. In the left corner the mark of a piano and music stands; on the walls the patterns left by paintings, mirrors, hangings, told the story of richness, civilities, dancing, balls, men and women costumed to surprise and delight.

The one table, perfect roccoco, both sturdy and dainty, had

been covered with a green blotter and faced the garden. It was set up neatly as a desk with folders, sharp pencils, ink, a telephone, an apple on a blue plate. I went to look at a photograph in a leather frame. A small girl dressed in boy's pants on a sun dappled chestnut tree smiling—my smile. Peering out behind fanlike monster finger leaves, my tousled head, my owl face from the water castle watching, tree-climbing days. On the lookout, in danger and safe, the climber who climbs too high. Skier who skies too fast and rarely falls, safe from indiscriminating carpet beaters of my time. I have remained the unpunished one who looks on. Safe from the holding, the kissing, rumping, pumping, grabbing, killer men. Wild as a Russian rapist, chaste as a young owl. That's what he likes to see. That's what I want to be for him.

I could hear footsteps coming down uncarpeted stairs. He was coming. Sitting here Arnold's eyes would wander from the child balanced on the top of a tree, ready for a false move, to the marvel of the garden which had taken no punishment, an untrampled solitude. I buttoned my hood as though I had just arrived and were ready to leave. He came through the door in a panic, tripped over an untied shoelace. I saw him unguarded, all that had been dapper, proper, typical, *echt* German, the military tautness had vanished. He wore an open necked white shirt, brown velvet jacket with leather patches at the elbow and looked like a sleepy young student. A pillow crease like a duelling scar marked his left cheek.

"What happened? What happened to you, Reyna? Are you all right?" He opened his arms wide for a child toppling from the tree. I was caught, hugged and kissed, held securely, and far too happily.

"I did something lousy!" I said. "Do you know about it?"

We stood near the window. The sun came and went. I leaned against him and he drew me closer. I confessed. He enfolded me as if he wished to absorb any harm I had done or known with his own body.

"Nothing has changed," he was saying when I had told him everything. "I'm still watching you come back from where you should not have been." He pointed at the table. "I took this picture from a gestapo file. That was when you were about eight or nine."

"Ten," I quickly corrected.

"You had gone to the Romberg house and came across a group of carousers who drank themselves to death on poisoned Meinert wine. You must have seen a man with a camera and decided to make a get-away to the top of the tree. The informer took this picture. I had to talk to your father and persuade him to move you and your mother to the country. I feel as helpless now as I did five years ago."

"Almost six. I'll soon be sixteen."

"If there were any safe place in the world and I could send you there . . ."

"I don't want to be sent anywhere!" I said. "You must never say a word to my father."

He let go of me. Paced back and forth and hitching his trousers. He had dressed in such a hurry he had forgotten his belt. "If Hitler had not taken over Austria, the house across the street from yours would have been the home of dear friends. I was part of the Hitler movement when I was not much older than you are now. But one is responsible."

"Social conscience," I said.

"*Richtig,* right, Reyna. You allow yourself to become part of a system. Everything else follows. I, the fifteen-year-old Hitlerjunge, in a sense brought about the occupation. What can you expect from soldier boys, our own, and everyone else here in Vienna, all over Europe?" He looked at my face. "And if it hand't been for the Hitler movement you would never have met an American soldier."

"I wouldn't have met you either." I had to laugh because I remembered Frau Boschke's: "No scum no suds. No Russ no Tony."

He responded with an undemanding kiss that made more sense to me than anything else. Then he said, he knew how I felt. He had American friends. One wants to be obliging. "If there hadn't been a war, I might have met Americans, British, perhaps even Russian students at a university. Now, there is always a certain condescension. A German, good or bad, is always a German."

"An Austrian, an Austrian. We are the enemy too," I said.

"Not you. Never you!" He kissed me as if I had belonged to him for years. "I have been thinking about Webern in this empty house," he said, "because he used to come here all the time. An amazing modern composer. He was in Baden. There was a curfew. He stepped just outside his front door to smoke a cigarette, an American soldier shot him. A mistake. So much has been lost. And it's not over. The Russians want to overrun Europe. Anyone who they think might get in their way will be killed or simply vanish. They will never stop. Russian uniforms really are not funny here in Vienna. Lieutenant Kaufman is not just average. He has a conscience, but he could have shot all of you in self-defense. It wasn't a joke."

He hadn't seen Tony wearing a big Russian hat! Nor had he seen the Mongolians in the courtyard of the little palace. "A horrible joke!" I said. "All of it."

He understood me at once, held me close, stroked my hair and my cheeks. Told me all over again I was never to blame; he was responsible for everything. Germany had been defeated but the regime had not been put down. Under Hitler everyone had been suspect and suspicious. The Fuehrer had surrounded himself with suspicious men. For his own safety he got them to watch one another with secret distrust which radiated down into the ranks and later into occupied lands, especially Austria. "And here in Vienna, the lowest of low. Those who looted under the Nazis, put on red arm bands and led the Russians to Nazi apartments. Russians were kind-hearted compared to them. The Americans use Nazis against the Russians—"

"Like the Schmiedlers," I interrupted. He ignored this. "People like Schmiedler are to blame. Not you. How could anything possibly be your fault," I said.

The tunes we sang to each other were "atonal" as any Webern composition that had once been heard in this room. We found ourselves repeating this or that phrase for each other. Then we kissed and he promised me a safe world. Pulled down my hood and kissed my hair. I nuzzled his bare neck and it had the flavor of walnuts. He shuddered. "Child, *Kind,*" he said to keep himself from loving me as a woman.

Rapid footsteps banged down the stairs. A burst of shrill laughter came towards us and then went on.

"We had to take her in," Arnold said. "She was afraid of the Americans. She thought they might somehow blame her because she knew where the colonel kept those Russian uniforms." He dreamily pushed a curl off my forehead and smoothed my hair back. "After all, she's only a child."

Else whistled to her dog. It barked. Then I heard Herbster-Krummerer. They seemed to be leaving. "The entire prank was her idea," I said. "And she told the Amis to use me as the *Lockvogel.*"

"Well, forgive her. After all she is a sitting duck all the time. Her father turned her into a *Lockvogel,* his decoy. Sometimes I think that was his biggest crime. Now that he has vanished, he is getting the blame for everything so that others can get off lightly. No Nazi wants him to suddenly show his face, believe me. His own wife and daughter perhaps least of all. They are better off without him, although Else keeps saying she is waiting for her Vati."

"Because she knows the Amis are waiting for him," I said. "I hate the girl!"

"You, hate? Impossible. You know she's been hurt just like the war children, even if it doesn't show. Don't you see? If Hitler had not taken over Austria her father would have been a nice-looking good-for-nothing, borrowing money and speculating. Always living above his means. Or a bit player. She would have been an ordinary schoolgirl. Poor child, can you imagine! Her mother had influenza and they had no food early this winter. Else took to the streets to get enough money to feed her. It makes one shudder. One feels duty bound . . ."

"I don't see why," I suddenly felt as irresponsible as he was responsible. It was carnival, 1946. Everything was crazy. Why worry. I hadn't really done anything. Events rushed towards me like the carnival street with its shadowy people. It had all happened to me like a dream and I had nothing to do with it. Fate, or Hanna Roth prediction, or American agents, Russian spies, Hitler agents and the evil girl Else had control over me while Father in heaven sat on his throne of clouds and looked down like a theater director on a time as messy and dangerous as Kaufman's bedroom.

"Just now she had no where else to go," Arnold was saying.

I could imagine her arrival at his gate. Exquisitely haunting like someone who carries a disease without symptoms and passes it on. Her frailty would make Arnold's head spin with goodwill.

"She's in love with you," I said.

He shook his head. "She doesn't know what love is," he said and kissed my hair.

Else had known him when she was a child. I could see her

reaching out and taking his hand as I did. Children, like dogs, can sniff out a good person.

"She called me *Trottel,* fool. I'm still just that."

A fool because he knew no compromise. German was our mutual language but he was a stranger in Metternich's Vienna with the cozy little compromises, the live and let live—or let perish.

"Don't you know what she's really like?"

He took my hand. "What difference does it make?" He said smiling to the child in the tree.

He would never let go of my hand. I knew it. Where would it lead us? He was a stranger and the most familiar person at the same time. I never wanted to leave him. Once more we kissed each other Auf Wiedersehen, without mentioning how we would meet again.

I came home and Mother took me aside and told me Mort had telephoned. He had to leave Vienna. Did not know when he'd be back. I went to my room slowly as though I had suddenly grown old and stiff. My body felt too heavy. I flung myself onto the bed and cried for a few minutes, not liking myself too much.

The graphology book Frau Boschke had brought for me was lying on the bed. I fingered through it. Took my blue notebook from a new hiding place under the rug. There was the answer. My handwriting. Illegible small letters: unformed personality. I dried my tears, blew my nose and decided to transform myself at once. From now on let the C.I.C. former gestapo agents, Russian agents, any expert read my notes on carnival 1946; let the experts marvel at the exquisite personality of the new writer who now took over in the schoolgirl's journal.

Upright letters: sincerity. *Arnold.*

Flowing round letters: positive, cheerful. *Bertl.*

Using a dash instead of a dot: venturesome, original: *Mort.*

Plenty of space between words: imaginative, brilliant. *Eli Romberg.*

And, finally, that buxom S: mysterious, daring: *Rudolf Hess.*

I disguised myself. Acquired in my new handwriting all the qualities I had bestowed on my assorted loves. It took several days of practice. Baffled teachers came to look over my shoulder to watch me write as a monster of perfections—graphologically, at least. . . .

# NINETEEN

# *Winter Hyacinth*

A RAP, RAP AT THE DOOR and tapping on the window awakened my grandmother, the Countess Reyna. "Come in, *herein!* Come in," someone seemed to be waiting. "Please do come in!" she said.

It couldn't have been the wind. Trees stood motionless and delicate twigs carved filigree patterns into a gray morning sky. She was about to close her eyes again. A whiff of sweetness and a flicker of blue against snow banked up outside the window made her sit up. There, on her escritoir, winter hyacinth had opened.

Her legs felt stiff as stilts, the floor was icy. She hastened to the window, bent over the blossoms and inhaled the perfume. And then she heard it again: rap, rap, tap, tap. "Come in spring," she said and fainted.

My grandmother had been tiring herself preparing for her little monarchist house ball. The doctor came and said her blood pressure was high. She promised to rest, but she couldn't possibly uninvite her friends. As soon as we were alone, she said: "Reyna, I'll be all right when I'm able to get my drawing of the horse back. You know the doctor's protégé, the poor fellow who was in concentration camp, Frank? He really liked my drawing and he gave me three hens for it. But then, Frank and his friends are not ordinary black-marketeers. The doctor says, he gets his supplies from charitable organizations."

I couldn't believe that three hens could have come from a charitable organization. They were worth a fortune. The actress, Frau Hillie had been offered a diamond the size of a small hazelnut for one duck.

"The doctor must have told him you worked against Hitler." I said. "He wanted to give you something. And he knew you would be too proud to accept."

"No, no. Frank studied art history and painting. He really likes my work and he is dealing in art."

"Then why don't you let him keep it. You have many more drawings. About thirty or forty of the horse."

She looked very white. "I must have that drawing back. I made a mistake," she clamored. "I must reach this young man at once. Don't you understand? I had been driven to my limits when I drew that last picture. I even shot at the Russian officer on the white horse."

"The horse was really gray. Mottled." I said and hoped she had forgotten the threat of her own Falkenburg violence which had inspired this last and most masterful drawing of the horse, the Lipizzaner stallion her mad father had forced to leap into a quarry. She had depicted in a final Capriole the terror of a noble creature driven against ancient and inherent traits. Frenzied nobility. A dressage of death.

"I feel as though I had sold my soul for three hens," she said.

"You'll get the drawing back. Frank will bring it back and we'll give him something else," I said.

I spoke to the doctor when he came to examine my grandmother. Frank, he said, had left Vienna, and should be back within a day or two. "Try to get her to rest," he said. "If you can get her mind off the drawing it would be of great help. Please don't tell her, but Frank doesn't have the drawing anymore. Someone saw it at Frank's place and he gave Frank five kilo of flour for it. I'll see what I can do to get it back."

Father arrived in his old truck and unloaded wine at the little palace like a delivery man. "You didn't allow me to help you out with food, Countess. You can't say no to this. After all, Meinert wines are a tradition when you give a party. You mustn't be mad at me. You've got to understand, a peasant like me doesn't fit into such high company. Annerl has been suffering from migraine headaches. The foehn-wind, you know . . . Anyway, you have Reyna. And she can't wait for her first ball."

He shouldered a heavy crate and carried it down to the kitchen stairs embarrassing me with his peasant deliveryman act. I had overheard him call the monarchist ball risky when he discussed it with Mother. He had to get along with all the allies. Actually Mother, the former illegal Nazi, supposed Hitler favorite was risky among Grandmama's Monarchists. I was walking behind him and saw him pass his hand over the stone walls. "They knew how to build a foundation." He had said that to himself the first time he had come to the little palace acting as a deliveryman. At the kitchen door he paused to regain an inexplicable hesitancy he had experienced the first day he came here thirteen years ago. Then he knocked twice.

"No one in the kitchen," I quickly said and opened the door.

He put the heavy case down with a sigh. "I always feel as though my little Annerl is sitting with her back to the tile stove waiting for me down here."

My sympathy was now with Mother, a lonely child, taken out of school to get married. A bride trying to please a husband who was happiest when she stayed at home doing nothing, nothing at all but wait for him. My empathy, however, was with Father. I had inherited his gusto for reliving his great moments. Boundless gratitude made him unique, radiantly happy during this time of miserable uncertainty. A grateful man is always a winner.

"Girls are as varied as flowers." He sounded like the court doctor. When he had something on his mind and wanted to make me understand, he became sentimental these days. It was like putting sugar on spinach to make me eat. "One has to watch out for little girls and yet let them grow up."

Statement of the obvious. "I am grown up," I said.

He took in my splendid height. "A veritable hop-pole. That's not what I mean. Sit down with me. Sit down." We sat on the stove bench where Mother used to sit with her doll. He took a pipe from his pocket and consoled himself by sucking an empty pipe. He seemed to be out of tobacco. It was sad. "An American interpreter and investigator called on me at the office and asked all kinds of asinine questions. Then he wanted to know whether my fifteen-year-old daughter had lovers . . . I showed him the door. He had hardly walked out, when a certain young German

was announced. No stranger. Someone I like and respect. I think
his ideas of united Europe are impractical. All the same, I made
some precious coffee for him on my spirit stove and was looking
forward to talking about the future of the world to get away from
all the ghastly problems one has to face every day. What does he
want to talk about, but my fifteen-year-old daughter. He wants
to know about her school, her girlfriends, hobbies. I say to him:
I thought you were interested in helping war children . . . My
Reyna is well looked after as a girl that age can be in present
day Vienna. Then I told him that he wouldn't recognize you anymore. You had grown up during the last year. He became as
embarrassed as a schoolboy. I could tell he had seen you. How
on earth did you turn his head?"

"Years and years ago," I said in my grandmother's voice. "He
came to the farm, remember. He was supposed to catch Eli and
didn't want to. We made friends. Now I just ran into him by
chance."

"You never mentioned it, did you now?"

"It was private. I'm not a child anymore."

"You are my only child!"

He leaned back against the stove. It had been lit in the morning and was still warm. I like to make myself cozy when I am
uneasy and I snuggled against him. He did not respond. I felt
him heave a deep sigh.

He was jealous! I couldn't believe it at first. He wouldn't have
believed it either. Had he not allowed Mother to run around with
her playmate Bertl, ride wild horses, join the Nazi party? And
when she fell off that horse and was confined, during the Blitzkrieg, all kinds of men had come to our house to worship Mother.
He never seemed to be jealous.

"Well, at least they come and let me know they are interested
in you. Can't expect much more these days. Then there is our
little officer, Mort. To tell you the truth, I'm quite glad he's been
transferred."

He produced his tobacco pouch, filled his pipe with tobacco
dust. Put his arm around me and waited for me to say: I love
only you, Papa. At this moment it was all too true.

"Men are as varied as flowers, too," I said.

He threw back his head and roared. I had not heard him laugh
like that for a while. And I covered his face with little kisses, one
for Arnold, one for Mort, one for Eli, one for Bertl. I got carried

away and added one for Rudolf Hess and one for Kaufman too. He hugged me so tight I could hardly breathe. "Thank God you're still my baby," because he knew, for the first time I was a woman. "Nothing but a big baby."

Pure self protection, like those American songs about babies, all the Viennese endearments, the diminutives, the Annerl, the Reserl, the Hillie, little one, little girl. Men chanting to themselves, telling themselves not to be scared.

Female power, new and ancient, allowed me then to luxuriate in being the helpless silly daughter which made him such a strong, smiling man.

The day of the ball, I kept buffing fingernails, furniture and silver. My grandmother had invited monarchist friends I knew as uncles and aunts. I sponged the leaves of the rubberplant as if it were Aladdin's wonder lamp. And I wished Bertl, or any young man would come and dance with me. A few young men did appear at the ball, but not to dance. Wishing too hard causes trouble.

You couldn't help feeling wishful in the *Fest-Zimmer*. The first winter of Hitler's war when I had shared lessons from a French governess with the Hohentahler sisters, I used to practice my cartwheels here or spread my books out in front of the old white porcelain stove. It stood on lion's paws, tall, pear-shaped, decorated with garlands of flowers. All the do-dads on the cast iron door glowed as it heated the big happy room, giving forth comfort from the seductive past.

The table had been drawn out and set. Sun shone in through the window on silver, china, crystal we had used during our last stand. I breathed in the dilapidated glorious coziness of the little palace and I kept fussing and cleaning.

In the evening I blew my breath onto the oval mirror and gave it one more rub. My grandmother came in carrying the Chinese bowl of blue hyacinth. We exchanged a smile in the mirror.

"You better stop. You'll get yourself dirty," she said.

"It hadn't been cleaned for a century," I said.

"I know. I feel funny about mirrors from way back. Girls in convent had spent too much time in front of the mirror. Especially little tiny Hanna taking a look every day to see whether she was changing and growing. So the Mother Superior, who was quite old, had it removed. I learned to get dressed, comb and braid my hair without a mirror. When we went for walks by the lake we would lean over the water to see our faces. Later, I would watch my Aunt Christina in front of this and that mirror, all over Europe getting herself and the doll ready for dinner, a party, a ball. I was horrified."

She placed the flowers in the center of the table and the blue of the blossoms reflected on silver and scattered into glitter of cut crystal. And all we meant to each other refracted into memory scintillating like that rare blue color and fragrance of winter hyacinth.

"Don't say a word about my fainting spell to the Rittmeister. He will be suprised to see the flowers in bloom just in time. So perfect. And don't mention the drawing. He would not approve of the three hens. He makes do with his food ration stamps."

He often stayed at the little palace and shared her warm rooms this winter but insisted on going to his cold apartment whenever I came to visit my grandmother. Her pleasure of having me with her was spoiled by his absence. They insisted on decorum so much, I had to wonder whether my lack of it had been discussed.

Frau Boschke had come and gone on the back on Tony's wobbly motorbike bringing with her American soap powders, coffee. There had no doubt been a cup for Grandmama. A court curtsey. "I am so free, I have the honor. Cup of coffe a day lifts the little heart up high. Nice sunny day. Bleach the table linen white as snow. Defrost it by the kitchen stove, and iron after lunch. Ami coffee and soap powder, you can depend on it. But not Ami fellows—some of "te poise"—tricky as monsters. *Ja, ja.* Vienna hopping again, all night long. All kinds of masquerades. *Die Maskeraden!*" I could just imagine how she would carry my carnival story along to the little palace. Frau Boschke never meant any harm, she just chatted.

Grandmama never said a word to me. Later on, I wished I had told her everything to put her at ease. We were standing in front of the mirror. "Everyone always said you look exactly like me," she said.

"I'm too pink," I said.

"It's the von Dornbach in you," she said ignoring all my ruddy faced staunch Meinert ancesters. "I felt it the very first time I ever held you, just after you were born. I took you into my arms. You were so tiny and red, waving your hands, a miracle of love. And all the jolly feelings your grandfather had once inspired returned. And I had to laugh and felt happy for the first time in years. And here you are dressed up for your first ball."

Black ruffles framed my flat chest and prominent colar bones. Black in the evening like my grandmother, and Great Aunt Christina . . . not just ordinary black, but iridescent as rose beatles I had admired, and our Nazi gardener Fritz Janicek had mashed.

She was fussing over me in front of the mirror, fluffing up impressive puff sleeves and sighed because I had borrowed her gown and did not have a suitable white or pale pink girlish gown. "I wore it once. And never again," she said.

I used to dip into her closet and vanish under that fantastic gown for "Where am I? find me!" games. Taffeta rustling in my ears. One day, one day. One day, one day, had arrived.

"The dress you're wearing came from Paris shortly before my wedding. I wore it at a decisive moment in my life. I think I once told you that I had lost my heart to a famous musician?"

"You once called him the prince of princes." I said. "You were in love with the Rittmeister and with grandfather too. All three of them, *nicht wahr?*"

She laughed. "In my days most girls accepted a suitable man like a verdict. But I had traveled with my Aunt Christina who obeyed only her own whim. I was still confused three days before my wedding. Your grandfather was at a stag party given by fellow officers. I put on this new dress and went to a concert all by myself, to hear my prince of music play once more. The kind of thing my Aunt Christina would have done."

"What happened at the concert?" I asked.

"My musician, of course, had no idea I was in the audience. Rudi was there. It was a beautiful evening. He escorted me home. I confided in him. Rudi loved me. He was a career officer and felt he did not have much to offer a wife. He knew I was confused and he actually advised me to go ahead and marry Karl."

"Why?" I asked. "This was before the war. You had money, Schloss Falkenburg and everything."

"Because my Rudi thought Karl was more fun than anyone else, and I would have a good life."

"Was he fun?" I asked.

"He could make me laugh even when he made me sad. Just like you *Herzerl*. That is the von Dornbach magic."

I became uneasy and played with tiny seed pearls that decorated the bodice of her black dress. Grandmama had lost weight again. She wore stays. Her gown hung as loose as mine. I helped fasten her moonstone and diamond necklace.

She reached into her pocket and took out a small diamond clasp shaped like a bow and clipped it into my curls. "This is not just a loan. I want you to keep it to remember this evening."

In the mirror our eyes met and I belonged with her so strongly my face took on her little Falkenburg frown; no one could ever kiss the line between my eyebrows away.

The *Hohe Herrschaft* arrived punctually, a polite fifteen minutes late and never more pleased with themselves. "Well here we are, here we are!" Dark cloaks came off and there they were in frock coats bedecked with medals, dazzling old uniforms. White tunics, blue tunics. Pinned up gowns were let down, shawls taken off tiara's. They had taken a chance, walked arm in arm together on this cold, damp night.

Pink noses, white cheeks, smiles, kisses, sachet fragrance. *Wie schoen,* how lovely. Admiring me, each other, shimmering in old silk, velvet, brocades, they pinned each other's broaches, straightened tiaras. High Gentlemen, outnumbered and self important, twirling waxed mustaches, brushing gray and white beards, wiping eyes, noses with handkerchiefs embroidered with crowns and crests.

"Well, child," the Rittmeister said to me. "These are real uniforms. And we looked just as good when we galloped into battle."

I noticed a few moth holes on his red breeches.

"You couldn't mistake us for a bush or a tree. We attacked like men. We showed our colors, carried the double eagle, sang at the tope of our voices when we charged. Here we are dressed up for carnival. *Fasching* indeed. To us everything that has happened to Austria since the first war is a masquerade."

The court doctor walked in, kissed Grandmother's hand. "I truly regret, my dear boy has not returned. I am sure within a day or two I will have the honor to bring the drawing back."

She thanked him. Her lips moved. Hardly a whisper. The doctor held her wrist as if by chance and felt her pulse. She turned to her guests with a smile. "The room is warm, really warm tonight!" she said to the ladies.

I felt grand and old with them. My role as female rapist, puerile

fancy dress, as satin Pierrot, voyeur—obscene schoolgirl escapades, imagined or real—all receded into nothingness. I breathed
in the courtliness, unconscious little gestures of inherent refine-
ment, simplicity, and lack of pretense, and cheerful affection.

They displayed themselves, hiding with the old glitter, pov-
erty, aging, and degradation. Bravado concealed loss of children,
grandchildren, the murder of fellow monarchists who had con-
spired against Hitler. For years I would not talk about the monarchist ball. Even now I find it hard to describe this gathering
and make any sense.

I could imagine the *Hohe Herrschaft*, the gentry, falling into
accustomed order and entering paradise according to eminence,
in much the same manner as they now entered the festive room
of the little palace. The outnumbered *Hohe Herrn*, the high born
gentlemen, had the honor of having a lady on each arm. I stayed
behind with Tante Hermine who had to be pushed in a wheel
chair by her husband, the monarchist peasant leader. Our Franzl
was dressed up in festive black country clothes. My own father
was only a von, but no matter where you belonged in rank, even
excluded, looking on, you felt grand, ridiculous, perfect.

In the corner near the stove, a family of three elderly musicians, a mother and two sons, struck up *"Gott Erhalte,"* God save
our Kaiser, the old Austrian anthem. I wished the whole world
could hear us sing, and see me standing there. The affirmation
of the moment made me proud, rebellious and sad: this could
never happen again as long as I lived. I knew it. One could say
it was a celebration of grandeur of life *ad infinitum* among those
who were dying.

I was seated between my grandmother and the Rittmeister.
The *Hohe Herrschaft,* used to the best, had faced the worst and
fought against it. I never heard one word of Viennese grumbling,
nor a word of regret during the monarchist ball.

Many of the faces from the days of the Austrian resistance at
Café Wiesner were missing. And they all had remained uncles
and aunts. It still wasn't too safe to be a prince or a baron. There
was "the playground," their underground network, in the event
of a Russian take over. Talking in code had become a habit. A
big lively old man with a lion's mane of white hair, know as *Buberl,* little fellow, called the political circle game Russians like to
play "the cat and mouse." And if they should, God willing, leave
Vienna, Austria, the circle would widen. Most of Austria would

then be encircled by former imperial lands that were now communist . . . As for Europe . . .

Agnes appeared carrying a huge, silver soup tureen and put an end to this veiled talk of the heathen invastions. *"Ja,* here she is, our Agnes, carrying the heavy soup. And we know it will be a treat." Agnes flushed with pride. Franzl took it upon himself to bless the meal as if he were at home on the farm, but he didn't take long. We were all hungry. Beef broth with liver dumplings, a blessing beyond belief.

In between courses the Rittmeister proposed a toast to youth: "To our young Reyna who resembles the countess in courage and in beauty like a young sister."

Actually my grandmother looked old for the first time. She was tired. Or she would have rebuked the Rittmeister's compliment instead of gazing at the hyacinth with that vacant half smile. I felt her cold hand grip my warm fingers under the table and I rubbed it. I whispered to her that I would join the conspiracy to keep the Russians from taking over. Later, after a glass of champagne, I told her I would ask Father to let me go to the Sacre Ceour, the convent school of her choice, which my mother had attended. That way I could always stay with her during the week.

"Young Reyna reminds me so much of the Archduchess Adelheid as a girl," said a certain Uncle Gerhard. "I had the high honor of taking her Kaiserly Highness and her young brother the Archduke Felix across the Hungarian border when Hitler struck."

I did not like being compared to anyone but Grandmama. "Then they got away." I quickly said to put an end to this kind of comparisons.

"There was no time to lose. I'll never forget that little border town of Sopron," Uncle Gerhard went on. "Without 'our Franzl' I could never have snatched the young Archduke away from the Academy in Wiender Neustadt." Everyone was listening politely to the story of how he got the two Kaiser children safely across the border. The lunch at the little inn at the border town of Sopron. They had obviously heard all this again and again." A Herr from the telegraph recognized us. A fugitive himself. Came over with tears in his eyes. And he told the young highnesses how their late father, Kaiser Karl and the Empress Zita had once landed in a plane in Sopron. The final heroic attempt to save the Empire.

After the First World War. They had marched on Budapest with fifty thousand Hungarian soldiers. You should have seen the young Archduke jump up. Give him fifty thousand soldiers, he would drive Hitler out of Austria, he said. And his sister said she'd march with him."

A toast to the Hapsburg family and Crown Prince Otto followed. We ate slowly. Relishing each bite of roast hen. A pink-faced aunt, known as Kaete, talked about Crown Prince Otto at his grandfather's funeral, toddling alongside his tall, lovely mother, the new Empress, in the procession. An adorable little curly head, so sweet in a little dress and sash. She told the story in her soft voice. Her hair was piled on top of her head like a scoop of whipped cream. She and her sister, an identical twin had worked for the Austrian resistance during the war. The sister had been killed.

The Rittmeister deftly led us away from funerals and sang my praise some more. My escape from the country Nazis. The last stand with Grandmama. I could not enjoy the admiration. My grandmother had hardly eaten anything and kept putting food onto my plate the way Eli Romberg often did when I sat beside him at the loaded Romberg table. I was not surprised when she refused to dance the first waltz with the Rittmeister. He had to dance the Kaiser waltz with me instead.

The mother at the piano sat upright in a frilled, frayed, satin dress. Her sons wore shabby old trousers and jackets. Russians and looters had stolen everything during the invasion, but no one could take away their music. And they had kept their instruments.

You are supposed to look into your partner's eyes or at his tie to keep yourself from getting dizzy during a waltz. I, for some reason, kept watching the door Franzl left slightly ajar when he went out to fetch more wine. My head began to spin, The musicians, the shimmering table, the candles, and the open door whirled around me. Then the Rittmeister changed directions and waltzed to the left, puffing a little. "I guess the Countess wanted me to show you off in this dress. I remember it well."

After I sat down he did persuade the Countess to dance. He turned her slowly, she leaned back looking into his eyes. When she sat down she sipped water and reached for her heart. I thought this had something to do with Hanna Roth. Ladies who were not dancing were talking about her carrier pigeons. There was a rumor that she had sold those Hitler pigeons to an American for a hundred and fifty dollars. Uncle Bubi said they couldn't be the same pigeons. Either they had died, or they had all been eaten. Tante Hermine disagreed.

The music was playing softly. It was time now for my grand-mother's speech. *"Nein, nein.* Please keep playing," she said. "It makes it all a little less formal and more discreet if you play on." She breathed deeply and said the fragrance of the hyacinth took her breath away and the old blue tunics dazzled her. She was interrupted by applause at once. Then she tapped her glass with her wedding ring. I had seen her call headwaiters to the table that way and always thought she had learned this gesture dur-ing her travels with Great Aunt Christina. And in the manner of this impatient Christina, she now came to the point too quickly: the letter to King George had not been effective. One should address oneself to Winston Churchill at once. He was a high aristocrat and would understand the Austrian problem. Sir Win-ston should be reminded that Prince Otto had offered to come to Austria during the crisis when Adolf Hitler was waiting to cross the border and take over Austria. "To think what Austria might have been spared!"

She sat down quickly. Too quickly. Applause was long because her speech had been nice and short. She was toasted. The music played on. The stout uncle *Buberl* said I looked bored and danced with me and led so well I did not miss a beat. "You follow so well, enchanting, enchanting." Suddenly the music stopped. Heads turned towards the open door. The pianists froze, hands on the keys, the violinist bow on his strings stared. The little palace was invaded.

A Russian officer bedecked with medals came into the room. Behind him Alexander and another officer of lower rank, although you could never be sure.

I whispered to uncle Buberl that Alexander had stayed at my house and that the one with the medals had been there when we were stopped in the street. He took me back to my chair with disgust.

The officer had gained more medals, no longer wore watches on his coat sleeve, but I remembered his pistol and when he reached into his coat I ducked. Out came binoculars. No one spoke while he surveyed us. He lowered the glasses, and spoke to Alex-ander.

"Uniforms. Conspiracy. Revolution!" Alexander's translated in an official, monotone Nüremberg Trial interpreter's voice. "An imperialist uprising here."

"No uprising. Carnival. Costume party. Ball. Costume parties all over Vienna. Uprising to dance not to fight. No revolt. And this is the British zone," uncle Buberl thundered. "I think you have been misled."

"We have come to ask the young Frau a few questions," Alexander pointed at me. "You come with us." They had left the door wide open. There was an icy draft. "Only a few questions. We go at once. Bring her back."

The Rittmeister was up and took his stand beside me. "The Fraulein will not go anywhere with strangers. She is too young to be questioned about anything."

Alexander translated this and the officer surveyed the Rittmeister through his glasses.

"I'm no stranger," Alexander said. "I sleep in this house and keep it safe. Then I live in the young Frau house too."

I was being eyed by some of grandmother's friends. "We know you are a kind man." Grandmama said too quickly. "If there is anything you need to know you can ask your questions right here."

"We take the young Frau for an hour, maybe less. You have the celebration." Alexander said. "We bring her back."

I did not like all this Jung-Frau, maiden, virgin. The officer kept his binoculars trained on me. And Russians snatch anyone they pleased.

"You take the young lady, and I come along." The Rittmeister produced a certificate from his pocket, to show he had been a Nazi victim. "At your service."

Alexander looked at the paper, turned it around and showed it to the officer who stuck it into his coat pocket and refused to hand it back. Uncle Bubberl, the Rittmeister, and all the high gentlemen rose following an unspoken command and formed a circle around me. The fiddler's bow slipped with a yowl. The piano clinked. "Ask your questions here!" Uncle Bubberl thundered.

The officer lowered his glasses, drew his pistol, gave a command so fast, I knew at once that he understood German. The interpreter like the binoculars were ornamental, so were the soldiers, pistols raised, taking on a marksmen stance.

"No one can answer questions if we're dead," I said.

Alexander translated.

Tiny Aunt Kaete rose and said something in Russian. A great smile passed over the Russian officer's wide face. He put his pistol away, so did his men. He sat down beside her at once picked up her glass and emptied it. She talked and kept smiling. He downed wine and put his arm around the back of the Tante's chair. The soldiers wandered around the room.

Alexander came and stood in front of me. "Perhaps you have a box in this house. Gold, silver, diamonds?"

In the mirror it all looked like a comic operetta scene: girl in a dark dress, diamond pin sparkling in her hair, surrounded by old gala uniforms, facing Alexander in shabby Austrian clothes with his bright gold toothy grin. "You are very kind," I said to Alexander in the tone of voice Olga had always used around Russians. "I really have no idea what you're talking about."

Alexander translated. The officer yelled: *"Unwahr!"* Untrue.

At that moment our Franzl came back quite unperturbed, carrying several bottles of wine. "Sit down comrade, sit down," he said. "Join our little celebration. The end of Hitler. Come, come."

Alexander hesitated. Then Agnes came in carrying a precious cake. The men were fascinated. One of them stuck a finger into the icing. And Alexander changed into the good-natured snout-nosed fellow he had always been. The officer surveyed Agnes through his field glasses.

Since she had brought the cake, he considered her to be in charge of this strange household. "Our commander says sit down," Alexander said.

Agnes and the high gentry followed the invitation. Our Franzl, who had dealt with Russians on his farm knew enough of their language to drink a toast with the officers. "All Russian officers have beautiful fiancées waiting for them." he said to us. We all drank to the fiancées waiting in Russia. The officer looked pleased. Downed a glass of wine a minute. Then he pulled a thick dirty envelope from his pocket. Evidence. An interrogation. I was preparing myself for the worst. Then he waved to the musicians. They struck up a medley from Waltz Dream, and he emptied the envelope onto the side board shuffled through piles of photographs. Came back for another glass of wine. Sorted again. No one said anything.

He returned in triumph with a "well, here you are." smile

and handed a picture to our Franzl. Tante Hermine grabbed his arm. "Beautiful, *sehr schoen,*" she said in horror. The picture was passed around. Forced smiles. Loud admiration.

"All Russians have pictures of beautiful fiancées." Franzl said for the second time.

"A bad joke," the Rittmeister whispered in French.

It was no joke. The officer was beaming, drinking to his fiancée. And grandmother was holding the picture of my mother and Puppe, the doll, in decolte evening dresses. Puppe, the creation of the sculpture Antonelli, like Great Aunt Christina and then Mother had well-shaped bosoms. Father had chosen this unsmiling, serene picture. And he had copies made for Mother's admirers. The photograph must have accompanied officers and perhaps even a general to the Russian front.

The dirty brown envelope had been full of photographs. The sideboard was now littered with pictures of women. Young fiancées, and also older women: the mothers. Many adorned with love messages in Hungarian, Viennese, German, Polish. Pictures taken from prisoners or the dead.

The officer, picture of his fiancée in one hand and a wine glass in the other, delivered a lecture in a sing-song voice, which Alexander translated in his official voice word by word: Russian man has to have a woman. Cultured fiancée far away. Russian man has to have a woman. The officer patted Tante Kaete's shoulder reassuringly. Woman is never finished, but a man becomes useless at an early age . . . He picked up the wine bottle after that and drank deeply.

The two soldiers were walking around the table and their eyes wandered from left over food, wine glasses, to the females in the room. The officer stood up and continued: Austrian men dead, in prison or too old . . . Austrian women are lucky. There were hundreds and thousands of young Russians. Healthy Russians. (Not much illness. Vodka cures it.) Hundreds and thousands of Russians, more than all the capitalist soldiers put together. Russians who enjoy all women.

My grandmother had told the musicians to play "What is mine is thine," the old Gypsy song I liked so much, after dinner. They now played it loud as an anthem, over and over again. The mother was playing the piano and singing: "Let the sun be your diamond, the hay our bed. Violins sing of castles where we will dwell-

until Eternity." And stomp, stomp, crash. The door was flung back against the wall. Russian, French, British and American uniforms came into the room. Steel helmets, guns. The international patrol. Liberation forces. Franzl had not only brought the wine, Agnes and the cake, he had also made a telephone call.

Little Tante Kaete said: "Gentlemen, this is carnival, our *Fasching*. I'm sure you understand." in English, then in French. She patted our Russian officer. Got up with him, kept talking to him. He took one step backwards, then another. His men walked backwards, retreating. They had come to us like a bad dream and they backed out of the room like courtiers.

Boys in the uniforms of four nations gaped. Did they understand that this was a fancy dress party like no other? Old Austrians in moth eaten uniforms entertaining Russians and in the British sector of Vienna?

I slept in Mother's old bedroom. Someone was playing Chopin on the piano. It was out of tune. Many of the guests had stayed and stretched out on cots and sofas. Grandmama did not tell me that she had given up her bed to Princess Hermine and would sleep on the chaise. She came in to say goodnight. "How lovely you looked dancing with Rudi. I wonder where the Russian officer got the picture of your mother? Do you think he picked it out to impress us because she looks more like one of us? or did he want to see how we'd react?"

I didn't know what to say. She kissed me goodnight and told me to sleep well.

The half moon shone in through the window. The canopy on the bed was decorated with clouds and angel heads. When Mother was my age and slept in this bed she must have believed that the heavens were somewhere up in the sky. I could imagine her in bed with her doll looking up to the angels in heavens of pink cloud. Where was heaven now? I looked out at the night sky. With this war the hierarchy of angels had been displaced. You could not raise your eyes to the sky in prayer without thinking of bombs, and mushroom clouds. I pulled the covers over my head. It was dark like the cellar days.

I woke up early. Helped myself to bread and tea. Looked in on Grandmama and found Tante Hermine asleep in her bed. And Grandmama on the sofa in the pink room. She had covered herself with an eiderdown I had used during the last stand. Head tilted, she half smiled in her sleep. I tiptoed out so as not to disturb her wonderful look of expectancy and softly closed the door.

Out in the cold the air gripped me like my grandmother's icy hand under the table. I wished she had been able to enjoy the house ball more. I pushed myself onto a ring streetcar. Two drunk men came along in costumes, one in Turkish trousers and Fez. The other had adorned a bald spot on his head with a crown. They jostled me and everyone aside, staggered in and fell into empty seats. "We ride free, Herr Conductor." They wore old uniform boots.

The conductor punched tickets and ignored them.

A jeep drove past the street car. "Amis, nothing but Jews," said the king.

"Something has to be done," the Turk said and spat.

"Spitting is *verboten*. You'll pay a fine or go to jail," someone said.

"Nothing is *verboten* to us. Shut your trap," said the king.

"A good goulash is what I need," said his friend.

"Jews starving us to death," said the king. "That fat sow Church-hell."

"The Jew Rosenwelt. Some president."

"He's dead," said a small man who was standing up trying to steady a snub-nosed woman. Outside in the street people were leaning into the wind, eyes to the ground, as if they hoped to find something that had been lost.

"I'm glad he's dead," said the Turk. "One American Jew less."

"Now we have Truman. Another Jew," snorted the king. He coughed, gagged. The street car stopped. The conductor and the little man with the woman, a couple of husky older housewives pushed them out. The king vomited into a waste paper basket and lost his crown. The Turk shook his fist and called the entire street car a dirty Jew.

I suddenly felt like getting off and spending the rest of the day with my grandmother. Perhaps Frank would come back to Vienna today and I could get the drawing back for her. I thought of her smile, the look of expectancy. She had been so tired she needed to sleep. Later I wished I had kissed her. I might have roused her. She would have opened her eyes for me when no one else could wake her.

# TWENTY

# *Wax Lilies*

THE COUNTESS REYNA VON FALKENBURG DORNBACH, my grandmother had gone to sleep and died in her unending dream of the return of the Hapsburg monarchy. Her head lay slightly tilted on a lace trimmed pillow under the crest of the Falcon perched upon the sun. The smooth white crown of braids and her unlined pale skin gave her a marble perfection. I saw my own short nose, high forehead, willful chin, a face like mine for the last time.

Rain drummed against colored glass windows of the funeral chapel. In a propped up coffin, which was lined with foolish confetti pink silk, my grandmother wore an ivory gown: light colors in dim weather. A tradition among von Kortnai women. I had insisted on this and also made sure she wore her moonstone necklace. Dreamers never look bored. She had smiled in her sleep and kept the soft smile with an air of vital expectancy.

She would have said: Reyna stand tall. My tall parents had lowered their heads for the blessing, I held mine high. I could not yield her up. Mother was trembling under her black veils and Father stepped between us and took her arm. A chorus of stifled sobs rose behind us. The Rittmeister stood guard beside sentinel wax lilies. His eyes dark marbles, lips pressed together. Grief had turned him into a startling effigy of himself which frightened me and seemed far less alive than the Countess in her coffin. During the last rites she might have sat up, to smooth her skirt and say: "What do you think you're doing Herr Pfarrer,

throwing water on me with your fat hand!" She never could abide
our local priest. Yet, water fell from his plump, white hand onto
her face like rain on stone.

I took my father's arm. Mourners filled the chapel. Those who
could not get in stood outside the entrance under umbrellas.
Someone said, "Pardon," in a loud voice. Mourners whispered,
making way. Raincoats rustled. Firm footsteps pounded the aisle,
an umbrella tapped the tile floor. Hanna Roth, upright, all in
black, drawn in at the waist as my grandmother had been for
the ball walked to the altar trailing a lace mantilla. She ignored
the sanctum and the Amen, the stifled sobs, pushed herself up
on her umbrella and stood on the toes of her platform shoes peering through the stalks of wax lilies into the coffin. Then she threw
back her veils with a caressing gesture from a face old as the
world and the smile of a newborn.

She had lost all her teeth since I had last seen her, but not
her smile, that blank cheerfulness. I felt in league with her at
once. She rescued me from the mourners as she faced my grandmother's unending smile with her own. I saw in her gesture
admiration, not sorrow. Nor did she wait for the closing of the
coffin. She had come to see the Countess. No one else. She brushed
the mantilla forward over her face and walked away. Her footsteps resounded like rhythmic hammer blows. The bells began
to toll.

Shocked mourners made way again. A tall young man stepped
forward and swung the open door back with a charming bow:
Bertl.

He had come. And he knew how to spare me the nailing of
the coffin, the unfathomable moment of parting. "Come, come. I
can't stand this," he whispered and resolutely drew me aside,
away from my parents. Then he sneezed three times. "Such a
spectacle." He could not stop sneezing and drew me out into the
soft rain. "I am allergic to funerals. Had enough of that monkey
stuff, what!" He opened his umbrella, took me under it, and as
though this were not enough, he shared his raincoat with me.
His deft one armed gesture both tender and rueful was typical
of my mother's cousin. "Your grandmother always indulged me,
I am her great favorite. Reminded her of the husband she lost.
Same kind of bounder, what."

He took me into hiding behind the chapel and we smoked and

listened to the rain drumming on the roof to the ding, ding, ding, ding of the funeral bell. The procession formed behind my parents. Monarchists fell into order according to eminence. Slowly the umbrellas moved uphill towards the little Grecian temple at the fringe of the woods: the empty poet's grave my grandmother had bought. We could not see the coffin.

"Look at Hanna!" Bertl said. The tiny black figure under the huge, black umbrella had reached the cemetery gate. An American Army car was waiting for her. "What a show off. I guess she just couldn't miss this opportunity of making an appearance. She always shows up at weddings, christenings and funerals, uninvited and unexpected."

Hanna Roth climbed into the car. It drove away. "She hasn't changed a bit. But you've grown up and are beautiful. I've grown old. I'll be thirty years old before long. None of this is real." He expressed my feelings with a sweeping gesture towards the tomb on the hill and a plain gold band on his hand caught my attention. "Reality is Aunt Reyna throwing me out the first time she saw me in my S.S. uniform and then running after me, offering me help, money to get away, go to a university in England. She knew me well. Knew what would happen. My old Pater ignored my black S.S. uniform and went on playing with tin soldiers on those old war maps."

"Your mother is great. She was in the resistance."

"She had her hands full with five Hitler maiden daughters and a Waffen S.S. son. No better cover, what!" Tears came into his eyes. He quickly kissed my cheek. "Too many girls, too many sisters. Now we have one less. We've had another death. We don't talk about it. Magda, poor misguided girl killed herself. Love affair. Big Nazi beast. A married man. Stupidity, disgrace." He always held his head so high it tilted back. "My father has had a little stroke, but he has not forgotten the little Reyna with the big strategic talent. He sends you this." Cigarette dangling from the corner of his mouth, he fumbled in his raincoat pocket and produced a small metal box.

I opened it and buried in cotton lay the tin officer on his white horse. "That used to be you, when your father and I followed the Hitler war on the old Austrian maps." Bertl laughed. "That should have been me. What? Flashy uniform, marvelous horse, beautiful women. I was made for the old Austrian army. All I can do now is talk about my escape to Italy, going over to the American army. They put me into their uniform. At the office in Salzburg I wear it. You would like that wouldn't you? Do you find me changed."

I told him he used to be terribly thin and now he had gained weight. He dimpled and beamed like my mother. "Fat old cousin, uncle, or whatever, *Ja?*" His sparce unruly hair stood up in the rain. I passed my hand over it and he preened like a cat. "Why didn't you write or telephone?" I asked.

"I don't write well with my left hand. Besides, letters are still censored and they listen in on the phone. Not very private, what? Come on."

He clasped my hand hard. His ring hurt. And he hurried me past graves, monuments, the tomb of Christina von Kortnai, her beautiful faded photograph; downhill past a pair of plump stone angels. Gravel crunched under our feet. With Bertl you never walked, you ran. The chapel bell went ding, ding, ding. Snow was melting everywhere. Rain turned into a drizzle. He had not mentioned my mother once. I felt I had taken her place. It was like a circle game. Running away with him from a world too dull and moribund for love games. He was my magician, the great conjurer who could create illusions of escape, and the promise of safe escapades.

We reached the gate behind the Meinert tomb. "Graves tell a lot about people," he said.

"The Meinert tomb looks like a wine storage house with a cross on top," I said.

"And our Countess, is buried in conspicuous seclusion," he said.

"She lived in conspicuous seclusion."

He put his arm around me. Drew me out onto the meadow lane between the graves and wine stalks. I had to get outside the gate to cry. He held me and I sobbed shamelessly: Grandmama had left me. He would leave me again. I had often laughed with him. Now he cried with me.

"Don't. We mustn't," he covered my face with kisses.

I liked the little kisses and sobbed on. He kissed my mouth and let go of me as if someone had yanked him away. "How old are you now?"

"Does it matter?"

"You were so far away from everything during the war, what? There weren't any boys around." He folded the umbrella, borrowed my handkerchief, wiped my face, then his own. "You're as fresh as a blossom." He tasted my mouth absentmindedly. "You must remember one thing. No matter what you feel. Never let yourself be touched by anyone who doesn't love you. Your grandmother said that to my sister. Magda wouldn't listen. Now remember. No matter how you feel. It makes good sense, what!"

His face was so close I could see a few red veins in his eyes and a small scar below his lip. I shut my eyes. Drizzle caressed my face. He loved me. I was waiting to be kissed.

I stroked his cheek. He stayed my hand with kisses. "What a mess. I'm in." He said in English.

I understood the words. Did not get his meaning. "You're not. You're wonderrrful."

My Pnevski English made him laugh. He put his finger to my lips. "You mustn't. It's the kind of thing she keeps telling me. Always trying to convince herself."

"Who is she?"

"Promise you won't say a word?"

"I won't talk," I said.

"My wife," he whispered. "Leni Gruenbaum."

"Wife?" I whispered.

"Remember the Jewish family. My father had to sell the Landsitz after the First World War. They bought it."

"You aryanized it back," I said.

"We bought it. Perhaps the price was low, but my own old Oma, you know the old highness in the wig? She helped us pay for it with her jewels. If we hadn't bought it, it would have been requisitioned. Madam Gruenbaum is French, a stylish lady. And I must say old Hanna was decent enough to sew diamonds into hats for her. And they all had pasports, I saw to that. But the Gruenbaums were afraid there might be trouble at the border. They had passage on an Italian liner. I had promised Herr Gruenbaum to take Leni across the border a couple of days early . . . She was terrified. All went well. In Italy she was able to breathe freely for the first time in months. She was more than grateful."

"In love with you," I said.

"She is small, soft. Eyes like a deer. And she told me she had danced with me once at the opera ball and fell in love with me. We had her little car. Two whole days. I took her to Venice. We stayed at the Lido. Same little hotel where we all stayed. You probably don't remember."

We took the wet lane towards the cemetery road and I thought of wet sand, a gangly shadowy figure of a boy in a beach tent. And my parents in black bathing suits twirling on the beach like children.

"I used to play with you and your mother in the water," he said.

"You kissed Mother," I said. "You were in the water. I was digging in the sand. "You dipped under and you came up kissing."

"I really did?"

"You don't remember?" I asked.

"To tell you the truth I don't remember not kissing her. She was five years old when I was born. My mother had lung trouble and stayed at a sanatorium after the delivery. Your grandmother and Agnes looked after me and your mother started pushing me around in her beautiful doll carriage with that doll. Annerl was my little mother, my sister, my great love before I even learned to walk."

Our faces glistened with moisture as if we had just come up from a dip. "I did not feel jealous when she married your father. But Venice was thrilling and awful. Your father had invited an entourage. Only in the water could I get her all to myself. And would you believe it. The owner remembered all of us when I arrived with Leni. He gave me the big room your parents had with the balcony. Leni had the one you were in. Right next to it. And Leni had bad dreams. Of course she ended up with me. She is five years older, just like your mother. A university student. She had traveled a lot. Gone to balls. I had no idea . . . She was innocent. My first untouched girl. She cried because she loved me and I made her so happy. After all the terrible things that had happened to her already, I just had to marry her."

"Does Mama know?"

"Of course not. With the war and everything, I didn't think I'd ever see Leni again. I only told one other person. This officer, the German prince. He came to see me in the hospital after my arm had been amputated. I told him everything, just in case I was killed. I had saved some of my money for Leni."

He held me at arms length. "Don't stare at me like a baby owl. *Ja, jawohl,* Leni was on a boat and on her way to America and I returned to the Ostmark, the Third Reich. I was quite lonely. Rescuing lovelies can become a habit. So I got Resi out of the gestapo hotel. And how can any normal man be around a grateful Resi Romberg for even an hour and not make love to her? She had divorced Rombert, you know. Because he had taken that Resi's masseuse, that Scandinavian little squirrel to Switzerland. As you know Reserl is in Salzburg now. We are old friends. I was seeing her. Then Leni arrived from America. Life has become complicated and confusing."

We stopped under the lichen covered old trees on cemetery road. Smoke rose from the chimney of the inn at the foot of the hill. Father had somehow bartered for venison. Mourners were always famished. After a funeral there had to be a feast. After the meal they would all talk about my grandmother.

"Leni has become a veterinary surgeon. She works for the army. Has a profession she loves. She thinks of me as some kind of a hero because I went over to the American army. What choice did I have? I had asked too many questions about Eugene Romberg in Salzburg. The gestapo was after me. I was saving my own skin. The Americans stuck me into their uniform. Now that the war is over I feel like a flunkey. An Ami *Schani.* I have no education. Then there is the fact that I was an S.S. Leni's father is a religious Hebrew man. Made money in America, and wants her to marry someone of her own faith, someone who amounts to something. Leni is going to be thirty-five years old. She wants children. I can't support her. I have to look after my parents and sisters, frankly, I can't tell my father that I married her. A mess, what?"

"What are you going to do?" I asked.

He looked into my eyes. Bare branches of wet trees swayed above us. "Kiss you."

I closed my eyes. Hoping that my wicked innocence—as Lieutenant Kaufman had called it—would bring about uncontrollable passion, a declaration of sorts.

His lips hardly touched my mouth. He kissed my eyelids, my cheeks. It started to rain again and the drops ran down our faces. "I look at you," he whispered. "And I see your grandmother. You know, she would have been the one person I could have talked to. She had good sense. Most people just see her as an old-fashioned idealist, a fanatic, eccentric monarchist, a dreamer."

He took my handkerchief from my pocket, wiped the rain from my face and his. "Don't stare at me like a baby owl. I feel inadequate. I'm not what I used to be. Leni expects so little and admires everything I do and say. And she is my secret wife and an American. All this helps . . ."

He looked up into the tree and went on talking about Leni: her important job with the army. Her independence. How tiny she was and strong. I should see her handle a horse. He became embarrassed. Took my hand again and twirled me away, then towards him, kissing the tip of my nose, spinning me around and back, umbrella swinging on his wrist. His raincoat slipped. I picked it up and like the wife of a one-armed man put it around his shoulders. He kissed me. I knew he was thinking of Leni.

"You don't know how to kiss yet, I'm glad." His second kiss was a lesson. I responded too much. "That's enough, what?"

I threw my arms around his neck and we held onto each other. "Why did she have to die?" he whispered. His words ended in a sob. I started to cry again. "I couldn't believe it," he said. "Why did she have to give the ball?"

"For me," I said. "Really for me." I said.

"Nothing will ever be the same," he sounded annoyed.

It did not make sense. We kept on complaining in the dirge of the young: she did not know how much we loved her or she would have lived. We felt abandoned as though she had jilted us with death.

Bertl came to our house only once, to see my mother. They never mentioned my grandmother as they wandered through the Meinert-Hof. He marvelled at how everything had remained the same, while I marvelled how they had both changed. I missed their childhood habit of laughing, teasing, whispering, which used to both exclude and attract me. Now they went to pet the deer. Hand in hand they wandered like tired children after wild games talking as grown-ups for the first time.

I kept a polite distance and played with my dog. Mother did not even try to keep her voice down, her need to tell him everything was so great. "*Ja, ja,* I met a few of the men who are now on trial. Schmiedler? More than likely one way or another. Nobody ever knew him. I had to go to Schloss Kiesheim if I wanted to keep my mother and Ferdl safe."

"Blackmail, what?" Bertl said.

"But it wasn't all that bad. Only rather dull, everyone uneasy, watching each other. The first two times I was summoned news of victories had arrived with me. I was considered good luck."

"Old Fritz Janicek raving about you, what. He is still at it you know, when the Ami question him. Goddess and all that. He consorted with men. Nazis sometimes punished that by death. Carrying on like that about a woman might very well have saved him," Bertl said.

"Nothing much happened until my last visit. The war was just about lost. Hitler kept looking for a magic weapon, a miracle. I was supposed to bring luck. I did not want to go to Salzburg. They sent a driver and he told me they had my old doll. Usually I just went for lunch. I had no intention of spending the night. This time I drank a glass of champagne. That's all I remember of lunch. They must have drugged me."

"You spent it alone?" Bertl, asked with solemnity.

She lowered her voice. "I dreamt that Hitler was with me. I know, I know. So did millions of women. Only I hated it, wanted to escape. He ordered me to just scat, get up, get out. I found myself standing up alone in the middle of the dark room. In the morning I knew I could walk, but I got back into my wheelchair. That's when I came face to face with Eugene Romberg dressed up in an S.S. uniform. I thought I was really going mad. He calmed me down and told me to get back into my wheelchair, stay there and say I was feeling feverish. They were all afraid of catching things and they would send me home."

She had embarrassed Bertl telling him what he had to know and didn't really want to hear. He sighed, kneeled down near the deer. Rita lifted her head expectantly flicking her tail.

"I never found Puppe; didn't bring anyone any luck. And God only knows whether someone came into my bedroom that night or not. But as I was leaving, I thought I saw Hitler, or rather two Hitlers. Servants had to lift me into the limousine and in the side mirror I had a glimpse of two Fuehrers walking in the back of the park with two dogs."

I was entertained by the two Hitlers, but Bertl was not. "We all went through some hopelessly ghastly things," he said.

"At least my mama never knew what went on," she said.

I felt like shouting: don't be too sure. I kept quiet because I had been neither included nor excluded from their conversation which broke the silence, the mystery that had surrounded Mother, not to spare her, but much more to spare us.

My grandmother in her white dress floated through my dreams. Sometimes Mother, Agnes, or I took her place: eyes closed, half smiling, hands folded stiff as a doll inside a box. Panic sent me reeling in darkness on a lone last stand.

During the day I lolled around the house, refused to go to church or to the graveyard with Mother. Finally Father loaded me into his truck and delivered me at school.

Girls surrounded me and said they were so sorry about the death of my grandmother. Stories poured out about their dead.

Ursel put her arm around me and promised to take me to visit her grandmother, who lived in the British zone. "My Oma always made her own sauerkraut and her own pickles. She had some hidden away. You'll have to have a taste. I was carrying a jar home the other day and I met the German Ami. He spoke to me and he knows all my father went through during the war. He said he felt sorry for us. I felt sorry for him because of the trick you and the Amis played on him. I gave him one of Oma's pickles. He said he had never tasted anything so good. I'm not afraid of him anymore. He even said he'd like to meet my Oma. And she doesn't care what people say about your Mama. She once saw her in a box at the Opera and she thinks she is beautiful. She wants to meet you."

Mimi had the final word. Her Jewish grandmother had vanished from her house and was exterminated. "Your grandmother had a big funeral. We don't even have a grave," Mimi said. I was disgustingly privileged as usual. My grandmother had died well.

# TWENTY-ONE

# Stone Bench

I HAD INHERITED the little palace. My grandmother had left instructions in her will to have the marble bench and the angel moved from the courtyard to the cemetery. Father insisted I should be there when the men came to pick it up. I had not been back since my grandmother died. With ownership, he pointed out, came duties.

I found Mother and an English officer walking around the courtyard in the warm sun, talking about a book they had both read. Mother kissed me. And I was introduced to Sir Hugh. He honored me with the fleeting glance of a professional and said: "Fine healthy looking girl."

The bench where Grandmama and I had often sat side by side was being pried loose by three men and carried out towards a horse-drawn cart. Mother with the doctor gave me the more powerful feeling of something being wrenched away and moved from a familiar spot.

I sat on the sunny steps ensconced behind my World Atlas and studied the doctor. He was tall, light-eyed, ruddy, just like my father and his light hair was turning white at the temples. His mouth was small and prim, not large and happy like Father's. He leaned against a tree and listened to Mother. I would always remember him like that, arms folded looking up into the intricate pattern of branches and new leaves.

She had inherited Schloss Falkenburg, the old family castle. It had been used as a rest home for German officers towards the end of the war. At that time, Grandmother had moved the most valuable furniture to Vienna. Then the Russians had taken the castle over and it hadn't been safe for her to go there. Vlado, the former partisan, had been there to take a look, and he had been able to persuade the Russian officer in charge to at least repair window panes that had been shot out. Soldiers had used furniture and books from the library to feed the stove.

The doctor said he might be able to go to Falkenburg with my mother. There would be no problems. Russians liked doctors. Many of them said they were doctors. He got to know them quite well during his stay in Hungary last fall. It was funny how they bragged. Here he would try to convince them he was just an ordinary country doctor, and they all bragged about being great surgeons, professors. He was fascinated by the way they all lied. They were great storytellers. It was absurd to put faith in any agreement with them.

The new mother I saw over the rim of my Atlas went on to calmly discuss Russian characters in the novels of Dostoyevsky. They talked about inherited and acquired obsession. No flirting, or teasing. "I guess I read Dostoyevsky to understand my own obsessions," she said.

Instead of rushing home to read *The Brothers Karamazov,* I slammed down my book like a Dostoyevsky character. What had happened to the mama who had galloped with Bertl and his pack of Theresianer schoolboys, taking the hurdle with a yodel? Or the pink cheeked mother using up all our priceless eggs to console the court doctor with a sweet mountain of fluff? I could no longer imagine her games with Father, wild with desire, barricading her bedroom.

I knew for the first time that the thrilling games of acquiescence and rebellion between my parents—which had involved me and, of course, the awful doll, Puppe—were over. She spoke softly, had tucked her hair into an old Roth hat in an effort to look plain, British beside her English officer. She wanted to be English, the way I had wanted to be American, especially around Mort. Germans had colonized us. And they had tried to purify our Austrian mish-mash language, take out all the foreign words. Now we were colonized again, by four nations. English words, the most useful for barter with the Amis, were fast becoming part of our language. I could imagine Vienna divided into four zones and we would become divided into British, French, American, even Russian paragons, pretending until we changed. An everlasting big masquerade. Would it ever pass?

I heard the bench being loaded with a thump, it sounded like a gigantic door being slammed on me the Ami Madl, Satin Pierrot. I sat and chewed my pencil. Mother just talked and talked the way men used to talk to her during the war. I had seen her surface for a moment with Bertl, from oceans of silence and secrets, but the English doctor, her true confidant, rescued her from drowning in guilt over what she had, or had not done.

With Sir Hugh Mother smiled, she never laughed out loud. And I thought of her as enslaved. Actually she was finally free to be calm, and did not have to exert herself. Sir Hugh, smitten with her as anyone, was not her lover, but her listener.

We were lucky that the little palace was in the British zone. And soon the Rittmeister would be moving into the empty rooms. Grandmother had given her Rudi the right to live at the little palace for the rest of his life. Nuns would use some of the downstairs rooms as offices until their convent was rebuilt. It had all been arranged according to the will. The boards would come down to allow swallows to return to their nests.

My mother and the English doctor had been coming here often to put things in order. He even went to the graveyard with her. I had stayed away. The cart rumbled over the cobbled pavement with the stone bench and the angel. I bit into the edge of the Atlas so that I wouldn't howl. My own discomfort made me more aware of the comfort Mother now enjoyed. Sir Hugh had remained curiously invisible until Grandmother died. Here he was now.

I shut my school bag with a loud snap. "Did you ever meet my Grandmama?" I called without getting up. "Did she ever invite you here?"

He was not in the least put out. "She entrusted me with her letter to King George."

My grandmother would use anyone who helped her monarchist cause. I got up and walked like her, holding my head high. "I hope you will work for a free Austria." This is what she would have said. I shook his hand. The moment I touched his cool, firm hand, I knew it had torn the letter to a king to shreds. Destroying for Mother's sake this evidence of obsession and family eccentricity.

The snowman I had built for my grandmother had melted. The head, or rather an icy grimy little lump with a huge grin and button eyes, lay under the tree. Sir Hugh kicked it playfully and invited me, to tea. "No, thank you." I excused myself in my grandmother's voice. Picked up the remains of the snowman, went into the little palace and put it into the refrigerator.

Father had donated a bench to replace one that had been destroyed by the bomb on our avenue. The plaque had been made of scrap metal found after the blast. Neighbors would now make a point of stooping to read: "IN MEMORY OF CHILDREN KILLED BY A STRAY BOMB." *Wie Schoen,* how beautiful. Tears in their eyes, although strictly speaking only one child, the foot doctor's Herbert had died with his family.

So seldom did I ever see Father at rest these days, it startled me to find him sitting in the sun with the two dogs. Krampus had curled up against his boot and aged Frica was leaning against his leg resting her head on his lap. Someone had brought the old black Alsatian back from the farm not long ago. She attached herself to Father as if she had never been away. The sun shining on Father took color from his cheek and the yellow from his graying hair, the green loden coat looked dusty and worn. He faded and lost substance before my eyes. I ran to him in panic, wind whipping my long, brown curls over my face. He stared at me and saw the dead girl. "Nadica!" he said to himself.

We could not relinquish the dead torn from us; we blamed ourselves, the Hitler mania, war. They had been torn away unprepared like displaced persons who can never return. We looked for them everywhere.

"Sit down with me. Sit down," he said. The dogs greeted me. He put his arm around me. "I have been sitting here and think-ing. Strange how that spot on the road was torn up by the bomb. Nazis used slaves to fill in the crater. And then Nazis them-selves had to work as slaves to pave it. Not all the slaves in the world could ever pave over what happened here. The very ones who stood and watched the S.A. do their worst, now stoop over the bench and read the plaque and say, *wie schoen,* how beauti-ful. I have given them a shrine."

I could see them fold their hands and mourn mostly for what they had once been. And they would walk away and whisper

about that young, young girl, who used to play the piano at
Father's house. Beautiful sonatinas drifting out of the open window. Beautiful . . . They all knew Father had created a memorial
bench for his childish, darling protégé. And here they could
remember days of music, romantic dalliance, harmless scandal.

"Just look at that spring sky. The Foehn wind has blown all
the dark clouds away. It's been a sad winter. But we have to
remember all the good things. Look ahead not back. You'll soon
have your sixteenth birthday." He lit his pipe on his memorial
bench. "The countess had planned a wonderful sixteenth birthday party for you. Did you know that? To make up for not having
a fifteenth. We'll have to do something about that."

Deep down in the cellar rooms, our last stand, my feverish
grandmother had slept a lot, but my birthday had become her
obsession. She had marked days on our calendar and she kept
opening her jewel box asking me what I wanted. I would look at
all the ancestral glitter and say: nothing. This had brought back
one of her favorite memories, my earliest birthday wish, when I
was two years old: bubbles, soap bubbles. I never wanted much
of anything, this had pleased her. But she had been quite wrong.
I had wanted everything. I wanted magic: endless iridescent
bubbles. She had said no matter what, we would light fifteen
candles on my birthday and celebrate. Vienna had exploded above
our heads like a monstrous firecracker she dropped her watch.
Soon our lights went out and my birthday was lost in the dark.

"You take after me," my clever father said. "I avoid funerals
and graveyards whenever I can." "A little birthday party will
cheer you up."

"I don't want to be cheered up. I don't want a party. I don't
want anything." For days and days I had felt the stone bench
and the angel with the von Dornbach smile waiting for me at my
grandmother's tomb. I had resisted and almost resented this
persistent invitation. The next day after school I went to my
grandmother's tomb for the first time. The air was mild and moist,
the sky blue and the lichen covered stone angel green against
the white tomb. Visitors had left wild primroses, "Heaven's-Keys,"
in masonry jars. An unusual wreath made from wax lilies, pine
cones and dry berries mixed with glass ornaments hung on the
gate. I had come empty handed.

Birds chirped in the budding shrubs and trees of the Vienna

woods behind her tomb. On a sunny day in March my grandmother would bring cushions out into her courtyard and we would
sit side by side on the stone bench to watch the nesting swallows
flit in and out of the corridor. She had learned to identify each
bird call and song around Lake Neusiedel from her favorite
teaching nun at convent. At an early age she got into the habit
of sitting still, listening and observing. We were never bored.

My grandmother had loved birds, butterflies, anything on
wings. I wished I could think of her as an angel, but my rosy
faith in triumphant goodness and heaven got lost in the dark
with my fifteenth birthday. I missed it as the most precious one
of all the luxuries the Hitler years and war had taken away.

I sat down. The stone bench felt like a block of ice. There was
a padlock on the gate to the burial chamber. Grandmother had
been nailed into a box and put away in there. What had happened to memories she did not share with me? How about my
own memories? I shuddered, stiffened, folded my hands. And
hands folded, eyes closed, I would be put away into a box one
day.

Something flapped inside the burial chamber. A song sparrow trilled and flew out and up over my head. I watched it carry
straw and fluff into the tomb, flit out again to perch on the head
of the stone angel. Throat feathers all ruffled it sang claiming
the nesting spot.

The slope before me was harmoniously patterned. Grave stones
studded the top half and neat rows of vinestalks, Father's vine-
yard, continued down to the vintner's village. No visible division.
Vintners were already at work. Someone was whistling the "Horst
Wessel" march out of old habit. Behind hedges on the left side of
the cemetery mourners coughed and then sobbed.

My grandmother would say: "If you are troubled, do some
work." I took out a notebook. My assignment in English was a
composition on democracy. I stared at the empty page, and lines
stared back. Prison bars. Rudolf Hess locked in behind bars. The
Countess Reyna behind bars. Irrational mad words of longing
and sympathy I felt poured out. Page after page. An appeal for
freedom and eternal life. I closed my book with a smack. I did
not have my grandmother's faith in omniscient, benign power.
My lips formed silent words praising my grandmother. Recom-

mending her Austrian style to a bureaucratic infinity where wickedly bungling officialdom ruled supreme. *Man tut was man kann.* One does what one can . . .

The female sparrow flew out of the tomb, twittered to the cock sparrow, and landed on the wing of the one and only cheerful angel in the cemetery. An angel of life not death. The cock sparrow preened and trilled serenading my sadness and horror away. The sun felt warmer, the tepid wind toyed with my hair caressingly, flipping my curls. I was putting my notebook away when I heard crackling sounds of footsteps on the gravel path below the tomb.

At first I thought it was a child hiding behind myrtle hedges. A tiny mourner appeared and started to walk uphill. Hanna Roth. Veiling tied into a bow behind her hat quivered like a giant moth. She saw me and waved her arms and her umbrella, as though she might take off and fly to me.

"Here you are at last, at last." She curtseyed to the tomb, the angel and finally to me. I got up and responded ceremoniously.

A smile from crease to crease of her old face displayed new, large white teeth. "Yesterday was warm too, but today is perfect weather. I have been expecting you. Almost your birthday, my congratulations." She handed me a bar of American chocolate. And we ate it at once.

"Are you staying in Vienna?" I asked.

"I am needed." She sat beside me dangling her short legs. The wind blew her veil towards me and I had a whiff of essence of violet, the perfume both she and the Countess Reyna preferred. "How do you like my wreath? I asked the sexton and he sold me a few of the wax lilies. Perfect with the dark pine cones. *Jawohl.*"

She asked me whether she had interrupted my school work with a knowing look at my school bag. I took out an apple and began to munch. Her gaze fastened to my lips and her mouth began to move like mine. I offered her the other apple I had taken to school with me.

"To think I can even chew an apple now. And I didn't even have to pay for my fine, American teeth. After all I am under their protection. But I don't want anything free. I happened to have an important document sewn into a hat for safe keeping.

And I let them have it. All for a good cause. But I will not part with the notes my Fuehrer sent me and signed with his own distinguished hand."

This last phrase, and the old formal tone was irresistably familiar. And she sounded enthusiastic, full of ideas and authority like my grandmother. "Isn't it nice that Christina von Kortnai is just a few rows down the hill. After all she did take our Countess and show her the world. She certainly knew how to wear a hat. I am planning to make her a little wreath. Such a beauty and such a doll." She looked at the apple core with tears in her eyes. Before I could decide whether she grieved for Grandmama, Great Aunt Christina, Puppe the lost doll, or the apple which had disappeared so fast, she remembered the very first time she had seen beautiful Christina in Schoenbrunn park. "I was in the park the other day. And in the castle. I was consulted, you know.

Ah, I'll never forget the first time Pierre Roth took me there. I was only a child. He had adopted me and wanted to show me off. Can you imagine."

Great wrought iron gates had flung open in welcome, to the sun-yellow summer palace: ornaments, balconies, green shutters, everything cheerful, open to gardens, formal and informal, harmoniously surrounded by freshly cut fragrant lawns, roses, gushing fountains, and all the life loving sweet and lavish exuberance which made Hanna smile to this day. And I smiled with her as she described strutting officers of the guard, red or blue or white gala uniforms; dancing, prancing horses. Liveried servants opening a portal to a Christina von Kortnai dressed in white. Court carriages unloading children on a special outing to visit the animals at the zoo. My grandfather Meinert, wine-grower to the court, personally supervising the unloading of choice Meinert wines, and chatting with a court gardener. And tiny figures in a green vista making their way up to the little temple on the hill, the Gloriette.

I could see Hanna walking up marble stairs holding onto the hand of the little master of hats, Pierre Roth, leaving behind forever the hush, the restraint and monotony of convent life. He had her dressed like a fashion doll. At the age of ten she couldn't have been any taller than a three year old, but she would insist on carrying one of the hat boxes to the Empress. Such a big hat box and such a tiny, smiling doll, would even make the stern liveried servants smile. She had been adopted by Pierre Roth and his little wife, and presented to the Empress because she was a darling dwarf, there she would be feeling taller by the minute as she walked proudly through endless mirrored halls, looking straight ahead. Never at herself. And she had been educated like a princess; the nuns had taught her to speak beautifully, even in French and English. Ladies hugged and kissed Hanna, gave her candy, and showed her the old nursery, old play rooms, the dolls cabinet where she would make herself at home.

"Where are you staying now?" I asked.

She untied her veil. Brought it down over her smile like a curtain, gathered up a beaded pouch bag and umbrella. "Nearby," she answered and kept me guessing. First she curtsied to the tomb, then the angel, finally to me. I stood up to respond and watched her vanish behind the hedges, reappear on the main path and scurry out. Her marvelous dark blue car with yellow spokes was back in Vienna and stood waiting under the weeping willow near the gate.

Frau Boschke came to do our laundry on Monday and brought the news that Hanna Roth was staying at the Romberg villa. Later that afternoon, Else Schmiedler's dog started to yip and snarl in the front gardens of the water castle. Both our dogs stuck their heads through the front railing and barked. Frau Hillie's duck sounded off. Else Schmiedler, back at the villa, was laughing. By the time Frau Boschke and Agnes and I rushed to the window, the miniature doberman was clinging to Hanna's skirt and tugging. She was in front of the house near the statues of the three graces, calling for help. Else looked on from Resi's old balcony in tight, black trousers and a loose Ami shirt. Colonel Fredericks appeared beside her and fired a pistol in the air to scare the little beast. Hanna either threw herself down or fell over with fright, the dog ran off with her hat shaking it like a rat. I expected secret documents, Hitler letters to come flying out. Tony came to the rescue, riding his roaring, spattering motorcycle, the dog dropped the hat and fled to the shed. Hanna stood up in terror, frantic to recover her hat and perhaps its contents.

Frau Boschke beamed. "You've got to give Tony credit. And

look at the way he's learned to ride that big bike."

Frau Schmiedler came running, a feather duster in hand. She wore a white surgeon's coat and a dashing green hunting hat adorned with pheasant feathers. Hanna put on her hat and allowed herself to be supported to the Rudolf Hess bench beside the statue of Icarus. Everyone stood around her.

Hanna did come to see Mother after that while I was at school, but never mentioned me. I never said a word either. How could I have explained that I enjoyed sitting on the stone bench beside my grandmother's tomb with Hanna Roth? We met in fair weather. I even did my homework sitting on the bench. She helped me with French and English and left the fragrance of violets on my school books . . .

Sometimes she would put on her glasses to embroider her gloves, her pouch bag, or a rip in her veiling with exquisite darning. Or she would have to stitch up the hem of her long, black skirt which had a way of catching on her thick soled shoes.

I now prepared my own school lunch and carried bread, whenever possible a hard boiled egg, cold meat, a piece of precious cheese for Hanna Roth. Funerals and cemeteries made her hungry as if she were one of the mourners. She cut death, wedding and birth announcements out of newspapers. "Nothing but funerals, mostly without feasts," she said. "A sad disgrace."

At my grandmother's funeral feast Father had asked about Hanna Roth. Mother didn't think she had been invited. And Father had remarked that one didn't have to invite Frau von Roth. Hanna had come uninvited to my birth and than she had appeared at my christening like the wicked fairy—as she herself once put it: half invited—far less distinguished than being left out . . . The cemetery was her park. No one gaped at her here among the graves. I said: "One day, when I get married, I'll invite you." When she did not respond at once, I hoped for a prediction. She merely tittered like a convent schoolgirl.

One day I was sitting beside her writing an English composition on spring: green grass and primroses grow wild among the graves. The funeral bell rang out. Chapel bells pealed and workers in the vinyard happened to be singing "*Ja, ja,* the wine is good I don't have a new hat. Rather than guzzle water, I'll wear an old cap."

"Christina von Kortnai certainly knew how to wear a hat. No matter what!" Hanna had said this before. "No one could ever stop Christina von Kortnai. She never listened to me. Scandalous. The sculptor Antonini exhibited a certain drawing of her wearing that beautiful straw hat with all the fruit and flowers."

"Nothing else?" I asked.

She ignored this question. "Half the society men of Vienna bid for it."

I don't know how often we met at my grandmother's tomb that spring. No arrangement was necessary. I arrived before she did and had to go home after an hour. Sometimes she stayed behind on the bench. I asked her whether Mort was in Vienna. "The little lieutenant with the big unhappy smile?" she said. "Here and there and everywhere. Always on the go. How can young men settle down after all that goes on in a war? No matter what side they were on they miss doing awful things and it makes them restless, ready for anything. All this talk about bravery. War weakens men. Women gain strength, they have to, just to live with them afterwards, or without them."

I thought of Arnold and shook my head.

"You might think you know better, but one day you'll remember what I said."

Then came a day when I found her pacing back and forth between the angel and the gate muttering to herself. "You just missed that funeral," she said. "And I had bought the grave. Not just rented it for a few years. The records were all lost and then they tried to rewrite them and made this mistake. Remember the beautiful monument of a little doll sitting on top?"

Rented graves were cleaned out when the lease was up and used again unceremoniously in Austria, especially at this time of high demand. "Imagine throwing hand grenades in a cemetery! They might have called themselves national socialists." The smiling lips curled back and her new American teeth clicked. "Nothing but traitors to the Fuehrer. Grave robbers. I bet it was Janicek. They put national socialists to work here. No punishment to him. A sleazy man was seen taking off with that precious coffin."

I saw it all like a doubly exposed photograph: Fritz in the mountains, the amethyst mine, planning to make the supreme sacrifice and blow himself up with Mother and all the museum art, and Fritz the professor in a slouch hat fleeing from the graveyard with a coffin. "But what was in the precious coffin, Frau Hanna?" She did not say anything. "And where is Janicek?"

"I feel his presence," she said in the tone of voice my grandmother always used when I asked too many questions.

"Here? Now? or just in Vienna?"

"Please lower your voice," she said.

I had brought for her bread and butter spread with our own honey.

"I thank you. *Danke, nein.* It has taken my appetite away." Her voice told me she was angry. Her mouth kept smiling. "Can you imagine, can you imagine. They put a murdered woman into my desecrated grave without asking me." She waved a newspaper before my eyes: "Butcher, Prisoner of War, Returns to Vienna and Slaughters Wife." I tried to calm her with a hard boiled egg. She said she would choke to death. For a while we sat side by side in silence. I read the notice. Vienna, as father always said, is a village. The butcher woman in Frau Boschke's house had been stabbed, I imagined because she had trouble explaining to her husband all those Boschke rings, especially the romantic forget-me-not which turned green.

"Vienna is no place for young ladies like us anymore. Civilization will come to an end without our Fuehrer." Hanna said.

This broke the spell. "Hitler and his men destroyed, killed and robbed all over Europe," I quoted in my grandmother's voice.

Hanna Roth gave me a sharp look. Her teeth clicked. "Men, men . . . But doesn't winter destroy and then we have spring?"

Before I could respond she was on her feet. "The car was supposed to pick me up," she said. By the time she had curtsied to the angel, the tomb, and me, Jan and his gang of children appeared on the main path walking in pairs behind a nun. The little girls carried bunches of primroses.

"War children," she said. "I better wait."

"They loved your storytelling," I said. "They hate Else Schmiedler. That's why they didn't stay at the party."

"It was just the big boy. He pointed at Else. The little ones, you never know. You, for instance, remember everything and from the beginning you were more than discreet. The truth is that I was only involved with war children once. And I was not to blame. Nor was Frau Schmiedler. She had been helpful to me on occasions through her husband—"

"When you wanted to take over the water castle?" I asked and was ignored. I had to think of Frau Boschke's saying: No reply is a good answer.

"Anyway, I wanted to be obliging. And Frau Schmiedler believed Else was helping to rescue little Slovene children who had lost their parents because the Fuehrer loved little children. Frau Schmiedler begged me to go along with Else. The trip promised to be pleasurable in that magnificent car. How could I suspect anything when Herr Schmiedler sent little Else. She was looking so sweet in a pale blue dress. I had decorated a hat with silk roses for her, but while I fitted it I had one of my spells and I saw uniform caps flying around the air and landing on children's heads like nesting birds. I told Else and she laughed so hard she wet her panties. She does that when she laughs. And she often laughed where other little girls would cry. A strange and heartless child. It was her third trip. She had been to Poland. Knew exactly what was going to happen. Considered it sport."

Hanna Roth turned and faced my grandmother's tomb, while the nun with her wards knelt at a row of children's graves. She kept on talking, depicting for me the magnificent sky blue car, the handsome driver, little toys they had carried as though they were going to a party. And then armed soldiers following in a truck to protect them from possible partisan attacks. They had all stopped on the road to feast on roast goose. I did not have to ask any questions. She needed to talk. And her story, like the creation and decoration of a hat, was personal, inspired and ornately tinged with the occult.

"I had dozed off in the cars after that great meal. When I woke up two flaxen haired little girls were sitting beside me and they were crying. I tried to talk to them but they didn't understand German, or French, only Slovene. We stopped and the officer handed the little ones over to the men who had followed us in a truck. Else said the children had seen me asleep in the beautiful car and begged for a ride with me. And now they had had enough and would be taken back to their village."

"Did they take the children back?" I asked.

"I saw them lifted into the truck and it turned around. We drove on to a small town and straight to the school. Kindergar-

ten children were playing out of doors. Else gave them soap suds
and straws and the blew bubbles and bubbles floated over us all.
The children laughed and danced around me. The driver and
Else lured all the fair haired ones, fed them candy and made a
game of letting them try on all kinds of uniform caps; Caps I had
seen in my dream flying around like birds of prey landed on those
children's heads. There was a prescribed master race size. Those
who were fair haired and found hats that fitted were invited for
a little ride with Else and me in the beautiful car. We drove off
at high speed. They loved that and clapped their little hands.
After a while they wanted to go back. The truck stood waiting
on the road. They were loaded on the back like cattle, met up
with the first group, and started to cry, holding out their hands
to me, asking for help. Else, again told me they would take them
back. And we drove away to Zagreb at top speed."

"At the hotel, Else told me not to get excited. It was Himmler's
idea to bring little blond children to the Reich and replenish the
master race. The S.S. used to look for fair-haired children in
Poland—not just orphans—in Russia too, until children started
to hide from them. After that some women had dressed up in
brown habits like nuns and that had worked for a while. Else
said she herself was better than anyone else and I had been simply grand. After all, they were just little peasant children. And
they would be treated well. Some of them would be adopted by
childless wealthy Aryans who could offer them everything."

"I felt quite ill at the hotel and simply took to my bed. The
officer came and told me he was very sorry. I would have to miss
the rest of the trip. They had to leave me. I would be taken to
the train and have my own first class compartment back to
Vienna. Close to the Austrian border, a group of S.S. officers
came onto the train looking for someone. I never travel light and
I had a trunk in the luggage room. I simply climbed into it. They
searched the train, perhaps for me. I'll never know."

"When I got back to Vienna Frau Traude and I had our big
quarrel. I wanted to inform Adolf Hitler. He with his dashing
dark hair would have been shocked at that cruel stupidity. After
all, many little blond children grow up to be dark haired. I did.
Traude would not allow me to send a pigeon to the Fuehrer. Said
it was too dangerous. And he probably knew all about the kid-
napping."

"Have you told the Americans about the children?"

"Incriminate myself and poor Frau Schmiedler who had allowed Else to go on these trips quite innocently?" She turned around and watched the war children follow the nun slowly along the rows of graves down the hill and out onto cemetery road.

"How did those children get maimed?" I asked.

"The war. The war. And I tried to stop it. so did Rudolf Hess," she said." She looked into my eyes. "In the end the innocent always get the blame."

And how guilty was the innocent one? I had to ask myself.

I had stayed longer than usual. The car arrived and honked twice. She jumped up. *"Lebwohl,"* live well to my *auf wiedersehen.* "You won't be coming here for a while now anyway," she told me. I watched her tiny figure disappear. The stone bench felt cold and hard as a block of ice. Like the little children in that school yard blowing bubbles, I had followed her. Had she led me astray without knowing it?

I watched her scurry downhill, veil flying in the wind. The amazing car was waiting.

# TWENTY-TWO

# *Trio*

SPRING WAS IN THE AIR and so was death. Art galleries opened in Vienna with black and white drawings. Skeletons and hollow-eyed ghouls danced the dance of death on ersatz paper. Flowers grew on graves; artists emerged. Pencil stumps swirling, pens scratching the dregs of India ink after eight years of this and that *verboten,* punishment, having to fight and being defeated, ashes, bombs, more punishment. What was there to depict, but the orgy of death?

Mother took me to a concert. We heard "Kinder Toten Lieder," "Children's Death Songs." Mahler's music had been banned, now it was played again. Mahler had written the songs after he had lost a daughter. As far as I was concerned the songs should have been banned forever because they made cotilllions of small skeletons dance in my head and made Mother weep openly.

The weather was bright. Mother couldn't face crowded street cars and decided to walk home. "I had to cry now for the baby I lost seven years ago. When they showed me the tiny dead boy, I couldn't cry, Reyna. I became paralyzed. Guilt gets in the way of mourning. Sir Hugh has taught me to understand myself better. He and I were worried that you might blame yourself in some way for Grandmother's death. We all knew she was not well enough to give a house ball. We should have stopped her. Just as Resi and Bertl should have stopped me from getting onto a horse when I had a six-month-old child in my belly."

Now I found myself humming the Mahler song's for dead

children as I walked in long strides under the linden trees on our avenue. Afternoon sun flared up weaving in and out of moving branches in a rhythmic medley of greens and velvet dark shade. A breath of linden blossom insinuated springtime in Vienna. And the song in my head—sweet melody of death—blended into all the miasmal triteness of "Roses from the South," "Spring Flower Waltz" and haunting melodies as yet unsung.

At the bombed house a solitary bush poured pink blossoms through the battered remains of a wrought-iron fence, forming a baldachin above Father's bench. Two men sat on it. The dark-haired one on the outside—too well dressed, beautiful like a young actor—had one of the pink blossoms in his buttonhole. He eyed me as I came along and got up.

I became uneasy and was about to cross the street.

"Reyna," he came towards me toeing-in a little. "It is you, isn't it?"

Eli. I ran to him, collided and stepped back.

"I've been waiting for you." The reproach of poor sick little son of the Splasher waiting at the water castle to play with his only friend. The deep voice of a slender, wiry man. His glossy black hair flipped forward in the wind and his large dark eyes reflected dancing spring greens, and bits of me. Everything about him had a silky sheen.

He looked so perfect. I was almost afraid I might spoil something with my hug and shy kiss on the cheek and big Viennese smile. "You're still the same," I quickly said.

"No, I'm not." He sighed a marvelous Eugene Romberg sigh. His sadness was startling and luxuriant as the nakedness of a native. He grabbed me, kissed my mouth. I tasted perfume, sweets, from a land of milk and honey. "We have changed. Isn't it wonderful!"

I stroked the sleeve of his vested dandified Eugene Romberg suit.

"But Vienna is a deplorable mess," said Eli, the boy who mustn't get dirty or too excited and happy, which, like unhappiness, might bring on an awful asthma attack. "You are the first cheerful sight. A picture. Isn't she remarkable Arnold?"

My Frog Prince discreetly preoccupied with a shoelace responded with a nod, an uneasy smile. The firm handshake telling me: Well here he is then. I had to take him away. I brought him back for you. Once more Arnold had done his duty, made amends, but he could not get himself to walk away.

I sat down beside Arnold. Kiss on the cheek again, Viennese smile. Eli took his place on my other side. Our trio was enveloped in the insidious fragrance of linden blossoms. And Frau Hillmar's duck qua, qua, quaed, greeting, or warnings to the strutting young doctor and his stern, female disciples. Chanting and panting, *eins-zwei, eins-zwei.* They passed by one-two, one-two, looking straight ahead. I laughed for the first time since Grandmama had died. And I kept laughing at everything that first day.

We started walking around Vienna arm in arm. I was always in the middle. For one week, or two, or three? The warm Foehn wind nudged and teased as we drifted around shattered Vienna in a state of aimless delight. I never asked Arnold how he found time every afternoon, or, how long Eli would stay in his mother's apartment on the Ringstrasse. The sun kept shining for us. We had found each other. Nothing else mattered.

We usually met just below my school. Girls watched me walk away arm in arm with the two amazingly handsome young fellows. They whispered about me and my two black marketeers and this helped my waning notoriety. I neglected Ursel and neglected home work.

The Friday Eli came to dinner at the Meinert-Hof, Arnold excused himself. "You won't miss me. You, Eli and your parents have so much to catch up on. I would only intrude."

I missed him that evening. And Father told Eli that the prince who had been confronted with unbelievable brutality had grown up into a self-reliant, strong man and was capable of the most delicate consideration, especially for children . . .

When it came to catching up that evening I had nothing to say. Mother had to fill my silence with talk about Charles Dickens. Eli listened eyes half closed. "How amazingly clever you are!" he said in a humble Eugene Romberg voice and kissed her hand.

My Father talked about reparation. Eli seemed disinterested and left the *Wiedergutmachung*—making-things-good-again, tedious reparation procedures—to Father and a lawyer who had the right connections. But in the reckless manner of a young heir he had taken over his dead father's modish style of dress, and that mad devotion to Mother.

A rich young fellow, in destitute Vienna just like his father after the First World War. He kept a secret pocket in his jacket stuffed with all kinds of money. Officially stores had nothing to sell but you could buy anything and most anyone in Vienna. My new Eli, the Switzerland Eli, made himself at home in Vienna among those who had less or were starving to death. Why should he care? They'd torn his parents apart, kicked him out, killed his father. Since he wasn't about to blame anyone in particular he must have blamed everyone in Vienna and Austria—even us—at the beginning.

At the same time he was in Vienna to enjoy himself with Arnold and me. Took us to eat in the back room of inns filled with smugglers and black marketeers. Outside, the sun kept shining. American wives had begun to arrive in Vienna; American children, too. You saw more and more American cars, bright as Easter eggs.

Then the weather changed and became unpredictable. I carried Agnes's big umbrella and my friends took me in the middle and put an arm around me; we turned green under the green umbrella in that tight huddle to stay dry.

The big umbrella must have kept us from seeing any "Entering the Russian Zone" sign that afternoon. Then it stopped raining. I closed the umbrella and we found ourselves near the bank of the Danube. The bridge had been blown up at the end of the war. Showers had darkened the dust and rubble of burned-out buildings on both banks of the swollen river. Bomb craters had filled up with rain water and reflected the racing clouds.

Arnold delivered one of his United Europe lectures to Eli and me: make the Danube an international river; persuade the Russians to go home. Invite all the famous artists, scholars, scientists in the world to meet every year and work on a plan for world peace.

While he talked I kept staring at the murky river rushing along and I felt myself drifting on the Danube so gray, so gray, towards the blue, blue sea: a great gathering of peacemakers in Venice.

Three Russian soldiers came along. And my hand gripped Arnold's. He stopped talking. They passed by. Suddenly the sun broke through clouds and a rainbow appeared spanning the Danube. The Russians stopped and shouted something. And on the other side of the river shabby children ran under a rainbow bridge and didn't know it. The mirage faded. Tears came into my eyes, as though the miracle of the happy time with Eli and Arnold, like the rainbow, was an illusion and nothing could ever span the gap my grandmother had left.

Arnold saw my sad face; forgot about uniting Europe, put his arm around me and kissed my cheek. An apology because he couldn't make the rainbow last for me. Too much sympathy made me feel worse. I quickly turned to Eli who had never learned to consider anyone, and passed the kiss on. Workers were piling up fallen bricks and shouting to each other. Eli said it was depressing by the Danube. Time for a coffeehouse. We held hands lightly after the kiss had passed between us. Arnold swinging my school bag, Eli a neat little brief case. They talked about money. Arnold always warned Eli about changing money in the black market. Now, it seemed, forged banknotes were in circulation. I only half listened. We came to a big puddle and they swung me over it.

"You're getting a lot of free time from the U.S. Special Services," Eli suddenly said to Arnold. "Are you watching me for them, or has Ferdl von Meinert hired you?"

We came to another puddle. Eli forgot me. Arnold put his arm around my waist, hoisted me over it and held onto me for a minute enjoying his own strength. "I feel so lucky to be with you both," he said. The wind played with his wavy, sand-colored hair. "I have never had such a good time." Then he turned to me and said: "I guess there is no need to talk about this."

Words had been unnecessary when I was seven years old. Nothing had changed. We looked at each other. Then we took off as if someone had given a signal, raced to the next corner laughing and shouting. He beat me by a couple of meters. We had reached the edge of the international zone. They took me in the middle again.

"I never had a chance for this kind of thing, Reyna," Arnold said. "I got myself into such deep water." He was almost a caricature of "Strength through Loyalty": high forehead, strong chin, straight back, powerful neck of a Nazi poster German.

"When are you going to get yourself out of deep water, Arnold?" Eli laughed.

"Arnold was in deep water when he saved you," I said.

"In Eli's case Ferdinand von Meinert was the real hero," Arnold said. "He was the one who saw to the passport."

"He was your father's best friend, Eli," I said. "But Arnold was a stranger. Had never even seen you and risked his life."

"I am compulsive and I just kept on doing whatever I could, which was nothing much."

"You are a hero," Eli said. "I know that."

"I don't want to be a hero anymore," Arnold said.

"You can't help yourself," Eli said. "Just as I can't help being nothing but Eugene Romberg's son. A rich boy. It's a habit."

Arnold laughed. "Let's break the habits or Reyna will get bored."

This was a cue for Eli. "I have a little surprise, little piece of nonsense. Hope you don't mind. Couldn't find anything better." A word by word imitation of Eugene Romberg as the apologetic beggar offering presents. There was always something for us in that brief case. A rare cake of soap, a golden bird for my charm bracelet, a silk scarf for me; and for Arnold, a book, a pair of socks, a shirt. And each time that Eugene Romberg apology spoiled everything for me.

"It's too much. I wish you wouldn't," I finally said. "It reminds me so much of your father. It makes me sad."

"It's not too much. Not this time." Eli said. Out came three pair of sunglasses. We laughed, but the moment we put on those black marketeer masques, the torn up Rotenturmstrasse was drowned in murky green. Now we could go to a café and fit right in and eat some secret cake, Eli said.

I should have said: No thank you, not today. I don't want to sit among smugglers and black marketeers, but I had always gone along with Eli's ideas. We ended up in the corner of the backroom of a café wearing our dark green glasses. And everything looked submerged, green: dark-haired young men wearing dark glasses, talking about money in Greek and passing green packages under green tables. Eli and Arnold talking about forgeries again. Germans had paid agents in foreign countries with forged money. Schmiedler's idea. Now it was circulating.

"Will they ever catch that scoundrel?" Eli asked. "I believe he was the one who had Father arrested."

"Everyone is looking for him," Arnold said.

"My father talked about him after his last trip," Eli was saying. "He was drinking. He was unhappy. It didn't all make sense.

He had been to Hitler's guesthouse at Salzburg, Schloss Kiesheim. Said it was all one big masquerade. And he went on and on about your mother, Reyna. He was crazy about her. You can't blame him."

Arnold put his arm around me. "Look at that cake. Mmm." He wanted Eli to stuff himself and stop talking.

Eli went on: "Father saw her at Hitler's guesthouse."

"Why bring that up," Arnold said. "Schloss Kiesheim was like a museum. Full of art treasures from all over Europe. Visitors came to see the collection. And she must have been bored in the mountains—"

Eli interrupted and said his father had mentioned pushing her around in her wheelchair when she was looking for a glass case in a reception room. She had expected to find her doll, and suddenly she had stood up and walked.

"It must have been quite a shock for her to see your father when he was supposed to be safe in Switzerland. At least it got her out of the wheelchair," Arnold said.

"I want to know what happened!" I said.

"Vati went to the castle because he had been told your mother would be there, Reyna." Eli said. "He came back to Switzerland in a bit of a state. Someone had been teasing her, promising her the doll. He didn't know how he could put an end to that and get it back for her. Then he found out about something I had done and this bothered him a lot. A telegram arrived. He took time to enroll me in a boarding school. Then he went back to Salzburg and never came back. Your mother says she doesn't know what happened to him. Perhaps she doesn't want to talk about it. I don't want to get into it either, because it was all my fault. I made him very angry."

"No. It was Mother's fault," I said.

Arnold and Eli looked at each other and didn't say anything.

"She probably got him all worked up again over that stupid old doll." And doll hating was not unlike Hitler's Jew hating, blaming someone or something, giving way to an ecstasy of ugly feelings. I had been gleeful when I had informed Mother that Fritz Janicek had shot the doll's head off. That's why she wouldn't believe me. And if those who wanted to destroy Hitler said he was dead no one wanted to believe that either. There was no end to Puppe and no end to Hitler.

A woman came to play a zither and sing: "This happens only once. Never again. Must be a piece of heaven." We ate cake that cost as much as one of my teachers would earn in two month. Sunglasses hid our faces, the smokey turgid green room made me feel submerged, and invisible. Before Hitler took over Austria the unemployed wearing dark glasses would stand around holding out hats begging in the street like blind men. I had once seen Eugene Romberg empty his pockets to fill a hat. The beggar forgot he was blind and counted the money. Eugene Romberg could have surprised Mother and she forgot to be paralyzed.

A flower woman came through the curtained entrance and looked around all the young men in despair. Eli and Arnold waved to her frantically and made her empty the tray. She tied all the bunches of violets into one large bouquet for me. Arnold pushed Eli aside and paid.

The song went on and on: "Happens only once. Never again." The violets, Grandmother's perfume, got the better of me. Instead of bursting into tears I turned into a wild girl. A flirt in a green smuggler's cafe. I put on my Rita Hayworth grin. Mixed English words into the conversation, laughed like Else Schmiedler, creating a stir among the dark-haired young men who moved hooded glances in the direction of my masqued face. I was rattling on about school, the Ami boys across the street, when I saw heads turn towards the door. Eli and Arnold sat close to me holding my hands as though the Ami boys were trying to edge in.

The man who came through the heavily curtained door seemed to have stepped out of another era in his impeccable riding habit, jacket slung over one shoulder, riding switch with an ornate handle. It was the von Kortnai groom. His mop of gray hair had vanished, he was bald and had changed into the kind of self important dashing older man General von Kortnai might have been.

He flick snapped his riding switch. "I like that song," he said and gave the zither player some money.

"Congratulations. Beautiful Hungarian horses. I understand you got quite a bargain," said a young man in a foreign voice.

"They changed hands a few times, are neglected and will cost me a lot of money." The groom had lost his accent and spoke softly. Some of the men made friendly sounds, others hasty departures as he settled down at a reserved corner table. He looked around the room, while the zither kept playing and the woman sang, "This happens only once. Never again. Must be a piece of heaven."

Affluence seemed to have aged the young man who had stayed at Salon Roth, and earned his living by making Nazi pants into little skirts. The knife happy von Kortnai groom and Russian agent had vanished, by changing into a self satisfied money man. His tired eyes found and challenged me, as older men often challenge one who is too young. I experienced an unsurpassed thrill of abhorance and thought of Franz Joseph Schmiedler.

Arnold, who always shared my feelings warmed my hand with both of his as though I had been out in the snow. Eli was laughing. He enjoyed seeing someone who looked affluent. "You see," Eli said later when they talked about that man. "My father was right. Someone asked him what would happen after the war to all the violent criminal types that have had the power under Hitler. He said, they'd get rich, fat, forgetful and old."

Arnold and I kept quiet like parents who don't want to scare a child. But it was Eli who knew where to find a taxi and bribe a driver. I always sat in the middle in the taxi. Our outings had come to revolve more and more around the parting at the gate, the kisses. I was not wickedly innocent, as Lieutenant Kaufman had put it, I was wickedly inexperienced. By the time we reached my district we sat in a tight huddle.

This month the Americans were in charge of Vienna. There was more traffic than usual on our avenue. An American truck had broken down and was surrounded by uniforms. The house across the street had been dark in the evenings as if the occupants were sleepy or had all gone away. Eli had been invited to look around his house once. He never talked about it. This evening windows were all lit up, as if Eugene Romberg had returned. Spotlights beamed down into the gardens, revealing nude statues of gods and goddesses in the maze of the now neatly trimmed ornamental hedges.

Both my friends always took me to the gate. The taxi would wait. First I kissed one, then the other. And never for too long. Grasping controlled only by having to share. In Vienna among the allies, as in our chaste trio, this provoked erotica of power struggles violating invisible demarcation lines.

This evening I had to give five kisses to Arnold to make up for Eli's long, spongy kiss. I wanted to be fair. That's how I came

to count kisses the way my Meinert ancestors, the chicken farmers must have counted their first gold coins. Meinerts inherit
perfect recall and keep their equanimity by never depending on
it for much more than a game of cards, or like Father, chess.
When it came to matters of gold or love they always kept records. Before the war, Father had filed little cards from flowers
that used to arrive for Mama after parties or balls. And he certainly must have remembered the silly ones like: "Roses to the
Rose of Vienna," signed Schmiedler with a big snakelike S.

I started my bookkeeping during the days of the trio. Mark-
ing each kiss with a cross in ink under the proud heading of
S.A.—sexual activity. The important kisses were darker, the long
ones larger. There was only one pencil mark. A kiss from a
stranger. Rows and rows of crosses filled the pages in my blue
notebook. I left white spaces for what might have happened. And
whenever I perused this log of kisses, I doodled. Those dots, flowers, tiny unicorns, monsters, gave the pages a hieroglyphic
splendor and anyone who didn't know that S.A. stood for Sexual
Activity, would have thought I had mapped out an S.A. graveyard commemorating large and small storm troopers.

I had not kissed much. The graveyard of kisses was funny
and sad like most anything that makes one laugh. Each kiss had
a beginning and an end like life itself. You have to be child enough,
ignorant and arrogant enough to create such a monumental farce.

Kisses that evening were different. Arnold put away his sunglasses and removed mine, folded them for me and put them into
my pocket. I saw longing in his eyes. He took me into his arms,
held me and did not want to give me up. Eli was looking on.
Arnold usually turned away when Eli and I kissed goodnight.

One kiss, twenty, or a thousand, I had stopped counting when
we were torn apart. Not by the distant thunder of Russian guns.
Not by Eli, but by a shrieking, laughing, Else Schmiedler standing close to the barbed wire, hopping about hugging herself, rollicking, crazy.

"How come you're sharing one girl over there?" She yelled
across the street. Shrill, brash, dancing around in the spotlight.
Her white dress flimsy, transparent, showing her small torso
and plump thighs. "*Du*, Arnold. You better come over here right
away. I have something to tell you."

Arnold let go of me and said he wouldn't be long. He took long
strides crossing the street. Then he pulled himself up, stiffened

into a German officer. I was about to run after him. Eli put his
arm around me and held me back. "Don't go after him. Stay! I
have not been alone with you once." We were standing close to a
grill covering a sewer. A foul breath of vapor rose as if a panting
monster cowered down there at the edge of those subterranean
corridors below our city.

"Arnold is decent," Eli went on. "I like him a lot. But he is
always mixed up in all kinds of rotten secret activities. I sometimes have a glass of wine with him after we take you home. He
shares a house with a weird fellow. My Vati used to say Nazis
were always fishing in murky waters, trying to catch big fish
with little fish. The Amis are doing the same thing. I told him
so."

"Arnold might be working for the Amis, but basically he always
works by himself, trying to help . . ." I said.

"Arnold is attracted to criminals like a fly to a piece of rot.
He wants to save everyone. Doesn't believe in death sentences
for the big Nazi hogs. He doesn't believe in executions."

I imagined Rudolf Hess being led to the gallows and my heart
sank. "There have been enough executions," I said. "My grandmother didn't believe in killing either."

Eli was not listening. "I will find Schmiedler. He had my father
arrested. Arnold knows how I feel and wants to protect even that
scoundrel. Lieutenant Kaufman is sure Schmiedler is in Vienna.
Kaufman is a German Jew and a realist. I'll get him to shoot
Schmiedler."

"A realist, Kaufman? How well do you know him?"

"I can count on him. He's in Nüremberg. One phone call from
me and he'll fly back to Vienna."

"To shoot Schmiedler?" I asked.

"Execute him."

"Vienna is full of suspicious types. You could make a mistake." I said. "Does Arnold know?"

"Probably. He might be spending all his time with us because
he is watching me."

"He is our friend," I said.

"He is an American agent. Don't forget that," Eli said.

The girl was laughing somewhere in his garden under the
trees. "The Schmiedler girl got mad at your father. And she was
the one who would have denounced him. You can ask Arnold
about that."

"I know more than he does," Eli said.

"The girl should be punished!" I said.

Eli smiled and dimpled. "Killing Schmiedler is enough."

Agnes had left the gate light on for me and moths circled around the lantern as they would circle around the spotlight over there. Vengeance was as futile as the dance of the moth. "It's rubbed off on everyone. Except Arnold. He was in the midst of it. He doesn't hate."

"Nothing much happened to Arnold personally. His mother and father in Germany are sharing their castle with a few American officers. My father is dead."

I couldn't say, *Du*, Eli. You know perfectly well Arnold is great, without belittling the prince. And I wanted Eli to forget what had happened to his father and leave the remembering to me. Wanted him to move back to Vienna and live in the house across the street. Throw the Schmiedlers out.

"There he is. He's coming back. Bother," Eli said. "It's early. I should have gone off with you. I want to go dancing with you. He won't go because he thinks you are too young to be seen in such places. There is nothing wrong with it. I love to dance. Remember when we used to dance to a gramophone in the attic?"

"They have your old phonograph over there and dance to the Hitler waltz."

Arnold had put on spectacles. His face looked taut and eyes strained. I had seen him that way when he had come to the farm as a German gestapo looking for Eli.

Else was in the front garden waving a piece of white paper over the edge of the barbed wire. "Come back here, Arnold. Come back Prince *von und zu,* Prince from and to, come back!"

"Give the paper to the colonel!" Arnold shouted back to her. "And stop making so much noise." Then he stroked my curls and said he was sorry. He had to hurry off. "Adieu, adieu! No need for the taxi!" He passed the empty bench at the bomb sight and vanished under the trees.

"I wish I had my car. Taxis are so scarce and a bore." Eli said. "I want to go dancing right now."

"Tomorrow," I quickly said.

"Tomorrow is always too late," Eli said in the sulky voice I remembered from our old games.

# TWENTY-THREE

# Cartwheels

ELI CAME WITH FLOWERS for Mother. We were having a little gathering that evening. Father took him downstairs into the catacomb for a wine tasting. I heard their feet going step, step, step, down the worn stone stairs to the woodpaneled cellar room. Eli had been in hiding down there and cared for by Frau Schwester, after his mother had been arrested by Fritz Janicek. Nothing ever changed that room. Resi's old mandolin, decorated with old faded ribbons weighed down by bells and charms from admirers, had remained on its hook from Father's bachelor days when she had been his protégé and his girl. Same old peasant furniture; same Ferdl Meinert would be briefing Eli: "Family is family."

He would remind Eli that his grandmother, Frau Traude Romberg and mine, raised in the same convent, didn't know they were cousins until Hitler laws—search for Aryan ancestors—had forced Frau Traude, to discover that she was the child of Christina von Kortnai and the sculptor Antonini.

Eli had never liked grandmother Traude, the fat widow, Hanna Roth's devoted candy eating assistant. Father would go from the family tree right on to me. The war years in the mountains. Father who had always wanted me to be a girl and as good as a boy, the modern father who had handed me the Uncle Ernstl gold keys when I was six, bragging about his sheltered and protected daughter, growing up as untouched as a convent girl . . .

I could imagine an eyelash-blinking Eli sampling Meinert

wines to choose one that had grown sweet and potent during the ugly years of war. They emerged ready to enjoy themselves thoroughly on this frenetically cozy Viennese evening. And I watched my father take the place of Eugene Romberg, forcing food on Eli: "Here, I was lucky to get a hold of some really nice ham, and how about another little bit of that great cheese. Here, here, here, you must taste this." He even filled his plate. Eli passed some of the food on to me the way he always did at the magic water castle table. He was teased. I was teased. By the end of the evening I was beginning to feel like just another one of these rare morsels forced on Eli.

There was a lot of joking, singing when Frau Hillie arrived with an elderly character actor from the Josefstaedter Theater. After a while playfulness became as oppressive as the warm Foehn wind. The actor was teasing Frau Hillie about her duck. Eli, who had my Krampus on his lap, wanted to know whether she wouldn't prefer a dog. *Ja,* she said, she had loved her wonderful black German Shepard, Rolfi. During the war Nazis were saying women who had pets instead of babies were treasonous. She had only one son. First she had received an anonymous letter, in verse form. Then some phone calls. For her husband's sake, she had to give the dog to the army. Tears came into her eyes when she thought of her Rolfi sent out to set off mines. But a kind fan of hers had surprised her with an adorable duckling. By that time she was widowed and keeping poultry was considered patriotic. No one could say a word.

Eli got up and went to the window. I followed. "Why does she have to bring this up? he asked. When I was in Salzburg with my Mother no one mentioned any of this. Here in Vienna I hear about concentration camps and all those awful things. I guess it's supposed to make me feel lucky that I had to get out of Austria . . . All these sad stories. Paul hates them . . ."

"Who is Paul?" I asked.

"Don't you know? A selfish fellow." Eli said. And the very next day he went off to visit his mother in Salzburg.

"Well, you did a good job. You got rid of Eli with that wonderful party." I said to Father.

"Not at all," he said. "He will be back."

On Saturday, I went for a long bike ride and passed the yellow villa twice; it seemed deserted. I went home. Father was taking a bath and singing wine garden songs in his off-key voice. He came down all pink and happy. "Guess who's been working in the garden with me for a couple of hours? your admirer, the prince. It's a good thing we have Rita to crop the grass, but there is a lot of weeding to be done."

"Is he going to garden with you again tomorrow?" I asked.

He smiled. Unfortunately they both had more urgent work. A reliable gardener was hard to find, but Mother's English doctor happened to be an expert with roses. "Some young fellows know nothing about gardens; too bad."

"Did you invite Eli to work in the garden? How about the Americans?"

"Gardening is good for body and soul," he said with satisfaction of one who was weeding out much more than flower beds.

Tall weeds hid Ursel and me in the neglected Schmiedler garden, where we were celebrated the last day of school by sharing an American cigarette and listening in on Else Schmiedler's conversation with Mimi Goldberg.

Else had appeared in the corridor with the final bell; her orange red dress glowing like a warning signal. Girls had crowded around her; she had waved them away and took Mimi out into the neglected rose garden of the ruined villa. They were sitting on a bench not far from us.

"You brought it for me, so why back out of it now?" Else was saying. "Hand it over or I'll just grab it. You owe me that little favor, Mimi Goldberg. And you can always tell your father your papers were stolen. Someone picked your pocket, grabbed your bag."

"You don't have to be so nasty about it," Mimi said. "I'll help you out." She opened her school bag and handed over a large envelope. "You don't look like me," she said. "You'll never be able to get away with it."

"I know a man who inspected those lovely English pound notes we used to print in a concentration camp. Fixing up those papers is easy for him and his staff. But you keep your mouth shut or you're dead."

Ursel had lately taught me the sign language of the deaf she had used with her sister in that one room apartment during the war. We had often communicated that way during class.

"Why would Mimi do this for the Schmiedler daughter?" I asked with my hands.

"Because they have been friends," Ursel signed in reply.

And what a harmless pretty picture they made walking away arm in arm. Ursel wanted to know whether she was my best friend. I said she was my best school friend.

She raised her fine eyebrows and broke the silence: "If your two admirers come along, right now, you'd leave me!"

"Wouldn't you run off and leave me if that Lieutenant Kaufman were in Vienna?" Ursel had secretly met Kaufman four times. And he had taken her out in his big car.

She shook her head. "It's all over. I have other plans."

"Another Ami?"

"Shhh. No, no. Plans, plans! Word of honor you won't tell?"

"Word of honor."

Her hands said: "I want to go to America!"

"Is that all," I made a so-what sign. "Who doesn't?"

"But I'm really going."

I didn't like her blank—going to America—stare. Those wild Dilly eyes that went with going to America talk. Dilly, the singer in our class had five Ami sweathearts during the winter, now she crooned "Loving Youuuu When You Are Far Away." She still used Ami slang, but she ran out of chewing gum. Her dirndl skirt had to be converted into a smock to hide the big belly getting bigger. Her face was getting smaller and eyes huge with sadness and longing and the "Loving Youuuu" song sounded operatic.

"Not like Dilly?" I said.

"No. Not like wild Dilly. I'm much too scared. And I'm disgusted. I wish I hadn't told Lieutenant Kaufman about her. It really bothered him a lot, and he asked a lot of questions. That's when he got the idea I didn't know what's what and needed to be enlightened."

"What did he do?"

A pause. Her eyes looking up into the trees. "It is too awful. And *Vater* really beat me up. He went too far. I'm leaving!"

"Kaufman took you to his apartment. The neat room or the messy one?"

She said no with her hands. Then she came and flopped down beside me. "He took me up the Leopoldsberg in his beautiful big car. Mother thought I was with my sister. At first it was really wonderrrful."

I stretched out on my back, head resting on my school bag. Sparrows nesting in one of the old paper lanterns chirped. And Ursel treated me first to memories of the good old unenlightened meetings with the lieutenant. Kisses, Coca Cola. Dancing at the American Clam Gallas club. Until, until. Rotten enlightenment. A drive uphill throught the Vienna woods. Stopping here and there . . . And finally the enlightment on the windswept Leopoldsberg, where hundreds of years ago a legendary unenlightened bride of a ruling Bamberger had lost her veils to the wind. Ursel had pointed down to the gray ribbon of water, the Danube and the monastery, built in fulfillment of the bridegroom's vow where the veil had been found.

"Then Herb's alarm-watch went off. He handed me the book. And he said it wasn't right for him to get serious with a girl who didn't even know what's what. He had gone to a lot of trouble to get that book for me. It's in German. It was too windy to read on a bench. We had to go back to the car . . . I should have thrown that book down Leopoldsberg.

"Worst of all, *der kleine* Sergeant Tony knows everything. He's seen me talking to Herb. And he had been the one who went off on his motorcycle and found that what- is- what doctor's book. Perhaps the little Ami knows Herb wanted it for me. And I bet you he showed it to your laundress that gossips. I'm so ashamed. Those sliced up naked pictures of what happens. Awful. Digusting. Ugly enlightment. After seeing that book I didn't even want Herb to kiss me anymore. And worst of all, the devil does not rest. Father was walking down to the street car after lunch. The Schmiedler girl with her dog was there, stopped him and asked whether he knew where Lieutenant Kaufman and I had gone. Everyone was waiting with an urgent message. When I came home there was Vater, and the carpet beater. Imagine being beaten up when you've done nothing but look at a book you hate. *Vater* made me swear by the Madonna I'll never as much as speak to an Ami. And he doesn't even believe in the Virgin Mary. I'm sick of it all. I'm going away forever."

"How? When? Where?" My mistake. "You'd be much too scared to go away."

"I am more scared to stay." Her thin legs scissored the air.

"I'll teach you cartwheels if you tell me everything," I said.

"Cartwheels, Cartwheels. O.K. O.K."

Skirts tucked into lace trimmed knickers sewn from old pillow slips made Dilly bellies. Hand over hand, crushing fragrant grass, leg after leg, turning like a sea star. "Like this. No, no. Up with the legs!"

Ursel collapsed. Tried again.

"Straighten your legs!"

Down she went, then up. "Going to America! Going to America!"

We were off. Oceans of sky flitting by with armadas of white clouds. Then lying on the cool grass, flattening our bellies we shared stories of daring escapades and escapes: German girls walking to Hamburg and smuggling themselves onto ships. Aryan girls selling themselves into harems. Desperate to get away from it all. One girl thrown out a hotel window by an Arab. Not Ursel. She would be sailing away towards a sunny New World full of Easter egg colored cars. A low flying plane droned over us and out of habit Ursel ran for cover throwing herself down behind an oak tree. Now her hands did the talking again, forming letters.

O R P H A N S. Gestured words, flickering between us and cabbage butterflies. Silent answers to silent questions. Then loud questions and loud answers behind the ruin of that house of many secrets.

After all, I had walked away after school going off to enjoy myself with my two admirers. No one to help her with homework anymore. At first her mother had taken her to the sunny playground with her school books. It seemed a safe place with women, little babies, old people watching swans on the pond, a nun with war children. Ursel had been allowed to go there by herself. Some of the war children, talked with their hands. Ursel could talk to them with her hands and they became friends.

Ursel made me swear by the Holy Virgin to keep my mouth shut. The children had found this tin box, shaped like a coffin. It had been full of old doll bodies. No heads. Under it all had been foreign money. English money. They were rich. And an American child rescue woman was taking them to Switzerland very soon. From there they intended to make their way to Italy and get a boat to America. And a man who felt sorry for them would help them. "One girl wants to stay in Vienna. I'm able take her place."

My hand found the little wooden trowel in my pocket. I thought of Italy, playing on the beach, spagetti. But Father was even worried about going to the mountain farm this summer because of the Russians at the demarcation line. People simply vanished and were never seen again. "How come you're suddenly so brave?"

"I hate my father," she grabbed my arm. "I think I like Herb so much, I'm scared of that."

"You have no visas. The Americans will send you right back anyway."

"No, they won't. They feel sorry for war children. Father knows a socilaist baker who went to New York when Hitler took over. Now he is a millionaire. He has written to him. I copied his address in New York. I can go to him. And I can work in a bakery and make cakes. And get rich. One day I'll invite you." She did a somersault in the grass and I did more of my cartwheels. Then she looked at her watch. She threw her arms around my neck; said she would write and send me packages. "It's late. I must run. Run. Run!"

A few days later Frau Prenner, Ursel's mother appeared at the Meinert-Hof. My Mother invited her. I found them sitting near the fountain drinking tea. Frau Prenner looked fragile like Ursel, had the same dreamy eyes and kept crumpling the apron of her old, blue dirndl dress, while she told us how lucky her little girl had been to get herself onto a children's transport to Switzerland. Herr Prenner having been an anti-fascist might have helped. But Ursel didn't want to worry anyone, and had arranged it all by herself. Ursel's mother hid her face in her dirndl apron and burst into tears. Mother and I cried with her.

Ursel was in Switzerland. Eli in Salzburg. Arnold stayed away. I needed company. Sophie, an old riding school mare, was another one of Father's clever chess-master moves. He had been trying to replace milk delivery cart horses when he found Sophie, and put her into the empty stable at the little palace. It certainly cheered up the Rittmeister. Sophie, brown and bony, her coat dull from starvation, sporting a snow white moustache, can-tered, or galloped on command. Mother was amused for one day, then she went back to riding the horses from the British stables with Sir Hugh. I was amused by Sophie as long as she lived.

Father got builders' sand to create a riding ring in the court-yard. Children and young people would come in to have riding lessons from the Rittmeister. There would be new life in the old courtyard. I wouldn't be moping around the little palace missing the countess. Mother's fall, losing her child, shaking up her brain and spending six years in a wheelchair, he dismissed with: "Your mother never had a teacher. She went riding with Cousin Bertl, that wild scamp. Never had any decent lessons. That's why she took chances and had her accident. The English doctor got her back into a saddle and he is as good as a riding master. A sensible fellow. When you were only four years old, you wanted to ride like your mother. I put you on a horse, you fell off and never wanted to ride again. I fell off a cherry tree when I was a small boy. Broke my leg. It remained a little shorter after it healed. I limped right back to that tree and I climbed it again. That's what life is all about."

"So you want to learn sidesaddle like your grandmother?" the Rittmeister said to me. "First you'll ride without a saddle." I rode back to front, climbed under the horse's belly and up on the other side without falling off, but I was so sore I could hardly walk. As a remedy the court doctor came and brought one of the first jars of Maltaline. (Back in production, thanks to the Americans. Full of vitamin B.) And he brought his boundless admiration for me and Sophie. The perfect cure. He often sat on his folded coat on the stone steps with two or three young riding students to applaud my antics and the effect of Maltaline.

The Rittmeister said I was a born horsewoman. It was in my blood, a true Falkenburg. I rode every day, and kept riding in my dreams. Once I even galloped over rippling sea water towards Venice without sinking.

One fine day I was riding sidesaddle, dressed up in Grandmother's gray riding habit and top hat. The Rittmeister went to the portal and let Arnold in. They shook hands and laughed and were pleased to see each other. Arnold greeted me politely. He had come to see the Rittmeister not me.

The Rittmeister said: "Isn't she a vision of the past? The image of the Countess." He tried to hide his tears by shouting: "Gallop!"

I was taken by surprise. Sophie suddenly behaved like a goat, ignored the command, nibbled grass, stopped in front of the hurdle and gave way to an enormous yawn. Arnold didn't notice Sophie trying to brush me off on the bushes. He just stared at his own shoes. I got her back under control, made her jump and she took the hurdle in great style.

Arnold sat on the stoop, scratching my dog Krampus behind the ears. I couldn't hear what he was saying to the Rittmeister. He didn't talk to me and avoided looking at me. Then he did his heel clicking, making excuses for having to go off with the Rittmeister for half an hour. Very polite, very German. Exactly as I remembered him when he had come to look for the Romberg boy on the Meinert aunt's farm and did not want to find him. I had been able to make him smile, when smiling could be dangerous. Now he just couldn't smile. I had lost him. Why had he turned away from me?

I took the saddle off Sophie. In the stable I threw my arms around her neck, sobbed and complained. Wanted my grandmother back. The horse nipped my shoulder. A Sophie nip—sharp reality—could bring me around fast.

I went into the little palace to change. Young swallows darted in and out circling over the old rose trees. They had learned to fly while I had learned to ride. Grandmama's old riding habit felt unbearably heavy, I slung the train over my arm and dragged myself upstairs. Krampus followed. Father had promised to pick me up in his truck. True to his word he had managed to have it repainted and it was now red as Amiercan army wife coats, cars, lips, fingertips.

I changed into my English dress and sat down in Grandmother's writing corner. The escritoire drawers were locked and I had the keys. All the neatly tied bundles of letters, the address books, and the poems had to remain exactly where they had always been. The mother of pearl inlaid pistol back in it's velvet lined case was locked into the big middle drawer. I flipped through the pages of her sketch book and admired the horse drawings, but had no notion how good they really were and how valuable they would become. I knew I had to get the missing drawing back.

Repairs had begun on the roof of the Hohentahler house. Charred boards were thrown down crashing to the ground. I closed my eyes and the pounding and tearing, took me back to the dark days of the invasion, the cellar days and Grandmother.

The window was open and when the builders took a break, I could hear the horse kicking against the stall, kicking against the confinement on this bright afternoon. Marks on her chest and head showed that she had been used as a cart horse in some way. She neighed three times, always hopeful for fodder. Some-one had walked into the courtyard. I leaned out of the window. Birds pecking near the stable flew up as though someone has passed close to the coach house keeping out of sight.

"Is that you, Papa?"

I walked to the landing. My dog was getting old. He stretched, shook himself and followed behind me. Only a few month's ago he would have run downstairs barking. I took my shoes off and tiptoed down the stairs. He followed, deaf and half blind, and licked the back of my heel testing the stairs with his paw. And I had been blind not to notice how he had aged.

I called again. No one answered and yet I felt the draft of the front door. Father had made me oil the hinges, water the rubber plant. Take responsibility for the little palace. I turned back, ran to the escritoire and found Grandmother's little pistol. Krampus was waiting and I crouched down and promised to take good care of him, always. And he sniffed in his world of darkness and silence. The tail wagged, he licked my hand. I was comforting myself, as much as him.

Soft footsteps tapped along the corridor. My temples throbbed. My temper rose. Thick walls wavered before my eyes. I raged down the stairs, turned, stumbled against someone, staggered back.

Mort was saying: "Hey, hey! take it easy," and fell into a foteulle, pulling me onto his lap. I jumped up at once. "Hey, babe. Stay, stay . . ." He was laughing. I later remembered that.

"In Austria we ring the bell before we go into a house," I said. "We don't break in!"

"I didn't break in. I asked to see you and they understood."

"They didn't understand you were going to come in and scare me."

"Surprise you," he said. "Make you forget you were mad at me."

"I might have shot you. And if you're coming in here to snoop around, or want to use me to get even with someone, just get out!"

He bent down. My dog sniffed his hand and wagged his tail remembering bits of chocolate. "I am an old friend, even he knows it."

"Are you?" I addressed him as 'Sie,' in formal German.

"I'm crazy about you."

Herb Kaufman in love with Ursel and now Mort crazy about me. His smile had not changed. The same great dark eyes. The sparkle. The same glorious American officer's uniform. I looked him up and down, and felt like giving way to an Ami whistle, one high note, one low. He reached out. I backed away.

"I'm no more a Negro than your friend the Romberg boy is a Jew. One of my grandmothers had a little black blood. And she was a real beauty. All the rest are white as you are . . ."

I took in his smooth, full lips, the uneasy smile. Lieutenant Curly-head, Frau Boschke had called him.

"You couldn't even call me a cross-over," he said.

"You didn't come bursting in here to give me your pedigree," I said.

"I just had to see you before I go to Berlin. I told the Rittmeister that there had been a misunderstanding with you."

The Rittmeister would do anything for an American. Mort had used him. I had to wonder about Arnold. Mort tried to pet my dog. I snatched Krampus up, and sat on the window shelf. Sweet air came in from the old courtyard. In between bird sounds I heard the first big bumble bees humming in a hedge. Mort smoked and watched me. I calmed down and waited, clutching my dog as Mother had once clutched her doll, gazing at this or that man.

His eyes followed my hand as I caressed the dog. He took in my tenderness, it touched him. I moved my eyes from side to side, like the mysterious eyes of Puppe, the doll. Solemn, expectant, wordless. His face changed, he stared at me and reached out as though he had lost his sight and had to feel his way towards me. Then he dropped his arms. "I can't get you out of my head. I had to speak to you alone." And for the first time I heard the trite word I had been longing to hear from someone, anyone: LOVE, LOVE, LOVE, LOVE. The spring air played over my hair. I did nothing to stop him.

"Look. I shouldn't have left you behind that night. I was really sorry. I lost my head. But you shouldn't have gone back up there to see Kaufman. He'd been drinking. He says nothing happened. In some ways he's not a bad guy. It's just that we used to be buddies . . ."

I waited, as Mother had waited, and I held my dog as she had held the doll without saying a word, while she had allowed this or that man to talk and talk. I listened to the tale of good comrades turning into bad comrades: Mort and Kaufman had become friends when they trained together in the U.S.A.

"I don't know what he told you. Perhaps it wasn't anyone's fault. Germany was much worse than Austria. That girl was already seventeen. I wasn't her first soldier either. The mother knew the girl took me to her room. They were more than willing. I don't think much of them." He kept his voice low. I could hear sparrows in the courtyard chirping during his vidication. "They wanted chocolate, food . . . You and your folks were so different."

"My father could afford to buy food in the black market," I said.

He threw his cigarette onto the stone floor where Maria Theresa the Empress had walked and ground it out. "I was the first one to get transferred to Vienna. Herb Kaufman got his orders about eight weeks later. The girl was crying her eyes out. I asked him to look after her a little, go to her mother and bring them a few things to eat. A month later I was back in Germany for a couple of days. I went straight to her house. For the first time her mother wasn't pleased to see me. She said the girl was sick in bed. I went upstairs to her room. She hid under the quilts. I touched her head. It was hot all right. She was burning up. I pulled the cover down. She was naked, all pink. I could hear the sound of a car pulling away from the back of the house. Kaufman had been taking care of her all right . . . She said she still loved me."

He interrupted himself, staring out into the courtyard. "The snowman is gone. And the statue. The bench too."

Father had always admired Mort's good ear, and his fantastic memory, which had helped him to speak German like an Austrian in no time. Although Mort had been trained to observe and note details, he never observed himself. Never sorted anything out until it was too late.

I listened and didn't say a word. Actually I could have performed an Austrian slapping stomping monster dance and he would have gone on with his story.

"Herb made out it had all been my fault. I hadn't written to her. She thought I was through with her and threw herself at him. He never liked girls who have been with anyone else. He

felt sorry for her. Herb drank a lot of beer. And he got more and
more disgusted with everything. Talked about being a Jew and
what it was like to come back to Germany. And I wanted him to
feel better. Told him I had a bit of black blood on my great grandmother's side. Reminded him of how Negros have been treated
and how they're still treated, kept apart from the white soldiers."

Mort got up and walked back and forth, back and forth. He
held his head high, slender, long legs, moving fast, pacing to the
stairs, to the window, to the stairs, as if he couldn't get away
and wanted to escape. "Before Christmas she sends me a letter
and says she's going to have a child. How should I have known
it was really mine? She told Kaufman she wanted to have that
child, wanted it to be mine. Her pop had been quite a Nazi. Herb
took it the wrong way. He thought she didn't want it to be his
child because he is a Jew. So he did everyone a big favor; told
her I have black blood. Knowing him, I think he actually meant
well. He gave her money. She went to a dirty doctor, got rid of
the child and almost died. That's when I went to Germany, at
Christmas, to get straightened out. I found her in the hospital.
She yelled at me that Kaufman was the better man. He at least
told her he was a Jew. I had never said a word about being a
black."

For a minute neither of us knew what to say. And I saw Mort
caught up in a never ending carnival: black man with the white
face running away from the unmasking. My love for him at this
moment was fierce and brief as unexpected pain. "Don't worry,"
I quickly said. "You know Hanna Roth? She might be my great
aunt and I might have dwarf blood."

He laughed. "You a dwarf?"

"It means I might give birth to one." I cradled my dog and
took on the guise of a young mother of a Negro dwarf, facing a
guilt-ridden, and reluctant Ami father. "Anyway, I'd never get
rid of my baby."

"I wouldn't ever want you to," he said.

I, the baby-hater, who had lived in dread of little doll-like
infant sisters and brothers, stood at the window cradling my old
dog, heart aching for the mothering of my unborn dynasty: black,
whites, Hebrew, dwarf, giant, hunchbacks or whatever. Everytime I blinked my eyes someone was murdered, made love, or

was born. In between blinks, I could imagine men everywhere talking confidingly and confessing and lying to women who are either innocent or corrupt enough to be trusted. I tried not to blink. And Mort went on and on about the German girl like a soloist, in a chorus of confessions as unending as the twitter of sparrows. It was soothing, like coffeehouse music. I understood how my mother had felt years ago. And in the end, I gave way to an enormous yawn.

He lit a cigarette. "I just wanted you to know my side of the story."

"Lieutenant Kaufman never told me his," I said.

He was taken aback. For a moment we did not speak, then he said he had some good news. "My" Rudolf Hess was going to live. The Russians wanted him dead, but a document in the hands of Rudolf's lawyer would do the trick.

And the moment Mort assured me Rudolf Hess would live, my idol, my Hess faded into memory of make-believe and died. Mort went on and on about the copy of a document that would save the Fuehrer's deputy. He said something about the pact Russia had made with Germany. Stalin had refused to accept a peace treaty with Britain because they would not promise him the control of the Baltic states. Adolf was willing to make a deal, so Joe Stalin had signed a treaty with him instead. Hess had nothing to do with any of that. Mort said, he found history fascinating, and would like to study languages and history when he got back home. He talked of the life he and I might have had together as students at an American University. "Of course, I'm no Prince." He clicked his heels and kissed my hand. I was not in the mood to be teased about Arnold.

He wanted to take me into his arms. And I simply said, "So long!" Afterwards I wished I had said Auf Wiedersehen.

# TWENTY-FOUR

# Hide and Seek

I HAD OFTEN ALLOWED MYSELF to steep in dreaminess, but fortunately the old "see all, hear all, say nothing" little me, was never far away and kept watching, waiting like an actor in the wing. Laundry day was a come back. I made my way down to the steaming and scrubbing. The realm of Frau Boschke, where grime and stains of any kind were examined, interpreted and dealt with dispassionately was about to reach a climax of goriness.

At seven o'clock in the morning Frau Boschke had the brick stove going and poured American soap powder into the big copper tub. I settled down on a pile of dirty sheets, sneezed and almost spilled my precious American cocoa.

Linen was simmering to a boil. Frau Boschke slosh, slosh, sloshed it around the kettle with a wooden slab and leaned into thick steam, because it was American, perfumed, good for the complexion. I missed the delicious odor of old pasty Smear-Soap.

"The Lieutenant Curly-head has gone back to Germany," she said with a crafty smile. "Did he give you that ring?"

"Ring?" I said. "No."

"Well, I happened to be picking up coffee cups when he was talking to that good looking German of yours. And he said he was serious about you and wanted to give you a ring. You had been serious about him. There had been a misunderstanding during Carnival . . . Misunderstanding! I felt like throwing a coffee cup at him. He could have had you and Tony shot . . ."

"What did the German say?" I asked.

"That you were very young. The lieutenant said so was he, but he wanted to get engaged.

"How about the German? What did he say?"

"He told him to go and speak to your father first. And the Ami laughed and said he didn't want to get engaged to Father Meinert. He had been trying to see you and he would be going back to Germany the next day. The German said he would try and find out where you were spending your time. I guess he never did and you never got your ring. And a girl should get rings," she added wistfully.

"Is the prince still in Vienna?" I asked.

"I would say so. Prince or no prince, he's got a nerve. I had to have a word with that bossy German the other day. Prince or no prince, who's he to tell my Tony what's right and what's wrong? I told him to leave my Tony to me. I know how to handle Tony. Wouldn't have my little Tony go after some of *that* stuff. Not for the *narrische* crazy colonel, or anyone else. Enough to make you gag."

"What's Tony been after now?" I asked.

"Lampshades," she said. "From Dachau concentration camp. Disgusting. Would you believe it. The camp commander and his Frau, the Kochs started that craze, Tony says. Anyone with a tattoo was slaughtered. Dragons, rose buds, pictures, that's what they liked best. Used to skin dead people like rabbits. Tony says Frau Koch had a lampshade with Hansl and Gretel on it. That witch."

Cocoa gurgled up my throat. I had a coughing fit.

Frau Boschke pulled pillow slips out from under me, stirred them into the tub. "*Ja, ja.* It's all come out in the wash."

"The Nüremberg Trial?"

"No need for that. The Kochs are already roasting in hell. I say they deserved all they got. Tony says that Koch woman went nabbing newborns from their natural mothers, making out they were hers. There she was fifty if she was a day. Would you believe it! Super wench. Himmler was wild about that idea, Tony says. Until he found out they'd fooled him. He packed them off to concentration camps. That was the end of the Kochs." She picked up a stained table cloth, contemplated it, gave it the treatment on the scrubbing board. Took a good look and that was that. All gone.

"How does Tony know so much? Could it be that someone made it all up?"

"It's a fact. My little fellow, he reads everything he can get a hold of. Remembers it word by word. Like you."

"And he's looking for lampshades?"

"It's that crazy, *narrische* colonel. I says to Tony. God preserve us. No way are you going around looking for something that'll spook you forever. No more Boschke Madl for you if you set foot in the house with that stuff."

"But you did find old Nazi uniforms, Hitler pictures and swastika pins and some of my stuff for him?"

"Just a few little things. Most of it he bought from a dealer. No harm done. Why not let Tony make the colonel happy? Colonel Fredrics is very rich. Director of the biggest advertising firm. He says, 'Tony, you can certainly learn from Adolf Hitler. There never was any better salesman in the world. Put his method to work and you can sell anything.' " She looked up from the scrubbing board and cackled. "He pays well, but there are some things I won't put up with. I says to Tony: either, or. No buts. Lampshades or Boschke *Madl*."

Eli returned. He said he had missed me and missed poor old dusty broken down Vienna. I took him to the little palace, but he was not interested in my riding. Horses, he said, made his eyes itch. The court doctor was visiting the Rittmeister.

"Remember the drawing my grandmother sold to Frank for two hens?" I finally asked. "She really wanted it back. Did you find out where it is? I would like to have it."

The doctor had written down the name of a gallery. They were springing up all over the place. A lot of art was for sale. Eli became interested, because so much had been stolen from his father's house. He said he had learned a lot about art from his father and would like to buy paintings as an investment. And he wanted to go to the gallery at once, but the court doctor could not remember the name. It was English and it was on the tip of his tongue. Eli decided to go to his villa and see what paintings and furniture were left. The piano was still there, most everything else had vanished. Else Schmiedler showed him around. A jolly girl, he discovered, who loved to play tennis, his favorite game. He told me we would soon all play together. He would be my teacher, and I would learn very fast. We'd play doubles.

"With Arnold?"

"Anyone," Eli said.

"Was Arnold over there?"

"He travels you know. He'll appear one of these days."

"Have you looked for him at the yellow villa?"

"Paul never likes the idea of looking for anyone. It's not a good idea."

"I don't think I'd like Paul."

Eli and I went to little theaters with my parents. I was bored with the Viennese skits, political inuendos about the occupation forces. Satire was not for me. And when I said to Eli, "I wonder what Arnold would think of this," he smiled, did his eyelash batting, blinking, big-little-poor-little-rich Eli bit. And somehow there was always Paul this and Paul that. As if the invisible Paul could take the place of Arnold.

I stayed behind curtains and used spy mirrors when I watched Else play tennis with the colonel early in the morning. She flitted around the court in a short pink tennis dress, screeching when she missed a ball, and laughing like crazy when he could not return balls she served with murderous smacks that resounded like pistol shots. She turned the game into wild combat. He was such a good loser, I could tell she was not the first girl he had allowed to get the better of him. Perhaps he let her win just to hear her scream: "Capitulate, America!" A man rarely capitulates to just one woman. It's a most insulting habit.

One day Else appeared in the garden wearing that old straw hat. A hundred years seemed to have passed since I had thrown the unlucky hat out of the window and Mort had jumped up in the jeep and caught it. I could imagine Else going into his room and taking the hat. She was used to taking anything she wanted.

She was playing "diabolo" in the garden, like a child, throwing her spool way up to the top of the trees. She had to tilt her head back, to catch it on the string fastened between the two sticks and the wind made off with the hat. Her dog gave chase. "Bring it!" she yelled. The dog shook the hat like a rat, then ripped it apart. I heard her laugh. Then she threw the wooden spool up very high and running to catch it she stepped on bits of straw, flowers, fruit; her silver sandals trampling on all the old salon Roth magic and bad luck.

The silver sandals infuriated me. My feet had grown bigger than Mother's. My shoes, Father's autumn surprise, shoes I once kissed with delight, had turned into worn-out clodhoppers, country bumpkin Meinert style. I was shabby. Never clean enough, perfect enough. I went to look for Frau Schwester. We didn't have much hot water, but nurse was always on my side and ever willing to heat water. She was washing my hair in the kitchen sink when an English soldier arrived to deliver a parcel from my Father's sisters, the English aunties.

Through the noisy tempest of the dryer, which we call Foehn after the warm south wind, I heard the soldier talking to Mother about nothing but the weather in England and the weather in Vienna, a non-fraternizing topic. By the time my hair was dry the soldier had finished the discussion of possible rain and had left.

He was right, it poured. Around noon a hot sun shone and sweet vapor rose from blooming lilac and jasmine bushes. Eli came. "Didn't you want a horse drawing? I called the court doctor and have the address. I want to go to galleries. I might even come across some of our stolen paintings. It's a perfect afternoon. I'll buy you a picture." It was French month. Russian month would have raised objections.

A fragrant south wind rumpled puffy clouds. I wore a new dress my aunts had sent. The full gathered skirt patterned with pale English flowers danced around my thin legs and made me feel like the girl from Shakespear's *Tempest:* a playful confused sheltered daughter hopelessly willing to be loved. And saved in the end by magic of some higher paternal power.

The sun created deep shadows in narrow streets of the first district. Birds sang on trees in ancient courtyards, perching on fountain figures, nesting on ruins. Eli talked about going to Switzerland and bringing back his car. "Paul won't walk if he can drive."

Street signs were missing. We got lost. Then the wind behind us almost swept us into a little square. There was the little gallery. An old sign said *Fleischhauerei-Selcher,* meat and sausage butcher. Art was available, meat was not. The window displayed unframed pen drawings. Dancing skeletons, costumed in cloaks, fancy shoes, boots, and Salon Roth spring hats decorated with flowers, bows, ribbons, feathers. As if the young men and women who had been slaughtered and skinned for Frau Koch were celebrating a ghostly carnival.

"Weird," Eli said and tried the door. It was locked. I rang the bell. "What's that on your arm?" he asked.

I had tattoed myself with an ink rose and forgot all about it. And I felt weird, both disgusting and disgusted, knowing about the concentration camp lampshades and what the Kochs had done. I wiped it off with spit staining my handkerchief. He watched and said: "Pfui." And I turned back into the unhygenic girl-child in leather pants that couldn't be washed, confronted by Frau Schwester, Eli's ever watchful nurse. Now a rejuvenated Frau Schwester, ready to leave the Meinert-Hof, stop washing my hair and scrubbing my back, and move into town to care for her boy, Eli.

"No one here. We can try later," I said.

We walked back to the Ringstrasse, hand in hand. A perfect day for sauntering arm in arm, hip to hip through the Stadtpark. Musicians on the terrace of Café Huebner played the "Spring Flower Waltz." We stopped and kissed under the trees and new leaves swooshed like silk skirts. Without Arnold I loved Eli less and wanted to kiss him more.

"Always wandering around the streets. Your father is so old fashioned. Doesn't even want me to take you dancing." Eli's hands danced over me. "Let's go and be cozy in my apartment. I want to be alone with you. This is uncomfortable. Too much Viennese wind and fresh air; that's not for Paul."

I ran away. Linden blossoms had fallen and shimmered like algae on the damp path. I turned and dipped into bushes behind the white arch at the Johann Strauss statue. Eli following slowly, hands in pockets, toeing in a little: a young dandy, foreign, untouched by war. I was proud to see girls and women on park chairs stare, drinking in the vanilla ice cream-colored vested suit, soft wool, shiny new shoes, a face like an actor. He made dancing skeletons, ruined houses and people, recede like a landscape in a film when the camera is trained on a star.

I had run away, as a young child and hidden in the big house whenever the water castle-Eli allure became too much. And he had always taken his time looking for me. I got bored and chirped to allow him to find me. Pouncing was forbidden in case he had an asthma attack.

Nothing had really changed, we still played our old game of hide and seek. Eli no longer had asthma attacks, but I still had to be careful. Talking to him about anything putrid or bad, would be like splashing him with mud. He might just leave Vienna, leave me. Mort and Arnold had gone from my life. And Grandmama had left a world of Buchenwald lampshades where children were lured and stolen, somehow linked with a grotesque artist, gardener, S.S. Fritz Janicek who had lured me with tales of horror and painted the blood of martyrs, and a huge, green Christ image bleeding on the cross in the family chapel orange red. And had once kissed a yellow rose with his tongue.

I was influenced by Arnold's: you see it, you're part of it, you know it and you are an accomplice. Sometimes I turned myself into a staunch guilty German Christian Arnold, as if thinking his thoughts, would bring him back.

"Reyna. where are you! What a child you are!" Eli called.

Women on park chairs watched Eli looking behind trees and had their fun too. "This way, young man, see. Down there towards the Old Danube. That's where she ran." They tittered. "You could just eat him up."

While Eli looked for me at the banks of the old Danube, I thought of the piano playing, smiling Mort, and composed a letter to him in my head. Before I could decide whether I should end it with love, a man in a wild hurry, turned, stumble-scrambled into my bushes and smack into me.

"Pardon," he doffed his black beret and with it a black wig.

He was bald, bearded, and wore a black leather coat although it was warm. "I'm hiding," I said.

"So am I," he said. He peeled off his coat as if he were playing this scene in a circus. Under it he wore a clownish, baggy, head-waiter's uniform that didn't go with the beard. The frock coat had seen better days. The shirt was frayed. I wouldn't have been surprised had he stripped it off and emerged in yet another costume. "Here they come," he whispered. "Not a sound!"

Two elderly men passed by walking arm in arm. Porky faces, sunglasses, same bowler hats and yellow chamois leather gloves. Determined twins. Off to a spring wedding, or funeral.

The bearded man was watching them. I was watching him

and admired the mephisto profile, especially the devilish eyebrows. "Do you owe them money?" I whispered.

He turned. Caught me staring at him. Grabbed my face with
both hands like a bowl and slurped my mouth into his. I tasted
American chewing gum and the beard scratched. The twin
brothers had stopped at the statue and looked all around. He
kept me in a tight grip. They walked on and I was released so
suddenly I staggered back.

"Pardon," he scraped his feet and this gesture was an odd
combination of old Vienna bowing and scraping and wiping shoes
after having stepped into dirt. "This is always the best way to
keep a pretty fraulein quiet and hide one's face. *Nicht wahr?*"

"Who are those two men?" I asked.

"One of them is a police informer from way back. The other
one comes along, and you can't tell them apart."

"Who are you?" I asked. "Are you Schmiedler?"

He trampled through bushes and I could smell crushed jasmine blossoms, fragrance of solitary old garden games. Make
believe hide and seek—before I knew Eli when I had caught unicorns with wings, furry pouncers that asked to be captured and
tied up with yo-yo string. I gave chase.

Eli caught me by the shoulders. I was talking too fast. He
blinked those long eyelashes. "Schmiedler. Hungarian groom.
Headwaiter, false beard, wig. Is that a fact? Kissing you. That
just isn't done. Where is that fellow?" he said in a high German
Arnold voice. Then he lost interest in me and my Schmiedler
fantasy and turned to the white arch behind Johann Strauss the
fiddler and studied the melange of female and male nude figures
swirling and diping in thick sweet creamy white marble. "See
the girl at the bottom? The one with the lovely breasts? She
reminds me of someone."

He wasn't thinking of me. Apples hadn't helped. And a doctor's daughter in my class had said sexuality made breasts. It
also made babies. I had to think of poor Dilly.

"Who does she remind you of?" I asked.

He closed my mouth with a kiss. (Best way to keep me quiet
and hide his face.) Music on the terrace of Café Huebner was
playing a Strauss polka. The building was under repair. The terrace crowded. Spring hats swayed to the music, ribbons danced.
And I was thinking of skeletons in hats kicking up bony legs.

"Why are you always running away," he asked. "Paul never liked skittery girls."

"When did you acquire Paul?" I asked.

A Eugene Romberg sigh. "Making love to Karin. Remember *Mutti's* Swedish masseuse? She went to Switzerland to be with *Vati*. Karin calls me Paul. It was Paul's fault that Vati left Switzerland and went back to Salzburg and never came back. I just didn't want to say all this in front of Arnold."

"How could it be," I said. "I saw your father during the war. He was dressed up as an honorary S.S. Told me he was helping to finance Hitler's Russia campaign. Sending the Nazi armies to doomsday for us."

"He was in league with Schmiedler," Eli said and hung his head. "Anyway, that's what Karin says. My father blamed Karin for seducing me. He stuck me into boarding school. Then he went back to Austira. He knew it was dangerous. He never came back, it was Paul's fault."

After the last ball at the water castle, Fasching before Hitler, Eugene Romberg and I had come across Karin as a pink ballerina asleep in the arms of a man in sailor costume. He had said: "I delight in her."

"What happened to Karin?"

"She married my Swiss doctor. Teaches gymnastics to patients who are fat. She had a baby boy and named him Eli."

"Not Paul." I said.

"Not Paul. He is a faithless one."

"I want you to be Eli," I said. "Not Paul."

"Paul is full of lust," Eli said. "A great lover."

Then we both laughed. The way we used to when we had just invented a new version of hide and seek behind Frau Schwester's back.

I think of Eli in Vienna that spring and it is like flipping pages of an old children's book and coming across a glossy picture that makes one remember an entire story. I see Eli in front of the gallery flushed as if he were facing a furnace. I always loved Eli best when he really wanted something. That day he wanted the drawing of the nude and he wanted me.

We had come back to the gallery. The window had been rearranged; dancing skeletons pushed back to make room for a pen drawing of a plump, half-naked beauty. Long hair rippling over her shoulders and bare breasts, stockings wrinkled around ankles tinted with sepia ink; so was the belly button, pouting lips and a thicket of curly pubic hair. Caressing black ink lines shaped the full, soft breasts, whisked around niples in a delirium, and whispered over the tell-tale mound of a belly, to a cream puff of a buttock. "Your mother!" he said at once.

"1886?" I pointed at the date.

Then he saw the Antonini signature. "My great-grandfather the sculptor. Marvelous. I'll buy this. Vati was quite a collector. He taught me a lot. This is great. So free. Really quite modern." And his hands absent-mindedly caressed my shoulders, passing over my breasts while he raved about the simplicity of black line drawings and those touches of sepia, that rust color. "The stockings . . . She looks as if she hadn't time to undress." He fiddled with the top buttons on my prim dress. "And pregnant, too. Must have been quite outrageous in those days. I wonder who she was?"

"Your great-grandmother," I said. "Frau Traude's mother. Christina von Kortnai. My ancestor too. She refused to marry Antonini, left him and he sent that awful doll."

"That much for the secret birth. He had to know there was going to be a child. I guess he was more interested in women than offsprings. One can't blame him." Eli said. Then he rang and rang again. His eyes wide open, breathing through his mouth. "My father would want this painting." Someone had been here to rearrange the display. Perhaps the owner had gone to sleep. Eli banged on the door. His face glowed and his dark eyes sparkled. He stared at the picture, pressed himself against me. His warm skin gave off a fragrance, reminding me of his perfumed father.

I didn't lose my head at once. At first I had to admire our hazy reflection on the window glass and felt proud of my sexuality. And an ever watchful Meinert in me kept a daily count of kisses. I had reached sixty-six when I became aware of a skeleton in the hat of a cavalier adorned with a swooping ostrich feather, thighbones raised in a ghostly polka: eyes fierce as a spurned lover's; dead eyes watching me kiss and count. If I told Eli that someone in the shop was peeking through those eyes, he wouldn't believe it.

Those were not the only eyes watching. Eli and I had attracted attention of neighborhood cronies gosipping at the corner. And they got the impression we were artists because of all the kissing in the street, and a large folio type briefcase Eli had brought along for the horse drawing. One of the women came over and told us that artists brought their stuff here after dark. Eli said he had come to buy, not to sell. She bleated like a goat. Such ugly pictures! Not for the young Fraulein, she hoped . . . The owner should be glad to get some business. No, she hadn't seen him. He had a workshop somewhere in the suburbs. She pointed to a small handwritten card on the door: Vienna Wood Art and Craft Association.

I knew that handwriting. Fine letters that leaned back as though they had toppled. My graphology book had taught me to recognize the hand of a deceiver. Had I not studied so many handwritings to perfect my own, I certainly would have remembered who that deceiver was.

Eli said he knew that place. "It's the cobbler's hut, just behind my house and up the hill. We'll go there." He drew me away from the women, turned the corner and pulled me into a doorway, where we kissed and caressed me as if he had to quickly reshape my angular body into ancestral erotica. We moved slowly from doorway to doorway towards the ring. I stopped counting kisses. We moved as though we were chained together. I saw nothing and heard nothing. We must have crossed at the opera among carts and wheel barrows of construction. Afterwards I did remember the caretaker, in a black shawl, dark circles under her eyes, dark lips, inside her glass cubicle knitting something black, saying "Good evening," on a sunny afternoon. She was counting stitches in a foreign language. We ran past her up the stairs. Eli let me into the apartment Father had furnished for Resi and we kissed our way towards her bedroom. He whispered something about my being the only reparation he wanted. "You were my first friend. The first girl. We're not living in the Middle Ages. And even my great grandmother . . . My mother was your father's girl before he married and he never gave her up."

Father never gave anyone up. I recognized rustic benches, a carved umbrella stand from the Meinert-Hof. Across the hall someone was clapping a rhythm and shouting? "Releve and hop, hop, leap. Turn, turn and again, repeat pattern, again, again."

That frosted glass panel on the living room door was patterned with clear roses. Through these rambling peepholes I had once seen Bertl coming out of Resi's bedroom. Everything we were doing, everything we felt, had happened here before and the outline of a female figure reclining on a sofa was vague as unwanted memory.

"Romberg, is that you?"

"*Bother,*" Eli said. "Else Schmiedler has parked herself here."

A dancing master was chanting: "Hop, hop, leap, turn, turn, repeat pattern."

I turned around and ran down the stairs. Eli followed me past a coffeehouse where couples sat watching work going on at the ruined opera. Wind was throwing dust into my eyes. All the way home Eli tried to tell me it was really business. Else was Colonel Fredrick's Nazi poster girl. She could get American coffee and such. Eli paid her in foreign money. She liked to play tennis and it was his favorite game. And he wanted me to come and play too. We'd all play together . . . He talked too fast.

"We'll go and find the art and craft studio and get those drawings!" he said.

What else could we do together now?

# TWENTY-FIVE

# *Moonrise*

ON TOP OF THE HILL Eli and I had a perfect view of the water castle and the Meinert-Hof, where gardens extended in a blue-green haze to distant vinyards, cemetery hill, the white speck on the fringe of the Vienna woods: Grandmother's tomb.

Women and old people were weeding in the garden plots. An elderly couple working side by side in an alotment garden looked up and greeted Eli and me. "What a beautiful pair!" she said as we passed by. The sun was going down as this day gathered momentum.

Eli was talking about the music festival in Salzburg. His mother would be singing. My family might be on our mountain farm in August and he could come and fetch me in his car. "Did you know that my father left money for you, Reyna? You have Swiss francs. And you can go to school in England. Next fall I'll be going to college in Cambrige, England. I asked your father whether you could go to a boarding school somewhere nearby. After all you have two aunts living in England. We could even get married one day," Eli said. "Your father wouldn't mind."

I thought with sadness of the picture Eli and I made standing there side by side like two young actors. No confusion, my grandmother had once told me. Playmates becoming friends and lovers. Nothing better. It reeked of compost. Wasps came and then left us. A white cat sat on a fence post licking it's paws. And on a porch someone was piping the Magic Flute theme. Grandmama had taken me to see the Opera at the beginning of the war: isn't it like a caress, that serene flute? can't you hear magic faith in love?

In a garden brown hens and yellow chicks all luxuriantly feathery, bustled and clacked around one small cockerel. There were the usual cock-a-doodle-doos and egg-boasting cackles. My own destiny could have been as predictable as life in a chicken coup.

England I guessed had been discussed with Father down there in the catacombs over the best Meinert wines. A good safe girl's school. The flutist stopped, and then started again accompanied now by hammering from the cobbler's hut. "TU FELIX AUSTRIA NUBE." The old Hapsburg slogan. You happy Austria marry. Did my father have plans to bring the Meinert empire and Romberg fortunes together? How about unhappy Austria taken over by the Russians? Impossible, everyone was saying. Now that the American wives and families were arriving to join husbands. General Clark's lady had moved into the house not far from us. All the same, Father, the chess master, could be thinking ahead to consider every possibility: should the worst happen and the Russians took over in Austria, Eli as a son-in-law could take all of us to Switzerland.

Father, the chess master, would ponder to achieve several advantages. And he would give Eli enough time alone with me; plenty of room for making the wrong move; it had simply happened too soon.

The wind flipped loose placards on a board wall which enclosed the back of the cobbler's hut. Peeling them off would have been a lesson in history. The Romberg baby milk, twins holding bottles; an old Meinert beer poster of a pretty waitress with foaming mugs, had been covered over by a Hitler maiden poster: a little flaxen-haired girl marching with a flag. Else had been the model. A white sign pasted at the top of the billboard said: *Kunstgewerbe*. Vienna Woods Art and Crafts Association. The arrow pointed at the cobbler's hut.

I had seen the dark shape of the cobbler at the window. Something held me back. "Wait!" I said too late. Eli had already knocked and entered. I followed.

"Good day," said the old cobbler and kept hammering the heel of a glossy black boot. He had a Kaiser beard. Loden cloak and a

green hat hung on a hook. I was looking at a Ferdl Meinert double.

"Can't get that kind of good leather anymore!"

Unmistakably the voice of Fritz Janicek. Teacher of art history and languages, who always spoke slowly as though he were
translating, trying to make himself clear to unwilling pupils.

He had been thin. Now, during a time of starvation he had
become stout. Nor was he as tall as Father, but from a distance
the Kaiser whiskers, leather breeches and loden, limping just a
little, he could fool most anyone.

"And here we have the Meinert daughter. Always had a way
of seeking me out." He could not help ogling a spectacular youth
like Eli: shiny hair, the marvelous face, fine clothes. "*Jawohl,*
young man. I used to work for a certain Herr von Meinert. Men-
ial work. Although I am an artist and teacher. Nothing has
changed. I am again considered unfit to teach the young. Same
thing all over again. I am working with my hands. Gravedigger,
mason, cobbler. But there is also art." He kept pounding, pounding at the boot made for marching, strutting, trampling for Reich
and Fuehrer. "How can I serve?"

Eli explained. Fritz watched him so intently his lips moved
with Eli's. "Drawings? An interest in art, then . . . Fine, fine.
*Sehr schoen.* Beautiful! We don't have much else in Vienna, but
we have art. *Jawohl.*" He turned away, picked up a nail. A mirror on his work table reflected the sharp pointed nose and the
old watchful Janicek half-smile that didn't go with Ferdl Meinert whiskers. With that wrong smile, the mirror caught a branch
of a potted rose tree.

Not a leaf not a bud. It was dead, dry thorny and loaded with
doll's heads. Such strange fruit: china heads of old dolls adorned
those spikey twigs. The flute played the same Mozart melody
over and over again. I was confronted by solemn child-faced dolls
a crack here and there, glass eyes staring, closed, or missing.
Two of them were bald as French girls shaved for having consorted with Germans. The others had wigs of women's hair, flaxen,
brown, or black, wavy or old time corkscrew curls, and braids:
red-gold matted braids made from the cuttings of Christina von
Kortnai's famous hair. I was confronted with the head of Puppe—
master portrait of a pouting enchantress—the heirloom of con-
tempt.

Draft from the open door shook the dry branches and set a delicate mechanism in motion and the violet blue glass eyes moved slowly from side to side, matted hair stirred. The cobbler's hammer pounded.

"Charming old dolls," said the art collector, Nazi professor, honorary S.S., head of National Socialist Art Recovery unit. "Most of them were buried in a zinc coffin in a graveyard. Not even graves were sacred to the Bolshevic Russians. Young heros, my former students, had sought sanctuary among the graves. Bolshevic savages threw hand granades at them and uprooted this lovely rose tree. I'm an artist, I repair, I salvage, I create."

Fritz Janicek, the creator of mazes had salvaged himself in the costume of a Meinert man. Had he secretly accosted Mother with this parody, driving her to seek protection in the company of Sir Hugh? Creator and part of his creation: dolls heads on the dead rose tree, and the hammer banging down on the S.S. boot. I saw him caught in the colossal maze of brutal self-deceptions, past, present and still to come.

"And then, imagine, thieves breaking into my shed and making off with the coffin. What would anyone want with a coffin full of doll's bodies? but I guess, nowadays anything is in demand."

I grabbed Puppe's head off the tree stuffed it into my shoulder bag and walked out.

"My respects to your gracious Mama!" Fritz shouted.

And as soon as I was outside I knew I should not have done this. Not in front of Eli. He came after me. "*Du*, Reyna. You were acting like a Nazi. How could you just snatch away that doll's head."

I mumbled something about Puppe, my mother. Heirloom, our mutual ancestor, Christina, his grandfather Antonini who had created Puppe with the help of a toymaker.

"Just an excuse to take something that isn't yours. Old dolls all look alike. He is a collector. I collect kites, stamps. My father collected paintings. I can understand this. The man obviously respects your family. He even dresses like your father and has the same beard. Give it to me," he said. "I'll put it back. Or I'll ask him whether I can buy it if you want it so much."

"He stole Mother's doll and I'm keeping the head."

"What would you do with it?"

Smash it or have it repaired? For a second I didn't know what to say. "Have it put onto a body and give it to Hanna Roth."

"Ridiculous! Now he'll never let me have the drawing!"

It was just one drawing now. The nude. An angry stamp and kite collector Eli who had to have what he wanted or else he'd stop breathing, went storming back into the hut.

The flutist had stopped practicing. Somewhere in the distance I heard the one-two, one-two, eins-zwei-eins. The health doctor and his followers trotted across the avenue. I walked around the back of the hut. Windows were covered with heavy wartime black-out curtains. One of them moved. We believe in fresh air in Vienna and windows are often left open.

Tools, dyes, sewing machines, paint brushes were neatly arranged on long work tables. Fritz Janicek's easel stood near the back window displaying his old, purple self-portrait. The workers had left. Hitler posters lay in piles beside the printing press. Gray identity cards everyone in Vienna had to carry lay brazenly piled in a half-open drawer. Enameled hook-cross pins and medals of all sorts and sizes had been stacked on shelves near a kiln. Tony did not have to go far to supply the colonel. I had one leg in the window when I glimpsed the black limousine Fritz Janicek the S.S. had aryanized then parked at the gate of the Romberg villa. It sat at the back inside a yard. Swastika pennants had been removed from the hood. Wheels had vanished and the black limousine which had once swallowed up a defiant little Resi, now served as a tool shed full of rakes and shovels. All around, in this sheltered spot, Fritz Janicek yellow roses bloomed.

Eli came out of the hut carrying the framed horse drawing.

"What were you doing in there?" Eli asked. "Sometimes you are quite strange."

My shoulderbag was open and the doll's eyes designed to gleam in the half dark moved slowly and ominously from side to side.

"Here," he handed me the drawing of the horse. "A bargain. A couple of English pound notes. The frame and glass alone are worth that."

I said *herzichsten Dank*. I felt relief, but my thanks were not heartfelt. How could Eli have forgotten hiding behind the tapestry with Karin and me. "Don't you remember Fritz and his gang? He arrested your mother," I asked.

Eli grabbed my hand, held it tight and said, "Stop it."

"I think we should tell Arnold. The Americans don't understand." I said. "Fritz Janicek is dangerous."

"You are gettings things mixed up," he said in the condescending voice of Paul. "You were only six years old. This poor old fellow couldn't have done any such thing."

Understanding, forgiving, or refusing the role of refugee, victim's son. Since he met Else he had given up the role of avenger who would punish Schmiedlers. I couldn't say to Eli, it was Else who had betrayed his father, although I was quite certain she did. I could not say to him, Fritz Janicek chained your father to the back of a truck in an ice cold mine and that was murder. Eli would not want to believe any of it, and I would send him away to Switzerland, away from hateful Austria and me.

"And if that man was a Nazi, that was not unusual, was it now? How about your mother. All this talk about her. Nothing . . . Anyway, you got your horse drawing. The cobbler promised to get me that marvelous old nude."

"Why not now?" I asked.

"He has to fetch it from the gallery and he is a perfectionist; wants to have the drawings properly matted and framed for me. I'll pick it up tomorrow. I've promised to play tennis with Else anyway." He went on and on. How I would really like Else if I got to know her. She was a lot of fun and had been forced to humor the colonel to protect herself and the mother. They didn't have anything left. Their home had been destroyed. Russians agents might just nab them, send them to Siberia just because they were Schmiedler's family.

"She helped kidnap blond children from foreign countries and bring them to the Reich," I said.

"Rumors. The colonel is a strange fellow. He likes those Nazi stories about Else. Anything wild. He is the one who told me a crazy story about you and an American lieutenant. I never believed any of it."

The next day Eli found the cobbler's hut locked. He decided to wait around and play tennis. Although I had refused to join the game as a loser, I watched the tennis court in an oversized spy mirror. Following the ball, ping-pink, ping-pink, I became hypnotized, and calliope merry-go-round music started up in my head. I felt weightless, suspended, and sick with longing for my good old days: the dress-up games with Eli in the attic when we had played in front of an old cracked mirror and our fantasies had intermingled like the limbs of lovers.

Games of make believe had been replaced by games of deceit, revolving around an invisible Franz Joseph Schmiedler. Crown jewels had been sought avidly. The American army had returned the treasure to Vienna, to guard, display and show how grand Austria had been century after century. And Schmiedler, the rogue, had to be found, locked up, guarded, displayed and blamed to make us blameless.

Eli did come back to the Meinert-Hof in the evening. Time to get his car, he said at the supper table. He was going to Switzerland at once and would bring it back. He never mentioned Else, Fritz Janicek or the drawing of great aunt Christine. I didn't either. And after he left, Father declared Eli wanted the car to please me. I couldn't say a word about Else in that apartment near the opera without giving myself away.

"He bears no grudges and he gets along with everyone," Father was watching me when he said: "That's the Resi in him."

Resi, the entertainer, the typical, sweet Vienna girl, like Paul, had been a faithless one.

"Where do you think Schmiedler is hiding?" I asked Frau Boschke.

"Who cares," she said. "The Ami boys asked Frau Hanna about him just before she went back to Salzburg. She said stop looking And she's right. Good riddance. Anyway, I had a big surprise today. You know how I love blood sausage? I don't know how your busy father remembered this and got some for me. What a feast." She joined me at the open window. A spotted moon hung above the Kahlenberg, like a faded Chinese lantern left over from bygone celebrations. "Look at that early moonrise. Don't go staring at it. I'tll drive you mad. And smell those early roses. A night for lovers and lunatics. And I have eaten too much." My open bag was lying on the chair. *"Lieber Gott,* what do you have in here? Where did you find that? You didn't tear that old doll apart? Not that I'd blame you. I sometimes felt like it. All the fancy ironing, those tiny things. Such a fuss—"

I interrupted. Told her about the shoemakers hut and she kept sorting my clean clothes quite unperturbed. "Everybody has to make some money to eat. Tony says, 'souply and temand!' That little workshop comes in handy right next door. As for Herr Janicek, he's always been a little plem-plem in the head. So was his *Seelige,* the mother. It's in the family. She had a knitting machine and made skirts and sweaters for some of the finest stores in town, I knew her from the park and she wore some of the clothes she had knitted. She was clever with her hands. So is he, there's no denying that."

Furs, hung out to air, swayed on the washing line. This did not deter a pair of tiny chickadees chirr-chirring over pink candelabra of blossoms back and forth between great Aunt Christina's fur hat and their nesting hole on the chestnut tree. I watched them line their nest and wondered why they chose the old sable hat I had worn during the cellar days.

"The colonel was certainly in a state today. He had been drinking whiskey, that's why he talked to me. He said he was quite sorry the war was over. He was at his best during fighting, and isn't cut out for dealing with this mess; sheer murder . . . I asked who was murdered. He ran upstairs, locked Else into his room and bellowed 'You're under arrest. Under arrest. Troublemaker.' And asked her what Lieutenant Mort had ever done to her, exept ignore her. Then he went to sleep for a couple of hours and now they are playing tennis as good as gold."

"What did Else do to Mort?"

"Don't tell me you've forgotten that."

"Where is Mort now?"

"In Germany. And he's had a car accident."

"He's hurt?"

"Never. Look at my little Tony, how many accidents did he have until he learned to ride that big bike? The Ami boys often have accidents, they drive too fast. You can't blame Else for that. But Frau Schmiedler wants to get out of Vienna."

"Where would she go; did she tell you?"

Frau Boschke put her arm around my shoulder. This was unusual. She reeked of blood sausage and perfume. "Just away, anywhere. I have to say quite honestly if a certain person asked me to go off somewhere, anywhere at all, I'd be off in two seconds. Before the war, I was often asked to go along with families for the summer. Never wanted to leave Vienna, but now, I don't have to be asked twice. Everybody has *Reisefieber,* Tony says I

have traveling fever because he's turned me into a Wild-*Madl*.
It's true. It was the invasion. That Russ first of all. Now Tony.
No scum no suds, I always say. No Russ no Tony. I am a new
woman."

The garden hose hissed. Agnes was watering flower beds where
vegetables had been planted to feed us. We breathed in the fragrance of roses and freshly cut grass. Rita the deer had become
trusting and was lapping water at the fountain and blind Krampus followed the deer.

Frau Boschke put my sun dried blouses on hangers. "Nice
and fresh for you. Tony admired my snow white starched blouse
the very first time he spoke to me. I said to him: 'You're the
sweetest fellow. You know how to make a woman feel good about
herself! And he said to me: 'I know how to make you feel good
. . .' And he did just that, right behind that big file cabinet."

The cupola glowed and the cupid weathervane began to turn
in the evening breeze. "Something is going to happen." I said in
a Hanna Roth voice.

"I would say so. American women are arriving. Children too.
The American apartments up near the park are already full. More
cars. A lot of whiskey. Big excitement. One of the swans is sick
They keep saying 'cute, cute, beautiful' and feeding it all kinds
of American stuff. The veterinarian had to come and he is scared
of swans, and the American wives.

"Tony isn't married, is he?"

"My Tony? Go on. Never."

We heard Else shrieking with laughter at the tennis courts.
There was a finality about this. Once more I saw her chasing the
ball. Colonel Fredricks batted it down near the net.

That night, just before I went to sleep I was tracking down
Franz Joseph Schmiedler in my mind and imagined catching him,
to punish that girl who was his evil creation. A trail of suspicions
led from the man servant at the Schmiedler villa to the groom,
the stranger who had thrown Hanna into the river. My hunt
might have gone on and on. I could hear my grandmother say:
"Reyna, Reyna. Just like the hunter stalks and becomes like the
beast he hunts. I have become like HIM." She had fired her pistol, not at the ghost of her father, but evil itself. I cried for my
grandmother and for Eugene Romberg.

He had been a monarchist, too, in his own way, because he

had admired a predictable order, punctual meals. One day when Eugene Romberg, had taken Eli and me out to lunch, he made the chauffeur stop the car in the Hohemarkt, a certain square in Vienna. A small audience had gathered waiting for the clock to strike. And high up between two tall buildings on a glass encased bridge great figures of Austrian monarchs and their spouses gleaming in red and gold Kaiserly coats, and gold crowns, began to move at the stroke of noon from one building to the next. We had attracted as much admiration as the clockwork Kaisers. Eli and I—such beautiful children—the white Daimler, Resi dressed in shocking pink from head to toe smiling to those who recognized her, but Eugene Romberg had made us leave. He did not want to be late for lunch. He had spoken English that one time and Eli had to translate for me: punctuality, he had said, is the virtue of kings.

In my dream Eugene Romberg in the black S.S. uniform is reclining in a gondola. "I'm sorry I couldn't buy that little wooden shovel for you, little Reyna. You wanted it, that's why that other little girl wouldn't part with it. I will find you some just like it and buy as many as you want. By the way, why aren't you wearing the little diamond studded watch I gave you? You'll be late for meals without a watch. Put it on, but don't overwind it . . ."

Time in dreams moves like a merry-go-round and my head spins when I think of what followed that dream. I had vowed never to wind up the watch until Eugene Romberg came back, because my Countess Grandmama had vowed never to wind up her clock collection until the return of the Hapsburgs. I woke up and the full moon was shining into my room. I took the watch from my treasure box, wound it up and held it into the white light to see it sparkle. Not even an owl, or cat was heard. Frau Boschke had left two white table cloths spread out on the grass to be bleached by the moonlight, but she would never again iron them. My little watch ticked, ticked. I was happy because I had been in Venice with Uncle Eugene who wanted me to have regal punctual meals and who would give me everything I wanted. I could feel him smile my hatred and fury away. I held the watch to my ear and like the heart of a killer or a lover it tick-tick-ticked me towards the end of the hunt, but I didn't know it.

# TWENTY-SIX

# *Love as an Epitaph*

You're only surprised once, repetition turns anything into slapstick, even love and especially murder. I had seen this happen before: lights at the water castle coming on from cellar to attic and a second later they all went out. Mort had said, turning on all those darned lights at once they'd blown a fuse—typical.

Only this time lights went out and the big house remained wartime dark. The moon and searchlights, with their own power source, shone down and turned the back of the great house into a stage. White beams severed from the dark a head of a love-Goddess, the hand of Apollo, and topped the wings of Icarus.

In this light I then saw how statues had been placed exactly the same measured distance apart, just like trees, flower beds, pagodas, benches, and the walks enclosed by the maze of hedges were all part a of a symmetrical pattern. Fritz Janicek, in his days as our gardener had been frustrated because the Meinert Hof woodland and orchard overgrown with wild flowers, wild strawberries and raspberries could not be tamed into the Meinert park he had wished to create as the proper setting for Mama. He had achieved a formal rose garden in front of the house. And there he had lectured to a five-year-old me on the beauty of symmetry, order. Hitler Germany, soon Hitler Austria, the ideal order in the world as in gardens. Symmetry then, required ruthless cutting down.

In the Romberg garden every flower and blade of grass had

been controlled to grow in it's proper place and never too much. Walks enclosed by those high, squared-off hedges lead to nude statues, pagodas and concealed seats, one of them with a marble chess table perfect for hiding, especially this evening.

Jeeps came racing along. Some parked in front and American soldiers climbed right over the railings. The back gate stood wide open; barbed wire had been removed. Three jeeps and a huge, red car had left deep tire marks on the moist soft grass. A mushroom patch of white M.P. helmets clustered below the French window of Eugene Romberg's secret room. The heavy curtains had been raised, windows opened; flashlights and candles flitted around in the dark.

To me it could mean only one thing: they had finally done it. Schmiedler had been trapped. I just had to see it happen: Schmiedler revealed, spotlights carving him out of the dark as judgment isolates shadowy crime and mutilates disguise, of a scraping liveried servant, hooded assailant, or bearded headwaiter who kisses girls to hide his face.

I did not feel like a trespasser. Every one else was an intruder and I remained Eugene Romberg's ever welcome guest. I sought him out as the moment of justice arrived, felt the presence of the most generous of all men at his marble chess table in the dark seclusion of his chess pagoda, which hid me and also gave me a box seat view of Ami boys climbing in and out French windows of that once forbidden room.

"Stand back! Stand back!" The voice of an American woman.

"Hey, careful, you better not throw that!" the colonel warned and was ignored. A large object came flying out, grazed my shoulder: a Hitler bust smashing against a post.

They had cornered Schmiedler in the dark house, and he had gone mad. The gramophone started to play the Hitler waltz. Candles stuck into empty bottles flickered. A strident woman in a tight, red skirt and fluffy white blouse strutted with piratical splendor over shredded swastika flags, torn Hitler posters, piles of old uniforms.

The colonel was dancing attendance on her with a glass. "Here. That's enough. You'll hurt yourself, baby. Have your drink. You don't like the collection, we get rid of it. Let the men do the job."

She drank, handed the colonel her empty glass; turned to the

Salon Roth Hitler picture. Two soldiers followed with candles and stood by. Light danced over Hitler as an Austrian peasant, wearing a green hat Hanna Roth had once called disastrous. The colonel's wife studied the Fuehrer breathing so hard her bosom heaved the frills on her blouse. Then she reached up with both arms, yanked the picture down and let it crash.

The colonel laughed. And the men in the room couldn't help laughing as she trampled on a Fuehrer dressed as an Austrian country man, and ground her high heels on glass splinters, tearing the picture. She revived for them wild days of victory and invasions, shooting chandeliers, old paintings and anything resembling Mussi and Adolf. Good old crazy times, bashing everything to pieces, better really, then looting or buying with cigarettes and chocolate and stockings.

Someone wound up the phonograph and the voice of the little nightingale of Vienna singing Hitler's favorite waltz drifted out into the moonlit night. This time Colonel Fredricks wasn't dancing, but on his knees in front of the tile stove to feed the flames with the torn up Hitler picture and other papers from his collection: photographs, letters. I could imagine the Fuehrer kissing Mother's hand going puff, up in flames. Burned paper flew up the chimney and out: fire birds, then paper ash bats circled down onto the trees.

During the war when I had hidden here in the back garden at dawn and spied on men dressed up in Resi's gowns, I had seen men sick of having to be men. Consul Hillmar at Resi's piano in a bright floral dress, had thumped out this same *Merry Widow Waltz* with impressive brutality.

And impressively brutal, sick of being a woman, was the colonel's wife in there confronting the symbols of male mischief, which she smashed and tore and shattered in a rite of pure female exorcism. She leaned out of the window. "Make the hole deep. Deep!"

Shovels clanged. The men dug a hole in the soft soil of an empty flower bed. Then Schmiedler—like the men who had once caroused here—had to be dead. The Ami boys were burying him in a hurry. Uniform coats came flying out. S.S. caps with the death head emblem to be buried in the pit. The colonel's wife ordered the men around like slaves, and they thrust spades down with all their power working as enchanted gravediggers.

The music came to a sudden halt. The colonel's voice clamored: "No, baby, not that. Worth a lot of money that recording." Not a hundred Mort songs of bad babes, sweet babes, cruel babes or loving babes could have stopped her from throwing the phonograph crash, at a marble Adonis. "A drink. Another drink. I need it. And bring me the Nasties. The mother and that girl, that girl of yours, now! I bet they've done something to the lights."

Candles flickered back and forth past dark windows. Frau Schmiedler wearing her white surgeon's coat and Roth hunting hat arrived like a pilgrim carrying a candle into the candlelit room. She kept her voice suitably low, I could not hear her.

The colonel's wife faced her arms acimbo. "What is this you're saying? Wires cut: Nasties, conspiracy. We need more help!" The colonel gave an order. A jeep took off in front just as Else appeared at the back, the servants entrance, near the rubbish heap. She had thrown her big sable coat over the pink tennis dress, wore that black hat and dragged a big suitcase. The little black monster-dog tried to jump out of the pocket and she stuffed it back and vanished behind the maze of hedges; only the glitter on her hat marked her progress to the gate.

I followed, tripped over a pile of tattered swastika banners, recovered, and was about to yell, "Here she is" and give myself away. Then, suddenly, for the first time I felt sorry for Else. Where would the fatherless girl go?

I stayed under trees and behind hedges reaching the gate just as my father's red truck appeared on the hill. I ran out into the street. Else was faster. The truck came downhill, and stopped near Else. Father reached down from the cabin: up went the suitcase, up the girl, glitter chain dancing. Else said, "well done!" snatched a cigarette from his mouth. The door banged shut and the black little monster dog yap-yapped and snarled.

I stood in the middle of the road shouting: "Stop Papa, halt!" The truck started up and came at me.

Else yelled: "Don't stop. Go, go on! Step on the gas!"

I was grabbed around the middle and pulled aside. "Reyna, Reyna, why do you always have to get into the midst of everything." Arnold half carried me inside the garden as though the driver who had killed General Patton, and the other one who collided with Mort in Berlin, an entire convoy of murderous trucks, might come after me.

"You're an idiot, Arnold!" Else yelled.

Arnold held me tight to keep me from running after the truck.

"The cigarette. Father hates cigarettes. It's Fritz Janicek. He's stolen the truck."

I allowed Arnold to tell me: It had all been arranged. The truck would be stopped by the Americans. But there was never just one arrangement in Vienna. Fritz Janicek could produce a forged Ferdinand Meinert identity card, perhaps even a passport. Real or forged? Nobody would ask. Money talked. Especially foreign money.

I allowed Arnold to tell me everything would be all right. He drew me under the dark trees, kissed me and called me his *Schatz,* his treasure. (Treasures certainly changed hands). But nothing ever happened twice to Arnold. He could never get used to love or malice and would remain an emissary of goodwill from a realm of his own ideals. I suddenly knew he was again kissing me *Auf Wiedersehen,* ready to tear himself away dutifully and send me home. I didn't know how to stop him, panicked, and helped myself to Frau Boschke's: "You certainly know how to make me feel good about myself." A parody, with slight variation, after all, is subterfuge, not theft.

"I want to devote myself to just that—" he was saying.

The colonel's wife leaned out the window and shouted: "There is someone out there. Schmiedler, that Nasty. Stop thief! Stop him!"

Guards came along the gravel walk and didn't see us. One of them was whistling, "Don't Fence Me In."

"Mort's tune," I said.

Arnold picked up my hand, the way Frau Schwester used to, checking for dirty fingernails. "You're not wearing his ring. Mort was wrong then." He kissed the hand as though I had hurt it, whispered to me that there might be false rumors. If Mort did have a car accident involving a Russian truck he would have been sent home.

"Was he the one who took evidence to the trial and saved Rudolf Hess?"

"I wouldn't know. But without it the Russians could have insisted on death sentence. After all, Hess flew to England and wanted the British to join Germany in a war against the Bolshevics."

I started to shake. Arnold put his jacket around my shoulders. Told me he was sure I would hear from Mort. He wanted to take me home. I refused.

A telephone rang somewhere inside the big house. Frau Schmiedler and two Ami boys with candles flitted past dark windows and vanished. The colonel's wife made herself heard above the din of digging, crashing, ripping and smashing: "Lets pour on the gas! And I'll throw a candle."

Poof, and flames shot up from the pit. The Ami boys formed a circle around the flames, "Juhuu, Yippee." One took a high leap over the flames, then another one swinging a spade. Pants caught on fire, there was slapping, rolling in the grass, laughter. Back and forth they jumped over the flames two by two.

We watched the ritual come to an end. Flames died down. Guards withdrew to the tennis pavillion, M.P.s drove away, spotlights were turned off. The back gate remained open like a mousetrap without bait. Neither Schmiedler nor his daughter would come back.

Arnold and I stayed in the chess pavillion. We could have played chess by the light of the moon on this night for lovers and lunatics. But that never was our game. "Dangerous game," Eugene Romberg had once said to me when I disturbed him here.

"I saw Eugene Romberg playing a game against himself at this table. He had to keep changing sides," I told Arnold.

"Both winner and loser," he said. "The game was more important than the player. That's his story."

"I dreamt about him last night."

Arnold released me and moved back to study my face. "What is the matter? Was it a terrible dream?"

"Very real. He looked ridiculous in that S.S. uniform. I saw him like that once at the beginning of Hitler's Russia Campaign. In my dream we were in a gondola and he told me to put on this watch he sent to me when you and Father took Eli to the Swiss border." I held it up and diamonds sparkled, put it against Arnold's ears and he looked solemn as the doctor listening to a heart beat.

"There is no Schmiedler," I said. "Eugene Romberg must have taken his place."

"When did you find out?" he asked.

"Just now. When you said both winner and loser."

"I am only slightly ahead of you. Frau Schmiedler was worried when the colonel's wife arrived, and she telephoned me. She broke down and told me she had found her husband dead in his dressing room; he was made up as a Hitler double. And that was just before our Russia campaign."

"Suicide?"

"No. Poisoned wine. He had an empty glass beside him, a bottle of Meinert wine. Frau Schmiedler could have been accused. Your father too. Eugene Romberg was in Vienna and she knew she could confide in him. He took over financial transactions as an invisible Schmiedler."

"Then, in the end Else gave him away to Fritz Janicek." I said.

"Who knows. Eugene Romberg could have given himself away with his devotion to your family, especially your mother."

On this night for lovers and lunatics I did not count kisses, minutes or hours we shared and had ahead of us. Soon Colonel Fredricks jumped out of Eugene Romberg's secret room and lifted down his wife. They strolled, arms entwined, to the biggest oak tree and kissed. She leaned back, became part of the dark trunk and the colonel looked as though he were hugging and kissing an old king-Kaiser day Austrian oak.

"That moon is driving me crazy," she said and led him back inside. Their candle moved from window to window and upstairs.

"It must be many years since a husband and wife enjoyed each other in that house," Arnold said. "I guess it had to be cleaned out first."

"But Tony can always get Fredrics more pictures, uniforms, anything." I said.

"The worst ones are those of Hitler stroking a dog, or a child," Arnold said.

."Probably Hitler doubles, perhaps Schmiedler," I said. "And everyone saying 'look at such a kind man he loved animals and children.' "

"Humanity of inhuman men always touches those who do not want to be responsible for evil," Arnold said.

It sounded like something my grandmama would have said. And an irresponsible collector of Rudolf Hess paper dolls quickly said. "Else is evil. The colonel knows and loves it. And everyone, including you sees her as a mere girl, because of her lovely face.

There she is with American papers she took from another girl. No matter what happens to Fritz Janicek, she'll somehow get into Switzerland and stay with Eli," I said.

"Not for long. She is the colonel's prize Nazi specimen. He's sure to ship her to America. He wants to photograph her face and make her into a model to promote all kinds of things. Colonel Fredricks calls it 'packaging.' "

"You argued with him?"

"Of course. Colonel Fredrics is not just eccentric, he is terrifying. He plans to use Nazi propaganda methods for selling cheese, toothpaste, books, politicians; anything good or bad. He wanted to hire me and take me to America as an expert; offered me great sums of money."

"You refused."

The diamond-studded Swiss watch ticked and ticked. "There are other moral considerations. I want to work for a untied Europe. And to be quite honest I have been alone so much." He sighed and I kissed his cheek. "At this moment I am so happy it makes me sad. I want you to be with me all the time," he said.

"Now, tomorrow, the day after tomorrow . . ." He looked at me and we both laughed. Was it really so simple?

"When did you know?" he asked.

"When I was seven years old."

"How does a seven year old chose a man?"

I could have said, Meinert instinct. A seven-year-old daughter and as good as a son chosing an equal in glowing good health and superior in powerful goodwill. The best dowry to be passed on to children and grandchildren. "I thought we were well-suited," I said in my father's voice.

He laughed and we kept on laughing when Tony's motorbike came sputtering along the main path in a straight line. His big helmet was slipping down to his nose, and Frau Boschke adorned with the ermine-trimmed Roth hat held him clasped around the middle. Did I see the glint of rings on her hand? She wore a huge rucksack. The dreambook would be inside it . . .

I waved, *lebwohl*, live well, to my Frau Boschke. She turned her head, saw me with Arnold, smiled, and vanished from my life clinging to Tony the deserter; not to escape, but giving chase. Lovers like haters are great stalkers; time itself a beast of fancy in a mirror maze.